SONG OF SHADOW

Ballad of Emerald and Iron Book 1

NATALYA CAPELLO

Cover illustration by Jackson Tjota and typography by Christian Bentulan.
Editing by Rainy Kaye

❀ Created with Vellum

To my husband, Jayson. Without you, there would be no Emerald and Iron.

I

With each wave, the docked boats called out to Lorelei like the sirens of the seas. She knew enough from her father's shipping business that she could take one and be off the Empire-forsaken island in moments. She glared up at the darkening clouds and the nuns surrounding her. It wouldn't work. If the sisters didn't stop her, the possible storm would. Besides, running away wouldn't help prove her case that she wasn't crazy.

With a sigh, Lorelei scanned the pier at the bustling faerie. A girl's laughter caught Lorelei's attention. It was a swift melody in its own right, brightening the dock despite the slate colored sky. Two phooka stood close together next to a small fishing boat. The girl's long, fur-covered ears twitched as she wrapped her slender pale arms around her lover and pulled his head down in a kiss. Her lover drew her closer, his bushy golden tail wagging as their kiss deepened. The two appeared oblivious to the activity around them as dockworkers, sailors, and fishermen prepared for the worst the darkening clouds could bring.

"Disgraceful," muttered one of the nuns near Lorelei.

Lorelei tore her eyes from the two lovers as the other nuns made noises of agreement to their sister's opinion.

The sea churned, its murky waves cresting white before dissolving and giving glimpses of the blue-black depths below. Lorelei's heart seemed to twist and turn in time to those waves. She blinked at the stinging of her eyes. Damn the sea salt. That's what it had to be. It certainly wasn't tears.

She cleared her throat of the knot making her breath ragged and brushed back a lock of her mahogany hair the wind had blown in her face. She stepped close to Prioress Abagail who stood a few feet apart from the rest of the nuns. The Prioress gave her the barest of nods before she continued to stare out at the sea. The skirts of her robe flapped about her legs, a stark contrast of red against the muted gray and blue of sky and sea.

"Am I really required for this?" Lorelei asked.

The Prioress stabbed her with a narrowed eyed glare. "Were you not listening, girl? The Apostle of Fire has specifically requested to meet you."

Lorelei ducked her head to hide her scowl. "Yes, but you never told me why."

"The Empress only knows. Perhaps she's come to request you join the Elemental Order, though I couldn't guess why." Prioress Abagail raised her face to the sky with the shake of her head. "You are only here with us at your parents' request, but in the past year I have seen little improvement on your attitude or your condition."

Her condition. Lorelei let out a soft snort. The Elemental Order had a name for it that rang in her head, taunting her. Reincarnation Sickness. According to the Order, everyone was reincarnated, though most didn't remember their past lives. However, some were plagued with memories, like Lorelei. Hers wasn't the worst. She mostly suffered from nightmares, and they weren't as bad as they used to be.

However, most of her life whispers had followed her and her parents had grown tired of those whispers, especially after she'd been expelled from the Aimsir.

Lorelei crossed her arms, slipping her hands under her elbows, and stared out at the sea. A small dot appeared on the edge of the horizon and rode the waves.

Lorelei pointed to it. "Is that the ship?"

The Prioress leaned forward, peering out. "I believe so. I only hope it reaches here before this storm hits."

As if brought on by her words, thunder rumbled followed by a downpour of rain. It came as a downpour of cold, hard drops. Shouts from the dockworkers mixed with the whoosh of the rainfall as people rushed about to secure the boats. In minutes, what had once been small crests grew into monstrosities crashing against the dock. One slammed into the wooden post near Lorelei and sent a spray of water over her and the nuns, soaking through her dress. She let out a shriek along with several of the nuns.

"Prioress," called a nun dressed in white robes of the Path of Air. "This storm is only going to get worse."

Prioress Abagail straightened her shoulders and stood to her full height. "All right, Sisters...we need your combined power on this. Sister Dina shall lead."

The nun in white nodded and stepped forward. The remaining sisters crowded around her and bowed their heads. Sister Dina stared out at the ship fighting against the waves and began to chant.

Lorelei grabbed the Prioress's sleeve. "I can help."

Prioress Abagail gave her a scornful look. "You would only break their concentration. Go find a place for shelter. We will come for you when we are done."

Lorelei's shoulders slumped and she trudged up the dock, towards the wooden buildings of the town with her arms wrapped around her.

"Lorelei." The Prioress's voice rang out through the storm. "Stay away from the wine."

Lorelei half turned and gave her an arched eyebrow. "Why? I've taken no vows."

"It wouldn't do to have you meet the Apostle drunk."

"I can handle my wine better than that." With those words, Lorelei turned and marched up the remainder of the dock.

She stood at the hill and scanned the one- and two-story wooden buildings with their coral rooftops. A line of small shops and huts strung across the main road. Most of the doors were closed and their windows shuttered.

Lorelei bit the inside of her cheek. None of those would work.

Her gaze landed on the sign of a structure at the end of the muddy road. Seacrest Tavern. Perfect. A flash of lightning split the sky, followed by a boom of thunder, causing Lorelei to start. The rain pounded harder against her skin, soaking her through.

She raced across the street and yanked the door open. Warmth and the smell of burning wood rushed over her as she stepped inside. The wind rattled against the windows of the tavern as the rain pounded on its roof. A murmur rose up from the patrons of the tavern as the hob barkeep tottered across the room on his short legs to close the wooden shutters over the windows. His pointed ears stood out from his head, behind a mass of wavy brown hair and his skin sparkled in the flickering lanterns that hung on the wooden walls.

He stopped at the door and he stared up at her for a moment before glancing at the puddle around her feet. "You done brought some of the storm inside."

She glanced down and gave a soft cough. "Sorry."

"No worries, lady. Why don't you find yourself a seat near the fire and get yourself warm?"

He disappeared through a door behind the bar along the right wall as Lorelei took in the room. A large hearth with a roaring fire stood in the center of the room surrounded by square wooden tables and chairs. Lorelei shivered and scanned the four tables closest to the hearth. All full. She would have liked to have sat near the hearth, but it didn't matter. She would warm up with a few glasses of wine at the bar instead. She settled herself on one of the barstools and huddled as she waited for the barkeep to return.

He came from the back, holding a mop with a handle twice as tall as he was. He scurried to the wet spot at the door. Lorelei turned to watch. How was he going to wield such an awkward mop?

The barkeep muttered something and flicked the handle of the mop with his thumb and forefinger. It shuddered and leapt from his hand. It danced around, absorbing the water as it went. With a nod, the barkeep turned and headed back to the bar.

Lorelei chuckled softly. She'd never paid much attention to the work the hob servants did at her parents' house. They were known to have the magic of hearth and home. That seemed to work for taverns, as well.

The barkeep stepped up on a stool behind the counter and leaned close. "What can I get for you, lady?"

"Wine, please." She pulled out a silver coin from her pocket, one of the few she had remaining. "The best this can get."

He climbed down and shuffled around beneath the counter. In a few moments, he popped back up with a dark, unopened bottle and a brass cup.

He poured the wine. "Don't see many sidhe here on the Isle aside from the Prioress. We're supposed to have a lord of some Great House looking over us, but I've never met him."

Not surprising. What sidhe would want to upheave their

life to look after some small island they'd been granted? Most preferred to stay in the heart of the Elphyne Empire on the central continent. It was where most of the political maneuvering happened. Few would want to travel to the outskirts. Bayacre, the island's one town, had nothing to boast about. Their biggest fixture was the dock and the attached boathouse. Moving here was a form of banishment. Lorelei knew that all too well. The Quorum wouldn't grant the Isle to one of the commoner races though. The sidhe were born to rule.

"Your mayor or town elder is probably responsible for reporting to him or her," Lorelei said.

"So, you're not them." The barkeep picked at his chin with a speculative gleam in his eye. "I guess that means you're the girl living with the nuns up there at Morningtide."

"That would be me." She raised her cup in a mock salute.

She gulped down the wine. The sweet liquid danced on her taste buds. Heat welled up from her chest and it felt like her veins were alive with tiny bubbles. Aether. Pure power. It was like a drug all its own and she'd had so little over the past year. She leaned against the bar, letting her head fall back, and exhaled a long breath.

"I guess you approve." A quick laugh burst out from the barkeep. "Want another?"

Lorelei held out her goblet. "Much obliged."

He filled the cup. "So, what brings you to the Priory? You don't wear their robes."

Lorelei chuckled and sipped her wine. "I suppose you could say they're gracious enough to look after me."

She tried to keep the bitterness. Here she was, stuck on an island in the middle of nowhere, sharing a moment with a barkeep.

Well, the barkeep thing wasn't much different from what she had got up to before she had been banished by her parents. It was usually the start of the trouble she created.

But then, she'd had Arryn to get her out of it.

Arryn...

An ache filled her chest as his face occupied her mind. She took another drink of her wine as thunder boomed loud enough to rattle the windows.

The door of the tavern flung inward and a tall female with a set of black leathery wings stepped inside. The wind blew through the tavern and caught Lorelei's hair, forcing several brown locks to slip from behind her pointed ears and whip around her face.

With a sigh, she pushed them back and leaned forward to study the new female. She was an ankou, a race of winged faerie that had an affinity with death. Her wings draped over her body as she pressed her spindly form against the door to shut it. Her chest heaved as she scanned the tavern. Her gaze passed over Lorelei and landed on the barkeep.

The ankou rushed forward, her voice coming out in a hoarse murmur. "Bardo, the Elkar is still out. It's caught in the storm."

Bardo paled, his eyes wide. "Aela...I'm sorry."

Aela shook her head. "I tried to get the nuns on the dock to help bring it in, but they're fighting the storm to bring another ship...They can't save both." She pressed her face in her hands and let out a sob. "My husband and son..."

It was strange to see. Even with their connection to death, the ankou still grieved the ones they loved. They still felt the loss.

Lorelei's chest tightened. Once again, Arryn's face flashed in her mind. This time it was deathly pale as he lay on the brink of death. A death she'd almost caused.

Aela didn't have to lose someone today. Not if Lorelei could help it.

Lorelei drained the rest of her cup and slammed it on the counter, causing Aela and Bardo to start. "I'll help."

Aela blinked at her. "Milady, are you a nun? Do you follow one of the Paths?"

Lorelei glanced at her wine goblet and let out a soft laugh. "Oh, not at all."

Bardo's brow furrowed. "How can you help then?"

Lorelei stood and stretched her arms above her head. "I happen to know a little bit of magic...especially, elemental. So, I'll bring your husband's boat in."

Aela's back straightened as she pressed her hands to her mouth and stared at Lorelei with a glimmer of hope.

Lorelei took a deep breath. "Would you show me the closest dock to where your husband's ship would be?"

With an emphatic nod, Aela rushed to the door and opened it. The wind tore the handle from her hands and the door hit the wall with a loud crack. Icy rain poured in, pelting the closest patrons' faces and arms as she stepped into the doorway. Aela strode into the storm with her wings curved above her head to shield against most of the rain. With a sigh, Lorelei lifted the hood of her cloak and followed.

The sky had become charcoal, filled with churning clouds that spat torrents of rain.

They came to the harbor, stopping along the wooden boardwalk that held a few stalls that sold fish, now abandoned due to the storm. The sea, usually cobalt, was gray green, with large waves crashing upon the pier and the shore that stretched beyond.

Lorelei shivered, wrapping her cloak around her as a frigid gust of wind blew against her. To her right, on the same dock she'd left earlier, the nuns stood clustered together. They stared out at the ship fighting against waves, almost as large as it. The ship was still several miles out.

Aela pulled at her arm and pointed in the opposite direction of the ship. A small boat struggled to avoid a stack of rocks that jutted from the sea. It shifted its small body towards the docks as a large wave slapped against it.

"Please," Aela cried over the wind as she clutched Lorelei's arm. "They can't make it past those rocks by themselves."

Lorelei untangled herself from Aela's grip and patted her shoulder. "Go back to the tavern. It's dangerous for you out here. I'll bring them home."

At least she'd try to.

"No," Aela shook her head, her hair whipping around her. "I want to stay here."

Lorelei pressed her lips together. She didn't have time to argue. "Fine. At least find a place to take cover."

She drew in a deep breath and stared up at the sky. If she could calm the wind, the waves would follow. She hummed the first few chords of a song, willing her magic to connect with the air currents. Her voice rose above the howling wind and she grasped control of the air currents. She could feel them in the back of her mind, urging her to be swept up in their dance.

Not today.

She forced the sense of serenity into the heart of the storm. It rampaged against her, trying to wrest control by increasing the winds. A large wave slammed against the little fishing boat.

Her heart pounded so hard it could have leapt into her throat. She couldn't control the storm. She wasn't powerful enough. She had to change tactics.

She shifted her song to a hypnotic melody, like the ebb and flow of the tide. With it, her will touched that of the water. She summoned a wave and caught the boat with it. Her voice overcame the wind as she used the wave to push the boat away from the stack and towards the harbor.

With each verse, she grabbed wave after wave, guiding the boat to safety. As it reached the docks, she calmed the surrounding water, keeping it from crashing into the wooden planks.

The faeries on board scurried about the boat, pulling at the sails while one stood clenching the wheel. A phooka tossed a rope around one of the dock's pillars.

Lorelei let the song die and stepped back to lean against a stall, closing her eyes and drawing in a deep breath. A smile danced on her lips. It had taken all the Aether she'd gained from the wine, but she'd done it.

She'd brought the boat home.

"Oh!" Aela leapt forward and gripped Lorelei's hands. "Thank you, lady. I would as sure as lost him without you."

She planted a kiss on each of Lorelei's palms and then let go to rush down the dock to meet her family's boat. On the other side of the dock, the ship that held the Apostle of Fire coasted into a space as well. The nuns had been hard at prayer while Lorelei had been struggling with the waves.

With a sigh, Lorelei straightened up. The wind had blown the hood of her cloak back during her battle with the storm and her hair was completely soaked through. It looked like she would be meeting one of the most important faeries in the Empire looking like a drowned waif.

2

The nuns had hustled the Apostle and her two sidhe companions back to the tavern to wait out the rest of the storm. Lorelei had trailed behind, exhaustion from her efforts to save the fishing boat dogging her steps.

All now huddled near the fire in the hearth. Bardo had cleared the other patrons from the four tables surrounding the fire before he had left to prepare transportation for the Apostle and nuns. The ousted faerie sat at the tables along the wall. Those who hadn't been lucky enough to take a chair, stood with their mugs in hand and murmured.

Lorelei slumped in her chair at one of the tables orbiting the Apostle's and rested her head on her arms. She hadn't performed such a feat of magic in a while. Not since the citadel.

Where Arryn had gotten hurt.

She sat up with the shake of her head. She wouldn't think about Arryn, or her family. There was an Apostle of the church to focus on.

The Apostle stood out from the nuns as she was dressed

in silks in shades of red, layered to give off the effect of a dancing flame as she moved. They were dry and unwrinkled as if the storm had not touched her. They should have clashed with her deep red hair, but somehow, they complemented it. A gold starburst pendant hung around her neck and golden ear cuffs adorned her long, pointed ears.

The two other sidhe sat on either side of her, dressed in ceremonial robes of white with gold trim. The rain had soaked them through, turning the white into gray.

The Apostle looked up from where she was staring into the fire and her gaze fell on Lorelei. She waved her over.

Lorelei stood, running her hands over her still wet clothing and trudged over. She gave a slight curtsey.

"You are Lady Lorelei ap Moura, correct?" The Apostle spoke in a smooth voice, like a violin.

"Yes, Apostle," Lorelei said.

How much did the Apostle know of her? The Prioress had told Lorelei that she'd been requested specifically, but why?

"I am the Apostle Evangeline," the Apostle said. "We heard your song through the storm. You have quite a talent."

"One can almost say it's enchanting," the female on her right said with a smirk.

She sat with her arms relaxed and her hand resting on her lap but an alertness surrounded her. Her black hair was piled on her head in an elaborate twist of braids. Her green eyes slanted over to her companion who gave a silent chuckle. Lorelei's gaze shifted between the three sidhe. They seemed to have some secret jest she wasn't a part of, or she was the butt of it. Heat suffused her cheeks.

Apostle Evangeline waved to the right. "This is Vaana." Then she waved to her left. "And this is Beth. They have been kind enough to accompany me."

Both nodded. Beth's hair was almost as elaborate as Vaana's.

Two pale blue streaks cupped her face while the rest of her black hair was pulled up. She studied Lorelei like she was some sort of creature the acolyte was not sure should be killed or not. The room became hot and Lorelei's breath grew even shorter.

"You must have had extensive training to have that effect on the storm," Vaana said.

"I did attend the Aimsir for a short time, but I was unable to complete my training," Lorelei said. "I practice quite a bit, though."

"Very impressive," Apostle Evangeline said. "I commend you on your dedication, Lady Lorelei."

Lorelei gave a small curtsey. "I am honored, Apostle."

The door to the tavern opened and the barkeep stepped inside. He approached the group and bowed to Apostle Evangeline before turning to address the Prioress who sat at a table to the Apostle's right.

"Milady," he said. "We have prepared a coach for you and the Apostle to travel in."

The Prioress looked down her nose at him. "Only one coach?"

He shrank beneath her look. "Forgive me, Milady, but your other coach was damaged in the storm. The coach can fit six of your party inside and another with the driver."

"It is alright. I'm sure a few would be willing to stay behind to wait out the storm." She gave Lorelei a conspiratorial smile.

Lorelei raised an eyebrow, but a grin spread across her face. She wasn't going to lose this chance for a little longer outside of the priory. "I will stay."

The Prioress gave her a sharp look. "Nonsense. You are under our care by the direction of your parents. We cannot leave you in the town alone."

"I will stay with her," Vaana spoke up.

“Vaana is one of my most trusted,” Apostle Evangeline said to the Prioress. “She will watch after Lady Lorelei.”

The Prioress looked between the Apostle and Lorelei with a pinched mouth.

With a sigh, she bowed her head to the Apostle. “As you wish.”

“Excellent,” Apostle Evangeline beamed at her.

She rose and the Prioress and the rest of the nuns followed suit. The patrons stood from their sitting positions and bowed. She raised her hand and murmured a prayer over the crowd, then turned her attention back to Lorelei.

Lorelei gave another curtsey.

“It was a pleasure meeting you, Lady Lorelei. I’m sure we will have time to speak again.” Apostle Evangeline turned to the barkeep. “Please lead the way.

The barkeep tottered out of the tavern with the Apostle and her entourage of nuns following behind. Once the door had shut, muting the sound of pounding rain, the crowd broke up into smaller groups, speaking with each other as they reclaimed the tables. Vaana stood near the table the Apostle had vacated.

Lorelei plodded to the bar and grabbed a bottle of wine and a glass. She would pay Bardo for it when he came back. She returned to the table near the fire, sank in one of the empty chairs, and let out a loud whoosh of breath. Meeting the Apostle had been intense and it seemed she wanted to speak more with Lorelei. What was her interest?

Vaana sat down across from her and smiled at her. “So, now that we’re alone, let’s get to know one another. What’s your life story?”

Lorelei blinked. “My life story? That’s a bit personal.”

Vaana shrugged. “I find small talk meaningless. It is such a bore that makes state events drag on forever. So how did you end up on a remote island like this?”

"It's a complicated series of events." Lorelei poured wine into the glass and took a deep drink. "What is your interest with me?"

Vaana tilted her head with a smirk. "What do you mean?"

"The Apostle asked to meet me specifically when she arrived. You stayed behind and now you are asking about my life. Doesn't seem like this is casual interest."

Vaana chuckled and leaned back in her chair. "Very astute. Well, let's get down to it then. I have a proposition for you

Lorelei studied her with a raised eyebrow. "What is this proposition?"

"The Apostle of Fire wishes to recruit you to travel in her retinue to the city of Nearon."

Lorelei's eyes widened. "I'm not with the Order. I'm only staying here under the care of the priory."

"Ah, but it is *your* talents we need, Lady Lorelei, not a member of the Order," Vaana said.

"I didn't even complete my training at the Aimsir. Almost any Magus would be overjoyed to work for an Apostle. What could I have that is so special?"

"You are a Moura. So, I'm sure you know of the story behind the Menhir Du Moura," Vaana said.

Lorelei's heart fluttered. As a child, she'd begged her father, her mother, her nursemaid, or anyone, really, to relay the story of Lady Moura and Lord Essus, the founders of two of the Great Noble Houses, to her repeatedly. When she'd gotten older, she'd read the story itself almost every night. It had been her talisman against the nightmares that plagued her. Lady Moura had been brave in the face of destruction and she had fought for the male she loved, even if had cost her life.

"Of course." Lorelei cleared her throat. "Lady Moura's lover Essus built the cairn as a monument for Moura after she was killed."

"By his wife," Vaana said. "Shame they had such an illicit relationship."

Lorelei bristled. "If I remember correctly, his wife had become tainted by the Miasma."

"True, but it's not known whether that was before or after."

"Still, their love is an epic romance," Lorelei said.

"What if I told you that there are wonders hidden in the Menhir? Would that pique your interest?"

Lorelei leaned forward, resting her arms on the table. "I'm listening."

"Well, the Apostle believes there are important artifacts that should be recovered. Some could be dangerous to the people of Threshold and must be kept in the Order's care. However, we are unable to access the Menhir. It requires a Moura, or an Essus."

"Why haven't you approached an Essus, then?"

Vaana waved her hand. "You know they are all cursed with madness. It makes them really unreliable."

"I thought that was just a rumor," Lorelei said. "Like their supposed ability to see the future."

Vaana smirked. "You haven't met an Essus, have you?"

Lorelei looked down at her hands and shook her head. Her family had never run in the same circles as any from House Essus. Their members tended to be more aloof than the other Houses.

"Trust me," Vaana said. "The rumors are true. So, we need a Moura, especially one with your magical talent. If you are willing, we can travel together. Of course, we'll pay for some equipment. After all, we need to be prepared to travel through Winderward. Once we have finished, the Apostle will declare you are fit to be free from the care of the Order."

"Winderward." Lorelei leaned back and crossed her arms.

"That's those ancient ruins attached to Nearon, right? From a city that existed before the Miasma?"

"Indeed," Vaana said. "Interesting that Lord Essus would build the Menhir there, isn't it?"

"I've always wondered," Lorelei said. "I mean, there are rumors the city has wild magic that causes it to shift."

Vaana leaned forward with a sparkle in her eye. "Lends credence that there is something there, doesn't it?"

Lorelei bit the inside of her cheek. Her gaze landed on a birdcage hanging above the bar. Two small brown birds hopped up and down along the perch inside. Her chest tightened. The priory was her own cage, but not forever. One month and her father would come for her. One month and she would fly free. Working for the Apostle, with Vaana, could take longer than a month. She'd be on a mission, exploring a place she'd only heard stories about, but she'd still be under direct yolk of the Order.

What are you wanting to go back to? A voice whispered in her head. *More pain?*

No, there was a chance that she could prove to her family, prove to Arryn, that she was well. That was why they'd sent her to the Priory. If she behaved, he would accept her. She looked up at Vaana and swallowed hard.

"I appreciate the offer," Lorelei said. "It is very intriguing, but my family will be coming for me soon. I'll be able to go home."

Vaana raised an eyebrow. "You think they will accept you?"

Lorelei narrowed her eyes. "What do you know about my family?"

"Enough to know you are the odd one, the adventurous one." Vaana shrugged. "Perhaps we were mistaken on that last part."

"You are," Lorelei said. "My thirst for adventure died two years ago."

Lorelei raised her chin and let her confidence in her words ring through. Still, in the back of her head a tiny voice whispered one word.

Liar.

❧

After a few hours, the rain lightened enough for Lorelei and Vaana to trek to the Morningtide Priory. Traveling on the muddy roads slowed them considerably and they didn't reach the priory until well after the sun had set. Luckily, the barkeep had provided a lantern for them before they'd left the tavern.

Lorelei entered her room and leaned against the door with a sigh, closing her eyes. What a crazy day.

She hadn't lied to Vaana exactly. She'd had to douse her craving for adventure when she'd nearly gotten her schoolmates, Arryn, and herself killed on an insane quest to find a way to control her magic. That mistake had led to her being stuck at the priory now which meant no more adventures. Her stomach twisted and the world appeared duller like the sparkle had gone out of everything just at the thought. However, if she wanted to win Arryn back, she needed to try to live a normal life, starting with finishing her time here at the priory.

With a groan, she stripped off her wrinkled dirty dress and trudged to the wash basin on an end table. She filled it with water from a pitcher next to it and washed off the dirt and grime. After her fight with the storm and hours of walking, the thought of running a bath seemed a monumental task. She would clean off what she could for now and have a bath in the morning.

She grabbed a chemise hanging from her bedpost, pulled it over her head and, collapsed into her bed pressed against the far wall of her room. The mattress was lumpy and hard, but the blanket was soft and warm. Her eyes fluttered closed and she drifted in darkness in a matter of seconds.

A rap on the door, followed by the muffled voice of one of the nuns woke her. “Pardon me, Lady Lorelei, but your family wishes to speak to you.”

Lorelei sat up and rubbed her face. The first rays of dawn slanted through the blinds of her window. She must have been exhausted. She barely remembered the nightmares except for the sensation of falling forever.

Her head snapped in the direction of the door as the nun’s words filtered through her sleep-muddled mind.

“Now?” she called.

“Yes,” the nun said with an exasperated tone. “They are holding the mirror communication open to wait for you.”

Lorelei looked down at the dirt smudges she had missed on her arms. She really should have taken that bath last night.

“I’ll be out in a moment.”

“You should hurry. This magic seems to be taxing on your sister.”

Lorelei huffed out a silent breath. “Of course, Freya would be the first to complain.”

Lorelei hopped from her bed, rushed to the wash basin, and scrubbed her arms and face. The night had cooled the water and it was like ice upon her skin. She grabbed a brush from her nightstand and ran it through her hair in a few quick strokes as she strode to her wardrobe and dug out a dress. It was a simple one made of white cotton with yellow embroidery. She lay it on the bed and stared at it for several moments, biting the inside of her cheek. Her mother and sister would expect her in something more elegant, but that would take hours. This dress would have to do on such short notice. She slipped it on, then emerged from her room, as ready as she could be to face her family.

The nun raised an eyebrow at her. Lorelei gave her a nod, and the nun turned and led the way through the stone hall and down a set of steps. She opened a door to a small room that held several chairs stationed around a large, full-length mirror. Lorelei took a deep breath and sat in one of the chairs.

"I'll give you some privacy." With that, the nun left, closing the door with a quiet click.

Lorelei focused on the mirror and clenched her hands on the arms of the chair at the sight in front of her. The shimmering reflection of the mirror didn't match that of the room. Instead, it showed the sitting room of her home.

Her mother sat in the leather high-backed armchair next to the stone fireplace with her eyes narrowed and a taut jaw that made her slender face even more narrow. She was dressed in a light green day dress with a lace bodice. Lorelei's father loomed over her chain with his hands behind his back. His dark brown hair, the same mahogany as Lorelei's, was combed back from his face, accentuating his long ears. Beside her mother sat Freya, dressed in a blue silk and white lace gown. Her hand rested on the sidhe male sitting in the last chair.

Arryn.

Lorelei's chest twisted into knots.

Arryn's blond hair was long enough to brush his shoulders, but he had it tied at the nape of his neck. He wore a dark blue overcoat stitched with a coat of arms depicting a ship and waves over a torch and sword over the right side of his chest. It was the crest of House Nemain, his house, and soon to be Freya's.

Lorelei sucked in a breath and closed her eyes, willing the whirlwind within her chest to calm. After a few moments, she opened her eyes and smiled at them with an expression of serenity.

"Hello, Mother, Father...Freya." Lorelei swallowed at the tightness in the throat. "Arryn."

"Hello, Nightingale." Her father's pale blue eyes warmed as he gave her a smile.

Her mother's gaze slid over Lorelei with cool disdain. "This is how you present yourself to us? Your hair is a mess. And what are you wearing?"

Lorelei ran a hand over the skirt of her dress, trying to smooth out the wrinkles as her face heated. "I had little notice that you had contacted me."

"I think there's even dirt on her cheek," Freya said in a scandalized tone.

Of course, Freya looked picturesque. Her golden hair was coifed in a series of elaborate braids that spiraled to a bun at the left side of her neck, just below her ear.

Freya was the radiant one. She shared the same soft hair as her mother while Lorelei had inherited her father's mahogany tresses. Of course, it didn't end there. Lorelei's eyes were two obsidian orbs, while Freya had the pale blue of her parents. Her cheekbones were more delicate, her lips more sculpted, and she was thinner while Lorelei had more rounded hips and breast. Freya had been the favorite of her family. More beautiful and gifted.

Except for voice and song, Lorelei thought. *For all the good it has done me.*

Her father cleared his throat. "How have you been?"

"Well enough, considering that I'm still here." Lorelei focused her gaze on him, willing herself not to dart glances at Arryn. "Have you contacted me about my return next month?"

Her father's gaze slid from her. "In a way."

Her mother lifted her chin and stared down her nose at Lorelei. "We've decided that it is best you stay at the Morningtide Priory indefinitely."

“Maybe even join the nuns,” Freya added in her high, fluting voice.

Lorelei’s mouth hung open as a gasp got caught in her throat. Her skin tingled with flashes of hot and cold.

“But why?” she sputtered. “I’ve done everything you have asked of me during my stay. I have behaved.”

“Yet, you haven’t improved,” her mother said. “Prioress Abagail says you are still prone to nightmares.”

“She believes that could change if you accepted your place in the Empress’s Order.” Her father let out a sigh. “We only want what’s best for you.”

“No.” Lorelei’s voice held a cold tone. “You want to hide me away.”

“Is it any wonder?” Freya asked. “After what you did to get expelled from the Aimsir. What you did to Arryn?”

Of course, she would bring that up. Lorelei hadn’t done it on purpose. She’d needed to go to the citadel to find something to control her magic. Things had just...gone awry.

Lorelei finally turned to Arryn. “You blame me, then? Is that why you chose Freya?”

Arryn closed his eyes and let out a long sigh. He turned to her family. “Would you allow me to speak to Lorelei alone?”

Freya narrowed her eyes and her jaw tightened. “Why? I can stay with you as your fiancée.”

He rested his hand over hers. “Please, just a few moments.”

Her mother stood. “I suppose it couldn’t hurt. She always seemed to listen to you.” She looked at the others in turn. “Come Freya, Dougan.”

With a scathing glare at Lorelei, Freya followed their parents out of the room. She’d never understood what she had done to earn Freya’s ire, but it was there with a vengeance. Freya had no reason for such animosity. Once again, she'd won. Lorelei's parents would sequester her away forever while Freya and Arryn lived in happy matrimony.

The sound of a door clicking echoed from the other side of the mirror. Lorelei stared at Arryn, waiting for him to speak.

"It's good to see you," he said. "You are looking well, though maybe as wild as ever."

She brushed her hair from her face. "And you. How are...things?"

"You mean my wound? It still hurts at times. I'm still unable to properly hold a sword without it flaring up."

She bowed her head. "Again, I'm sorry for what happened. I know it cost you your military tour. But, you said you had forgiven me."

"I have. You were doing what was in your nature, I understand. I was the fool for following you into that citadel. I was a fool for staying."

"But we had to stay. I had to go on. That vampire general would have ravaged the Empire." Lorelei bunched up her skirt between her fists.

"That was something for the Quorum to handle." Arryn's gaze turned colder. "I'd said that before."

"You know we didn't have time! The Black Herons were close to awakening the vampire. You were the one who knew of them."

"Mere rumors." Arryn waved his hand.

"Rumors? You saw the insignia on the swords."

Was he seriously pretending nothing happened?

He shook his head. "I don't know what I saw anymore. I think we all got caught up in one of your delusions."

An icy sensation spread through her core. "You know my visions don't work like that. You are lying. Who is covering this up and what did they offer you?"

Arryn let out a high laugh. "You never stop, do you? See,

this is why your parents wish for you to stay. You believe this conspiracy that isn't there."

Lorelei slumped back in her chair and glowered down at her hands. She wasn't crazy. They all had come across the secret sect that had been determined to take down the Quorum, the government that had ruled since the Empress had disappeared. They had all fought the agents, though Lorelei had been the only one to see and fight the necromancer attempting to awaken the ancient vampire.

"Why does everyone pretend that this didn't happen?"

"Look," Arryn said in a tired voice. "This marriage to Freya is the last chance I have to bring prestige to my family. Your sister's status as Magus is highly valued."

Of course, his father looked for prestige, as well as access to her father's ships. And her father had accepted because having connections to the legions of House Nemain was always beneficial. Her father loved her and sometimes doted on her, but he was a practical male. Freya was the first born and her magic was more useful.

Lorelei's whole body shook as heat suffused her face. With one quick slam of her fist, she could shatter the mirror. What did it matter anyway? No one was coming for her here. She swallowed and blinked at the pressure building behind her eyes.

No, she thought. *I won't cry. I'm not poor Lorelei.*

"Fine." She kept her gaze on her hands. "You can tell my parents I understand their decision."

She understood. But that didn't mean she would acquiesce.

She stood up and shot him a cold glance. Without another word, she strode out of the room, passing the nun who waited outside the door, and headed down the hall.

The nun caught up with Lorelei's quick pace. "You have finished already?"

"Oh, very much so," Lorelei said. "Tell me, where is the Apostle's entourage this morning?"

The nun shuddered at the hint of command in her voice. A wave a tightness fluttered through Lorelei's chest. She shouldn't have done that, but she'd been too angry to stop herself. All sidhe had the power to command lesser faerie and they had to be careful of what they said.

The words tumbled from the nun's lips with a whoosh of breath. "They are enjoying the cloister garden, I believe." She stiffened, her eyes narrowing. "Did you just command me?"

"Sorry," Lorelei muttered and turned from her.

"But you can't—"

Lorelei took off into a run before the nun could finish. She had tired of *can't* and *shouldn't*. Behaving had gotten her nothing.

She sprinted through the halls and flung open the door leading to the cloister. Apostle Evangeline sat with Beth and Vaana amid the flower beds of the garden. The morning sun streamed down from the sky as if the previous day's storm had been nothing.

Lorelei paused at one of the archways separating the covered cloister from the garden and cleared her throat. She may be sick of rules, but she wasn't foolish enough to disrespect the Apostle of Fire, especially when she was Lorelei's chance to leave. She cleared her throat.

"Pardon me, Apostle, but may I speak with Vaana for a moment?" Lorelei asked.

Apostle Evangeline looked to Vaana and nodded with a smile. Vaana rose and sauntered to Lorelei. She leaned against the stone archway with her arms crossed.

"Changed your mind?" Vaana asked.

"You said that once I went to the Menhir with you, the Apostle would deem me fit and free to be on my own?"

Vaana nodded.

“Then, yes. I accept your offer.”

A slow grin spread across Vaana’s face. “Excellent. You should prepare. We leave within the week. We’ll gather supplies for you when we reach Nearon. Winderward is a dangerous place, after all.”

“I’m not afraid of danger.”

She was a Moura. Brave after their founder. She would help Vaana retrieve whatever she needed and she would earn her freedom. Then, she would search for proof on the Black Heron’s existence.

She would prove she wasn’t crazy, no matter how perilous it was.

3

The Apostle only stayed a few days at the priory once she secured Lorelei's agreement. Most of that had been transferring guardianship of Lorelei to the Apostle. It was funny. At eighteen, Lorelei should have been old enough for her own autonomy. However, this wasn't so, since the Empire considered her unstable.

That wouldn't be for long. All she needed was to travel to the Menhir with Vaana for the Apostle. After that, she would be free.

Lorelei left with the Apostle and her entourage on the same ship that had brought them. They had been at sea for a week until finally reaching port at Nearon.

Lorelei ran her hands down the skirt of her purple dress as she stared in the mirror in her room. Her hair cascaded around her shoulders in wild, windblown locks.

Shouts and cheers drifted in from her open door. The noise had been going on since the ship had made port an hour ago. The people were apparently excited for the arrival of the Apostle. They'd even decorated the dock with banners. Surprising since Nearon wasn't officially a part of the Elphyne

Empire. Yes, the Empress had saved all of Threshold and not just the Empire, but Lorelei hadn't expected those outside of it to worship the Empress.

Vaana poked her head in the doorway. "We're ready to depart. Do you have your things together?"

Lorelei nodded and grabbed for her bags from next to the bed. "I don't have much."

"Don't worry about those," Vaana said. "They'll be delivered to the Temple."

Lorelei raised an eyebrow. "There's a temple here?"

"It's new. Part of the reason for the Apostle's journey was to christen the new temple with her presence."

"How long does that take?" Lorelei joined Vaana in the hallway.

"The entire ceremony takes three days." Vaana walked towards the wooden steps leading up to the deck. "You'll get to see some tonight. It starts with the lighting of the braziers and there's a huge party after."

"A party? So, is the Apostle like the nuns who disapprove of alcohol, or is she like the old priest in Hy-Breasail. He thought that wine was sacred...or he just liked the sacred wine."

Vaana laughed. "That sounds like an interesting priest. The Apostle abstains from alcohol herself, but that doesn't mean all who are in her entourage do."

"What about you?"

The side of Vaana's lips quirked in a smirk. "I occasionally like a drink and a male to bed."

Lorelei looped her arm in Vaana's as they ascended. "I have a feeling we are going to get along well."

"Just don't enjoy yourself too much," Vaana said. "You and I leave for Winderward in the morning."

Lorelei squinted against the brightness of the clear sky as

they reached the top deck. A slight breeze carried the scent of sea salt and roasted meat.

Lorelei gasped at the crowd gathered at the edge of the dock. It had doubled in size since she'd last seen it.

"Get ready to wave your hand off," Vaana said with a grin. "Looks like we're in for a parade."

❧

Hours later, as the sun sank beneath the horizon, Lorelei stood among a crowd of faeries on the marble steps of Temple of Resplendent Order.

She raised her gaze from the twining, marble columns to the frieze near the roof that depicted the Empress battling the Fomorians. Resplendent, indeed. The mural had been painted with bright greens for the Empress and dark red and black of the Miasma for her enemies.

She could probably spend hours admiring it and still miss details.

Her gaze lowered to wander over the procession at the top of the steps. On the left of the double doors, a line of priests dressed in red robes stood with their arms crossed in front of them. In the center of them, Vaana and Beth stood out in their white and gold ceremonial robes.

A group of seven males and females stood to the right of the doors, dressed in finery in an array of blue. Each wore a black mask with gold filigree. They chatted softly to one another.

Lorelei raised an eyebrow. She couldn't quite tell what race they were. It was as if their features were blurred.

Lorelei leaned close to a pixie male fluttering near her. "Who are those seven?"

The pixie raised an eyebrow at her. "You don't know of the Council of Peers? Where did you live? In a cave?"

"No." Lorelei fidgeted with her dress. "I'm from the Elphyne Empire. And I've heard of the Council before, I've just never seen them."

The pixie snorted. "First time here, then. They show up to big to-dos in the city. Except the Legate...He doesn't like parties. Oh! Here she comes!"

The pixie did an aerial flip and rose higher. Several of his fellow pixies joined him above the heads of the faerie. The double doors of the temple opened and the Apostle of Fire stepped out. A roar of cheers spread through the crowd. Lorelei's heartbeat sped up and her stomach flittered. The city's excitement was contagious. She'd spent a week with the Apostle, and yet she leaned forward with everyone else as the Apostle raised her hands and addressed the crowd.

Her voice carried on the air, and despite the people gathered around, it was as if she was speaking directly to Lorelei. "In the time of our need, the Goddess left her heavenly abode in order to save us. She saw the coming of the Miasma, and willed herself to be born upon Threshold.

"With her grace she healed those sickened by the Miasma and turned deadly iron into beautiful emerald. Those who possess emerald are destined to have their dreams fulfilled."

More like the emerald held the power to grant wishes. Even the greatest magi of Threshold could not replicate the effects of emerald. Many had tried with detrimental effects—most often, massive explosions that took whole laboratories with it. The Aimsir had forbidden experimentation on emerald in the university itself. Still, Lorelei remembered many of her fellow students with the ambition to recreate emerald.

"With the aid of the Elemental Dragons, she brought order to the chaos that marred Threshold and created the Empire. Thus, she became the Empress.

"Under the Empress's guidance, the Quorum was formed and it aided her in the rule of the Empire."

The Quorum was composed of the heads of each of the Great Noble Houses. Lorelei had met the leader of her own House Moura over a decade ago when she had been a girl of ten. He'd been loud and boasting of his exploits. Lorelei had sat rapt as he'd told her of his triumph over a Fomorian horde in the North.

Lorelei chuckled as she scanned the enraptured faces of the faerie on the steps. Several hobs stood in front of the crowd or sat on the shoulders of others. The phooka listened with their ears or tails twitching. The ankou had their wings folded around their spindly bodies. She could even pick out the red hair and muscular frames of several redcaps. There were even a few sidhe in the crowd, their angular faces raised in interest.

She wondered how much the people knew of the Quorum. It seemed that Nearon had a different form of government. She would have to ask someone when she had a chance.

"Alas, the Empress had to leave us and return to her heavenly home. However, she left the Elemental Order and the Quorum to guide those of Threshold," Apostle Evangeline continued.

Lorelei tapped her fingers against her skirt. From what she remembered from her history books, the Empress had retreated from public rule decades before she disappeared. The Quorum had continued to rule the Empire for the last eight centuries since her disappearance.

"We will all be welcomed into the embrace of the Empress for a rest, if we adhere to her teachings. Do not walk with the spirits, for they will lead you astray. Cultivate Aether, for it is our life's breath. And remember to follow your place in the grand order, for you will be rewarded in the next life."

Reincarnation. Lorelei dug her fingers into her skirt, forming a fist. What the Order didn't preach was how one's past life could invade the current one. She shut her eyes and gritted her teeth. Had she been something horrible in her past? Was that why nightmares plagued her?

The Prioress on Kiste Isle believed she had not followed the Empress in her previous life, and that wickedness was haunting her. Because of that, the nuns encouraged her to live a pious life. They believed it would cleanse her of the taint and she would be cured of Reincarnation Sickness.

She tried, but she found it so confusing. Drinking was looked down upon. Yet, it brought her a measure of happiness, which refueled her Aether. Wasn't the cultivation of Aether one of the tenants they adhered to?

Apostle Evangeline stepped forward between two braziers. "Tonight, we honor the Empress with fire!"

Flames burst forth from both her hands and into the braziers. With a bright burst of orange and yellow, fire roared to life in both of them. The crowd erupted in cheers.

Lorelei clapped, though the spark within her had dimmed with her thoughts.

The Apostle stepped back and turned to enter the temple. The priests and the Council of Peers followed her.

Many of the faeries remained on the steps, chattering in excited voices.

Lorelei descended the stairs and into the streets of the city. She would probably be allowed into the temple, but she wanted to have a taste of the city, including its wine and revelry, instead.

As Lorelei wandered the streets, she was drawn to the sounds of laughter and music coming from a sturdy brick building nestled between two unlit shops. Its welcoming yellow glow radiated from the windows.

The patrons inside sounded happy. Of course, the arrival of the Apostle of Fire had put everyone in the mood for celebration this day.

She gripped the handle of the sturdy wooden door and pushed. The door opened inward and peals of laughter spilled out from the tavern.

She smiled at the crowd of people that sat in the two long tables in the center of the room. They ranged from all races, some in traveling cloaks while others wore reds, blues, or white, depicting the celebratory atmosphere. Smaller groups sat around circular tables in the corners of the room, laughing and chatting over pitchers. The scent of fresh baked bread permeated the air, overpowering the underlying smell of ale.

Lorelei wove her way through the patrons and scurrying hob barmaids to the last open seat at the bar between a male pixie and a slender male with nut skin and a head full of yellow fluff. Lorelei had met plenty of pixies in various bars over the years. Freya would always say that Lorelei should have been born a pixie with all her love of revelry, drinking, and pleasure. Of course, Freya judged people on first impressions, so of course she would assume there wasn't much to pixies besides the generalization. Many enjoyed traveling and would tell her tales from different lands.

Though he didn't have ears or a tail, the other faerie had to be a phooka. In fact, his nose was elongated with a hooked curve, almost like a beak.

The hob barkeep strode over to her, using an upraised platform attached to the backside of the bar, and blew a tuff of black hair from his face.

"What can I get you, my lady?" the barkeep asked.

Lorelei tilted her head up and scanned the bottles on the wall shelf behind the bar. "What kinds of wine do you have?"

"We have some of the best wines from all over the Empire. If you're looking for something rich, we have a few bottles of the Imperial Red." The barkeep leaned close to murmur, "Though, I think our house wine tastes just as good. It's called Heart of the Lovers."

"Hmm, I like the name and I'm always willing to try something new."

The barkeep waddled off and returned a few minutes later with her wine.

Lorelei pulled a silver coin from a pouch on her belt and slid it across the bar. The barkeep tipped his head with a grin, revealing a missing tooth, and took the coin before heading off to another patron down the bar.

Lorelei turned to face the tavern, wine in hand. A phooka from one of the corner tables hopped up and danced to the center of the room while strumming a lute. Cheers filled the room as she sang the first few notes of her song.

Lorelei took her first drink of the wine and smiled. The taste of berries mixed with a hint of spiciness danced on her tongue. A tiny rush of Aether raced through her body. She let out a giggle and leaned back against the bar.

Her head bobbed to the music and a smile lit her face as she finished her wine. She tapped her fingers against the bar, the slight roughness of the wood scratching her finger tips. She tipped the glass back and was only rewarded with the last drop.

"Another round?" a smooth voice tickled her ear.

Lorelei glanced over at the phooka with a raised eyebrow, but he was already waving down the barkeep.

"A refill for the lady and another Sidesweeper for me," the phooka said.

"Thanks." Lorelei studied the phooka as the barkeep left to fill the order.

"Anything for a beautiful lady." He smiled at her. "I'm Hamlin, by the way."

"Lorelei." She shook his hand. "So, do you live in Nearon?"

"Not at all," he chuckled. "I'm from farther South, on the edge of the desert. You probably haven't heard of it. It's called Kurnach."

She shook her head. "No, I haven't heard of it. It's not officially part of the Empire, is it?"

"No, we're part of the Freelands of the South."

"Oh, so what is it like there?" she asked.

He shrugged. "Not much to talk about. It's a town like any other."

"Well, are there any stories about the town?" she asked. "There has to be something interesting."

He smiled at her. "We do have one about a warrior who defended the entire city from an invasion of Sluagh by himself. He died, of course."

Lorelei's heart raced. She loved stories like this. "What happened? Why were they attacking?"

"Well, it was said that whoever possessed the heart of the City would possess the desert and there were several Sluagh Princes who wished to rule the desert.

"Of course, the people of the city didn't want to be ruled by demons, and many a warrior rose to defend Kurnach. They were all defeated in battle except for Kieran. He stood tall with his spear and slayed many that day. Unfortunately, he gave his life in that defense, but his sacrifice stopped the attacks."

The barkeeper placed their drinks in front of them.

"How?" Lorelei asked Hamlin. "I mean, if the really strong

warrior preventing the city from being taken died, why didn't the Sluagh double their efforts?"

Hamlin shook his head, then took a sip from his glass. "I don't know, really. It all happened during the time when the Miasma came, so all we have is the tale that was passed down."

"Oh." Lorelei picked up her wine and took a drink to mask her disappointment.

"What about you?" Hamlin asked. "Are you from the Empire?"

A smile spread across her face and she giggled. "Hy-Breasail, actually. How did you know?"

"That's a port, right?"

She nodded. "It's the closest port from the Empire proper to Nearon."

"It must be a great place," he said.

As long as the faerie acted the right way.

She glanced away and sipped her wine. "So, were you at the fire lighting?"

He perked up. "I was. It was a great show!"

"It was entertaining," Lorelei said, slightly less impressed.

His face scrunched up. "Though I was a little confused on a few things."

"Like what?"

He raised a brow. "Is the Quorum run by all sidhe? No other faerie?"

"Well, no," Lorelei said. "Other faeries are allowed to join the Houses, but the leaders are all sidhe. We're born to rule, after all."

"We don't do that back home. Whoever is strongest rules."

She chuckled. "You don't have many sidhe there, do you?"

"Not really. Why?"

"Because they'd most likely find their way to the top. As I said, born to rule."

He shrugged. "If you say so."

She glanced at his drink. "What is that?"

"It's a mix of whiskey and a cinnamon alcohol," he said. "It's smooth, but it sneaks up on you."

She waved to the barkeep. "I'd like a Sidesweeper, like his."

Hamlin raised a brow. "You sure? It's a bit strong."

"I can handle it." She grinned at him. "I'm not the delicate flower you think I am."

His gaze traveled down her body. "Oh, I'm sure you're not."

One side of her lips lifted in a smirk as the barkeep brought a small glass of amber liquid. She held Hamlin's gold-eyed gaze as she tipped the glass and drained it.

He gave a low whistle. "Brave of you."

"Of course," she said. "I'm a Moura. Bravery is in our blood."

"A Moura, hmm? So, did you come to see the Menhir?"

"Is it that obvious?"

"Why else would a Moura come from the Empire?"

"I have my reasons." She glanced at the phooka minstrel, who had started playing a lively jig. She returned her gaze at Hamlin. "Want to dance?"

He stood and gave an elaborate bow, then offered his hand. "I'd be honored, my lady."

She took his hand and they moved to the open space that had been made for dancers. She whirled about in his arms, laughing and singing the repeated chorus with the rest of the tavern. They danced for hours, stopping only to relieve their thirst with a few rounds of Sidesweepers.

The city was dark and quiet by the time they left the

tavern. Lorelei barely noticed as the buildings passed in a blur.

Giggling and making shushing sounds, she followed him up the stairs of the inn he was staying in and into his room. Their lips met in fevered kisses, and they pulled their clothes from their bodies and dropped them about the floor. They fell upon the bed and into each other, and for a moment of ecstasy, Lorelei forgot the constant ache in her heart.

Later while he slept, she slipped out of the inn and returned to the temple. On her way to her room, one of the priests at the door raised an eyebrow at her, but she gave him a salute.

Inside her room, she laid in her borrowed bed and stared up at the tiled ceiling. He'd asked why she'd come. Yes, she had her own reasons aside from the Menhir. She would find the Black Herons and prove their existence. Arryn, her parents...hell, the Quorum themselves would have to admit she was right.

She just had to survive Winderward first.

4

The cacophony of cheering and music filled the city streets. Red and orange banners fluttered in the air, strung together along the street posts. The scent of roasted meats and sweet breads drifted along the breeze. Thousands of Nearon's citizens had turned out for the parade honoring the arrival of the Apostle of Fire. Every one of them impeded Vandermere from his destination.

He pressed his back to the wooden wall of a tavern as a group of three faerie—a pixie, a phooka, and a hob—ambled past him, laughing and talking excitedly with each other. Luckily, the Apostle and her entourage had already passed through the neighborhood surrounding the docks at the beginning of the parade. He'd fought his way through the worst of the crowds. He only had a few blocks more until he reached the ships. There, he hopefully could find the girl he was looking for. The Nightingale.

He ducked his head down and quickened his pace. The scent of sea and fish assaulted his senses before he rounded the street corner that led to the docks. He wrinkled his nose and pushed on until he reached the buildings that lined the wooden planks of the harbor.

He stopped and surveyed them. They didn't look like much. They stood in a range from one story to four stories, with their wood dried and cracked from the salty air.

He wrinkled his nose as the stench of fish overpowered the sea air.

The docks were nothing like the center of the city with its immaculate houses of stone and ebonwood. There, the homes stretched up several stories and sat upon roads of new cobblestone.

Vandermere sighed. He'd grown tired of the backstabbing and politics of the city run by the Legate and the Council of Peers. They weren't part of the Elphyne Empire, but their scheming and backstabbing reminded him of the Quorum. His duty had been to watch the Menhir, but soon it would be over. He needed to find the girl first.

Seven ships sat floating in the sea next to the docks. One more than yesterday.

Vandermere's heartbeat sped up. Today had to be the day that the Nightingale arrived. His gaze drifted over the sails and name symbols of the ships. The newest one sat at the end of the dock. It was simpler than what he expected for a sidhe noble to travel on. However, the symbol of a four-pointed star surrounded by flame was emblazoned on the sails. The mark of the Apostle of Fire. In his vision, he'd seen the Nightingale surrounded by flames.

The boards creaked under his feet as he strode to the gangplank. Two sailors, a phooka and redcap, were carrying a large crate down. They set it to the side and looked down at him. The red narrowed his eyes at Vandermere as he pushed his red hair from his forehead. The phooka's rabbit ears twitched and he tilted his head at Vandermere with a look of curiosity.

"Anything we can help ye with, milord?" the phooka asked, giving a respectful bow.

"Have the passengers disembarked already?" Vandermere asked.

"Aye." The redcap flashed his sharp teeth. "They left about an hour after we arrived."

"Did they mention where they were traveling to?" Vandermere asked.

"Why?" the redcap asked with a growl.

"I'm looking for a girl. She has mahogany hair and likes to sing," Vandermere said.

The phooka shrugged. "She left with the others, including the Apostle."

Vandermere rubbed the back of his neck. Of course, it wouldn't be that easy. "Thank you."

He turned and scanned the thatched roofs of the shops and taverns.

She'd left with the Apostle, but they could have just been traveling on the same ship. Once again, his vision hadn't been specific on who she would arrive with, if anyone. Still, he should check the newly built Temple of Resplendent Order near the heart of Nearon in case she'd been a part of the Apostle's entourage.

He groaned. Those wishing to hear the words of the Apostle would crowd the temple. She herself would have many guards. If the Nightingale was a part of her retinue, he would have to use his influence as the only member of House Essus in the city. That meant possibly showing his hand.

Why was he even doing this? Searching for a girl in hopes she would help him. His visions were suspect, at best. They were never wrong, but the Shadow lurked on the edges, waiting to take control.

Shouts from the sailors on the deck of the ship pulled him from his reverie. He hurried down the wooden pier to the cobblestone street. Dock workers milled about hefting cargo onto ships in the bright sunlight. A winged pixie girl stood in front of the door of a tavern and beckoned him towards her as he passed by. With the shake of his head, he turned left and strode towards the center of the city. He would search the more refined taverns on his way to the temple. After all, the girl was sidhe and had to have some of her family money.

As he strode farther into the city, the wooden buildings gave way to brick and the scent of baked sweetbread from a nearby bakery overtook the smell of salt and fish.

Vandermere scanned the corner of the cobblestone street with a sigh. Banners of different shades of red were tied to the streetlamps, though some had fallen into the street, trampled by passing carriages.

How could the girl be the key to unraveling what he had seen? How could she know more about the Shadow than he?

He should just return home. It wasn't far from Nearon in the first place, because of his duty.

However, the visions were growing stronger and becoming more frequent. He had to understand what they meant. He was responsible for the events he prophesied. How could he alone carry so much upon his shoulders?

The Shadow was moving faster. Vandermere could feel something looming in the future that could shake the foundations of everything.

He turned right and walked down the sidewalk towards the center of the city. A female hob stood beside a cart of fruits, calling out to those who passed her.

The worst part of the vision was the tower of Iron that rose out of the sea. He shuddered at the thought of such a thing of pure poison. It had to be a symbol for something. Was the Miasma returning?

As if his thoughts called to it, cold fingertips prickled at the back of his mind. He shuddered as a weight filled his cheek, stifling his breathing. No. He couldn't have an attack here. He needed to find the girl first. She could save him. He'd seen it once. The Nightingale could push the Shadow from his mind.

He raked his fingers across his forehead, his nails leaving a tingling aftershock as he stared up at a sign across the street. It was of a dancing hog with a mug of ale in its hand. The Jigging Pig. This would have to do for a start. Perhaps she had stopped by.

He sprinted across the street and yanked open the door. The long wooden tables were half filled with patrons hunched over steaming bowls. The smell of stewed fish and vegetables permeated the tavern.

A hob with blue green hair paused from scrubbing the counter to look up at Vandermere.

"Welcome, my lord," he called. "Can I get you a bowl of stew and a pint?"

Vandermere shook his head and strode to the bar. He kept his voice low and even, fighting off the tremors that wanted to pulse through his body. "Actually, I'm looking for a sidhe girl. She would come to my shoulder with mahogany hair. Maybe she asked to sing?"

The barkeep studied him with narrowed eyes and then made a sucking sound. "Can't rightly say, my lord. There's been a lot of folks in from all over for the coming of the Fire Apostle. A few of them sidhe, even."

Vandermere's shoulders slumped. "Is this an inn?"

"Nope, we're just a tavern. The closest inn is the Dented Shield up the street."

"Thank you, I—" Vandermere gasped as the hob and the tavern began to fade to blackness.

The barkeeps voice sounded far away. "My lord, are you all right? Perhaps you should sit down?"

Vandermere stumbled towards the door and escaped

outside. He needed to get to his house and to his protection. Everything dimmed and the roaring of waves filled his ears.

From the roiling sea, a burst of steam shoots forth a massive iron tower that twists itself into the night sky, rending it like a spear would pierce flesh.

He rushed through the streets as the vision stood semi-imposed over the city itself. He stumbled into a cart, knocking the vendor to the ground. The faerie's shout was muted as he rushed onward. He gulped in a steadied breath as his feet took him closer to his home.

Within minutes, he reached the door to his red brick townhouse and climbed the stairs. The door slammed against the wall, and the paintings on the wall rattled. He dashed into the foyer and through the doorway on his right, his study, and raised his hands in front of him, reaching...searching.

Howls of agony fill the air as a monstrously large, thorned vine winds its way up and around the tower, drinking the red blood that pours from the wounded sky.

The grain of wood brushed against his fingertips. There it was, his cabinet. He swung the doors open and reached inside, groping until he felt the glassy smoothness. His helmet. It would keep the shadow at bay. He'd devised it with spells of misdirection. It had to work. He slipped it over his head.

The thorns reach their apex and bloom into a crimson colored rose, from the petals of which emerge a monstrous snake that begins to devour the rose and wind its way back down the tower.

Vandermere swallowed back the bile rising in his throat. No. Why wasn't the helmet working? It had always worked before. Vandermere stumbled towards the chair at his desk and sank into it. The roaring of the ocean deafened him to the sounds of the city.

The cries of agony are replaced with shouts of triumph as the serpent makes its descent.

With that last image, the Shadow took control.

5

The next morning, while the citizens of Nearon gathered for a special Mass given by the Apostle, Lorelei trekked with Vaana to the outskirts of Nearon where the city pooled over into Winderward.

Most of the buildings were shoddy wooden shacks that looked like they would fall over with a strong enough wind. They had no doors, only scraps of cloth, old blankets, or even ship sails draped in front. A few people squatted outside the dwelling, watching as she and Vaana walked by. Vaana paid no attention to them. Lorelei kept her hand near the pommel of her new sword, just in case.

Vaana had dressed in black leather pants and a tunic that came to mid-thigh and was slit up the sides to her waist. The backpack she wore sagged as if it was mostly empty. Strapped to her leg was a sheath that held a short, thin sword. She'd bought similar clothes for Lorelei, though Lorelei had opted for a leather skirt rather than the pants. Vaana had raised an eyebrow and shrugged, stating Lorelei would regret it once they entered the swamp. Maybe Vaana was right, but Lorelei found pants to be too confining. Vaana had given Lorelei her worn backpack full of supplies before leaving.

As they passed by, an old hob female peered up at them with squinting eyes. Her generous mouth worked into a frown. "Ya'll not going into that cursed city, are ya?"

Vaana paused and glanced down at the hob with her nose wrinkled. "What business is it of yours?"

"None, milady." The hob shrank closer to the dwelling she sat against.

Lorelei took a deep breath and stepped forward. "We are. We're looking for the Menhir Du Moura. Is there any information you can give us?"

The hob peered at her with wide eyes and opened her mouth in a toothless smile. "The Dark Lord has returned. He's been wandering the Marsh. Ya should steer clear of him. And of the Mourner's Hill. Something wicked is callin' people there."

Lorelei raised an eyebrow. "What is the Dark Lord?"

"He's a dangerous thang," the female said. "Some folk say he takes littles. Others say girls. Never saw him myself."

Lorelei glanced at Vaana. "You ever heard of the Dark Lord. Or Mourner's Hill?"

"Mourner's Hill I have. Supposed to be a hill filled with graves. We shouldn't have to pass through there. As for this Dark Lord." She patted the pommel of her knife on her belt. "You shouldn't worry too much. With this and the Empress on our side, we can deal with anything there."

"Thank you." Lorelei pulled out a small loaf of bread from her backpack and handed it to the female. It wasn't much, but it was what she could spare since she didn't know how long she would be in Winderward.

The hob's smile reached her eyes as she tucked the bread into the layers of her clothing. "Blessings of the Empress upon you, milady."

"And you," Lorelei said.

Vaana gave a small hiss and stalked down the street. Lorelei rushed to catch up to her.

"You could be nicer to people," Lorelei said. "A little honey attracts flies."

"I don't want to attract flies. They are pests," Vaana said. "And you should be more careful of what you tell others. That could have been a trap."

Lorelei blinked. "Why would I need to keep where we are going a secret? I'm sure others have passed through here to visit the Menhir."

Vaana stopped at a crumbling wall and shot her a withering look. "These people probably know the best places to ambush and rob us. We don't need to make it easier for them by telling them where we are going."

Lorelei crossed her arms and stared past the wall. There were no wooden shacks on the other side and the road all but disappeared, leaving only patches of cobblestone mixed in with mud and tufts of grass. A short distance away, copses of weeping willows stood among pools of murky water.

"That's it?" Lorelei asked, her stomach fluttering. "That's the beginning of Winderward?"

"Welcome to the Weeping Willow Marsh." Vaana stepped through a large hole in the wall. "It's a short trek through here to get to the Menhir."

"Let's go then." Lorelei surged forward, moving ahead of Vaana.

As she passed through the tree line, the sounds of the city disappeared and the chirping of insects and frogs filled her ears. Walking became more difficult. Most of the ground was muddy, and they had to pick their way through the pools of water that surrounded the weeping willows. The trees drooped with long chains of leaves dripping from their black branches like a stream of tears. Moss draped across the wizened trunks. The air smelled strongly of lilies, which was strange because Lorelei hadn't seen a lily at all.

"So, out of curiosity." Lorelei ducked under a branch and glanced back at Vaana. "Isn't the Elemental Order about helping the downtrodden?"

Vaana smirked. "You really don't know much about it, do you?"

"A little," Lorelei said. "I know that the Miasma almost wiped out our entire race and the Empress was the one to save us. She was able to heal the afflicted and turn iron to emerald."

"That's how the stories go," Vaana said. "But the Empress is more than that. She was the reincarnation of the True Goddess. It is by her grace that we exist and we all must learn our place in her order. For some, their place is below others."

"That doesn't mean they have to starve," Lorelei said.

"Oh, they don't have to starve," Vaana said. "They can go to any church and ask for aid. However, my place isn't to stop and offer aid to every downtrodden person I come across."

"So, what is your place?"

"We're not that close for that personal of a question." Vaana pushed past Lorelei and threaded through a dense set of trees.

"Maybe. But you could at least tell me what Tradition you follow. Most priests aren't secretive about that." Lorelei hopped over a large root. "Are you with Fire, like Apostle Evangeline?"

"No," Vaana said. "I was assigned to the Apostle of Fire by the Voice of Wisdom."

"Really? Does that make you special? Like you're from the Tradition of Aether?"

"There are certain individuals who are talented enough to earn a place under the Voice of Wisdom."

"And you're one of them?"

Vaana stopped, panting, and scanned the swamp. "Like I said, you and I aren't close enough for you to know my life story."

"This isn't really a life story." Lorelei leaned against a weeping willow, pulled a small waterskin from her bag, and took a drink of water. "So, whatever your duties are, they have to do with the Menhir? What are you looking to retrieve?"

"You'll have to see when we get there." Vaana continued on, leaving Lorelei behind.

Lorelei capped her water, returned it to her bag, and rushed forward to catch up to Vaana. Somewhere in the distance, a bird cried a mournful hymn, and a shiver wiggled down Lorelei's spine. Something was off about the marsh. It appeared like many others, but something heavier than moisture hung in the air.

Vaana kept her swift hike. She seemed determined to get to the Menhir as soon as possible. An ill feeling settled in the pit of her stomach. What did Vaana want with the Menhir? Lorelei had been caught up in her chance at gaining her freedom and what she would do beyond that, she never bothered to ask.

"You know, you're being really secretive about your goal at the Menhir," Lorelei said when she caught up to Vaana. "What if you are the one to betray me?"

"I suppose you have to ask yourself if it is worth the risk for your freedom." Vaana pointed to a small hill rising up from the trees surrounding it.

Lorelei let out a small gasp. At the top of the hill stood a group of standing stones.

They'd arrived at the Menhir Du Moura.

* * *

Lorelei panted as she reached the top of the hill.

The oranges and pinks of the setting sun had faded to

dark purple as the light began to wane from the world. Even in the gloom, the Menhir took Lorelei's breath away. The circle of stones towered above her so that she would have to stand on someone's shoulders just to touch the tops.

She ran her hand along one of them, her fingers pressing into the intricate inscribing. It ran from the top down the bottom on all sides. In the center of the circle was a stone disk encased in the earth. Pictures along with words spiraled towards the center. The first picture depicted a female with her finger pointed in the direction she looked and energy beams extending from the back of her head. Before her, masses of creatures, their bodies twisted, cowered.

"That has to be the Empress." Lorelei kneeled for a closer look.

The pictures spiraled on to a male and female facing off with each other. Something like lightning was depicted between the two. The female's hair was carved with intricate flowers woven through it, and the male had a strong face with high cheekbones. The story continued as the two fought by the side of the Empress, and then together later on.

"Moura and Essus." Lorelei's voice sounded like a sigh even to herself.

How long had she known of this story? How long had she dreamed of a love like theirs? She thought she had found it in Arryn. What they had was supposed to last forever.

Her heart squeezed tight until she had to stop and take a deep breath. Their parents had thought differently. Arryn's had found a better match with her sister. After all, Freya was the eldest, while Lorelei was the mere second daughter.

Vaana made her way up the hill, then leaned against a waist-high rock and crossed her arms as she caught her breath.

She stared at Lorelei and gave a soft, silent laugh, just the exhalation of air. "Enjoying yourself?"

Lorelei barely spared her a glance as she stood and made her way to another one of the tall stones. Her fingers ran over the embossment of Essus holding a dying Moura in his arms. She frowned in thought. Perhaps her love with Arryn was more like the legend than she wanted it to be. After all, Essus and Moura had been separated by his jealous wife.

The cracking of branches shook her from her reverie. Vaana stood and pulled her sword. Lorelei was on her feet and over to the side of the hill in a moment. The marsh loomed below, its shadows growing heavy at the loss of the light.

She unsheathed her own sword, gripping the pommel as she scanned the trees.

Who knew what kind of monsters roamed this area at night? Wild creatures or even Fomorians. Lorelei shuddered at the thought of those twisted creatures, victims of the Miasma that had spread millennia ago. Whatever it was, she was prepared to face it. Her father had taught her the basics of defending herself until her mother had deemed it enough. They hadn't known that Lorelei had snuck off to learn actual sword fighting alongside Arryn. It had been one of their many secrets.

A smile came to Lorelei's lips as she remembered lying back in the tall grass of the meadows that surrounded her town and planning to escape into a life of adventure with Arryn. They would take a ship and set sail for the Star Islands of the West, or perhaps for the deserts of the South.

The rattle of rocks sounded from behind her. Lorelei spun around with a gasp, her sword raised. The figure shuffled forward, blocking the dying light, and Lorelei's chest constricted.

It loomed, standing nearly as tall as the stones themselves, dressed in a black flowing cloak with black clothing underneath. The oddest thing was the globe it possessed for a head. The thing seemed to glow with an eerie yellow light.

Lorelei's sword shook in her sweaty palm and she took a step backwards.

Why was she so frightened? She was a Moura, and Mouras were fearless.

A dark, stifling atmosphere emanated from the being, reaching out as if the aura itself wanted to strangle the life from Lorelei one gasp at a time. Whatever this thing was, it didn't mean them any goodwill. It had come to devour their souls. Or they had tread upon its territory, and it had come to get rid of whoever had trespassed.

They were going to have to fight the thing off.

Vaana must have felt the same way. She nodded at the creature and pointed to her knife before crouching and disappearing behind the closest standing stone. Did she want Lorelei to attack it while she snuck behind it?

Lorelei hoped that is what she meant. She stepped forward, taking a fighting stance with her sword pointed at the creature. The figure drew closer and stopped, as if seeing her for the first time. It turned her direction and the weight of its regard weighed upon Lorelei even though it had no real face.

She felt rooted to the spot. She tried to make her legs move, for her body to attack it, but her feet wouldn't obey her silent commands. She had to do something, anything.

But what could she do? This creature was something greater than she and it was displeased at her presence. She could feel its ire washing over her like a dark flood. She swallowed hard, her dry throat contracting. Soon it would do away with her and she couldn't even move.

Sing, Lorelei, a voice whispered in her mind.

She closed her eyes and sent her voice forth. At first, it

trembled at the task of performing for such a fearsome audience, but it grew stronger with each passing word.

"The shadow of the moon hides my sorrow. For the whisper of your name is a thousand voices."

She sang the song that had taken hold of her heart for months. She'd written it after she'd arrived at the Morningtide Priory, when all her feelings for Arryn had been swirling around in her mind.

The figure stiffened and the sphere-like head tilted slightly. The pressure in Lorelei's chest eased and a shiver ran down her spine.

"The moon herself cries tears of silver since you have left my arms." Her voice echoed off of the stones and filled the night.

The figure raised its hands to the globe and it staggered back to rest against one of the great stones for the Menhir. Was that a ragged gasp she'd heard between her verses? The stones themselves gave off a soft blue glow.

"The moon mourns our love in my place, for my heart now lies with you."

Lorelei let the song fade with the last verse. The stones continued to glow around her. She stood and placed a hand on the closest one. The light held a sparkle that danced around her fingertips.

She stared at the figure, panting in a mixture of anxiety and exhilaration of the song. The being raised its glowing globe in her direction and she stiffened. The look wasn't stifling this time. She let out a breath of relief and straightened up with her sword relaxed at her side.

"Why have you come?" A strong male tenor echoed from the globe. It sounded muffled, like something blocked it.

Was that a helmet?

"I came to see the Menhir." Lorelei kept her voice steady.

The anxiety that had overtaken her was dissipating now. "Is this your territory?"

The figure bobbed its sphere in a nod. "It is."

"Winderward doesn't belong to anyone." Vaana's voice rang out from behind him. She stepped out of the darkness with her sword still drawn.

"On the contrary, many stake claims of different areas in Winderward." The figure leaned forward and removed the globe from his head, revealing a cascade of black hair and the face of a sidhe. "In this case, it is under the protection of House Essus. I am Lord Vandermere."

"Lady Lorelei ap Moura." Lorelei nodded to Vaana. "This is Lady Vaana..."

"Of the Elemental Order." Vaana continued to watch him with narrowed eyes.

"A pleasure to finally meet you," Vandermere said.

"Finally? How do you know me? And what just happened?" Lorelei pointed to the globe. "And what is that thing?"

"I suppose it's true that all of House Essus are mad." He ambled up to the stones and inspected them with narrowed eyes. "Interesting."

"So, this was all your madness? And you still haven't answered how you know me?" Lorelei snapped her fingers as she glanced around. "Wait, are you this Dark Lord the people of Nearon are talking about?"

"Unfortunately. It's a rumor that has come from my bouts of madness." He let out a loud breath and held up the globe. "I'd hoped this might stave them off, but alas you found me in a poor state. As for knowing of you...well. House Essus are prophets as well."

Lorelei's eyes widened. She'd heard the stories, but to be a part of some vision... A shiver raced down her spine. "You were here because you saw it?"

"Our meeting? Not here exactly. As I said, this is my territory," Vandermere said. "I'm tasked with watching over it until a certain time."

"What time?" Lorelei asked.

He smiled and looked to Vaana, who was still walking around the stones, running her hands over the glowing carvings. With a soft groan, he sat on a rock, set the globe down, and rubbed the back of his neck. He closed his eyes.

Lorelei sheathed her sword and turned back to the stones and bit her lip. "Do they do this often?"

"What?"

"Do the stones glow often? Is that a trick of the stones or Winderward?"

He chuckled. "Oh, no. I believe that was your doing. Your singing."

"Great." It had been a long time since her magic had done something unexpected. She'd sacrificed much to have it fixed. She didn't need that kind of thing happening in Winderward.

"You don't sound happy about that," Vaana said. "Surely, you had some training as a Lyrist at the Aimsir?"

Lorelei averted her gaze. "Not enough."

"Pity, you have a natural talent. More than I've seen from even the most skilled bards."

Lorelei's shoulders stiffened. "Does that mean you are going to arrest me as a heretic?"

"Maybe. Are you consorting with spirits or Sluagh?"

Lorelei snorted and shook her head.

"Are you sure? It would explain your singing."

"No."

"Good. Then we have no problems," Vaana said.

She stepped in the middle of the stones to inspect the inscribed disc with a furrowed brow.

"What are you doing?" Lorelei moved to stare at the inscriptions as well.

Vaana bent down to run her hand in the center of the spiral. "You are the daughter of Lord Dougan and Lady Morgaine, correct?"

"Yes, but I'm not sure..."

"By blood?"

"Yes."

Vaana smiled. "Excellent."

"What does it matter?"

Vaana stood and strode over to the outer stones. She traced her fingers across the glowing inscriptions on one, mumbling to herself. At the tallest stone, she halted and pressed symbols on the stone. They sank with the grinding of rock and the hill began to rumble. Lorelei grabbed onto the nearest stone to keep from tumbling to the ground. The spiral in the center sank, forming a staircase.

"Hmm, that wasn't as difficult as I thought it would be," Vaana said.

She pulled a long rod from her backpack and whispered a word. The tip lit into an orange glow.

Lorelei moved forward, trying to keep from gaping at the stairs. Vaana had told her there was something beneath the rock before, but the whole idea that the Menhir was something other than a monument was almost too much to believe.

Vaana glanced at her. "Shall we see what's inside?"

Lorelei turned towards Vandermere. "May we?"

"By all means." The corner of his mouth lifted in a smirk as his gaze swept over Vaana. "It's what you came here for, after all."

Lorelei gave Vaana a conspiratorial grin. "Let's go."

Vaana handed her the torch. "Lead the way."

6

Lorelei took the light rod and began her descent down the stairs. Her footsteps echoed in the darkness surrounding her. The narrow walls opened up as she reached the bottom. The air was surprisingly sweet for hidden ruins, like a cinnamon musk. The edges of her light barely reached the walls.

Vaana moved to one, pulled a flint and steel from her bag, and lit a sconce. Reddish fire flared for a moment, and Lorelei gasped.

The room appeared to be circular and made of a greenish stone. She moved closer. Was that emerald? No, it was too dull to be.

Circular disks That spanned from ceiling from floor stuck out from the walls with writing carved on them. There were large bars jutting from the middle of each. Lorelei grabbed the bar to the disk on the far left and turned it to the right so that the bar was vertical. A loud click echoed through the room followed by the scraping of stone. The disk glided back, so it was flush with the wall and slid to the side, leaving a large doorway.

Vaana took the torch from her and held it up. "It looks like we begin to the left."

Lorelei followed her into the room with her heart racing. Vandermere trailed behind with his hands in his pockets.

Being underneath the Menhir seemed almost forbidden, like a sacrilege. When had that ever stopped her before? Perhaps she could find more about Essus and Moura. Too bad Arryn wasn't here.

She swallowed the knot in her throat and shook her head. Arryn wouldn't be joining her for any more adventures. She had a new companion, although she was a little strange for an acolyte of the Order.

Past the doorway, pedestals lined the sides of the rectangular room. Lorelei stopped at the first one and bent to inspect the object resting on top of it. It was a ruby the size of her fist. Tiny flames danced inside the heart of the red stone.

Vaana glanced back at it before moving to the back wall. "A heartstone."

"Oh," Lorelei exclaimed. "I've heard of those. Isn't there a story that they are actually the hearts of spirits?"

Vaana shrugged. "That's the belief. The more powerful the spirit, the more magic the stone will hold."

"So, this would have been a fire spirit." Lorelei sighed. "It's almost sad. They had to die for us to have this magic."

"Why? They were our enemies once."

Lorelei blinked. "When?"

"Before the Miasma."

"How do you know anything that happened before the Miasma? All that was lost."

Vaana smirked. "The knowledge is there...if you know where to look."

"And you have looked in a lot of places?" Lorelei studied her. "I doubt you are much older than I."

"Old enough to have seen the world. The Voice of Wisdom saw fit to send me into the world early," Vaana said.

She picked up a bracelet from one of the pedestals, wiped it on her sleeve, and stuck it in her bag. With a small shrug, she headed towards the door they entered. Lorelei scanned the trinkets on the pedestals. She ran her finger along the surface of the one that held the ruby. Her finger came away clean.

"This place is well maintained for being almost forgotten," Lorelei said.

"And?"

"And these aren't ruins. This is someone's vault."

"Actually, it would be both," Vandermere said. "It has been in the keeping of my House since the Miasma. We use it to store dangerous artifacts."

Vaana frowned. "You should turn them over to the Order."

"Not all of us believe the Order should have that much power," Vandermere said. "Besides, your Wyld Hunt brings you enough."

Lorelei swallowed as her throat went dry. The Order had called for the Wyld Hunt to reclaim dangerous artifacts and rid the Empire of heretics. They claimed it was to ensure something like the Miasma never happened again, not that anyone knew how it had started. Lorelei had heard a few tales, whispered in the darkened corners of taverns, of the Wyld hunt taking people who weren't heretics, of whole families disappearing. Lorelei shuddered and wrapped her arms around herself. They were just rumors though. The Order was there to guide and protect the people. That's why the Empire sought to stretch wider, beyond the central continent, to bring safety and protection to the world. After all, Threshold still had pockets of Miasma and Fomorians roaming around.

Vaana raised her chin as her face went taut. "The Wyld Hunt protects the faerie."

"Perhaps that was true when you fought the Fomorians, but we both know the Order has moved beyond that."

"So, you would rather allow Sluagh to run amok, stealing souls or enslaving whole towns to their will?"

Lorelei shivered. She had loved to sit with Freya and Arryn as children and share haunting tales of the Sluagh, the demons who used faerie souls as bargaining chips. Many a mage had summoned Sluagh intending to enslave them, only to be enslaved themselves.

They didn't live on Threshold, but another realm far to the South. If someone could survive the trek through the Fire Plains, one would become lost and fall into the domain of the Eternal Desert. Beyond the Eternal Desert stood the Demon City, home of the Sluagh.

"Perhaps," Vandermere said. "But what about the spirits and little gods you hunt?"

"Little gods?" Lorelei asked.

Vaana pursed her lips. "Upstarts who believe they can steal worship away from the Empress with a little bit of power."

Vandermere sighed and covered his eyes with his hand. "The lies you have been told have blinded you. Everything in existence has an essence. Sometimes that essence gains sentience. They would be the god of their small area."

Vaana glared at him. "How far are you willing to go with your blasphemous speech?"

He smiled. "Forgive me. You are not ready. Shall we return to the reason you came?"

She crossed her arms. "With the way you have spoken, I can have your property seized by the power of the Disciple of Fire."

"Oh, I wasn't planning on stopping you from searching.

By all means..." He waved his hand to the open door she stood beside.

She gave him one last condescending look before stepping inside the hallway. Lorelei moved closer to Vandermere. Her heart was racing and she wasn't sure if it was because of his presence or the whole event. What was she thinking? Was she so ready to fall for another handsome face? She had sworn her eternal love for Arryn.

And where did that get you?

"They are fallible, like you and I," Vandermere said. "You shouldn't revere them, Nightingale."

She paused. "How did you know that was my nickname?"

He smiled and ambled to the doorway, peering out it to where Vaana must have been.

Lorelei raised a brow. Damn House Essus. She now understood why many considered them unsettling.

Besides the madness, of course.

She turned back to the red gemstone on the pedestal. "Can I take this?"

"Sure," he said. "It will be useful for what's coming."

"It must be nice to know everything," Lorelei muttered.

"I don't know everything," he said in an annoyed voice. "And my visions aren't always straight forward."

"Visions?" She frowned at him. "Are they always of the future?"

"Sometimes the past, but it tends to be even more confusing."

"Have you had any visions of me?"

Vandermere smiled. "We should see what Vaana has gotten into and make sure she doesn't claim too many artifacts."

He turned and stepped out of the room with his arm resting on the doorframe.

She took the ruby, pocketing it in her side satchel, and

strode to him to poke her head under his arm. Vaana had moved past the remaining circular doors to a wall in the back. She rested one hand on her chin as she studied it, mumbling to herself in a soft voice.

"Speaking of trust," Lorelei said, "are you really going to let her take whatever she is after in here? She gets no admonishments about things being dangerous?"

Vandermere sighed. "We can only hide things for so long. Eventually they become unearthed."

Vaana glanced back at them with an anticipatory smile lighting on her face. "I think I found it."

"Found what?" Lorelei asked.

"Come and see." Vaana crooked her finger in a "come hither" motion.

Lorelei slipped under Vandermere's arm and joined Vaana. The bricks of the back wall had slid from their places to reveal an embossed depiction of a sidhe female with long flowing hair gazing up a sidhe male. The artist had captured the looks of adoration and devotion. Their hands were joined between them.

Lorelei sucked in a quick breath. "Moura and Essus."

Vaana stepped back with her arms crossed. "Indeed."

"Why was it hidden?" Lorelei asked.

"Hmm, that is the question," Vaana murmured.

Lorelei raised an eyebrow. "I have a feeling you already know the answer."

Vaana chuckled. "I have some suspicions."

"Well, what is it?"

Vaana pointed to the entwined hands. "Touch it and see."

Lorelei gave an annoyed sigh. Why did Vaana have to be so cryptic all the time? She was worse than Vandermere, and he was a seer. She placed her hand over Moura's and waited. Nothing happened.

She looked back to Vaana. "Well? Is it supposed to light up or something?"

Vaana's brow furrowed. "That should have worked. I have a true blood descendant of Moura..."

Vandermere ambled up behind Vaana and studied the wall. "You seem to be missing half."

"The scrolls said one or the other." Vaana crossed her arms and glared at him. "Don't tell me you knew about this all along."

Vandermere chuckled. "Do you think our ancestors would make things so simple if they wanted this to stay hidden?"

"I'm really starting to feel left out of this conversation," Lorelei muttered.

"Allow me," Vandermere said.

He stepped forward and placed his hand on Essus's stone fingers so that his thumb brushed Lorelei's. Her pulse raced as their gazes met. The stone beneath their hands warmed.

A seam appeared in the wall, separating Moura from Essus. The irony was not lost on Lorelei. The embossment slid forward and to the side, covering the bricks of the wall. Lorelei coughed and covered her mouth as stale air rushed from the opening.

A narrow hallway led into darkness. From the darkness a female voice sang in a language Lorelei didn't recognize. It was soft, with hissing vowels, like the rustling of silk.

Vaana pushed past Vandermere and Lorelei and hurried down the hall with her torch lifted up, leaving a trail of disturbed dust behind. Vandermere gave Lorelei's hand a gentle squeeze and pulled her down the hall in Vaana's wake.

The voice continued to sing as they made their way down the hall. It ended in a round room filled with a soft white light from that seemed to be everywhere at once. Six pedestals stood in a circle in the center of the room, each holding a large stone tablet.

Vaana circled them with a calculating look on her face. She moved between the pedestals and pulled her bag from her back. Her hand reached out for the first tablet on her right.

"Are you sure you wish to do that?" Vandermere asked. "Are you willing to pay the consequences?"

Vaana smirked and nodded to Lorelei. "I know what I'm doing. This isn't my first time delving into secret places."

Vaana reached out and grasped the first stone. Small bolts of lightning raced from the edges and covered her hand. She screamed. The tablet crumbled into dust and the lightning zapped the two adjacent tablets as it continued to climb up Vaana's arm. Lorelei darted forward to try to knock her free from the circle but Vandermere pulled her back.

"She has made her choice," he said.

"But it will kill her." Lorelei waved a wide hand in Vaana's direction.

The lightning covered the remaining tablets. They shook and then crumbled into dust, each sending a new bolt that struck Vaana. Her scream filled the room and she fell to her knees. The lightning raced along her entire body and traveled up to fill her eyes with a light that flashed a multitude of colors. She collapsed in a heap as the light faded and took a long shuddering breath.

Vandermere's grip tightened on Lorelei's arm as a guttural sound left his throat. He slid to the ground, clutching his head.

Lorelei stared between the two with a thrum in her ears pounding in time to her racing heart.

What had just happened?

7

Vandermere sat on the ground with his fingers pressed into his temples as blackness covered his vision. His heart pounded in his chest. He could feel that familiar tingling behind his eyes. A vision was coming on. Music, heavy with drum and guitar, filled his ears.

He stands surrounded by blackness. A leather book, seven foot by four feet and one inch thick, appears in front of him. A tarnished silver chain hangs at the bottom. Seven lidded eyes adorn the front. The left eye opens, glowing a deep purple. The book fades, leaving only the purple glowing eye. It flashes.

Vandermere finds himself in a great hall. Tapestries hang along the walls filled with creatures he doesn't recognize.

A female with long black hair and immaculate robes stands in the center of the room. A silver and amethyst crown adorns her head. Her gaze travels upward and Vandermere's vision follows to the ceiling where a hexagon is set in the middle of a starscape. At the points where the lines meet there are pictures: an erupting volcano, rolling clouds, a pool of water, dancing fire, wood, and a set of crystals. In the center is a lidless eye.

She speaks to the Eye, but Vandermere can't hear her words. The eye doesn't seem to respond. When she finishes, the eye vanishes.

Blackness. The gem flashes purple and an ankh unfolds in the center of the darkness. There is another flash of purple.

The crowned female stands in the same room with six others. The lidless eye is gone. She moves her hand to the ceiling above as she says something to the group. They watch her with contemplating looks.

A white-haired female shakes her head. Her eyes narrow behind the violet light produced by two thin bands of metal, one above her eyes and one below. She steps forward and pounds her fist into the palm of her other hand to punctuate her words.

The crowned female motions to the ceiling again in a sharp jerk and speaks words Vandermere cannot hear. A winged male in red, carrying a sword as tall as himself, stands beside the white hair female. He waves his hand in a flat swipe and shakes his head.

A blond male with white glowing eyes, standing with his hands clasped in front of him, nods to the crowned female. She smiles at him and looks back to the white-haired female with a raised eyebrow. The white-haired female moves until their faces are inches apart and speaks slowly. The crowned female turns her head and says something in the direction of the three quiet ones. A male with long hair and an obscured face laughs and nods to the crowned female. Beside him, a blue-haired male in gray robes speaks but keeps his eyes on the floor. In the corner, a tall thin female, half of her body black and the other half white, shrugs and stares at the ceiling.

The male in red puts a hand on the white-haired female's shoulder. She glances back at him and takes a deep breath. The crowned female glances around and speaks again. All nod and then they disappear.

There is a flash of purple light and a ruby gemstone hangs from a chain in a black void.

Vandermere's vision pans over thousands of beings. Some are made of living fire, while others are made of water, wood, wind, or crystal. The spirits.

A flash of light.

Millions of people. They look to be sidhe but more. Their ears are more pointed, and they stand with a regal stance.

Flash.

A sword appears, piercing down.

Vandermere stands in the middle of a battlefield. On one side stands an old male and behind him are the seven beings from the room. The crowned female has a chain on her wrist of a dark twisted metal.

Vandermere's heart pounds. Iron.

At the other end floats the hexagram with the eye in the center. Behind it are many of the spirits he had seen.

Flash.

A mirror turns before him, reflective on both sides.

The dead cover the battlefield. Only a few hundred of the spirits remain. The millions are as they were as are another group that looks similar, only with gray skin.

Flash.

All faerie. Society with churches flourishing.

Flash.

Butterflies of all colors fly around Vandermere.

Flash.

A shadow rises over the society. It cripples, kills, and destroys. Metals turns to iron. What was once the crowned female walks the world. Her crown is gone, and her hair has changed to blue and her eyes are white. Blood trails from her lips and down her alabaster skin. Wherever she goes, the shadow follows.

Vandermere's chest tightens. He knows this shadow. It still hovers over the world now. The Miasma.

Flash.

The remaining six confront the once crowned female. Her hair has changed to a powder blue and her skin is as pale as ivory now. The fight takes them from Threshold and across many realms. The white-haired female fights fiercely, but she is the first to fall as the shadow strikes her and she is no more. The male with the obscured face turns to find the pale female beside him. She strikes him and he is no more. The male with glowing white eyes attacks the pale female. She tears him to shreds. The blue-haired male raises his sword and appears in front of her. The shadow strikes out and destroys him. The male in red drives his sword through her back. She turns to face him, charges forward, and impales him on his own blade. She pulls the sword from her back and turns her attention to the last one—the black and white female.

The black and white female grins at her. The shadow comes to strike and she tears the Miasma from it. Its body warps and twists, beginning to grow. She tosses it away and turn to the pale female. They fight but the black and white female overcomes the pale female. She stands over the pale female's fallen form and sways. Small bits of corrosion appear on her skin. What is black and what is white splits into two separate beings. The shadow will eat the black part of her away. The white falls through the realms and hits the site of the future Imperial City.

A beautiful female will emerge from the crash and begin her trek, turning iron to emeralds as she walks.

Vandermere gasped, waving his arms in front of him, his entire body stiffening. The glow of the torches came into focus, followed by the stone of the secret room.

Lorelei was leaning over him with a frown on her face.

"I'm fine." He pulled himself up with the help of the pillar behind him as he tried to chase away the scenes dancing behind his eyes. What did any of it mean? He had seen the Miasma, but the Shadow hadn't driven him over the edge, for once.

Lorelei breathed a sigh, stood, and squeezed his shoulder gently. "I wasn't sure what was happening. Especially since Vaana collapsed at the same time."

Vaana lay in a heap in the center of the pedestals, twitching. Little bolts of lightning raced across her skin occasionally.

"She found what she was searching for," he said. "She didn't know the consequences."

"Is she dead?" Lorelei raised up on her toes to peer at Vaana.

"No, she is probably acclimating to the new presences within her."

"The lightning from the stone? Were they spirits?"

A flash of the faces of the six beings passed through his mind. "No. Gods."

Lorelei stared at him with her eyes wide. She opened her mouth to ask him to elaborate but a sharp crack drowned out her words. An ice blue light swirled into being on the far wall. It grew larger and larger until a disk covered the wall, stretching from floor to ceiling. The pale female with blue hair stepped out.

Vandermere's heart plummeted.

8

When Vandermere's face paled, Lorelei turned to see what had caught his attention. The creature that stepped out of the portal could barely be called female. She was not sidhe or any other race Lorelei knew. Her blue hair flew about her wildly. From the neck down, she wore some sort of form-fitting armor made of bone and flesh that wasn't her own.

Lorelei shivered. The being tilted her head and studied Lorelei and Vandermere with her crimson eyes before turning her gaze to Vaana. Two sharp fangs poked out from her lips as she smiled.

"Such an obedient girl," the creature murmured.

She took a step in Vaana's direction.

Vandermere darted forward to stand in between the creature and Vaana. She stared at him as if he was some sort of insect. He drew the sword at his side and pointed it at her.

"You won't be taking her, or them, today," he said.

She laughed. "You would dare stand in my way? Move aside, boy. I wish to be reunited with my siblings."

Lorelei swallowed, her mouth going dry. What in

Gehenna was this thing? Could it be a Sluagh...or even a Fomorian? She didn't know, but it wanted to take Vaana and she couldn't let that happen, even if she had no idea what Vaana had gotten them into.

Lorelei strode to stand beside Vandermere. "I don't think anyone here is related to you, whoever or whatever you are."

The creature smirked. "You shouldn't get involved in things you know nothing about."

Lorelei felt her cheeks flame. Throughout the exploration of the vault, she had felt like a passenger in a carriage that she had no idea where it was going.

She took a deep breath. "I know enough to know you're not welcome here."

"I go where I please."

"Not here," Lorelei unsheathed her sword.

This was her chance to prove she was a true descendant of Lady Moura. Her House was fearless, after all.

"And you plan to stop me?"

Lorelei raised her sword.

The creature threw her head back and laughed. "Who are you to believe you can defeat the Mother of Vampires?"

Lorelei's heart raced in her chest. She had heard tales of vampires, Fomorians that could drain the very essence of the faerie. Daan, the Mother of Vampires, had become twisted by the Miasma. She had spread her contagion wherever she went, creating more and more children. During her adventure with Arryn in the Citadel of Night she'd found vampires. It had taken everything for her to prevent an ancient one from awakening.

Now, Lorelei stood face to face with the original. She swallowed and straightened her shoulders.

"I am Lorelei ap Moura," she said. "Remember it in your death."

Vandermere glanced at her and frowned.

"I was going to save you for after," Daan said with a snarl. "However, I think an appetizer before the main course is more fitting."

Lorelei swung her sword and connected with Daan's shoulder. The blade scraped against the bones and bounced off with a show of sparks. Daan smirked and swiped her hand at Lorelei. The knobby claws sliced through Lorelei's sleeve and sank into her shoulder. Lorelei screamed and yanked herself backwards. She covered her wound with her hand, and her royal blue blood seeped through her fingers.

Vandermere jabbed his sword through the thin opening in between the bones that covered Daan's chest. Red ichor oozed from the wound. Lorelei's heart pounded in her ears. Only Fomorians had red blood. Daan's gaze traveled from the wound to Vandermere, and her face twisted in a fearsome scowl. Her backhand sent him flying across the room.

Lorelei lunged forward, aiming her sword for Daan's breast. Daan knocked the blade to the side with one hand and swiped at Lorelei's chest with the other. The bones that made up the shoulder pads in her armor stretched out and buried themselves in Lorelei's shoulders and arms. She screamed. She could feel a pulling sensation that started with the blood in her veins. She choked out a gargle as her entire body burned. Her sword fell from her numbing fingers.

Lorelei heaved herself up and gripped one of the bones imbedded in her arm. The world had taken on a surreal quality. She twisted her wrist and the bone snapped under her hand. Pain shot through her arm as a spurt of blood gushed across her chest and once again, she was swinging in the air. The air became so heavy, she had to suck in long gasps.

She shifted to grab the next bone but Daan's hand snaked out and caught her in the throat. Vandermere swung his sword at the remaining bones. Daan batted the blade away with the back of her other hand. The bones retracted from Lorelei's arm.

"You taste different." Daan narrowed her eyes. "There is something more to you than just a sidhe. Did your mother have a dalliance with a little god?"

Vandermere rammed his blade through the fleshy part of Daan's armpit. Lorelei hit the ground and the breath was knocked out of her. Her fingers brushed against her sword's handle.

Daan grabbed Vandermere and rammed him into the pillar. He slid to the floor as she dropped him. Lorelei lunged at Daan. She buried her blade between the bones covering her abdomen. Daan gave a little choke and glared at Lorelei. Her shove sent Lorelei skittering across the floor and into Vaana.

Vaana moaned and sat up as Lorelei climbed off her. Daan strutted towards the two of them with an anticipatory smile. Lorelei struggled to her feet. Blood that flowed from the holes the bones had left behind streaked her dress. Thank the Empress, the protrusions still stuck in her had blocked the other wounds or she might not even be able to stand at this point. The world was spinning as it was. However, she wouldn't die on her knees.

The wounds she and Vandermere had inflicted on Daan were already closing. The sword was all but useless against this creature.

She needed something more magical. She glanced at her bag. Vandermere said the heartstone would be useful, though he'd inferred for later. Still, she didn't have much of a choice. She yanked the ruby from her bag and held it in front of her like a medallion.

Daan threw her head back and laughed. "What are you expecting that to do?"

Lorelei pursed her lips. She had no idea how to activate

such a thing. The Order had confiscated most of the heart-stones. She had to think of something.

Sing.

A song to call fire that she'd learned from the academy came to mind. She hummed and the lyrics sprang from her lips as she concentrated on coaxing fire from the stone.

Fire burst from the ruby in an explosion that slammed into Daan and her, sending them flying in opposite directions. Lorelei crashed into one of the pedestals and hit the ground. With a groan, she picked herself up and ran her hands over her body. Other than her clothes being singed, she'd taken no harm from the flames. The ruby had to have protected her.

Daan was another matter. The fiery blast had left a giant burn across the flesh parts of her body and scorched the bone along Daan's chest. She hobbled to her feet and glared at Lorelei, raising her bone wings for a strike.

Lorelei trembled as a wave of exhaustion hit her. This was it. She would die now.

A blur of motion in her peripheral caught her attention. A female with a white hair and some sort of metal visor that glowed violet marched past her.

Where had she come from? The spot Vaana had lay was now empty.

Daan stiffened, her eyes fixed on the female. The white-haired female hand extended as she continued to stride towards the Daan. A large axe appeared in it. She gripped it with her other hand, spun, and swung the axe at Daan's midsection. Daan leapt back and the blade of the axe missed her by inches. She glowered at the white-haired female as she backed towards the open portal.

"Leaving so soon?" the white hair female asked. "We have much to discuss."

Daan gave her a sour smile. "Another time."

"I'll be waiting," the white-haired female said.

Daan stepped back into the portal with her gaze locked on the white-haired female. The portal shrunk until it became a tiny dot and disappeared.

Lorelei stumbled back against the wall, her body sagging. Her veins were still singing, but nausea rose from the pit of her stomach.

She turned to study the female. She was taller than even Vandermere and held herself as if she was larger than life.

"Thank you," Lorelei said. "Though I don't know who I should be thanking."

The female studied her with narrowed eyes. "You don't know the Morrigan?"

Lorelei blinked. "Who?"

The female gave a disgusted snort. "What has the faerie come to, they forget their own gods?"

"The only Goddess I know of is the Empress," Lorelei said. "I guess you can thank the Miasma if we lost anyone else."

The female snarled.

"So, I'm guessing you would be the Morrigan?"

The Morrigan took a step closer to Lorelei with her axe gripped in her hand.

Lorelei's heart pounded. Now she had done it.

The Morrigan staggered and paused to rest one hand on a pillar. She let out a gasp as her entire body shuddered. It shook again and continued until her entire form became a blur. It shrank upon itself.

Lorelei took a hesitant step towards her. Would touching her be bad? Tiny bolts of lightning raced across the form and the vibrating ceased. In her place, Vaana collapsed to her hands and knees with her chest heaving.

Lorelei rushed to her. "What is going on? This whole night is insane."

Vaana looked up at her with exhausted eyes. "You have no idea."

Lorelei stood and scanned the room. She hadn't seen Vandermere since Daan had knocked him across the room. Her gaze fell upon his still form on the floor and her chest squeezed painfully.

❧

Lorelei rushed to Vandermere and knelt beside him. His skin was cool to the touch. She stared at his chest, praying for some indication of movement.

There it was. She let out a sigh of relief and pulled his head into her lap.

"You shouldn't move him," Vaana said in a hoarse voice.

Her entire body was leaned against one pillar with her palms flat against it. She looked as if it was supporting her along with the ceiling. She took several unsteady steps and all but collapsed beside Vandermere.

"Move," she said.

"You're a healer?" Lorelei asked.

"One of the skills of the Order is healing."

Lorelei leaned back and closed her eyes as the dizziness flared up again. "You're a female of many talents."

The sharp sting across her cheek caused her to jump. She blinked at Vaana leaning over her. When had she lain down?

Vandermere was sitting up rubbing his temple, a large white bandage swathed his head. Vaana was wrapping bandages around the bone shards still protruding out of Lorelei.

"Fall asleep and you may never awaken," Vaana said. "I will have to remove the shard later."

"Will she be able to make it through the Marsh?" Vandermere asked.

Vaana raised an eyebrow at him. "Not alone."

"Very well." He stood up. "I'll carry her."

"Someone please tell me what just happened. Why was the Mother of Vampires trying to eat me?"

Vaana stood and pulled Lorelei to her feet. "It's a long tale. One we don't have time for."

Lorelei frowned. "What do you mean?"

"She'll be sending her minions to finish us off," Vandermere said. "We don't want them to find us here while you're in this condition."

"We should go to the Order," Lorelei said. "They'll want to know the Mother of Vampires is in Winderward."

"I can't now," Vaana muttered, looking away.

"What do you mean?" Lorelei asked. "Aren't you a priest or something?"

Vandermere cleared his throat. "Vaana has found herself in quite a predicament."

"Things didn't go as planned," Vaana said.

"All of which can be discussed at a later time, when we are safely away," Vandermere said.

Lorelei took a step and the world tilted. She reached out and grabbed onto Vaana's arm. Vandermere took her shoulders and steadied her. When she found her balance, he guided her through the hall, toward the exit.

The rooms became a blur. Soon, she found herself outside, staring at the moon with the fresh air sending chills down her back. She wandered to one of the large rocks and sat down. With a groan, she leaned forward, resting her elbows on her knees, and willed the world to stop spinning.

Vandermere hovered over her, but he turned to Vaana. "Shut the entrance."

The rumble of sliding stone echoed through the night. Vandermere jerked his blade across his palm in a swift motion. He let his blue blood drip on the spiral writing of the stone pillar. Purple light shimmered across the surface, followed by a soft pop.

"That should keep them out," Vandermere said.

Vaana crossed her arms. "Not forever."

"Long enough for the head of my House, Lord Lorenz, to receive my letter." Vandermere sheathed his sword, pulled a small handkerchief from his pocket, and wrapped it around his hand.

He took Lorelei by her elbow, nudging her to her feet, and guided her through the treacherous maze of rocks set on tripping her on her way to the bottom of the hill. Vaana was already halfway down. They seemed to be leaving the opposite way they arrived though Lorelei couldn't be sure. The dizziness seemed to grow with each step. Once they made it to the Marsh, Vandermere lifted her into his arms and cradled her against his chest. Her arm brushed against his and sent a sharp bolt through her body.

"Just a little longer," Vandermere murmured in her ear.

Time slowed to a crawl. Every step Vandermere took seemed to take an eternity. Lorelei longed to close her eyes, but she couldn't. Her mind was racing. Each question she had was like a layer of an onion being peeled back to reveal a new one. Who the hell was the Morrigan and how had Vaana changed into her?

The Mother of Vampires had been afraid of her. Why? This all started with the stone Vaana had been after. What were they, really? Vandermere and Vaana would come off with what they knew as soon as the world quit spinning.

When they finally stopped hours later, Lorelei slid off out of Vandermere's arms and to a sitting position on the ground. Vaana marched over and knelt beside Lorelei. She drew out a rolled-up leather case from her backpack, opened it, and pulled a large pair of tongs and a piece of flat wood.

"This will hurt." Vaana held out the wood to her.

Lorelei shook her head. "Just get it over with."

Vaana positioned herself next to Lorelei and pulled the first bone shard from her arm. The world turned sideways. Lorelei bit down on her tongue to keep from screaming. The tang of copper filled her mouth and a new pain joined the rest.

By the time all the bone shards were removed, she was flat on the ground with Vandermere's hands on her shoulders.

"Sit her up and remove her sleeves," Vaana said.

A cool wet cloth touched the bare flesh of her arms. The burning started as the liquid seeped into her wounds. She winced. It was nothing compared to what she had just felt, though.

Vaana began chanting in a soft tone and the burning in Lorelei's chest and shoulders lessened to a soft tingling. Gone were the deep gaping holes and claw marks, replaced by thin scabs. They looked weeks old instead of one night.

Vaana held a flask out to Lorelei.

"Drink it. It will help with the rest of the healing," she said. "Healing the both of you has taken a lot of Aether."

Lorelei took a long gulp. The nutty bitterness stung her tongue and made her eyes water. A strange warmth settled in her stomach and began to spread through her limbs. She yawned as the world dulled around her. The ground invited her to rest her head upon it.

Vaana gathered her things and stood. "You should get some sleep."

"Not yet," Lorelei struggled to form a coherent thought. She would get to the bottom of this tonight. "You will tell me what is going on. What happened with the stones, and why were we attacked by the Mother of Vampires?"

Vaana shoulders stiffened. "This can wait."

"It's waited long enough. If we're safe to sleep, we're safe to talk," Lorelei said. "Both of you know a lot more than me. If someone doesn't explain, I'm leaving."

Vaana turned and crossed her arms with her eyes narrowed. "I don't give into threats."

"It's not a threat..."

Lorelei swayed. What had she been saying? She looked down at the flask in her hand then back to Vaana.

"Did you drug me?" she asked.

Vaana smirked.

Vandermere pulled her up from the tree stump. "We will talk tomorrow, when you can comprehend things better."

Lorelei's eyelids drooped and she gripped Vandermere's arms just to keep upright. He helped her lay down on a bedroll he'd rolled out. She wanted to argue, but being defiant seemed like too much effort. She reached a hand out as he left her, leaving a sudden coldness in his place. She was always cold and alone.

As the world drifted away, she hoped she didn't dream.

9

Vandermere stood with his back against a tree and watched the sun peek over the horizon, turning the sky light pink.

Nearby, Lorelei whimpered in her sleep and rolled in his direction. Her face scrunched in a grimace. He half rose with a hand stretched out to her. With her injuries, she needed as much rest as possible, but this didn't seem like good sleep. She'd slumbered fitfully in the last few hours that he'd taken the responsibility of keeping watch from Vaana.

He sighed. He'd waited many years of his life for this moment. Now that it was here, he wished she hadn't come into his life. No longer did he have the isolation of his home and or even the Menhir to rely on when his visions were at their worst. Would she be able to cope when the madness struck him? Would Vaana decide he was too much of a danger and eliminate him? His visions left more questions and few answers.

Whatever was a part of Vaana now was connected to Daan. The reaction of the tablets had drawn the Mother of Vampires to them.

He shuddered. She hadn't always been like that, if what he'd seen had been true. She'd been a god. The Shadow had twisted her into a monster. He'd recognized that thing as it had attacked the other in his vision.

He ran his hands partway through his long hair, then tapped one heel of his boot against the tree trunk. Daan. Those other gods. There were giants and he was a mere insect. If they fell so easily to the Shadow's machinations, what chance did he have? What chance did Lorelei have?

With a soft groan, he pushed away from the tree and strode to Lorelei. Dawn was here, regardless. They needed to be on the road soon enough. The farther from the Menhir, the better.

He leaned down and rested his hand on Lorelei's shoulder. His vision shifted for a second. Platinum blonde locks that seemed to glow with their own light had replaced her mahogany hair. Her cheekbones became sharper and her nose more pointed. Around her forehead extended an intricate golden headpiece.

His heart pounded in his ears. What was this? Had Lorelei touched one of the stones when he'd been lost in his vision?

He blinked and the headpiece disappeared. Lorelei lay before him, same as the day he had met her, except for the desperate look of terror on her face. Her body shook and she sat up with a small shriek. He leaned back with his hand still hovering. She panted as she stared at him with wild eyes.

"I was just going to wake you." He stood and brushed off his pants. "Whatever you dreamed didn't look pleasant."

Her fingers caught in the tangles in her hair. "It never is."

He took a cup from beside her backpack and poured the soup that had been heating by the campfire in it. He held it out to her. She looked at it with narrowed eyes and pursed lips before raising her gaze to his.

He chuckled. "Just soup. You need something to help you gain your strength."

She took it, cupping it between her hands, and sipped from it.

He walked to where Vaana lay against the fallen tree stump and touched her leg with his boot. She opened one eye and looked up at him.

"Dawn already?" she asked.

He nodded. "We should leave soon."

"Not before you tell me what is happening." Lorelei stood, crossing her arms. The cup sat on the ground at her feet. "I may have been drugged last night, but I meant what I said. I will leave."

Vaana tilted her head. "So?"

Vandermere rubbed his temple. The visions had never foretold what a headache either female would be. This would be a trial just to keep them together.

"She's not asking for anything unreasonable," he said. "Besides, how far do you think you would get alone with them?"

Vaana crossed her arms and glared between him and Lorelei. "It sounds like you know quite a bit already, Lord Vandermere."

"I know enough." He turned to Lorelei. "The stones held the remaining essences of old gods."

Lorelei's eyes widened and she spoke in a halting voice. "What? How...how is that possible?"

"Believe me, I'd like to know that as well," Vaana said through gritted teeth.

Lorelei looked to Vaana. "You came to steal them for the Order?"

Vaana shrugged. "They are objects of heresy."

"She didn't predict they would use her as a vessel," Vandermere said.

Vaana cut her gaze at him. "And you did?"

"I warned you."

Lorelei frowned. "So, you knew they were there?"

Vandermere sighed. "Not exactly. I knew something would be uncovered last night that would begin this journey. I didn't have the specifics."

Lorelei bit her bottom lip. "Why was Daan there?"

"I think she came for the gods Vaana now has within her," Vandermere said.

Lorelei let out a strangled cough as she looked from Vaana to Vandermere. "I'm sorry, what?"

Vandermere held up his hand. "Let me try to explain. I had a vision...of the past, I believe."

Lorelei and Vaana looked at him expectantly. He took a deep breath and described the events he'd seen. As usual, the scenes were ingrained in his mind with near perfect detail. He recalled the way Daan had slaughtered the others.

"Oh." Lorelei glanced at Vaana. "I remember the white-haired one. Vaana shifted into her....She called herself Morrigan...How is that even possible? Phooka can shift into other people, but you aren't one."

"More like she took control." Vaana laced her fingers together, her knuckles whitening. "I felt them enter me...the essences, at least. I was weak, but she...she's the strongest of them and her hatred for Daan is palatable."

Lorelei leaned forward with her eyes intent on Vaana, as if she was trying to absorb every word. "You're aware of them? Can you speak with them?"

Vaana frowned and stared off into the distance with narrowed eyes as her jaw tightened. "No. And I'm not interested in knowing them. I don't intend to have them inside me long."

Lorelei cupped the sides of her face with her hands,

tangling her fingers in her hair, and squeezed her eyes shut. "I…This all seems so impossible. How can this even happen?"

"That's what I plan to find out." Vaana's voice remained soft, but her white knuckles betrayed her, as did the glazed look in her eyes. "As well as how to get rid of them."

Neither of them seemed to be taking this well. Vandermere couldn't blame them. He'd had years of seeing unbelievable things, many of which had already come true. For Lorelei, this had to a mind-blowing revelation. Vaana had known what those stones contained, but not what would happen. They needed him to guide them.

"We," he said.

Lorelei held up her hands. "Wait. I got you into the Menhir. Whatever patsy I played, my job is complete."

Vandermere's chest tightened. He could lose the Nightingale now. She was key to the events to come, or at least fighting them. He closed his eyes, willing himself to see something, anything that would keep her with them.

A black heron with its wings curled around its head like an umbrella stands in a churning river. The Nightingale flies along the river in search of it.

"Do you really think the Apostle is going to just release you? You're a part of this. The Order will be after you as well," Vaana said.

"I get that." Lorelei clenched her fists in her lap and glared up at Vaana. "That doesn't mean I have to go along with you. I have my own goals I need to accomplish."

"If you travel with us, you will come across the Black Herons again. You'll find your proof. What you choose to do with it remains to be seen."

Lorelei dropped her hand and looked at him. "Seriously?"

"Black Herons?" Vaana asked.

"Group of spies and mercenaries set on bringing down the

Empire." Lorelei turned her attention back to Vandermere. "They're a part of this."

"We have stumbled upon a tangled web we will have to unravel," Vandermere said. "First, we must learn more about these beings Vaana carries. They are part of the key."

Lorelei chuckled. "The Order is going to love this. Shouldn't you turn yourself in or something?"

Vaana glared at her.

"Lorelei." Vandermere tried to keep his voice patient. "I think we should go to the Lord of Fate's tower. We can find a ship in Nearon."

Vaana snorted. "I doubt he's even real. That's a long way to go for someone that hasn't been seen in decades."

"He is real," Vandermere said. "And his library is said to be vast. He will have answers."

"Have you met him?" Vaana asked.

"I've not had the honor."

She waved her hand. "Then you don't know what he knows. It could be lies."

The world faded around him and a purple light flashed.

He stands in the middle of a large bed chamber. The furniture is shattered and the curtains of the bed hang in tatters. Shards of iron are imbedded in the walls and floor. Someone lays in the remains of the bed.

Vandermere gasped and blinked up at Vaana, who was staring at him with raised eyebrows.

"Well?" she asked.

"What was it you said?" he asked.

Lorelei leaned forward with a strange light in her eyes. "She wants to explore more of Winderward."

"There is an old chapel here that holds many secrets of the Forgotten Ages. It may be connected to these gods." Vaana nodded to the East.

"Winderward also holds a lot of unstable magic and

possible Fomorians which are worse the deeper we go," Vandermere said.

"They can't be any worse than Daan," Lorelei said. "We need the information, and it's on the way to Nearon. Why don't we stop there first?"

Vandermere's stomach twisted. The thought of entering the lost city caused a clammy sweat to break out across his skin. His visions had not given him a clue on which path he should take, but this felt like the wrong one.

"Very few come out of Winderward alive," he said. "It gets worse the deeper we go."

"You seem to come and go as you please." Lorelei smiled. "And now we're traveling with gods, right?"

"What remains of them, anyway." Vaana smirked at Vandermere. "I think you're outvoted."

"It appears so," Vandermere said. "We should set out. The quicker we get through this, the better."

He gathered their scattered equipment with his jaw set. They had a destination. Still, he couldn't shake the feeling of doom that accompanied the decision.

❧ 10 ❧

Evangeline knelt in front of the brazier and rested her hands on her knees as she stared into the fire. The rest of the room was covered in darkness. She preferred it that way in order for her to focus and commune with the flames. She inhaled, breathing in the musky, floral fumes of the amber incense that filled the room. She felt her consciousness raise and shift to the flames.

"I give my heart to the fire, so my will becomes strong." Her chant reverberated against the stone walls of the prayer room. "The fire fills me with its power."

She shifted to ease the ache in her knees from the cold marble beneath her. She shouldn't feel it so acutely; she needed to focus more.

"The fire burns away my impurities," she intoned. "I am left pure and righteous."

The dancing of the flames was all she could see, the mixture of yellows, reds, and oranges. They shifted and twisted, switching this way and that.

"Truth lies in the Eternal Flame," she continued. "I implore the eternal flame to show me the way to ascension."

She needed to know how to take the next step of her journey. This was her only path now. She was the Apostle of Fire, after all, the reincarnation of the Elemental Dragon of Fire. She would rise up as the great Dragon again. She just needed to know how.

The flames seemed to solidify, becoming sharp panes of glass, rigid and unchanging. Evangeline gritted her teeth and willed them back to their fluid form. They shook and shattered into thousands of tiny fractures. As they fell, Evangeline could see a reflection of herself in each one.

She pushed herself away from the still burning fire with a frustrated mutter. The vision was always the same. No matter how hard she tried, she could never get past it. What did it mean? Was her reincarnation not complete?

She rubbed her temples and took several slow breaths. She would rest for a few moments and meditate on what she saw. There had to be some sort of clue to lead her to the correct path.

"You seemed troubled, my child," a female voice whispered from the flames. "I sensed your distress and came. What guidance can I give you?"

The flames weren't the only place she heard it through. She could hear it throughout her every essence. It was the Voice of Wisdom speaking to her.

Evangeline bowed, pressing her forehead to the floor, even though she was the only one in the room.

"Oh, great Voice," she said. "I am lost. I wish to find the path to ascension in order to better serve the Empress. However, I find my way blocked by the vision of shattering glass."

"An interesting predicament," the Voice whispered. There seemed a ragged, tired edge to it that was not usually there.

"Great Voice, is something wrong?"

The sound of the crackling flames filled the silence for a moment.

"You are astute, my child," the Voice said. "There are many things wrong. The Empress has spoken of the awakening of an old corruption. I believe this may be the obstruction keeping you from your ascension. For how can there be great purity while this corruption moves?"

Evangeline gasped. "You speak of the Miasma? It is returning?"

"Not yet. Old gods have awoken," the Voice said. "If they are allowed to strengthen, I fear the Miasma will return. They have already caused the fall of one of their own. By taking these gods into herself, she has become an Anathema."

"Something must be done." Evangeline stood. "I will root out this impurity."

"The task will be difficult, for it is someone you care for deeply."

Evangeline felt a twisting in her gut. There were two of the church who still held her affections deeply. One remained by her side while the other had left for a mission given by the Voice herself.

"Yes," the Voice said with a hint of sadness. "Vaana has failed us. She must be purified."

Evangeline's throat tightened. Vaana had been her first friend since they had arrived at the temple in Iath, the imperial city for training. Both had been lost, feeling abandoned by their family into a world of strict rules. They had clung to one another through their initiate training and had learned together the purpose behind those rules. The purpose of order set forth by the Empress herself.

They had parted ways as Vaana was chosen as one of the special few to train under the Voice of Wisdom, the head of the entire Order, while Evangeline went to the Path of Fire. Evangeline had felt a little jealous of Vaana's position until she learned she was the reincarnation of the Great Elemental Dragon itself. Still, they had remained close friends who worked together often. After all, the Elemental Order was all one Order in service to the Empress.

Now, she would have to end Vaana's life.

Evangeline closed her eyes and called upon her strength of will, forged in fire. "I will do what needs to be done, in the name of the Empress."

"She is traveling with two others. A male and a female, both sidhe. Eliminate them, and bring her to me for purification," the Voice said.

"It shall be done, by the Great Flame."

"I leave it up to you," the Voice whispered.

The room was filled with the crackling of flame.

Evangeline stared deep into the fire, debating what to do. She could not send a group of monks to retrieve Vaana. Nearon was a dangerous city and the Order's power was tenuous.

The Council would love to see that one of the Order's own had fallen. No, she needed to do this quietly. If Vaana had become an Anathema, she would not return to the Order on her own. Her training would provide an advantage to her as she knew how the Order hunted.

A smile lit Evangeline's lips. Who better to send after Vaana, but the very person who trained her?

Evangeline rose to her feet, crossed the room to the door with its ornate bronze handle, and swung it open.

The initiate standing outside her door jumped to attention and gave a stiff bow. "Your Grace?"

"Send for Beth," Evangeline said. "I have a mission for her."

II

Buildings appeared at the horizon as Lorelei broke through the tree line. From this distance, the city looked almost complete and not ruins. It was an illusion hiding the secrets that had lain buried for centuries.

Lorelei licked her lips as her stomach fluttered and her chest filled with a light air.

Vaana and Vandermere came up next to her.

"How is the swamp considered part of Winderward?" she asked. "I'd always heard that the city actually bled into parts of Nearon."

"It does in some places," Vaana said. "However, the area around Winderward was affected by a spell long ago, such as where the Menhir was located."

"The city has a tendency to shift as well," Vandermere said. "We should be cautious."

"It's said that the laws of reality are different within the city," Vaana said. "Some sort of magical catastrophe caused it to happen."

"The Miasma, right?" Lorelei asked.

Vaana glanced at her with narrowed eyes. "Supposedly, it took place after the Empress had defeated the Miasma."

"But the city was in the grips of the Miasma." Lorelei's voice took on an almost trance quality. "The people called to their gods, and in their need to help, the Three in One fell from the heavens."

"That's not in any history I have heard," Vaana said. "What are the Three in One?"

Lorelei opened her mouth and then paused for a moment. She didn't have an answer for Vaana. Where had she heard that name? The story had felt so familiar, like she knew that story from heart, but where had she heard it?

An echo of screams and cries for mercy filled her head. A flash of white light stuck behind her eyes and dimmed.

Lorelei blinked and smiled at Vaana. "It must have been a tale I heard somewhere."

"The Empress came and saved Winderward from the Miasma, like she did with many cities," Vaana said.

"But it's still like this," Lorelei said.

"Magic can be volatile, especially the wrong kind," Vandermere said. "With the scars of the Miasma, the magic they cast caused the city to twist."

"What sort of magic was it?" Lorelei asked.

"Some say it was a time spell, others say the mage tried to summon a Sluagh." Vaana moved closer to Lorelei. "Either way, it's dangerous and Fomorians like to use it as a place to hide."

"I'm surprised Nearon allows that so close to their gates." Lorelei nodded to the large walls of the port city not even an hour's ride from Winderward.

"And risk the manpower of going in?" Vandermere snorted. "They prefer to guard the gates from anything that comes out."

"As interesting as this history lesson is," Vaana said, "we're wasting daylight. Shall we?"

"You're right," Lorelei said as her veins seemed to sing.

She had to see the city up close. Now.

With a grin, she rushed towards the city. This was what she'd wanted in life—a way to discover the things lost to the history and bring them to light. The danger didn't matter. She would overcome it and her name would be known throughout the land for the deeds she did. It could be one of her many escapades people talked about on her quest to find the Shadow Court.

She stopped and waited for the others to catch up to the gate, or what should have been the gate. Now only small pieces of brass remained. The wall had fallen in many places and lay in piles of broken bricks. The cobblestone of the road had worn away to broken chunks and dust. No one had traveled this path in ages.

Vaana joined her a few moments afterwards. She stared up at the city with a gleam in her eyes. Her fingers traced along brass hinge still embedded in the stone. Vandermere was the last to join them. He leaned against one of the few remaining parts of the wall, panting, and looked to Vaana.

"Well, where are we headed?" he asked.

"We have two choices," Vaana said. "There should be a temple where this little god was worshipped. There was also supposedly a library."

Lorelei stepped through the threshold of the gate.

Vandermere grabbed her arm before she could take another step and hissed. "What do you think you are doing?"

Lorelei tilted her head. "I wanted to get a better look at the city. I thought we could see which was closer."

His fingers tightened around her arm. "You have no idea how dangerous this place is. Running off will get you killed, or worse."

Her lips pressed together as she narrowed her eyes at his hand on her arm. "Let go."

He released his grip and looked at the ground, clearing his throat. "Forgive me. I shouldn't have been so forward."

"I'm aware this place is dangerous. You and Vaana have stressed that to the point it's ingrained in my mind," she said in a cool voice. "However, we are never going to get anywhere standing at the gates."

"She has a point," Vaana said as she trotted past the two of them.

Lorelei scanned the dilapidated buildings lining the main road with a thoughtful look on her face. The inside of the city looked as much in ruins as the outside. Large holes were in many of the rooftops. Some walls looked like they would collapse at the slightest touch. If the whole city was this way, how would they find anything that hadn't already fallen prey to time and destruction?

"I don't see anything that looks like a temple or a library," Lorelei said.

"These were most likely shops," Vaana said. "The others should be further in. Maybe closer to the center."

Lorelei pointed to the tallest building, or what would have been, if it was whole. The top half of the tower was missing, leaving only an angled point.

"What do you think that was?" she asked.

"It's a place to start." Vaana continued marching down the street.

Vandermere nodded. "Please be careful. I cannot carry the two of you out of here by myself."

Vaana smirked. "If I remember correctly, I was treating your head injury last night."

"Only because I had to defend you from Daan."

Lorelei shook her head. "Well, we all got beat there. A god had to save us."

"One that used my body," Vaana said.

Lorelei shrugged. "Maybe you shouldn't have touched the stones. Either way, we're here and the city's not getting any less dusty while we try to one up each other."

Vaana pressed her lips together in a thin line and stalked down the street. Every so often, she would stop and peer up at the tower before turning down a smaller side street, and then another. Soon, the gate disappeared behind a maze of turns and buildings.

"Do you know where you are going?" Lorelei asked.

"Towards treasure," Vaana said. "I can hear it."

Lorelei raised an eyebrow. "Really?"

"Family gift," Vaana said.

"So, is this treasure anywhere close to this tower or where we need to go?" Vandermere asked.

"Who knows?" Vaana shrugged. "But I'm sure it will be worth it."

"That depends on your definition of worth," Vandermere muttered.

A low growl emanated from an alley to Lorelei's right. A pair of red eyes stared out of the dark at them.

Vandermere stepped in between Lorelei and the alley with his hand on his sword.

Another growl sounded from above them. A black monstrous hulk crouched on four legs in the remains of the second floor of a building. Its maw drew back into a snarl as its gaze locked onto Vandermere.

Lorelei gripped his arm as she drew her sword with her other hand. Four other beasts joined their two pack mates. They must have smelled a fresh meal.

Lorelei raised her sword. She would make sure it would be the hardest meal they ever fought for.

Vaana muttered a curse and drew her blade. "Barghests."

The barghest on the building lifted its head and let out a

keening howl, chilling the blood in Lorelei's veins. The four on the street rushed towards them with snarls and barks that echoed against the buildings. The one in the alley growled again.

Lorelei slipped around Vandermere and rushed towards the creature before it could pounce. She jabbed her sword out and it bit into the creature's shoulder. A rotting stench emanated from its black fur, and she gagged.

It growled and then shot forward with its jaw snapping. Its fangs sank into Lorelei's hip. She bit back a scream at the sharp burning that raced along her side. She slammed the pommel on its snout. The barghest yelped, releasing her from its maw. She took a couple of steps back and glanced up at where the other one had been in time to watch it leap from its perch onto Vandermere.

Lorelei sprinted towards the alley with her heart pounding in her head. She needed to save Vandermere from these things.

Another barghest appeared from around the corner with its front body crouched down and its lips lifted in a snarl. By the hells of Gehenna, she was trapped. She glanced behind her at the wounded barghest padding closer. The second barghest lunged at her with it fangs bared. She spun to the side and ran her blade across its muzzle. It backed up a few steps, glaring at her with its red eyes—the sign of a Fomorian creature if anything she had read was true.

Her gaze darted between the creatures to the alley. She could hear Vaana's and Vandermere's grunts and the growls of the other barghests, but they'd moved past the alley and beyond her sight. A dark blur in her peripheral was her only warning of the first barghest's attack. She glanced back to see it leap at her. She hit the ground, rolling into a ball. The creature flew over her and landed next to its companion. Lorelei's stomach sank. She was even more trapped, separated from Vaana and Vandermere.

"Lorelei!" Vandermere's voice echoed from the street.

"I'm here!" she called. "A little busy, now."

The second's eyes flared red. A heaviness filled Lorelei's limbs as tears sprang to her eyes. She couldn't win this. Why was she even trying? How had she thought that coming to Winderward was a good idea? She was going to die here, a meal to these creatures, and be forgotten by all.

No.

She shook her head. What the hell was she thinking? These were just two stupid dogs. Yeah, Fomorian dogs, but dogs nonetheless. She wasn't going to lose after a few hours in the city.

She glared at the creatures. Those thoughts, that despair, had to have been a mental trick from the barghests to get her to drop her guard. She had no time to be playing around with these things anymore.

She backed away from them and drew in a deep breath, letting it settle in her diaphragm. The scream she released sent a wave of force down the alley and slammed into both the barghests. It lifted them in the air and slammed them into the ground. The two buildings shook with the force of her cry and large chunks of rubble began to fall into the alley.

Lorelei ducked into the corner and covered her head with her arms. Her voice never did quite what she wanted. After a few seconds, the sounds of falling rock stopped. She peered through her arms at the end of the alley. The front of the alley was now filled with chunks of rock, towering over her to what would have been the next stories of the buildings she stood between. The majority had fallen on the barghests, crushing them. However, it also blocked her way back to Vandermere and Vaana.

She rushed to the pile of rubble. "Vandermere! Can you hear me?"

The sounds of battle came from the other side, along with his strained voice. "Are you all right?"

"Yeah, but I can't get through from here. I'll have to find another way around."

"Wait!" Whatever he was going to say was cut off by a growling bark.

She needed to find another way to them. She backed towards the other end of the alley. A dim light shone in the distance. If the alley came out to another street, she could backtrack through the street to them. She ran past the fallen rocks and pieces of refuge that littered the ground towards the light ahead of her. Her pulse sped up as did her pace. She barely registered the stone beneath her giving way to moss and mud. She gasped as she broke through the alley.

Before her lay the murky pools of the swamp with the weeping willows standing on sparse patches of mud. Lorelei turned back towards what should have been the alley. Her heart sank into her stomach.

She was surrounded by the marsh with no building, no city in sight.

12

She gripped her hair with both hands and let out a short scream.

This wasn't possible. It couldn't be. How was she back in this damned marsh?

This had to be what Vandermere had meant when he'd said the city shifted. She'd assumed, well, she hadn't really known what to think. Maybe that a building would disappear, not the whole city! How was she ever going to get out of here?

Her eyes narrowed as she peered into the distance. A hill rose up just out of the horizon. It seemed to be the only thing visible, aside from the marsh and willows.

She let out a sigh. At least she could climb the hill and try to get a better view of the land. Perhaps she could see the city, though if the land changed on a whim like before, she may never find Vandermere and Vaana again. She might be better off looking for a way back to Nearon.

She trudged her way through the sloshing marsh with the perfume of lilies clinging to the inside of her nose until she almost wanted to gag on the sweet scent.

The sound of a sob echoed from in front of her, causing her to start.

As the hill had grown closer, Lorelei could make out several figures standing atop it. Far too many to be her companions. Maybe these people were there waiting for them. She stopped at the base and took a deep breath.

These people could also be dangerous, a group of Fomorians, even. Still, she wasn't going to find out unless she climbed.

Her hands dug into the black gritty dirt as she gripped the stones buried in the hill. She gasped when her gaze landed on one of the stones. It was jagged, like a part had been broken off, but the remaining portion had something written on it.

Died 5th year of Emerald.

Beloved Wife.

These were gravestones.

Lorelei gulped and continued her ascent. She'd heard of Mourner's Hill before the hob in Nearon had mentioned it. It was supposedly a cursed place where those who traveled to it were never seen again. If the unease growing in the pit of Lorelei's stomach was any indication, she had found it.

"Well," Lorelei muttered, "I'm already halfway there and it's not like I have anywhere else to go."

She exhaled and pulled herself up the rest of the hill. As she stopped to catch her breath, she took stock of what was at the top of the hill. A group of nearly two dozen faeries stood in a circle around a large altar. They were from different races: sidhe, hob, phooka, redcap, pixie. Even the deathly ankou.

Floating just above the alter was a curved sword with its point down. Intricate green writing ran along the blade in a language Lorelei didn't know. Green jewels decorated the pommel.

Lorelei's heart sped up for a second. Could those be emerald? If so, that would solve a lot of her problems. Emerald granted wishes.

A green light emanated from the sword and surrounded the faerie. Their gazes stared off in the direction of the sword, and tears streamed down their cheeks. Some must have been on the hill for a while, from the look of their emaciated faces. An occasional sob escaped the slack lips of one of a pixie as she stood on a small rock.

Lorelei circled the group, trying to keep herself out of the light as she searched the faces for Vaana or Vandermere. No one seemed to notice her. As she drew closer something echoed in the back of her head. Some sort of slow music, that held a melancholy air. She blinked as her eyes began to water. Why was chest feeling so heavy?

She bit the inside of her cheek. "Hello? Can any of you hear me?"

"They cannot hear anything but the song of the Light of Lament." A figure stepped out of the crowd and turned in Lorelei's direction. "They are caught in its mourning song."

The figure, an ankou, pulled her hood back to reveal a pasty face with sunken cheekbones and deep shadows for eyes. Of course, this was how all ankou looked. They walked with death and showed it.

Lorelei raised an eyebrow and pointed to the sword. "I take it that's the Light of Lament?"

The girl nodded, one single, slow head bob.

"Why aren't you affected?"

"My will is stronger than theirs," the girl said. "But I fear that it isn't strong enough to claim the Lord."

"What happens to them if they remain here?" Lorelei asked.

"They will die," the girl said, "and the Lord will claim their souls."

A coldness crept through Lorelei's stomach. These people didn't deserve to have their soul claimed by some entity.

"So to stop it, all I need is to claim the sword?" Lorelei strode forward. "No problem."

"You will be lost in his song," the girl said.

"We'll see about that," Lorelei stopped in front of the sword.

Her hand itched to touch it. She wanted to wrap her fingers around the pommel with its skull head and feel the weight of the sword in her hand.

The world around her faded, the sounds from the surrounding faerie becoming muffled. The light of the setting sun dimmed to darkness and the sword hung before her, glowing with a green light.

Are you strong enough to claim me? A male tenor filled her mind.

Lorelei shook her head. "What are you?"

Battle me and I will give you my name. I am he who can cut down your enemies and leave a river of blood at our feet.

Lorelei raised an eyebrow. "How am I supposed to battle a sword?"

We pit our wills against each other. If you are weak, I shall claim you.

Lorelei crossed her arms. Now even swords were challenging her. Was she such a pushover that she could be a doormat for anything that came along? No. The blood of Moura flowed in her veins just as much as it did in Freya's. She wasn't going to let a weapon get the better of her. She reached out.

"Good luck," the ankou girl whispered.

Lorelei glanced at her with the sword gripped in her hand before the green light encompassed her.

The moon hung high in the sky and the cool breeze carried the sweet scent of the roses that surrounded Lorelei. She stood on her tiptoes and tried to peer over the looming bushes. It was no good. She would have to keep moving forward.

Where was Arryn? He'd promised he would meet her here tonight.

Tonight would be special. Butterflies fluttered in her stomach at the thought of it.

Tonight, she would tell him.

A green light flickered from around the corner of the rose maze. Lorelei's heart pounded in her chest. Could that be him? She picked up her skirts and raced forward. She rounded the corner and stepped into a circular clearing.

A male stood in the middle. He wasn't Arryn. His black hair was pulled back into a topknot that was banded every few inches and dragged across the ground as he moved. His chest was bare, revealing brown, tattooed skin. His viridian eyes seemed to glow.

"This is what you dream of, little girl?" He chuckled. "Why do you play at an adventure when there are battles to be had?"

This wasn't right. Where was Arryn? Could this male be one of the spirits said to haunt this place at night?

Lorelei swallowed the unease inside her. The surrounding roses wilted into blackened husks, their petals dropping to the ground.

No spirit would do that.

In an instant he was in front of her, his hand clutching hers. She gasped at the black veins that raced up her arm.

"You have already taken me up," he said. "Surrender to me and become my vessel."

She tried to yank her hand away as the blackness continued to climb in her veins. "Who are you?"

The world flashed green. She blinked to find herself before a great sandstone wall. Shouts and clamors of metal filled her ears and warriors trampled over their fallen to assault the barrier. The sun beat down on her from above, casting a red sheen over the desert. She licked her parched lips and scanned the dead. Where was she?

The voice echoed over the shouts of the men. "I was once The Harvester of the Fallen."

Most of the warriors gravitated towards a giant gate to the left. She shouldered her way through with a large spear gripped in her hand. A small part of her wondered at this, but the part than controlled her body thought this was normal.

A bright green arc burst from the center of the battle and bodies flew past her, disappearing in the hoard behind her. A male stood in front of the gate, facing the army with a viridian sword in his hand. His hair, spotted like a leopard, was plastered to his forehead and his leather armor hung in shreds on his body. In two quick slashes, he brought down five more men. With a roar, she lifted her spear and rushed towards him.

He slid to the side and ran his sword through her. Pain coursed through her chest as the blade pierced her heart. The spear fell from her limp hand and she fell to her knees with the sword still stuck in her. It shimmered green in the sun. She gasped as the black in her veins covered her shoulders. This wasn't right. She'd never seen the desert, let alone fought in any way.

"Who are you?" Blood splattered on her lips as she choked the words out.

Green light filled her sight.

She stood beside her mother's chair in their throne room. Her heart raced as she looked down at Arryn and his father.

The time had come. He was going to ask for her hand. She couldn't keep the smile from her face.

Arryn's father bowed. "Lord Moura, I have come before you to propose a joining of our families."

Her father straightened up with a smile. "This is wonderful news. Arryn, whose hand have you come to ask for?"

Arryn avoided Lorelei's gaze. "Lady Freya's, my lord."

The world began to spin around her. She gripped the back of mother's chair and stifled a gasp. She must have misheard. This couldn't be true.

Freya beamed down at Arryn from her place behind her father's seat. Her mother nodded with a smile of approval as her father accepted the offer. The world seemed to have forgotten Lorelei's existence. Time froze and her gaze fell on the curved, viridian sword lying on the pedestal before her.

"I am the heart of The Forger of Infinite Fires. Take me up and slaughter them." The voice echoed from the sword. "They have betrayed you. Let them be the first in the sea of dead we shall create."

She stretched her hand towards the sword and paused. How would this change things? It wouldn't give her Arryn.

"It will give you vengeance." The sword said.

"I don't want vengeance." she said. "I want Arryn. I love him. I would never kill him."

The sword's voice grew heavy with sorrow. "You know nothing of love, little girl."

"Who are you?" she asked.

The green light spread from the sword, glowing brighter and brighter.

She found herself floating above the desert battle. The leopard haired phooka now stood on a pile of bodies as he cut down more. He was panting and bright green blood was pouring from the deep wounds in his torso. He gripped the sword as he scanned the oncoming warriors and gave a slight nod. He spun, letting the blade of the sword follow his path. A viridian wave emanated from the blade and swept across the army. Men clutched their throats and howled in pain. The light faded into the horizon and the army lay dead before the gates of the city.

The male collapsed atop his fallen enemies. The sword tumbled from his hand. It flickered and the brown skinned male with viridian eyes stood in place of the sword. He lifted the phooka up and cradled him in his arms. A green tear trailed down his cheek as he carried him through the gates of the city.

Lorelei's heart ached for him and she swallowed the lump in her throat.

"You loved him and he died," she said.

The viridian eyed male appeared before her and bowed his head. "I am the Light of Lament."

Lorelei crossed her arms. "That's your name?"

He smirked. "It is who I am. You have bested me. What is your name, little girl?"

"Lorelei ap Moura."

"Interesting." He bowed. "Lorelei, you are now the wielder of Murgleis."

He disappeared, and Lorelei held the sword in her hand.

"For now." His voice echoed in the encroaching darkness. "In the end, we shall see who wields who."

13

The murmur of voices pulled Lorelei out of her reverie. Murgleis's spell had broken and the surrounding people were rubbing their faces and gazing around with confused expressions.

A shout echoed as a young male and female pixie embraced each other. Others began chattering to each other. The ankou Lorelei had spoken with earlier was holding the hand of a phooka boy with long locks of brown and black hair. Two wolf ears poked out atop his head. The ankou nodded in Lorelei's direction and the phooka's gaze followed. The side of his mouth curled in a lopsided grin and he trotted over with the ankou trailing behind him.

"Ora says we have you to thank for freeing us. I came here to release these people, but I got ensnared myself." He raised one hand to scratch the back of his head as his grin turned sheepish. Then he held out his other hand to her as if an afterthought. "I'm Wes, by the way."

"Lorelei ap Moura." She took his hand.

Ora bowed her head. "Thank you for your help."

"So, what do you plan to do with that thing?" Wes's gaze

slid to Murgleis with an expression mixed with disgust and curiosity.

"I'm not sure, yet," Lorelei said. "For now, it stays with me."

"Are you sure you can control it? I mean, it's a Sluagh, right?" Wes asked. "I might know someone who could take it off your hands."

A Sluagh. Lorelei bit the inside of her cheek. In contesting this thing to save the people, she'd somehow bound herself to a Sluagh. She would have to be careful. If the tales were true, such a thing could devour her soul.

She straightened her shoulders. "That's all right. I have pitted my will against it and won. I'd rather not have another incident like this happen."

"Yeah." Wes sighed. "Well, you should be careful. Sluagh are vicious tricksters, and *I'm* saying that."

"I will." Lorelei glanced around, then murmured almost to herself, "These people will probably need help getting to Nearon."

"Oh, Ora and I can do that. We come and go through Winderward all the time. Well, before..." He nodded to the sword. "We can get you back, too."

"Thanks, but I can't leave yet." Her gaze fell on the horizon. Were those buildings out there? "I still have friends I need to find."

Wes gave a soft whistle. "Good luck with that."

Lorelei let out her breath in a soft laugh. Even the phooka was dubious.

Ora nudged him and whispered in his ear. He nodded, reached his pocket, and pulled out a silver coin with a serpent embossed on it. "Look, if you make it back to Nearon and need help, just pass this to one of the beggars. It'll get back to me...or someone who can repay what I owe ya."

Lorelei closed her hand around the coin and smiled at

him. "Thanks. I'll keep that in mind. Do you have any idea how I can get to the city part of Winderward?"

"Walk toward the horizon with your goal in mind," Ora said. "Winderward seems to work on the principle of will and desire."

"Great," Lorelei muttered. "Well, thanks for the advice. I need to start looking for my friends again."

She waved at them and moved to the edge of the hill. Wes's voice rang in the air, calling to the other faerie on the hill.

Lorelei paused at the edge and stared down at Murgleis then to her belt. The sword was sharp enough that it might cut through her belt. She had some rope in her bag. Did he even have a sheath?

I do, his voice whispered in her mind. *It has been lost to me, though.*

Lorelei jumped and glanced down at Murgleis.

Surprised? Did you expect me to remain silent from now on?

"No," she whispered. "That just takes some getting used to."

You don't have to speak. Your thoughts are open to me. Your deepest fears and greatest desires.

"Great. I'm carrying an extreme voyeur around. Right now, I desire to find my companions. Can you help lead me through Winderward?" She asked.

I am not a compass which would never work in Winderward, anyway. The ankou girl gave you the best advice.

"Fine." That still left the issue of how to carry him.

She pulled off her backpack, set the sword on the ground, and opened the flap of her pack. Digging past her water, food, and lantern, she pulled out a length of rope. It was longer than she needed. Vaana had probably intended she use it for climbing, but she could use a little. She cut a small length and used it to tie Murgleis to her belt. Now ready to move, Lorelei hopped from the small ledge and landed on the incline.

She envisioned Vaana and Vandermere as she picked her way down the hill. The memory of Vandermere's husky chuckle sent warm shivers down her spine. Vaana's smirk always appeared on her face in every image. Though she hadn't been smirking when the stones had struck her when the power of gods had entered her. A chill ran through her as something danced on the edge between her consciousness and subconscious. A sensation of falling from an infinitely high space filled her and she pitched forward.

The ground came rushing towards her and met with her shoulder, shooting a spike of pain through her. She yelled, trying to grab onto a root or rock to no avail as she continued to tumble down the hill. Instead of the mud of the marsh, she was met with hard cobblestone at the bottom. With a groan, she picked herself up then halted. Her mouth gaped as she stared at the wide road and buildings that surrounded her.

She sputtered. "What in Gehenna is going on here?"

Gehenna, indeed, Murgleis's voice echoed in her mind. *This city shall remain ever shifting so no faerie will rule it again.*

"Why? What happened?"

A college of sorcerers sought to bind what they could never comprehend, much less control.

"My companion Vaana mentioned little gods. So, it would be one of those?"

Murgleis's laugh rattled around in her head. *No, I know nothing of what ruled this city before. I speak of Abaddon.*

"Let me guess, a Sluagh."

Of course.

Lorelei crossed her arms with a huff. "I'm not stupid, you know."

Just ignorant.

"Ignorance can be remedied by knowledge, so enlighten

me."

Murgleis remained quiet for several moments. Lorelei scanned the street in front of her. It looked similar to the street they'd entered the city on, except the road continued on in both directions instead of the gate and wall.

She wasn't going to find the others if she just stood here. They'd either traveled to the church or a library. She would have to search the city to find either.

Which direction should she choose, though?

Very well, Murgleis said.

"Oh, good," Lorelei muttered as she strode down the right street. "A story to make my walk more interesting."

The College of Sorcery sought to bind Abaddon for their power. However, they did not realize the power she had. She crossed the Eternal Desert and appeared in Winderward. When she did, the binding meant to hold her in place broke.

"So, she killed them?" Lorelei asked.

Oh, no, she had much worse planned. The whole city would pay for their ignorance, Murgleis said. *She danced. With each footfall, the earth cracked open and with each sway of her body, lightning rained down upon Winderward.*

As Murgleis weaved his story, Lorelei picked her way through the rubble-ridden street, keeping watch for her companions or any Fomorians waiting to ambush her. Goosebumps pricked at her arms. She didn't like the silence of the city, especially with Murgleis's words ringing in her mind. It also didn't mesh with the memory she had. It seems like she'd been wrong.

"That doesn't explain why the city shifts." Lorelei paused at a crossroads before turning left. A wave of familiarity washed over her, like she'd walked these streets before.

The magic went wild with her dance and in one night, the city fell. It will remain this way until Abaddon or one as powerful as her removes the curse.

"Could you do it?"

Murgleis gave a bitter laugh. *No. I am mighty, but she is something else. Abaddon is the child of something else. Perhaps a god.*

She stopped. "Gods? And how are they different from little gods?"

Power.

"Is it normal for these gods to have Sluagh children?"

No, he said. *Abaddon was not always that way. Something changed her.*

"What?"

"I know not."

Lorelei's lips curved up. "It looks like I'm not the only one who is ignorant."

Murgleis remained silent.

Lorelei chuckled to herself as she turned a corner around a four-story ruin. Her chuckle shifted to a gasp. Rising up at the end of the street, several blocks away, stood an ancient temple, gleaming in the sunlight.

❧

Lorelei's heart raced at the sight of the temple. It took up a majority of the square it stood in, looming over the other buildings by several stories.

There was a lot to explore in such a place.

"This had to be the temple Vaana was talking about," Lorelei murmured. "If they are anywhere, they would be here."

Unless your friends have become lost, Murgleis said. *Forever trapped in ever-changing Winderward.*

"No." Lorelei gulped and pressed her lips together. "Vandermere knows how this place works and Vaana came in prepared to find...things."

She chewed the inside of her cheek as she stared up at the

temple. Its walls held the sheen of a metal Lorelei had never seen before, pale but brighter than silver. A stone bridge created a road over the flowing stream that surrounded the temple to the wide steps that took up the entire street, large enough for a caravan to travel. At the top of the steps was a diamond shaped entryway.

"Well," she said, "I should check to see if they are inside. Vaana would not wait for me."

She crossed the bridge, searching for any sign her friends had come this way. Vines had overtaken the sides of the bridge and moss had grown on most of the cobblestone bricks. There were no footprints. Could she really be the first one here? She had to have wandered through the Marsh for a while and who knew how long her battle with Murgleis took.

She shook her head. She refused to believe that Vaana and Vandermere had become lost in Winderward. Either way, it was foolish to go searching for them more with the city shifting. Vaana had planned to find the temple. Lorelei would wait for her here.

She climbed the steps and stopped in front of the diamond shaped double doors. A sense of nostalgia filled her as she placed her hand on the large metal handle. How long had it been since she graced these halls?

Lorelei blinked and took a step back. She'd never been to Winderward before now, much less to this temple. How had she thought such a thing? She stared up at the temple. There was something familiar about it, like out of one of her dreams. Nightmares. Most of her nights were filled with visions that would make most sidhe's blood curdle. Was this place the source of her nightmares?

There was only one way to find out.

With a deep breath, she pushed the doors open. The inside of the temple took Lorelei's breath away. She opened her backpack, pulled out a small lantern, and lit it. The floor was made of a dark stone that reflected the light from the lantern she'd lit. Twelve columns, made of the same stone, lined the giant hall in two rows of six. Time had worn away the column, leaving cracks and large chips in their surface.

The ceiling, also of the same stone, was filled with diamonds that glittered in the lantern light. They had been arranged to represent the constellations. Lorelei had spent many nights on the roof of her house as a child along with Freya and Arryn. They had tried counting the stars and Lorelei loved recounting the tales of what each star cluster represented.

Now, she smiled up at Neefa, the Constellation of Silence. She was supposed to have served as the Empress' hidden hand and spymaster.

Lorelei's footsteps echoed on the stone floor, sending a feeling of loneliness through her, as she approached the back wall. Filled out in a series of tiles was a fresco of a trio of women. They weren't of any faerie Lorelei knew of, though it was difficult to tell because their forms seemed to be composed of stars. They were like constellations of themselves.

She'd never seen a constellation like this in the night sky.

"Murgleis, do you know of these women?" she asked.

I believe they were a trio of goddesses of some sort. Long dead. This temple is most likely dedicated to their religion.

"Strange," she said. "I don't remember ever hearing about them."

Have you heard of many gods? They fell from the heavens long ago, Murgleis said. *Forgotten like most gods after the Miasma struck.*

"I suppose many of these gods fell to the Miasma," Lorelei mused. "They didn't have the Empress's power to turn Iron into Emerald."

Many fell before then and after, but a few have survived, despite your Order's efforts to wipe them out.

"Really? Like who?"

Murgleis remained silent.

Lorelei sighed. That looked like all she was going to get out of him at the moment.

She turned her attention back to the room. The side walls each held a closed wooden door. She stepped up to the door on the right and opened it. Dust from ages of neglect swept up from the walls and floor and clogged her nose and throat. She coughed and sputtered. After a final sneeze, she rubbed her nose and stepped through the doorway. Beyond it lay a long hallway.

Several doors lined the hall, just waiting to be explored.

A buzzing sound echoed from the door at the end of the hall. She crept forward to it. Her hand hovered over Murgleis as she turned the handle.

The room was laid out oddly. There were seven alcoves that ended in points. The door she had opened stood in one of them and what looked like statues stood in the others. In the center of the room was a dome of white energy, which had to be the source of the buzz. Seven staves with glowing crystals surrounded the dome, correlating with each of the alcoves. Inside the energy, a pale female lay upon an alter with her eyes closed.

Lorelei rushed to the edge of the dome. The female was not only pale, but her hair was white as well. She had a thin frame that reminded her of a swan. Perhaps she was a phooka, though what a phooka would be doing behind a dome of energy she had no clue.

It's a binding circle, Murgleis said. *That is no faerie, but some sort of spirit masquerading as one. You should leave it alone.*

"That's not what I did for you," Lorelei said.

And now you are bound to me, Murgleis said. *Do you want to be bound to something else, or worse, end up as its meal?*

"Why would it matter to you if I did?" Lorelei tilted her head down at the sword.

It has been a while since someone was not caught in my song, let alone dared wield me. I do not wish to be trapped in this tomb if you die.

"It's a temple, not a tomb."

It may as well be a tomb for all it is visited.

Lorelei looked back to the sleeping female. Something about her was familiar, but she couldn't quite place it. If the female had been trapped here, perhaps she knew of the history of the place and the goddesses that had been worshipped. If they were one of the ones connect to Vaana, they would need that information. She would get no answers letting her lay here though.

You're going to ignore my advice, Murgleis said.

"How do I remove the binding?" Lorelei circled the dome, staring at each of the staves.

The energy is being channeled through the staves. They are acting as a focus. Removing the power of one would break the circle and the binding. However, it may have adverse effects.

"Can you drain the energy?"

Most of the Aether I consume is that of souls, little girl. Murgleis chuckled. *Besides, I would not risk a backlash if that circle is meant to hold a Sluagh. Such a thing would be detrimental to me.*

"Fine," Lorelei muttered.

She'd studied the principles of channeling at the Aimsir. She herself channeled Aether to perform her spells through song and music. Perhaps she could do the same thing and channel Aether out of one of these staves. Where would she put it though?

The heartstone!

Excitement buzzed through her like bits of electricity tingling her skin as she pulled out the ruby from her bag. She stared down at it, chewing the inside of her cheek. The last time she'd tried to use the heartstone it'd had explosive results. Now she was going to try something experimental again. She'd needed to prepare herself better.

She closed her eyes and chanted a soft song, summoning the Aether from the well deep within her to form a mystical cloak. Light blue energy shimmered around her body. Her heart leapt. She'd successfully created a fire protection mantle. If only her instructors could see her now. They would just shake their heads at the insanity she was about to attempt. She could barely master simple spells and here she was about to try something experimental.

She drew a deep breath to her diaphragm and shifted the melody of her song. Her words reverberated off the stone walls, overpowering the buzzing of the dome. She sang of the loneliness of the stars and of being forgotten.

All the while, she concentrated on pulling the Aether from the stave into the heartstone. It resisted her at first, like trying to pull a stop out of a tub if the tub was the size of a pond. Then, it gave with an inaudible pop and the energy rushed through her and into the heartstone.

A hole appeared in the dome where the stave she'd been concentrating on stood, and the other crystals in the staves began to spark. The air pulled her towards the dome for a second before a wave of force burst from the circle. Lorelei was knocked off her feet and into one of the statues in an alcove. Her head slammed against the base of the pedestal and the stars from the ceiling in the great hall danced before her eyes.

She rolled over with a groan, rubbing her head. A shadow blocked what little light was left in the room. The pale female loomed over Lorelei with her hands on her hips and her platinum hair falling about her like a halo.

"What have we here?" she murmured.

14

Vandermere paused at the corner of their fifth crossroads and rested his hand on his knees as he caught his breath. He and Vaana had been trekking through the city ever since their fight with the barghests. They'd started with searching for an alternate way into the alley that had blocked them off from Lorelei, only to discover she wasn't there.

Vaana had then directed them towards a tower they had seen. Despite every street they traveled and every turn they'd made, they drew no closer. The damn city was moving and forcing them to choose new paths after several blocks. It seemed like they'd been walking for hours now, though the sun was just reaching its high point in the sky.

Vandermere wiped the sweat from his brows. If only he could wipe away his pounding headache as well.

He scanned the street ahead, looking for a wisp of movement like Lorelei's dark clothes or her brown hair, and straining his ears for the lilt of her voice. The city remained eerily silent. Not even the birds or insects dared to make a sound in here.

"Let's just give up on the tower and look for Lorelei," Vandermere said. "If we can't get there, I doubt she can."

"No, we're not here to look for her," Vaana said. "She'll have to survive on her own."

"So, now that you got what you wanted out of her, you're ready to just forget about her?" He laughed, low and bitter. "Typical."

Vaana cast him a glare before scanning the city. "She's better off without us, anyway. You're mad and I'm carrying around heretical gods inside of me."

He shook his head. "When are you going to realize that other gods existed besides yours? That's not heresy. It is the way of the world."

"Pretenders." Vaana sniffed. "The Empress is the True Goddess. The scriptures speak of her rebirth to save us from the Miasma."

"And where is she now?"

"Once she fulfilled her purpose, she took her place back in the Heavens, of course."

Vandermere opened his mouth to retort when the dulcet tones of Lorelei's singing interrupted him. It was soft at first, like it'd been carried on the wind for some distance. He tensed and glanced around as an airy feeling filled his chest. It was coming from his left.

He spared Vaana a glance. "Well, you can depend on your Empress to guide you alone. I'm going to find Lorelei."

He rushed down the street toward the sound. In the distance, a metal spire stood above the dilapidated rooftops. How had he not seen it before? He shook his head, trying not to ponder the wildness of the city.

He concentrated on his steps echoing on the broken cobblestone which were soon joined by another set of lighter, rapid footfalls. He glanced back at Vaana's scowling face, locks of her black hair whipping about in the wind as she ran, and a smirk lit his face.

As much as she wanted to talk about the heresy of other gods, she wasn't prepared to return to her Order with her problem and she wasn't willing to go alone.

Where the tower had eluded them, Lorelei's song seemed to guide them to her. After several minutes, the road curved to the right and led to a large courtyard that held a giant temple with the metal spire. Lorelei's voice came from inside the open doors.

A group of hulking Fomorians stood on the bridge leading to the temple steps. These were different from the others, more humanoid. Before the Miasma touched them, they would have been redcaps, judging by their size. However, they were now twisted with wrinkly grey skin, elongated ears that flopped to one side, and jagged, sharp teeth that jutted from their mouths.

"Trolls," Vaana murmured in Vandermere's ear. "We're not the only one attracted to our songbird."

"Looks like we're going to have to go through them to get to her," Vandermere said.

Lorelei's song stopped abruptly followed by a ripple of force that emanated from the temple. Rubble skittered across the ground, kicking up dirt. The trolls growled, creeping back from the temple as they muttered amongst each other.

"That's not good," Vaana said.

"We need to dispatch them before they decide that the temple is worth inspecting," Vandermere said.

"Great. You distract them off the bridge and I'll sneak around."

"So you can leave me to fight all of them?" Vandermere snorted. "I think not."

"You really think I'd leave you?"

"I wouldn't put it past you." Vandermere stiffened as one

of the trolls raised its head and turned its red eyes in their direction. "We've lost the element of surprise."

The troll gave a guttural cry and slapped the shoulder of the one next to him. The others turned in their direction. The biggest one grinned, showing off its teeth, and skulked towards them.

"New plan," Vaana said. "Stay alive."

The trolls rushed towards them. Vaana whispered a chant under her breath and pointed a finger at the largest troll, their leader. A beam of yellow light burst forth and struck the troll. He staggered back and shook his head. His shoulders slumped and he seemed to collapse in on himself as he backed away from them with a whimper.

"You can cast fear upon others?" Vandermere raised an eyebrow at her.

Vaana smirked. "Fomorians should fear the power of the Empress."

Vandermere unsheathed his sword as the other four continued to charge them. "Well, can you do that to the rest?"

"Not in enough time." Vaana pulled her sword out, a thin short blade.

The first troll rushed towards Vandermere with his clawed hands raised. Vandermere ducked and spun to the side of the troll. He jabbed the blade into the soft spot in the troll's flank. A second troll swooped in to attack. Vandermere dipped and instead, the second troll's claws raked the first one. The first yowled and swiped at the second.

Vandermere backed away from the bickering trolls and glanced at Vaana. She had two of her own trolls to deal with. She dodged the slash of one troll only to be caught by the swooping claws of the second troll. Her face took on a grayish pallor as she staggered back. Blue blood ran from the four claw marks that had cut through her armor and into her skin. The troll laughed, low and guttural, as he stepped closer, separating Vandermere and Vaana.

Vandermere cursed under his breath as he glanced at the trolls. They were outnumbered and who knew what was happening with Lorelei. Something had cut off her song. Vandermere circled around his trolls to try to find a way to get back to Vaana. They had a better chance together.

Vaana raised her sword as she took a couple slow steps back. Her other hand covered her wound and her mouth moved in a soft mantra Vandermere couldn't hear. Color returned to her cheek and her shoulders straightened as she took a defensive stance against her trolls.

Vandermere dashed to the side of the first troll he had been fighting as it raised its hand at its companion and slashed its lower back. He turned and swung on the second troll. It grabbed the blade of his sword, engulfing half of it in its oversized paw, and backhanded Vandermere with the second one. The blow slammed into his face, and bones cracked. He was sent flying back several feet and landed on his back. The taste of blood filled his mouth.

The first troll glared at him, then roared and beat its chest. The wound on its side had closed, leaving only a trace of crimson blood. Coldness filled the pit of Vandermere's stomach.

"That thing can heal!" His words came out slurred as he tried to speak through his broken face. He pushed to his feet.

"It's a good thing we have the Empress on our side." Vaana spared him a glance. "Don't talk anymore, you'll only make things worse."

She ducked under one of her trolls as it reached for her and jammed her blade into its belly in a quick succession of jabs. The second swiped at her. She dove to the ground, tucked into a ball, and rolled in between the first one's legs.

Vandermere grabbed a rock and flung it at the hand of the troll holding his sword. The rock slammed into its wrist. The creature released his blade with a screech. It pounded his chest and rushed towards him.

Vandermere ducked behind a large piece of rubble. The troll rushed by him, its momentum carrying it into its leader, who cowered at the foot of the bridge. These things did not have tactical minds or a lot of coordination. The leader yowled, shoving the other away. It turned its head in Vaana's direction, standing, and stomped towards her. She tried to dodge its hands, but it grabbed her, lifted her over its head, and hurled her.

Vaana gave a gurgling sound and went flying through the air. She hit the side of one of the one-story buildings with a loud thud. Her body bounced to the ground. She lay still.

An ominous chill rushed through Vandermere. He sprinted to Vaana and knelt beside her, placing his fingers on her throat. He let out a breath of relief at the faint thrum of her heartbeat against his fingertips.

The trolls closed in on him.

His gaze darted to his sword lying across the courtyard. He would have to do some crazy maneuvering to get past the troll just to get to it and he would be leaving Vaana alone. If he didn't though...

One of the trolls licked its lips with a thick black tongue, its shoulders shaking with a laugh.

The flash of a bluish light from the entrance on the temple caught his eyes. Blue flames, in the shape of a snake, slithered in the air from the temple. It darted forward and struck the leader in the back, then forked to hit the two adjacent trolls. Their screeches rang out along with the stench of burning flesh. The other trolls jabbered amongst each other, their gazes darting from Vandermere to the entrance of the temple as they backed away. A pale, platinum haired phooka female sauntered out of the temple, tossing a ball of flame from one clawed hand to another. She stood at the top of the stairs and smirked down at the trolls.

Their gibbering increased, and as a whole, they turned and fled down one of the streets, disappearing into the city. The phooka chuckled and glanced at Vandermere.

"Looks like the two of you need some help," she said. "That is, if you're willing to step into my parlor."

15

Lorelei held a cold cloth to the back of her head and glanced around the room Amara, the phooka or the being disguised as a phooka, had chosen to place a wounded Vandermere and Vaana in. The room was shaped like a seven-pointed star as was the other. However, it appeared to have been some sort of dormitory at one time. Each of the alcoves held the remains of a bed, the wood brittle and the mattresses almost rotted away. They were probably bug filled.

Lorelei wrinkled her nose. It was a good thing she'd had a bedroll that she could lay out and sit on. The thin cushioning did little to harden the stone beneath her, though.

Amara knelt beside Vaana, who was stretched out on another bedroll, still unconscious. She had pulled out bandages and ointments from Vaana's bag and tended her wounds. She'd already tended to Vandermere's broken face.

After the energy had released from the binding circle, Amara had helped Lorelei up and introduced herself. Before Lorelei had much of a chance to ask questions, a distant roar had echoed through the temple. Amara had smiled and said she would handle it. She'd returned a short time later, carrying Vaana with Vandermere's help. They had settled in this room.

Lorelei glanced at Vandermere from under her lashes. Aside from a few bruises, he didn't appear to have any wounds. Lorelei's chest lightened with relief. Not that Vaana's injuries weren't bad, but...

She pushed the thought away before it could continue and glanced back at Amara. She'd barely had time to give her name. Why had she been trapped here?

You shouldn't trust her, Murgleis whispered.

You are a Sluagh, Lorelei thought back. *You shouldn't be trusted either.*

That's the point. There are stories of a Sluagh known as Amara. She is duplicitous. So much so, there's a debate that she's even a Sluagh.

How could you not know whether she is a Sluagh or not?

Vandermere moved closer to her. "You seem to be staring hard at that sword. It's new."

She glanced up, tearing her attention away from Murgleis, and flashed him a smile. "Yeah, I found it when we were separated."

He chuckled. "Seems like you had an adventure of your own."

"This city is insane." She set Murgleis beside her on the bedroll and drew her knees up to rest her elbows on them. "What about you? Seems you got into a big fight."

"We were wandering around for a while. Vaana was never able to get to that tower. Then we heard your voice and followed it. The trolls seemed to have the same idea."

She glanced at the ground and scratched the back of her head. "Yeah, sorry about that. I was helping Amara...get free."

He raised a brow. "Care to explain?"

She bit the inside of her cheek. Should she? She didn't

want a lecture on the dangers of releasing things from Vandermere as well as Murgleis. Still, he was looking at her like that and she didn't want to lie to him.

"She was bound here in a circle. I'm not sure on the details because she left to help you before I could talk to her."

"I see." He rocked back on his heels with his eyes narrowing. Was it a vision? "I suppose we will have to ask her, then."

Lorelei's shoulders straightened. "That's it? No, 'that's a reckless move, Lorelei'?"

"Oh, it was reckless," he said. "But for good or ill, we don't know yet."

Vaana moaned and shifted where she was laying. Amara scooted back and sat with her feet tucked under her and her hands resting on her knees. Vaana sat up with a wince, her hand going to her head.

"What happened?" she asked in a hoarse voice.

"The trolls felt like tossing you around," Amara said. "Luckily, Lorelei helped me out and I was able to do the same for you."

Vaana stiffened, her eyes narrowing at Amara. "Who are you? And where are we?"

"I am Amara. And this..." She waved her hand around the room. "This is the Temple of the Stars, or a room in it, to be precise."

Vaana stilled. "This is the temple in Winderward."

"What's left of it," Amara said with a sad sigh. "Most has been raided from those who seek riches in Winderward. I see several have even tried to pluck the stars from the sky though I doubt that turned out well for them."

"And how do you know this?" Vaana lowered her head in a tilt to stare at Amara.

Lorelei cleared her throat. "Does it matter? She saved you and tended to your wounds."

"For what price?" Vaana kept her gaze on Amara.

Amara raised her hands up. "No price. Like I said, I owe Lorelei."

"Why?"

"She freed me."

Vaana crossed her arms. "And how were you trapped that you needed Lorelei to free you?"

"I have many enemies." Amara looked at her hands as a bitter smile formed on her lips. She glanced back up at Vaana. "After failing to kill me, several joined forces and bound me here."

"Faerie can't be bound." Vaana's jaw set. "So, what are you? Sluagh? Little god?"

"Does it matter?" Lorelei broke in. "She saved you and isn't asking for anything in return."

Vaana jabbed a finger in Amara's direction. "She's most likely an Anathema. She may not want something now, but in the end, we'll have to pay."

"Or she may actually be a boon to the world," Vandermere said. "After all, this world is going to need all the help it can get."

Amara glanced at him and her shoulder trembled for an instant before she straightened and gave him a slight nod. Lorelei's heart sank as she looked between them. They knew something she didn't.

"What do you mean?" Lorelei asked.

Vandermere shook his head and turned to Vaana. "You shouldn't be judging, given your current predicament."

Vaana huffed and stood up, brushing off her pants. "Fine. At least we've reached the temple. I'm going to see if there is anything useful here."

"I doubt you'll find much here," Amara said. "This place had been well ransacked when I was trapped here." She pressed her lips together and her gaze stared into the distance.

Vaana glanced at the door with her brow knitting. She spoke in a low voice. “I’ll take my chances. I can’t leave without searching.”

Lorelei rose to her knees. “You’re still wounded though.”

Vaana closed her eyes and chanted a few words. Color returned to her skin and the shadows that had hovered under eyes disappeared. She unwrapped the bandages around her head and side, revealing fresh whole skin.

“The Empress still provides for those who believe,” she said, casting Vandermere a glare.

With those parting words, she left the room, closing the door with an authoritative clack.

Lorelei lowered herself into a sitting position and stared at her hands. Vaana had a drive to seek out things like this temple, but at the same time she looked down on Amara and others with disdain, bordering on hostility. She had to wonder if Vaana liked her and Vandermere, or just tolerated them because she was stuck.

Vandermere put his hand on Lorelei’s arm. “She’s confused. This whole thing has jarred everything she believes and she’s trying to desperately cling to it.”

Lorelei smirked. “Is that part of your seer abilities?”

“Prophet. And not exactly. I suppose it helps, but I have good insight on people.” Vandermere stood. “I’m going to find her and make sure she stays out of too much trouble. You should get some rest.”

A small smile curled on Lorelei’s lips as she watched him leave. He may not have been overly muscular, but he was fit. He was probably a lot of fun in bed.

What was she thinking?

She shook her head and glanced at Amara.

She cleared her throat. "You said you were bound here by enemies. Will they come after you again?"

"The ones that bound me? They've probably mostly died out," Amara said with a chuckle. "Though there are others that are still alive."

"You've been here for a while," Lorelei said. "So, Vaana was right that you aren't a faerie."

"But you already knew that," Amara said.

"What are you?" Lorelei asked.

Amara winked at her. "That's my secret"

"What about your enemies? They must be powerful."

"They're not your enemies, so you don't need to worry about them," Amara said. "You should enjoy the finer things in life. Not be forced to sleep on a hard floor in a dusty old temple. After all, enjoyment is what makes your magic stronger."

Lorelei tilted her head. "What do you know about my magic?"

Amara blinked at her a few times before she smiled. "That was meant more of a general case. Aether is replenished by doing things we love."

Oh. Amara had meant that.

Ever since coming to Nearon and joining Vaana on this adventure, she'd been able to do some amazing things she hadn't thought possible. Of course, her spells hadn't gone exactly how she had wanted, but she was being more experimental. She no longer had a school to study at. Lorelei stared down at her hands. Drinking and sex had both been Lorelei's favorites for refilling her Aether ever since she'd been at the Aimsir. Arryn had been her chosen partner until he'd left her for Freya.

She met Amara's gaze and spoke in a flat tone. "The finer things in life, as you say, have never brought me much joy. They come with too much heartache."

Amara leaned forward and touched Lorelei's cheek with a tender expression. "No, they wouldn't."

Lorelei's breath caught in her throat as she stared into Amara's dark eyes. Something about her touch was so familiar. There was an instant connection there. They'd just met, but Amara felt like the sister she had always wanted.

Before she could say anything, Amara stood and stretched her arms above her head, glancing around the room.

"Well, as much as I'm enjoying this, I've been staring at these walls for far too long," Amara said. "I'm itching to see what's become of the world."

"You're leaving already?" Lorelei tried to push the disappointment down.

"I've been resting long enough. Don't worry though. You and your friends will be safe here."

Lorelei nodded, her shoulders slumping.

Amara leaned over, grasped her hands, and pulled her to her feet. She towered over Lorelei. Had she gotten taller? She planted a small kiss on Lorelei's forehead.

"Don't look so sad. We'll meet again," Amara said. "After all, I still owe you."

"But you saved my friends," Lorelei said.

Amara laughed. "Scaring away some Fomorians and healing a few wounds doesn't make up for what you did for me."

Lorelei smiled. "I look forward to seeing you again, then."

"To the future." Amara gave a two-fingered salute and left.

Lorelei let out a loud sigh and looked around the empty room. The quietness seemed to become more deafening as each second passed. Once again, she was alone.

Well, not exactly; she did have Murgleis.

I'm not going to comfort you, Murgleis said.

"Fine," Lorelei muttered, stood up, and packed her equipment into her backpack. She picked up the heartstone and stared at it for a moment. Vandermere was right. This had been useful so far. She'd better keep it somewhere accessible. She stuck it in the pocket of her skirt. Last, she picked up Murgleis and tied him to her belt before crossing the room.

She flung the door open and stepped into the empty hallway. Most of the doors now hung open, a sign of Vaana's search most likely. Judging by the silence of the hall, she and Vandermere had already moved on.

Lorelei headed towards the grand hall. Vaana's voice reverberated through the air as she opened the door. Vandermere and Vaana stood against the far wall. Lorelei quickened her step to them.

Vaana glanced at her. "Where's your friend?"

"Amara left. She decided she wanted to see what's become of the world," Lorelei said. "Did you find anything?"

Vaana crossed her arms and huffed. "Most of the room are empty. What's left is useless."

Lorelei raised an eyebrow. "You searched this entire temple already?"

"Unfortunately, much of this wing is inaccessible." Vandermere nodded to the door on the left Lorelei had not taken. "Looks like there was a cave in."

"All of it?" Lorelei asked. "No way to the second floor?"

"No, we found stairs and we were able to reach a library on the second floor. Most of the books are ruined. All I got was this." Vaana pulled out a set of scrolls. "They look like their tenants to whatever this religion was."

Lorelei stared at the yellowed paper in Vaana's hand. Her fingers itched to get a hold of them. Vaana's brow wrinkled and her lips pinched in an expression of frustration.

"I'm guessing they aren't any of the gods you're carrying around," Lorelei said.

Vaana shook her head. "Some star religion."

"Well, it is proof that other gods existed," Lorelei said.

Vaana glared at her. "I'm aware there are other gods. The Order has sought to weed out the heretics for centuries."

"But why are they heretics?" Lorelei asked. "The Order has always stated the Empress was the One True Goddess, obviously, but what makes these gods any less?"

"The Empress saved us from the Miasma," Vaana said in a low, cold voice. "Don't forget that. These other gods could do nothing."

Lorelei looked to the floor. She couldn't refute that. She didn't know enough about any other gods to say different.

"Either way, this place doesn't have what we are looking for," Vandermere broke in. "Perhaps we can now make a journey to see the Lord of Fate."

"Why do you want to see him?" Lorelei asked. "How can he help?"

"He is of my House. And he was the one who originally placed the stones in the vault," Vandermere said. "He probably knows the most about the gods contained within."

Lorelei threw her hands up. "You didn't say he was the one who put them there."

"Vaana appeared adamant on searching here." Vandermere looked away. "I thought it was a good idea to humor her."

"Well?" Lorelei glanced at Vaana. "This Lord of Fate is probably your best option for finding out if you can get rid of these gods."

Vaana's jaw ticked as her gaze traveled the hall. "Fine. I suppose we'll go see the crazy wizard in his tower."

16

Vandermere and Vaana decided the group should stay the night in the temple to rest up before heading out, and Lorelei had no objections. They left in the morning, and the trek back to Nearon was uneventful. They arrived at night, long after the sun had set.

Lorelei stopped at the wall and glanced back to the Marsh she'd spent so much time in. It was as if Winderward was done with them.

She stared down one of the streets with its broken cobblestone and shacks made of wood. Pieces of trash tumbled on the ground, blown about by the soft breeze which also carried the faint stench of refuse. She glanced at one of the alleys they passed. Anything could be hidden there.

"We need to hire a boat to take us down the river," Vandermere said, coming up next to her. "The Lord of Fate's tower is—"

"In the middle of nowhere," Vaana interjected. "Whatever captain is willing to take us is going to want a lot of money. I suppose I'll be the one paying?"

Lorelei held her hands up. "My family mostly cut me off when they sent me to the priory."

"I'll pay for it," Vandermere said. "After all, it's my suggestion."

"Why are you even coming?" Vaana asked. "I understand why Lorelei is, with her predicament—but you?"

One side of Vandermere's lips curled up. "Well, to start with, you are carrying around something old that I was given the duty of watching over. Perhaps I want to keep you out of trouble."

"Who is going to watch the vault?" Lorelei asked. "You still have all those artifacts there that Vaana didn't take surprisingly. And the Order knows of it."

Vaana shot her a glare. "I was a little occupied after."

"I'll send word to the Head of my House to send a replacement," he said. "Sometimes it's needed when the guardian falls ill, or something."

"Why don't I think these things in me and keeping us out of trouble are the only reasons?" Vaana muttered.

She quickened her pace, moving ahead of Vandermere and Lorelei.

Lorelei glanced at Vandermere with her heart speeding up. Did Vaana mean that Vandermere wanted to stay because of her? He winked at her, then followed Vaana toward the alley ahead.

An arrow flew from the alley. With a grunt, Vaana twisted her torso to the side and shoved her palm out to slap the arrow out of the air. A female figure stepped out of the alley, shouldering her bow.

Lorelei gasped at the sidhe with the two-toned hair dressed in black. Beth, the other companion of the Apostle of Fire, stood in front of them with a bow in her hand. She'd stayed with the Apostle when Lorelei and Vaana had set off for Winderward.

"Beth." Vaana's face paled.

"I'm pleased to see you still remembered what I'd taught you, even though you've decided to turn your back on the Order." Beth barely spared Lorelei and Vandermere a glance.

"I haven't turned my back," Vaana said. "I just have some things I need to work out."

"We know what has happened. You have given into heretical gods. You have become an Anathema." Beth lifted her chin to look down her nose at Vaana. "Surrender yourself to the Order to be cleansed."

Vaana gulped and stared at the ground.

Lorelei scowled. "What happens in this cleansing?"

"The fire will burn her body to ash, but her soul will be clean and rejoin the reincarnation cycle," Beth said. "The two of you will be taken in for aiding and abetting her."

"No, there has to be another way." Vaana drew her blade from its sheath, lifting her head. "I'll find another way."

Beth sighed and drew a small thin sword of her own from a sheath on her belt. "So far you have fallen."

Vaana ran her hand along the flat of her blade, whispering softly. The blade shimmered with a soft gray light, even in the dark of the night. Vaana shot Beth a look mixed with triumph and pleading.

"The Empress hasn't abandoned me yet," Vaana said.

Beth let out a laugh. "How dare you mistake our Empress with the heretical gods you carry within you. They won't save you."

"You obviously haven't seen these gods in action." Lorelei pulled Murgleis from her belt. "Besides, she has us as well."

"Then you all will die as heretics." With those words, Beth lunged at Vaana.

She swung her sword at Vaana's side. Vaana pivoted and brought her blade up to block the swing. Her pivot took her right into Beth's closed fist. Vaana gasped and staggered backwards. Lorelei sprinted forward and yanked Vaana behind her. She swung Murgleis at Beth.

Beth batted the blade aside with the back of her fist and drove her sword into Lorelei's side. She shoved her foot into Lorelei's midsection and sent Lorelei stumbling back into Vaana.

Vandermere had moved to the side to flank Beth. She spun and planted a kick to his chest. She moved gracefully, like flowing water and wind.

I wish I could move like that, Lorelei thought as she covered her bleeding wound with her hand.

I will handle this, Murgleis said. *You can lick your wounds later.*

"Wait," Lorelei tried to cry out, but her mouth was no longer her own.

Lorelei's body thrust forward and delivered a blow that sliced through Beth's black armor. Beth recoiled. She looked down at the wound, her breast crackling with a green light. She turned her attention back to Lorelei.

"Sluagh tainted," she hissed. "You have corrupted my Vaana."

She rushed forward with her sword swinging low to eviscerate Lorelei. Murgleis flashed forward dragging Lorelei's arm along with it, glowing viridian, and deflected Beth's hand. Lorelei felt like a caged animal. This was her body. She wasn't going to let this Sluagh dictate what it did even if it was doing a much better job. She focused on her hand, willing it to obey her commands.

A blur of motion in her—or *their*—peripheral distracted her from her battle of wills. Vaana rushed from around Lorelei and sliced into Beth's arm. Beth cried out as her fingers flexed and she dropped her blade. She glared at Vaana.

Let me do this, Lorelei thought to Murgleis.

She felt her fingers obeying her commands again and relief washed through her. She pulled the heartstone from her pocket and held it out, singing a small song to summon a gout of flame. The fire poured from the gem and hit Beth.

It fizzled on her chest.

She let out a laugh. "The power of the Fire Dragon protects me."

Vandermere jabbed her in her side with Beth's sword. "It doesn't protect you against steel."

Beth shoved her open palm into Vandermere's chest, knocking him off his feet. She spun on her heel, throwing one leg out which plowed into Vaana's legs, sending her to the ground. She hopped back several paces, her gaze darting between the three of them. Her hand flicked to the side and a flash of metal flew through the air at Vaana. The stench of it sent a wave of nausea through Lorelei's stomach.

Iron.

She had to get to Vaana and deflect it somehow. Murgleis took control again. Her body flew into action and the world seemed to blur. Her arm came up and Murgleis met the point of the iron dagger with his flat side. The dagger flipped in the air and was flung off course. It landed a few feet away in the street.

Lorelei stumbled a few steps as Murgleis released his hold on her. She gaped in disgust at the dagger then to where Beth stood. Only, Beth was no longer there.

She'd disappeared.

"She took off into the alley." Vandermere got to his feet with a groan. "We should get off the street before the guard catches us."

Lorelei turned to give Vaana a hand up.

A shout echoed from the hill at the end of the street. Six

men in the livery of Nearon's city guard were marching in their direction.

They hadn't been fast enough. If the guards caught them, they'd be locked up. There would be no escape from the Order then.

17

The lead soldier, a redcap in a helmet came to a halt and stared down at Lorelei and the others. He studied each of them with narrowed eyes, and Lorelei's stomach dropped. She pressed her hand hard to the wound in her side, hoping to stymie the flow of blood.

"What are sidhe doing in this part of the city at this time at night?" he asked.

Lorelei swallowed hard and lifted her chin. "We're adventurers returning from Winderward."

Vaana shot her a glare and Lorelei shrugged. At this moment, it was better to throw a little truth into things. That part was at least believable.

"Sidhe adventurers?" one of the other soldiers, an ankou, scoffed.

Lorelei shot him a glare. "I'll have you know that many sidhe risked their lives fighting the Miasma. Lady Moura died fighting it."

"A Moura. That explains things," the lead soldier muttered. "Do you have any paperwork? Are you registered with the Delvers?"

Lorelei flicked her gaze at Vaana. Had she registered with them?

Vaana shook her head. Of course not. Vaana had had the blessing of the Order. She hadn't needed to get anything official from the Delvers. However, that blessing no longer applied.

"Well..." Lorelei said.

"Do they really need that?" a soft male voice called from one of the alleys.

Wes stepped out with his arms crossed. He winked at Lorelei before turning to the group of soldiers.

"Mullen, they assign you here again?" Wes addressed the lead soldier with a chuckle. "What did you do this time?"

Mullen gave him a quick grin. "One too many drinks and someone in the Heaving Maiden mouthing off too much. You know how it goes."

Wes laughed. "I do. So, about my friends here. You don't need to worry about them. They're with me."

Mullen glanced at them, then raised one eyebrow. "They don't look like Serpent material. The opposite, really."

Wes nodded to Lorelei. "Show him the coin, Beautiful."

Lorelei's brow furrowed. What was he talking about?

Oh! She slipped her hand in a belt pouch and pulled out the coin Wes had given her at Mourner's Hill. She held it out to the guards.

Mullen took it and flipped it between his fingers. He let out a short huff of breath in a laugh.

"Ain't that a crazy thing," he said. "I thought your group didn't take in sidhe."

"There's a time for everything." Wes pulled out a small pouch from behind his back that jingled and pressed it into Mullen's open hand. "So, you see, you have nothing to worry about here."

Mullen nodded with a grin and tossed the coin back to

Lorelei. She caught it in midair and was met with a few whistles of the guards.

"Nice catch." Mullen looked to the other guards. "All right, men, let's see if there are any disturbances near Pike Street."

Laughing and mumbling to themselves, the guards spun and headed the way they'd come.

Wes turned to Lorelei with an easygoing grin.

"Looks like you needed me after all," he said. "It's good to see you."

"Thanks for that." Lorelei could help respond with a smile of her own. "I guess this means your debt is paid?"

He tilted his head at the retreating guards. "Them? Nah, I think I owe you more. You saved my life. They probably would have just fined you."

"Then do you have a place we can lie low? Maybe tend to our wounds?" Lorelei glanced down at her blood covered fingers pressed against her side.

"Sure thing, follow me." He sauntered towards the alley he'd come from.

Vaana grabbed her arm. "You're seriously considering trusting this rogue?"

"He did just save us. And we don't have much choice," Lorelei muttered. "It's not like we can go to the Order."

Vaana let go of her arm with an unintelligible grumble.

Lorelei caught up with Wes, with Vaana and Vandermere trailing behind.

"So, what are the Serpents?" Lorelei rubbed the coin in her fingers. It gleamed in the moonlight. "I guess they're connected to this?"

His gaze dropped to the coin. "They're a group I'm a part of. We mostly run the slums and the docks. And you should be careful with that. Come on. We should get off the streets."

Lorelei tucked the coin away in her belt pouch and

followed him. Wes led them through a series of winding dark alleys until he reached a ragged wooden door of a house squeezed between two larger buildings.

He gave a series of knocks. After a few minutes, a green-skinned hob male opened the door. Wes leaned close and murmured a few words to him. The hob stepped back, opening the door wide enough for them to enter.

Wes nodded inside towards a narrow hall.

The house had obviously been made with the hob in mind. They had to squeeze in one at a time, push through the hall with several doors, and duck through the one at the end. At least that room was larger than Lorelei thought it would be. All four of them were able to fit in comfortably. There was one bed and a small end table beside it with a single candle atop it.

"We use this place as a safe house from time to time," Wes said. "Rourke doesn't mind the occasional visitor. You can tend to your wounds here. Do you need anything?"

Vaana shook her head, pushed Lorelei to the bed, and sat beside her. Her hands ran over Lorelei's side and she closed her eyes, her voice lowering to a murmur as she spoke a quick cadence. The pain vanished, replaced with a soft warmth that spread through her torso.

Lorelei let out a soft breath of relief. She turned back to Wes. "Thanks again."

"No problem. I've been watching the street for you to come out of Winderward for the last day or so," he said. "Figured you might need some help. You seem the type."

Lorelei crossed her arms. "And what type is that?"

"Trouble."

Vandermere chuckled from the back. "It seems you are well acquainted with Lorelei."

Lorelei wrinkled her nose and mock glared at both of

them. It wasn't like she tried to cause trouble. Things just tended to end up that way.

"Forgive me for no introduction, my lord and lady. I'm Wes." He gave an exaggerated bow with a flourishing hand toward Vandermere and Vaana in turn. "Lorelei saved me from that demon sword on her hip. So, I owed her a favor."

"Vandermere ap Essus," Vandermere said. "A pleasure."

Vaana's gaze shifted to the sword and then to Wes. "Charmed."

"Well, I'll leave you three to get some rest and clean up. I'll be in the next room if you need anything."

With a wave, he stepped out and shut the door with a quiet click.

Lorelei lay back on the bed, sighing, and closed her eyes.

"Is anyone else hurt?" she asked.

"Mostly bruises," Vaana said. "They should be able to heal with rest and some ointment I have. You're going to have to remove your shirt so I can get a better look at the wound."

Lorelei glanced at Vandermere as her fingers touched the edge of her leather jerkin. In the candlelight, it seemed that his cheeks had turned pink. He walked to the edge of the room and sat with his back to them.

She hid a smile and slipped off her jerkin. Vaana rubbed the cool ointment on the bruise at her midsection.

"What did the phooka boy mean about a demon sword?" Vaana asked in a quiet voice.

"Well..." Lorelei bit her bottom lip. "I came across Murgleis on a hill. It had a lot of people in thrall, including Wes. But I managed to beat it down in a battle of wills."

"As in the Sluagh Murgleis?" Vandermere partially turned his head in their direction, his voice taking a concerned edge. "That's a dangerous thing to carry around."

"Why do you still have that thing with you?" Vaana asked.

"Do you want your soul to be taken? Or to end up like those people you saved?"

Lorelei bunched her skirt in her fists as she glared at the two of them. "Was I supposed to leave it lying around? At least with me, I'm the one in control."

"It's probably lulling you into complacency," Vaana said. "It will trick you. It's what Sluagh do."

Lorelei stared down at her hands with her jaw tight and her eyes stinging. Vaana wasn't wrong exactly. It had taken control of her during the fight with Beth.

You wanted to move more gracefully, Murgleis said. *I was giving you what you wanted. It would have gone better if you didn't fight me.*

I'm not your puppet. She ground her teeth. *Don't ever do that again without my permission.*

But I am your tool? You lent no thought to raising me against the assassin.

You are a sword. You were made for that.

I was created for so much more, little girl. So many of your kind have wielded me with the same belief and they became my thralls.

Lorelei bit her lip. She had first picked him up with the intention of claiming a weapon. That had changed when she had seen part of his past. He may have hidden it under the sarcasm and sharp words, but there was pain. She hadn't even known Sluagh could feel loss. Most stories she had heard were of their trickery.

You're right, she said. *I assumed I could use you. So, let's make an accord. We work together. You obviously still like battles, and this won't be the last time we'll see it.*

You do seem to attract trouble. He sounded amused. *Why should I help you? I can just wait to wear your will down."*

Her eye twitched. *What do you truly want? To travel the land, leaving a trail of dead behind you?*

He went silent.

Her side ached from her wound.

Do you even know what you want? she prodded.

Of course. His voice took on an annoyed tone. *I'm not some wishful faerie child, full of baseless dreams.*

She let out her breath in a silent laugh. *My dreams aren't baseless. This isn't about me though. What do you want? Do I have to ask you a third time?*

I wish to return to Kurnach. He said softly. *I will continue to protect it in his stead.*

Lorelei blinked. Kurnach was one of the cities of the fire plains. Its walls had withstood countless armies. The greatest tale had been of the lone warrior that had protected the gate from a horde over a century ago.

You loved Kieran, right? I saw in the vision the way you acted at his death.

Murgleis remained silent. An ache formed in Lorelei's chest as she remembered the expression on Murgleis's face. He'd looked so lost, so helpless. She'd felt like that before, when Arryn had been wounded by an iron blade. Lorelei swallowed the lump in her throat and looked down at her hands.

Very well, she said. *I have a proposition. If you agree to let me wield you without trying to take over my will, I will take you to Kurnach when I can.*

And when will that be?

It may not be immediately, but I give you my word I will bring you there.

He didn't reply for a long moment. Then, he said, *I accept those terms.*

Good. Now there will be no more of you taking control of my body against my will.

I saved your life, he said. *You should be grateful.*

Your expertise was useful, but you should have asked first.

He didn't respond.

Lorelei blinked at both Vaana and Vandermere. Vaana had

pressed her lips into a thin line of disapproval while Vandermere had turned around, brow furrowed.

They both looked at her expectantly.

"I'm fine," Lorelei said. "We have an agreement. And no, it's not to kill or enthrall everyone in sight. He'll behave."

"You think that for now," Vaana said.

"Well, if something bad happens, you'll be there with your Order skills to handle it," Lorelei said.

"Sure, I'll clean up your mess." Vaana shook her head and stood up. "I suppose I owe you for sticking by me and helping with my mess."

Lorelei looked to Vandermere. "You'll watch over me too?"

"Of course, little Nightingale," he said softly. "I just wish you'd rethink this."

"If gods aren't what we believed them to be, why not Sluagh? I want to see the end of his story."

Vaana opened her mouth and then pressed her lips together and shook her head. She sat down beside her backpack, reached in, and pulled out a small brass ball with moving pieces attached to the surface. Her fingers pressed down on a triangle and slid it up until it was flush with another triangle.

Lorelei straightened and craned her neck for a better look. "What is that?"

"It's a puzzle ball," Vaana's brow wrinkled as she stared down at it. "The mystery and the challenge of solving puzzles help me regain Aether...much like drinking does for you, I suppose."

"You know, that actually sounds like a good plan." Lorelei stood. "After all the craziness of the last few days, I could use a drink." She shuffled to her backpack, pulled an unopened bottle of wine from it, and held it up to the two of them. "Anyone wish to join me?"

"Indeed." Vandermere got up from his corner and walked across the room to her.

Lorelei glanced at Vaana. "After what you've dealt with, I'd say you could use a drink. What do you say?"

Vaana stared at the bottle for several moments before letting her head fall. "Why not?"

"Great." With a grin, Lorelei pulled out three wooden cups from her bag, opened the bottle, and began to fill them.

Vaana eyed the cups. "You consider wine and cups essential gear?"

Lorelei looked up and huffed out a laugh. "Yes. And I see I was right, considering what we went through."

With a sigh, Vaana sat on the floor and took a cup from Lorelei. Vandermere settled himself with his back to the wall with his own drink.

Lorelei held her wine out. "To finding hidden secrets and creating new tales."

"To getting out of the mess we are in," Vaana muttered.

"To the future," Vandermere said. "May it be worth saving."

Their cups clanked together and each sipped of their wine. Vaana made a face, but then took a longer drink. Lorelei drained her cup dry and poured another.

"You know," Lorelei said to Vandermere. "Sometimes the things you say makes me think you know something we should."

He shrugged. "I know many things. Some of it you should know when the time is right."

"And that's not now?" Lorelei reached over and refilled Vaana's vessel.

"Not yet," he said.

"How about now? Maybe if you'd told me, I wouldn't be in this situation." Vaana's knuckles whitened around her cup as a growl threaded her voice.

"There is no stopping Fate," Vandermere said. "There is a story my House tells its children of one of our ancestors."

Lorelei leaned forward, waiting for Vandermere to continue. She'd never heard a story about any ancestors of the House aside from Essus himself.

"In the time of the Miasma, there was a seer named Brayden." Vandermere stared off with a distant gaze. "He'd had visions of a town being destroyed by a Fomorian beast. He tried several times to warn the town, but every time he thought he had averted the destruction, he would have the vision again. Finally, he understood, in order to destroy the Fomorian, he had to let Fate play out. He had to let the town die.

"He watched from a hill as the beast came. He heard the screams of the people, but could do nothing to save them. When the beast was sated and slept in the ruined town, Brayden struck and killed the beast. The cost was great, but he'd learned there was no other option."

"Wow, that was...depressing." Lorelei took a gulp of her wine. "Thanks for the inspiration."

"It's more for you to understand that what I see comes to pass. I knew something would change Vaana in the Menhir. There was no stopping it."

"Wait," Lorelei said. "This was at the time of the Miasma. The stories I remember put Essus around that time."

"Our House is older than Essus," Vandermere said. "The Empress renamed in honor of Essus."

"You're still not revealing what else you know." Vaana glared at him.

Vandermere sighed. "I've told you everything I know about the godstones. The other things should wait as you are already dealing with this crisis."

Vaana drained her wine and held out her cup again. With

a raised eyebrow, Lorelei filled it again, finishing the bottle off.

"You should be careful," Lorelei said. "You probably don't have much tolerance."

"If I get drunk, all the better," Vaana said over the lip of her wooden tumbler.

Lorelei pulled another bottle, her last, from her bag. "Guess I'm going to have to resupply when I get a chance."

Vaana's head bowed and her shoulders slumped. Her finger rubbed the edge of her cup. "Beth was my mentor. I can't believe she would be so ready to kill me. She didn't even ask for an explanation."

"Would you have done the same thing in her position?" Vandermere murmured.

Vaana opened her mouth to speak, but paused. She took a deep drink of her wine before continuing. "I want to say no, but before all of this happened, I would have eliminated my target with no questions of my orders. It's how she taught me."

Lorelei's brow knitted together as she poured more wine for both Vaana and herself. "How does the Order even know?"

"That's a good question." Vaana rubbed her face with one hand. "I'm officially an anathema now. And what's worse is I'm not sure if it's a bad thing. These things inside me keep whispering..."

"Whispering what?" Lorelei leaned forward with interest.

Vaana finished her cup instead of answering and set it on the floor. She stood and smiled down at them.

"I think that's enough for me tonight. Thanks for listening." She turned and tottered to the bed.

"I think we should all call it a night," Vandermere said as Vaana flopped on the bed. "We should talk in the morning about what to do when we are less inebriated."

"You've barely drank," Lorelei pointed out.

"I didn't need to." He nodded to Vaana who was already snoring softly. "She needed some sort of release."

He stood and pulled Lorelei's bedroll out. After laying it out, he rolled out his own.

"You act more like our caretaker rather than a companion." Lorelei shook the bottle. It was empty. Had they really drunk that much?

"That's not exactly true," Vandermere said. "I think we all take care of each other when the need arises."

Lorelei stretched out on her bedroll and closed her eyes with a smile. "That's a nice thought."

She relaxed, feeling warm and accepted, like she belonged somewhere for once.

Even though they were most likely criminals now, wanted by the church as heretics.

She let out a soft laugh. She had never thought her place in life would be as a heretic. She had thought it would be with Arryn, forever convincing him to go on little adventures. Eventually she would settle down and they would have children. She'd been wrong about that, though. Freya had gotten that life because Freya was better.

At least I'm not alone, she thought to herself as she drifted off to sleep.

She woke to a loud knock on the door. With a groan, she rolled over and looked up at the door as it opened. Wes peered down at her before his gaze traveled over Vandermere and Vaana. He expression was closed off, different from the easygoing demeanor he'd had last night.

He looked back to Lorelei. "The leader of the Silver Serpents wants to see you."

18

The tavern Wes took them to stood out from the surrounding buildings as it was made of stone instead of wood, with hardwood beams as support. Tatters of old sails were used as curtains, covering the openings that served as windows.

Lorelei eyed the building dubiously. Wes paused at a wooden door and glanced back at the group.

"Well?" He huffed with a bit of impatience. "We shouldn't make him wait."

"I'm not sure we should go in there," Vandermere said. "It looks like it might fall over with the puff of breath from a large wolf."

"Don't let the outside deceive you." Wes patted the side of the building. "The Black Salt has stood up to a lot."

"Why does this gang leader want to see us again?" Vaana asked.

"He's heard how Lorelei helped me and the others and wants to thank her," Wes said.

"This sounds like a trap," Vaana muttered. "We should be

leaving the city, not meeting with someone that may turn us over for a bit of coin."

"Hold on, Wes." Lorelei gave him a quick smile and stepped closer to Vaana and Vandermere, lowering her voice. "This may be a chance for us to get a boat. If he's actually grateful, I might be able to get another favor out of them."

"Or he'll sell us out," Vaana said. "You should know not to trust this type."

Vandermere stared at the door with narrowed eyes. "I don't believe we'll be betrayed."

Vaana raised an eyebrow. "You got that in a few moments? Why couldn't you sense the Fomorians so we could have avoided them?"

"I don't get visions for everything. When they come to me, it is in flashes. I can concentrate on a particular instance, like now, but it takes longer," Vandermere said. "Besides, the visions I do get will happen. There is no avoiding them."

"Fine," Vaana said. "Let's get this over with."

Lorelei straightened up, turned back to Wes, and strode towards the door. "We're ready."

Wes shrugged and opened the door. "I don't see the big deal. It's not like you're meeting the Empress."

"That would be difficult since she is gone," Vandermere said.

"She'll return one day," Vaana said.

Lorelei stepped into the tavern. The inside was not much better than the outside. There were several long tables with abandoned mugs and empty wooden plates. They were barely occupied with one or two people spread out leaning over their drinks. The stench of stale ale and old food wafted up from the floor. It probably hadn't been cleaned since the place was built. The bartender, an old redcap, poured ale into a mug that was dwarfed in his hand.

He glanced up and nodded at Wes as he passed the bar with a wave.

Lorelei followed Wes with quick steps, Vaana and Vandermere behind her, to the door in the back which held a staircase. They filed down in a row. The wood stairs creaked with each step. Barrels of ale were stacked on the left and right of the small room. At least it appeared to be cleaner than above.

Wes strolled through the room to a wooden door in the back and knocked. A muffled voice came from the other side of the door. Wes pushed it open and nodded to Lorelei. She shuffled past him and stepped into the room, followed by Vaana and Vandermere.

An ankou sat behind a large wooden desk looking at a scroll. He wasn't like any ankou Lorelei had seen, though. His hair was pure white, gleaming in the dim light of the room, and his wings were composed of white feathers with black fringe. She'd never seen an ankou who had feathered wings. Most tended to have dark hair as well.

He glanced up and smiled. His gaze scanned over each of them and his silver eyes locked on Lorelei. A shiver snaked through her

"You would be Lorelei?" he asked.

"Lorelei ap Moura." She nodded.

"I'm Silvereyes," he said. "I heard what you did for Wes and the others who were trapped. That is commendable, and surprising for a sidhe."

Vandermere crossed his arms and tilted his head. "Why do you say that? It is our duty to look after the people under our rule."

"But Nearon is not under her rule," Silvereyes said. "I believe she is an outsider to the city."

"They needed help, so I helped them," Lorelei said. "I was glad to help."

Silvereyes's gaze shifted to the sword on her hip. "I am

grateful for your help. I'd all but given up on the agents I'd lost to that thing."

"What do your agents do?" Lorelei asked. "Do you have goals other than earning money?"

Silvereyes chuckled. "Are you asking if we're common thieves? Not at all. We wish to free the people from the rule of the Legate and Council of Peers."

Lorelei's eyes widened. The Apostle had explained some of the politics of Nearon on their journey to the city. It was different from the Quorum's rule of the Empire, but still eerily similar. The Legate was the mysterious entity that rose up at the end of the time of Miasma to take control of Nearon. He formed the Council of Peers as a set of advisors, but many believed they were mere puppets. He was the one who made the laws of Nearon, and the laws changed on his whim, sometimes without the rest of Nearon knowing before it was too late. One rule always stayed the same and it was punishable by death: one must never interrupt the flow of trade.

"So, are you doing this by breaking the main rule?" Lorelei asked.

Silvereyes chuckled. "More like redirected the flow of trade."

"Sounds dangerous," Vandermere said. "The Council themselves don't like their plans meddled with."

"Say you do succeed," Vaana said. "Do you have something that will fill the vacuum of power?"

"We have some things in mind, but that is Serpent business," Silvereyes said.

"You must have a lot of connections in the city," Lorelei said. "Is there any chance you can get in contact with a ship captain we could hire to take us up the Silverbourne River? We'd like it to be quiet."

He raised an eyebrow. "Run into some trouble?"

Lorelei shrugged. "We've hit a few rough patches."

"Where are you headed?"

Lorelei glanced at Vandermere who nodded. She turned back to Silvereyes. "The Lord of Fate's tower."

"That's quite a distance away." He tapped one finger on his chin. "I have a few ships at my disposal."

"We have the money to hire our own ship," Vaana said.

Silvereyes chuckled. "I doubt you have enough spare coin to hire a ship to take you the entire trip. You'd have to pull money out from a bank, and that would lead to you getting noticed."

Vaana's jaw tightened as she glared at him. He was right though. They hadn't worried about paying for the ship before Beth. Now, the Order was watching any account, especially Vaana's.

"What do you want?" Lorelei asked Silvereyes. "I'm guessing it's not money."

"Of course not." A smile slid across his face. "A favor, really. There is a town called Ebonshire a few days up the river. My contacts there have stopped reporting in over the past year. In fact, I seem to lose anyone I send in there."

"Sounds dangerous." Lorelei crossed her arms. "I mean, you've already lost people."

"It shouldn't be a problem for someone who can deal with a Sluagh," Silvereyes said.

Lorelei glanced at Vaana who had her arms crossed. She threw her hands up.

"We don't have a better option," Vaana said.

"And there are three of us," Vandermere said.

Lorelei turned back to Silvereyes. "We'll do it."

He nodded. "Good. The Winddancer leaves tonight. Be at pier nine by midnight."

"That's not clandestine at all," Lorelei muttered as they left.

They arrived at pier nine a little early to scope it out, only to find others had arrived even earlier. The lanterns of the pier had been lit, staving off the darkness and bathing the ship and dock in a yellow-orange glow. Faerie dressed in dark clothing moved crates and boxes onto the ship, stacking them atop each other.

Lorelei expected shouting and the crash of wood against wood, but they were surprisingly quiet with just the sound of footfalls and the creaks of planks.

The ship was smaller than most others in the dock, forty feet long with three masts.

"A caravel," Lorelei murmured.

Her father had a few of the ships in his fleet. Their small size meant they weren't good for cargo or passengers, but they were fast and their elliptical frame made them very maneuverable. Her father tended to use his for messengers and such, as one ship cost less than hiring a mage.

Lorelei breathed in the salty night air, a wonderful change for the filth and refuse that clung to the slums of Nearon. She weaved her way through the workers to the gangplank. Footfalls sounded behind her, and Vandermere and Vaana joined her on either side.

"I hope the captain is capable," Vaana said.

"More than capable, if I say so myself." Wes's voice drifted from behind them.

They turned to face him.

"You?" Vaana asked in an incredulous voice.

Wes shrugged. "I've sailed up and down this river a number of times. The Winddancer and I are well acquainted."

"You would think you'd want more time to recover before you went looking for trouble again," Lorelei said with a grin.

"What can I say? I get bored easily. And traveling with a bunch of sidhe? This should be a tale to remember." Wes strolled past them and led them up the gangplank. They stepped onto the deck. "Alright, you should pick your rooms while the boys are getting our supplies loaded. Most are free except for the Captains quarters. They're mine."

"What about the rest of the crew?" Vaana asked. "Am I going to have to worry about a knife in my gut?"

Wes grinned at her. "Only if you piss me off, I suppose. I am the crew."

Lorelei blinked. "Just you? Doesn't it usually take at least seven to sail a caravel?"

Wes tilted his head with an expression of respect. "You know your ships. That could come in handy. Yes, usually it does take seven, but the Winddancer is a special ship."

Special usually meant magical in some way. Was there some sort of spirit that resided in the ship? She would have to check that out when she was settled.

Wes pointed to a door at the bow of the ship. "Stairs are down that way. We'll be leaving in an hour or so."

He glanced down at the men on the pier. They had finished stacking the boxes. Silvereyes leaned against one stack with his arms crossed, watching them. He nodded.

"'Scuse me. Looks like I have a few things to discuss." Wes pushed past them and sauntered down the gangplank to Silvereyes.

They spoke, nodding to the boxes and the ship, but Lorelei could not make out what was being said. She turned to Vaana and Vandermere.

"Well," she said. "I guess we should find places to sleep."

Vaana tossed her long braid over her shoulder and sauntered to the stairs. Vandermere patted Lorelei on the shoulder and then followed behind Vaana. With a sigh and another glance around the ship, Lorelei trailed after them.

Below deck led to a narrow hallway with several doors. Hinges squeaked as Vaana opened the door on the right closest to the stairs. Vandermere took the room three doors down from her. Lorelei chose the room next to Vandermere and pushed the door open. A layer of dust covered the small end table and the bunk bed bolted to the floor. A simple wooden chest stood at the foot of the bed.

Wes hadn't been on the Winddancer for a while, it seemed. No one had.

With a grimace, she pulled out a blouse and a waterskin from her backpack. She didn't have much since most of her clothes were still at the temple and she wasn't going back there. They were just clothes, after all.

She wetted the blouse with water from her waterskin and attacked the dirt, starting with the table. The mattress was going to have to be beaten to get the dust off. Maybe she could find something to use as bedsheets somewhere. After she finished dusting, she set to work batting cobwebs out of the corners of the room.

The ship lurched.

They were moving!

Lorelei dropped the blouse, now covered in dirt, and rushed to the top deck. Wes stood at the wheel, guiding the ship from the dock. A strong breeze ruffled her hair. She turned from Wes and wandered to the railing. Despite the dark of midnight, Nearon glowed on the horizon, giving a purplish haze around the city.

She sighed. She hadn't even had a chance to ask anyone in the city about the Black Herons. She'd intended to make a few discreet inquiries. How had she ended up sneaking out like a criminal?

You should have chosen better company then, Murgleis said. *And not trusted the Order.*

She chewed the inside of her cheek gently. True. This had

happened due to Vaana's machinations. But Vaana hadn't planned for this to happen and something in Lorelei's gut told her that the Order was up to something. Had they just wanted the tablets for safe keeping or was it for something else? She wanted to see where this thing with the tablets took them.

The shadow of something moved on the shore at the edge of Nearon. The light glinted off a white mask.

Lorelei leaned forward on the rail and peered into the darkness. The mask was attached to a cloaked figure that was hard to make out in the darkness.

Footsteps sounded behind her and Vandermere leaned on the rail beside her. "What are you staring at so hard?"

"There's someone on the shore watching us," she said in a low voice.

Vandermere gazed in the same direction for several moments before giving a huff of surprise. "I think that's the Legate."

Lorelei did a double-take at the figure. "You're joking."

"He supposedly is always seen in a mask."

"So? Someone could be impersonating him. I mean, why would the Legate be watching us leave?"

Vandermere shrugged. "I don't know."

"You could look," Lorelei said. "Use your nifty prophet powers. You know, to make sure it's not going to send us some nasty surprises."

"I'd rather not," Vandermere said. "I don't want to risk an episode."

"Like what happened at the Menhir where you were all crazy? That's brought on by your visions?"

Vandermere sighed and looked down at the rail. "They are linked. Sometimes the visions come and I can't stop them. With them comes the madness."

Lorelei rested her hand on top of his. "I'm sorry. That's a terrible thing to live with."

He squeezed her hand gently but didn't say anything.

"The rumors about the Dark Lord. You mentioned that was you...before all the craziness with the tablets and Daan happened. The people seemed afraid of you. Have you ever... done anything?"

Vandermere sucked in a deep breath. "I don't know honestly. The helmet was supposed to deflect...the madness... and it sometimes helped...at least enough for me to get away from people. I tried to stick to the Menhir since it was in Winderward, a place most sane people avoided. Still, I don't know what I've done when I'm fully taken."

Lorelei swallowed at the sudden dryness in her mouth. Vandermere could be dangerous to them. He could have murdered people.

He turned in her direction. "You wanted to know why I'm traveling with you and Vaana. It's because of you."

Lorelei blinked. "Me?"

His hand brushed her cheek, causing her heart to speed up. "You freed me from the episode at Menhir Du Moura. There is more to you than you believe. And from what I've seen, you may be my hope."

"Vandermere, Lorelei," Vaana called from the stairs. "Could you give me a hand? I found some things in the hold that could help salvage our mattresses. At least, if yours are anything like mine."

Vandermere gave Lorelei's shoulder a gentle squeeze before stepping back and turning in Vaana's direction. "Sure."

He joined Vaana and they headed below deck. Lorelei stayed near the railing for several minutes, trying to calm her pounding heart. Vandermere seemed to have put such faith in her, but she was a mess and constantly screwing things up. How could she be anyone's hope?

* * *

Lorelei yawned as she stood at the helm and guided the ship along the river. She narrowed her eyes as she peered into the night, the darkness only cut by the lanterns that hung on the ships.

They'd been traveling for several days and this was the first night she'd taken over for Wes so he could get some much-needed sleep. She'd learned the basics of sailing from her father's sailors when she could slip past her father, but most of that had never been hands on. Over the last few days, Wes had taught her how to sail diagonally and catch the wind in order for them to sail upstream. It had taken her some time, but she managed to succeed enough for him to give her free rein. It helped that the ship had some magic to it. She'd asked Wes where they'd gotten such a ship, but he'd only winked at her.

Vaana stood on the forecastle of the deck with a lantern in hand. She kept watch out at the river. She'd been annoyed to draw the night lot. However, they needed all four of them to run the ship, even with the magic on it.

The smell of sea salt caused Lorelei to wrinkle her nose. The scent had faded not long after leaving the dock, so why was it returning?

She glanced to the side of the ship with narrowed eyes. The song of a beautiful female soprano filled the air. Lorelei couldn't make out the words, but the sweet singing filled her mind and her soul. The world faded away and all that mattered was the music.

No, something wasn't right.

She let out a small gasp as she focused on the ship's wheel. Its wood grain dug into her palms as she tightened her grip on it. Someone in the water was using song to lull her into a trance.

Not someone, but a creature.

The same sailors that had taught her about sailing had also told tales of the sirens of the sea. Their voices were so beautiful they could lure a male to his death under the waves. Some argued they did it to find a mate to bear them children. Sailors who fell under their enchantment were never seen again. Those who braved the water to dive after were never able to find their shipmates.

Different sailors had argued that sirens must have been Fomorians, and that was why they sought to kill sailors. Others had ended that argument that their blood was the green of seaweed, not red like Fomorians. They were elementals of the sea.

The crash of a lantern echoed over the sound of the song. Lorelei's heart raced.

Vaana.

Vaana shuffled toward the rail with her eyes half closed. Her shoulders were tilted forward as if she was being led. Without thinking, Lorelei raised her voice into the night in a song of her own. The songs clashed. When one would gain dominance, the volume of the other would raise to overcome it.

Still singing, Lorelei raced down the steps of the deck and grabbed Vaana's arm as she reached for the railing. A glowing formed peeked out from the surface of the river. It was female, and her appearance matched the beauty of her voice. Her bluish white hair had a glow that illuminated the water around her for a few feet. Her eyes had the same whitish luminesce as she glared up at Lorelei with her soft full lips moving with her song. Lorelei dug her nails into Vaana's arm deep enough to draw blood and yanked her back from the rail.

"What?" Vaana blinked, then looked down at her arm. "What the hell, Lorelei?"

Lorelei released her and pointed to the railing. The siren

had risen from the water enough that her bare breasts were visible. She hissed at Lorelei, revealing a set of pointed teeth, and the surrounding water began to ripple.

Lorelei pulled the fire heartstone from a pouch on her side and switched the cadence of her song to match that of the spell she knew to call forth fire. Flame burst from the ruby in her clutched fists and flew into the river to hit the siren in the chest. The siren's song broke, and her screech of pain filled the air. She vanished below the water, and her glow faded into the black depths.

Lorelei shifted her song to a slower melody as she trod across the deck, keeping her gaze on the water. The ship bobbed on the river, but the waves remained dark. She let her song fade and turned to Vaana.

"Siren," she said.

Vaana's eyebrow raised. "Aren't they sea creatures?"

"Usually. I've never heard them living in any freshwater. Those are usually claimed by other water creatures."

"So, what is she doing here?"

"Something must have driven her from the sea."

Lorelei returned to the helm and took control of the wheel. She had to maneuver the boat back on course. The encounter with the siren had probably lost them a few hours of travel. As she wrestled with the ship, her mind wrestled with a question.

What could have driven a siren from the sea?

19

The Winddancer made port in Ebonshire early the next afternoon. Lorelei stepped off the gangplank and yawned as she stretched, raising her arms above her head. They'd had no more issues with sirens or any water creatures that were actually supposed to reside in rivers. Still, she'd tossed and turned in her bed during the early hours of the morning, barely able to get much sleep.

She smiled at Vandermere as he stepped onto the dock. He rubbed his face and returned her smile.

She looked up at Vaana who was watching them from the rail. "Are you sure you don't want to come with us?"

"The local Lord is connected with the Order in Kirkwall up the river. I'm known there, so I should stay. Don't want to ruin this little mission by getting recognized."

Lorelei nodded. "You have a good point."

Wes stuck his head over the edge of the boat. "I have a few things to do here, but I'll meet you at the Swift Swan. It's the inn just off the harbor."

Lorelei nodded. "All right. Hopefully, we won't be too long."

Vandermere held out his arm for Lorelei. "Shall we?"

Lorelei rested her hand in the crook of his elbow and they strolled from the pier and along the wooden dock. She gazed up at the ebony wood buildings that filled the town. Rising above them was a black guard tower that had to have sat in the center of town. The smell of fish drifted from the sparse market stalls along the harbor. Groups of faeries glanced their direction with cautious gazes before turning back and whispering among one another.

"You'd think they would be used to people," Lorelei murmured. "They are a port off the river, after all."

"Hmm, perhaps it has been a while," Vandermere said. "They are at the fork of two rivers."

"Have you been here before?" she asked.

He shook his head. "I didn't do much exploring of the West after moving to Nearon. My duty was to watch the Menhir and keep unwanted intruders out."

"But not any longer? You haven't abandoned your responsibilities for us, have you?" Lorelei felt a mixture of dismay and something else she could not quite identify in the pit of her stomach.

He patted her hand that was resting in his elbow. "No. My watch is done there. Another of House Essus will take that up."

The wooden planks of the harbor ended and a dirt road started. Across the road stood a two-story ebonwood building. A small oval sign with an image of a flying swan hung on a post to the right of the door.

"I guess this is the place," Lorelei said.

"Indeed," Vandermere said.

They crossed the road and opened the solid wooden door of the inn. The heavy aroma of spiced fish and baked bread greeted them. The inn appeared to be filled with the lunch crowd. Dock workers sat with merchants at small tables around the walls. Two large trestle tables filled the center of the inn and at them sat various faerie in twos or threes. A set of stairs in the far left corner led to the second story. In the far right was the bar.

The barkeep, a hob with dark mustard colored skin and brown hair, nodded to them as he continued to clean glasses. A few of the patrons glanced up at them before returning to their conversations.

Lorelei took a stool at the center of the bar, and Vandermere sat next to her.

The barkeep smiled at them. "Good morrow, folks. Did you just arrive on a ship?"

Lorelei nodded. "Who can we talk to about getting a room?"

"That'd be me, Arry." He pointed to himself with one hand, still holding a mug. "But our inn is too humble for the likes of such a lord and lady. We've only one room to spare aside from that."

Lorelei glanced around the inn with a raised eyebrow. Most of the patrons appeared to be locals. "Really?"

"We're expectin' a ship in any day now," he said. "Been savin' some rooms for the men on it."

Lorelei sighed and glanced at Vandermere. "Well, we could stay on the ship...or we could share."

The last part held a hint of hopefulness.

He chuckled. "Why don't we start with lunch and discuss it when Wes arrives?"

"What are you serving?" Lorelei asked Arry.

"Fish gumbo. My wife just pulled out a fresh loaf of bread to go with it." Arry puffed his chest out with pride.

"Two of that then," Lorelei said with a smile. "And two glasses of wine."

Arry poured their drinks before he shuffled off towards the kitchen.

Lorelei turned to glance back at the patrons. Her gaze caught that of a phooka merchant who stared at her with wide eyes. He ducked his head to whisper something to his companion on the right.

"I'm not sure if there is something going on, or if they are just unused to seeing many sidhe," Lorelei said in a low voice.

"The lord and his family may be the only ones here," Vandermere said. "That doesn't mean there isn't something happening, though."

Lorelei leaned closer to him, lowering her voice to a murmur. "Have you been able to see anything?"

Vandermere shook his head. "No, but something feels off. I feel it in the pit of my stomach."

"Great." Lorelei leaned back and stared up at the ceiling. "I hope Wes knows someone we can talk to here."

"We should probably visit the lord as well to see if there has been anything he is aware of," Vandermere said.

The door to the kitchen swung open and Arry came out carrying a tray filled with two bowls and a loaf of bread wrapped in a cloth. He climbed back to the bar and set their food before them.

Lorelei dipped her spoon into the bowl and scooped out a large bite of the stew. Fish was mixed with vegetables and rice in a white cream sauce. She took a bite and immediately sucked in air at the heat that filled her mouth. She sipped her wine to help her swallow and then continued to drink while she waited on the food to cool. Vandermere chuckled at her and broke off a piece of bread. The second bite was much cooler temperature wise, but the stew itself was spiced to give a different sort of heat. Lorelei found she liked the balance of spiciness with the cream of the sauce.

Halfway through the meal, Wes entered the inn. He took a seat beside Lorelei and after eying her food, ordered a bowl of his own.

When Arry left, Wes turned to Lorelei and Vandermere.

"I've found a contact," he said in a low voice. "We're to meet tonight."

"Good," Lorelei said. "Have you been here before? Does it seem any different to you?"

Wes shook his head. "I haven't visited Ebonshire in a year or more, but everything seems like it was."

"What could have your leader been talking about then? What's the big disturbance?"

"I don't know," Wes said. "Maybe that siren you saw?"

Lorelei sat up straighter as Arry returned with Wes's food. "This is such a nice town. Seems to have a lot of history."

Arry beamed. "It does. That guard tower you see was built nigh seven decades ago by a band of revolutionaries. 'Course, they faded out when the Order and Lord Zaos Nematona came."

He glanced around uneasily and turned back to cleaning his glasses.

Lorelei's shoulders stiffened at the name Nematona. Decades ago, House Nematona had been caught trying to overthrow the Quorum. They would have been executed, but they sought sanctuary with the Elemental Order and were granted it. After years of negotiating, the new High Lord was admitted a seat back on the Quorum, though few trusted the house.

Lorelei tilted her head at Vandermere with raised eyebrows. He shook his head and shrugged, the slightest lift of his shoulders.

Lorelei finished her wine and set down her glass. "Arry, have you heard about anything strange going on in the town?"

Arry scratched his chin. "Well, I hear Martin's got a weird rash, but that could be from—" He stopped, his eyes widening as he glanced at Lorelei and Vandermere. "Well, never mind. It's not for such company."

Lorelei let out a soft laugh as Arry left to serve one of the tables. "So, nothing the innkeeper knows of except for a possible sexual disease."

"Oh, maybe it's some sort of sex demon." Wes's eyes got a glazed look.

"You know they kill you and steal your soul with sex?" Vandermere said.

"Yeah, but what a way to go," Wes said.

Lorelei shook her head. "Haven't you had enough experiences with Sluagh?"

Wes shuddered. "True."

The door to the inn opened and an ankou in green and silver livery stepped inside. He scanned the room with a lifted chin and narrowed eyes before his gaze landed on them. He marched to the bar and gave a stiff bow to Vandermere and Lorelei.

"My lord and lady, Lord Zaos ap Nematona requests your presence at his manse."

Lorelei blinked. Word certainly traveled fast in this town if the lord already knew of their presence in the span of lunch.

"I suppose we should pay him a visit." Lorelei slipped off the stool and glanced at Wes. "Are you coming?"

"Nah," he said. "I'll stay and look after the ship. I'm just hired help after all."

Lorelei nodded and took Vandermere's arm. They followed the ankou out of the inn. A carriage waited for them on the road. The ankou held the door open for them. Lorelei stepped inside first followed by Vandermere. The door shut behind them. As they settled on the cushioned seats, the carriage jolted forward. The town passed through the window in a slight blur and they traveled a few miles outside the city to stop at the gates of a large manse centered on a small hill.

The gates opened and they were moving forward again. After several moments, the carriage stopped and the door opened.

Lorelei stepped out and stared up at the manse as Vandermere got out. It was several stories high, made of the same black wood as the town with two large spires, one on either side. Steps lead to a set of double doors with stained glass windows.

Lorelei took a deep breath and followed the ankou up the steps. The doors opened at their approach and a male hob in the same livery bowed to them.

"Welcome, lord and lady?" The hob paused and looked at them expectantly.

"Lord Vandermere ap Essus and Lady Lorelei ap Moura," Vandermere supplied.

The hob blinked at them. "Oh. Very well, follow me. The lord awaits you in the sitting room."

They followed the hob across the black marble of the foyer and through a door on the left. The sitting room was decorated in forest green with a couch and two armchairs near a fire. A tall sidhe male with wavy blond hair sat in one of the black cushioned armchairs with a sifter of amber liquid in his hand. He stood as they entered. His eyebrows raised as the hob gave their introductions.

"Welcome, I am Lord Zaos Nematona," the sidhe said. "Please have a seat. Can I offer you an afternoon refreshment or tea?"

Lorelei chose the couch while Vandermere sat in the second high-backed chair.

"Tea would be lovely," Vandermere said, glancing at Lorelei before she could ask for anything else.

She smiled at him innocently. "Yes, tea."

"Excellent." Lord Zaos nodded to the hob. The hob scurried away, and Lord Zaos turned back to Vandermere. "I must admit, I'm a little surprised. I expected you both to be married. A lord and his lady traveling together."

"Well, we are traveling together but not in the way you thought," Lorelei said.

"Interesting." Lord Zaos studied her with his sapphire eyes. "And what brings you to my humble town?"

"This is a stopover more than anything. We are traveling farther up the river." Lorelei paused, wracking her brain for another town along the river. She didn't want him knowing they'd been hired to investigate the town by a group of rebel thugs, nor did she want him to know their true destination.

"We are traveling to Damerel for business purposes," Vandermere supplied.

"Ah." Lord Zaos smiled. "I heard that Damerel was really starting to expand. I would be remiss not to offer my hospitality. You are welcome as my guests in the manor as long as you are staying in Ebonshire. The Swift Swan is quaint, but it isn't fit for sidhe."

Lorelei smiled at him. "That would be lovely."

And it would give them a chance to learn more information from the lord and the household about if something was truly amiss with the town.

The hob returned, pushing a tea cart.

"Excellent. Please inform Jillin on where to find any belongings you want brought up." Lord Zaos nodded to the hob. "Now, you must excuse me, but I have some business I must attend. Please enjoy your tea."

❧

Several hours later, Jillin, the hob butler, led Lorelei and Vandermere into the dining room. Lord Zaos stood at one end of a long, black wood table and a lady with short red hair cupped around her face stood at the other.

Lord Zaos nodded at them a tight-lipped smile. "Welcome. Lord Vandermere, Lady Lorelei, this is my wife, Lady Verrona."

The lady dipped into a slight curtsy, the voluminous skirt of her gold and green gown swishing. "I'm pleased to meet both of you."

Vandermere dipped his head. "My lady."

Lorelei curtsied as well though her dress had less layers to it. "Thank you for hosting us while we are in Ebonshire."

"Our pleasure," Lady Verrona said.

Lord Zaos clapped his hands. "Now that's out of the way. Shall we eat, then?"

Lorelei and Vandermere took places across from each other, between the lord and lady. Once they had sat, servants came trailing into the room. They dished out the first course, a fish bisque. Lorelei smiled at the ankou serving girl who poured her wine. She took a drink, savoring the delicate bouquet of spice and fruit.

"This is very good wine," Lorelei said.

"Thank you," Lord Zaos said. "It's a special wine made within Kirkwall. I have a special connection with the Elemental Order, so I'm able to get a casket now and then."

"My lord has many connections," Lady Verrona said in a high, giggly voice.

Lord Zaos cleared his throat. "So, what sort of business are you looking into in Damerel?"

Vandermere set his spoon down after taking a sip. "I have a cousin there who is running a house. I was thinking of setting up a trade route with him. Lady Lorelei agreed to accompany me as her father is successful in ship trade. I'm lucky she has decided to visit the West at this time." He shot a secretive smile in Lorelei's direction. "Very fortunate."

Lord Zaos looked at Lorelei. "And how are you liking the

wild West?" He chuckled. "I'm sure you think it's all very uncivilized compared to Elphyne."

"It's interesting," Lorelei said. "There have been some unexpected events, but I've enjoyed my time here for the most part."

"Is your father looking to expand, then?" Lord Zaos asked.

"My father is always looking to expand. He has yet to decide what would be advantageous to him." Lorelei glanced at Lady Verrona. "How long have the two of you been married?"

The lady's lips curved into a smile, stretching across her thin pointed face. "Oh, Lord Zaos and I have only been bound for a short while."

"We're still in the honeymoon phase," Lord Zaos said quickly.

Lorelei cast him a glance. The lord appeared calm and affable despite his quick response. He tipped his glass of wine at her with a nod.

"Your home is very lovely," Vandermere said. "Such a unique wood."

"Ebonwood," Lord Zaos picked up his glass and took a long drink. "There is a forest several miles away."

"Ah," Lorelei said. "That explains why most of the town is crafted of it."

"Ours is of the finest wood," Lord Zaos chest puffed out as he leaned back in his chair. "We've recently been renovating since my marriage to my lovely Verrona."

"Have you been here a while?" Vandermere asked as he picked up his glass of wine.

"Only for about a decade. I was granted lordship of Ebonshire shortly after the Elemental Order built their church in Kirkwall."

Lorelei paused with her wineglass at her lips. "Isn't the

Quorum the ones with the authority to grant titles and land, not the Order?"

Getting such a title would have been difficult for Lord Zaos under the correct circumstances, considering how most of the Empire felt about his House. Even if they had been recently accepted back in the Quorum, no one really trusted House Nematona, at least not enough to grant them lands they Empire didn't fully control.

Lord's Zaos's eyes grew cold as did his voice. "My dear Lady Lorelei, I think you'll find things are very different here in the West."

"I'm learning that," Lorelei murmured.

"We are in an untamed land," Lord Zaos said. "Spirits and heretics abound. The Order stands between us and the danger."

Lady Verrona gave a high-pitched giggle. Lord Zaos glared at her, and she covered her mouth with her napkin.

He turned back to Lorelei and leveled his gaze at her. "You should be careful, my lady, or your lack of knowledge of this land will surely kill you."

20

Lord Zaos parted from dinner with barely another bite or word. The lady didn't bother to keep up any conversation. She only stared at Lorelei and Vandermere with a creepy smile while pushing her food around on her plate.

Lorelei glanced at Vandermere, and they hurried to finish their meal and excuse themselves. Something was amiss in the household. They convened in the foyer and, after a brief argument, decided Lorelei should be the one to sneak out and find Wes to see if he'd learned anything about what was happening in the town.

She waited until well after midnight, when the house had settled down and even the servants had gone to sleep, before pushing the large window in her guest room open. The moon hung high in the sky, casting a strange luminance over the yard of the manor below. Using a rope from her bag, she climbed down from the second story. She landed softly on the grass and scanned the yard. It appeared empty. Only the sound of chirping insects filled the cool night air.

She ducked low and trotted across the yard to the small

door in the outer wall of the manse. It made a small creak as she opened it, and she winced. Once out, she was on the road. The trek back to town was a little long, but she hurried her steps. She needed to get to Wes and find out what he knew and then get back to the manse for a few hours of sleep.

The ship bobbed in the water at the harbor. A single lantern was hung out and the gangplank was missing. Lorelei paused at the edge of the dock and bit her lip. Why had they pulled up the gangplank? She walked to a nearby post where a single bell hung and rang it. After a few minutes, Wes's head peered over the side of the ship.

"Oh, good, you're here." His voice reverberated out over the water.

His head disappeared from view and a few moments later the gangplank was lowered, hitting the dock with a small crash. Lorelei boarded the ship and raised an eyebrow at Wes who was standing on the deck, rocking back and forth on his feet.

"Something happened." A chill shot through Lorelei. "Is Vaana alright?"

Wes started, snapping his head in her direction "What? Yeah, why wouldn't she be?"

"I don't know. You seem like you're about to flip out. What happened?"

He shook his head. "I can't explain it. You have to come see."

Lorelei followed him below deck to one of the cabins no one had chosen. Vaana stood over a bunk that held the body of a phooka male. His dark hair was mussed and had blood caked on it and his skin was ashen.

"Is he dead?" Lorelei leaned closer for a better view.

"This wasn't supposed to happen. Ferro and I met to talk about the town."

Lorelei blinked at him "He's your contact?"

Wes rubbed his face with one hand. "He was. We met up and talked for a few moments. When my guard was down, he came at me with a knife. Luckily, my reflexes were quicker than his. I had to fight him off. I only meant to knock him out..."

"You didn't kill him," Vaana interjected. "Not exactly."

Lorelei raised an eyebrow. "How can you not exactly kill someone?"

Vaana leaned down and pulled the phooka's shirt aside. One lone thin red line ran from his collar to his navel. It looked sealed, but not scarred over. As if it hadn't even healed, just been closed by some other means.

"I had a look at it while Wes was gone. It seems to be held shut by some sort of spider silk. It's so fine it's nearly invisible. Someone cut his chest open, and I think they took something out."

Lorelei swallowed as her stomach roiled. "Something like an organ?"

Vaana gave her a look. "Of course. We need to know which one."

"You're planning to cut him open, aren't you?" Wes's face paled even more.

Vaana pulled a dagger from a sheath in her boot. "It shouldn't be too hard, There's already a line."

"I'll wait outside the room." Wes stumbled out in haste.

Lorelei rested against the wall and crossed her arms. Vaana shrugged and leaned over the body. She leaned forward and ran the blade over the incision line on his chest.

Lorelei swallowed again, gripping her arms. She could take this. She fought monsters, after all. A little blood shouldn't be a problem.

Only there wasn't any blood.

"Interesting," Vaana said as she leaned closer. "His veins

seemed to have shriveled. There is no blood pumping through them. He should look like a shambling corpse."

"So, it's just his blood?"

Vaana reached into his body, pushing organs aside. "No, he's missing his heart."

Lorelei shuddered. "How was he even walking around?"

"Most likely whatever creature took his heart is able to keep him animated as a puppet."

There is a Sluagh that can do that, Murgleis's voice sounded through her head. *She is known as Arachne, the Spider Queen.*

Lorelei started and stood up with a shiver. "A Sluagh?"

Vaana glanced at her with a dubious expression. "Maybe. We'd need more information."

Lorelei pointed to Murgleis then stretched her thought out to him. *You think this Arachne is here?*

I sensed something in the manor that felt...kindred.

Lorelei gritted her teeth as gooseflesh rose on her arms. *Why didn't you say something before?*

I wanted to avoid detection. Besides, you didn't ask.

Lorelei gulped and turned her wide eyes to Vaana. "We need to get to the manor. I think Vandermere is in danger."

If Lorelei was quick to travel to the ship, she was as swift as the wind in her race back to the manor. She outpaced both Vaana and Wes by several yards. The entire time a mantra kept repeating in her mind.

Please be safe.

The rope was where she'd left it. So, it appeared no one had been alerted to her sneaking out. Hope fluttered in her chest. Maybe she was wrong and the Sluagh, Arachne, wasn't after Vandermere. Having a sidhe as a puppet would be useful to her or Zaos.

She glanced back at Wes and Vaana, who were sprinting across the yard, and climbed up the rope. Her chest tightened and her arms ached as she climbed into her window. She placed her hands on her knees as she caught her breath.

What was she thinking? She didn't have time to rest. She ran across the room, yanked her door open, and ran down the hall to Vandermere's room, just two doors away. She flung the door open so hard it slammed against the wall with a loud bang.

A metallic stench mixed with the heady aroma of perfume hit her nose. Her stomach sank. The room was dimly lit, but it was enough to paint the picture. Lady Verrona stood over Vandermere as he lay sprawled on his bed with his legs hanging over the side. Blood had pooled around him, staining the pale sheets dark blue. As Verrona— Arachne—turned, her skirt rustled and a large, hairy spider leg poked out from beneath it.

With a scream, Lorelei yanked Murgleis from his sheath and rushed toward Arachne. How dare she touch Vandermere? The blade slashed into Arachne's side splitting the fabric and flesh. Arachne's screech reverberated through Lorelei's head like a thousand knives slashing through her mind. Lorelei clutched her head as something wet tricked from her nose.

Arachne skittered over Vandermere and the bed to the other side of the room with the clacking of many legs. As she moved away, the agony inside Lorelei's head subsided. Lorelei straightened up and wiped the blood from her nose, her gaze darting to Vandermere. He laid so pale and still on the sheet.

Please let him be alive, she chanted silently.

The stomp of two sets of footsteps grew louder from the hall behind Lorelei. Wes burst into the room, followed by Vaana. He cursed and then sprinted across the room as he drew his sword. He brought his sword down on Arachne's skirt, cutting through the layers of cloth and into one of her many hairy legs.

Arachne screeched.

Vaana narrowed her eyes at Arachne and chanted under her breath. A light left her fingers and raced towards Arachne. It slammed into her chest, but fizzled out. Vaana's eyes widened and her mouth opened and closed, as if she didn't understand how she had failed.

"Tend to Vandermere!" Lorelei called to Vaana and dashed across the room to Wes and Arachne.

She slashed Murgleis at Arachne. When the blade met flesh, the agony in Lorelei's brain flared up. It was like a cacophony of screams filling her mind, impeding her ability to think, much less move.

Murgleis' voice echoed through the screams though it sent a spike of pain down her body. *You are being mentally attacked. Any pain you cause Arachne will be visited upon you triply.*

How am I supposed to kill her then?

"You can't kill a Sluagh."

Lorelei stumbled at those words. *What?*

Two of Arachne's spider legs burst out from the tattered remains of the dress and grabbed Lorelei, pulling her in. Arachne wrapped her arms around Lorelei and dipped her head, fangs piercing her shoulder.

Lorelei gulped back a scream as a burning sensation spread through her shoulder and below. Dizziness swept through her, muting the screams in her head. Everything started to move in slow motion.

Wes darted to the side and jabbed his sword into Arachne's open back. Arachne screeched and released Lorelei.

Lorelei tried to turn, but her legs slid out from under her and she fell to the ground.

Arachne skittered backwards to the window. Her red-eyed glare darted over them.

"This isn't over," she hissed.

The shattering of glass filled the air as she burst through the window and disappeared.

21

Lorelei swallowed as the dizziness swept through her. Vaana leaning over Vandermere seemed so far away.

Wes pulled a pistol from a holster on his hip and hurried to the window. The breeze blew at his hair as he scanned the side of the building and ground below. He shook his head and stepped away before holstering his pistol again.

"She's gone," he said.

Lorelei crawled towards the bed, the dizziness making it difficult to even pick her head up. Perspiration beaded on her forehead.

Wes muttered a curse. Seconds later, his arms were around her and she was lifted into the air. The distance passed in a blur and he laid her on the other side of the bed. She turned her head toward Vandermere.

Vaana's hands hovered an inch above his chest, glowing with a soft light. As she chanted, her hands moved above the wound, sealing it as she went. From the looks of it, she was about halfway finished.

Lorelei closed her eyes as dizziness took over again. It

made her head feel like it was three sizes larger. She floated on the waves of darkness that flowed behind her eyes.

Vaana's voice snapped her back to a semi-conscious state.

"There," Vaana said. "I think it's done. Though his body is still combating the aftereffects of the poison. Looks like you are too."

"Mmm?" Lorelei tried to push herself to a sitting position, but the world blurred around her. "Okay...give me a moment."

The sound of cloth rushing against cloth filled the air, and the bed shifted as Vaana sat down beside her. "Drink this."

Vaana pressed the smooth glass lip of a small bottle to Lorelei's lips. Lorelei let the liquid run into her mouth and winced at the biting sour taste that invaded.

She pulled her head back, swallowing. "Ugh, that is vile."

"Not all medicine is sweet," Vaana said.

"How is it you have an antidote for a poison of a demon spider?" Wes asked with a trace of suspicion in his voice.

"It's not a particular antidote. It's water created by the Apostle of Water. This particular kind can cure all poisons." Vaana held the vial up, now only half full. "It's also very rare and this is the only bottle I have. So, try not to get poisoned again."

Lorelei blinked as the room became clear. "Oh, wow. That stuff is powerful."

Vaana glanced back at Vandermere with a frown. "Hmm, the antidote should be working for him as well."

Lorelei rubbed her face and stared at the shattered remains of the window. "What now?"

"I wonder if the great lord knows his wife is a monster from beyond," Wes muttered. "Seems a bit irresponsible of him not to and diabolical of him if he does."

"Someone had to have summoned her. Most likely it was him," Vaana said.

Lorelei looked down at Murgleis. *How did you get to Threshold without being summoned?*

I was summoned a very long time ago and was never sent away. His mental voice sounded smug.

A shadow passed near the open door and a slender ankou girl with long leather wings stepped into the room. Her brow knitted and her eyes narrowed as her gaze passed over each of them, pausing on Vandermere and then stopping on Lorelei.

Oh, great Gehenna, they'd been found out by the help.

Lorelei stood and raised her hands. "It's not what it looks like."

The girl crossed her arms and tilted her head. "Oh, so a Sluagh didn't attack your friend then?"

"Oh, well, yes," Lorelei stammered and blinked at the girl. "You know what's going on here?"

The girl chuckled and closed her eyes. Her form shimmered in a blur of light. There was a bright flash that blinded Lorelei. She blinked several times. Where her vision cleared, Amara stood in the place of the girl.

Amara grinned.

Wes sputtered, raising his hands in front of him.

"I'm surprised to see you so soon, and here of all places," Amara said.

"Oh," Vaana muttered. "I'm not sure if she's a better option than the Sluagh."

Wes pointed between Lorelei and Amara. "You know each other?"

"We've met," Vaana said.

"I owe Lorelei my freedom," Amara said.

Wes laughed and looked at Lorelei. "This a thing you do often?"

"It seemed to come up in Winderward." Lorelei shrugged at him and turned to Amara. "What are you doing here? I thought you were going to explore the world."

"I was, but imagine my surprise when I came across one of the very sorcerers who bound me," Amara said.

"Sorcerer?" Lorelei's brow knitted together. "So, not the Sluagh."

"No, the one that summoned her. Zaos Nematona."

"Well," Wes said, "that answers my question."

Amara leaned against the doorframe and raised her left hand, flipping it palm side up. "So, I'm here for a little vengeance. Hence the maid getup."

Wes stare at her. "Normal phooka can't shapeshift the way you do. What are you?"

"That's one of those impolite questions you shouldn't ask a lady. Besides, we have more pressing things to discuss. Such as the rogue lord and his Sluagh wife."

"Did you learn what he was up to?" Lorelei asked.

Amara let out a sigh. "Unfortunately not. The Lord is picky who he lets into his private chambers."

Lorelei's shoulders slumped. "Well, we need to find out soon. Our cover is pretty much blown...or their cover is. Both, I suppose."

Amara pulled out a key from her pocket and dangled it on her index finger. "Luckily, the chamber maid who cleans his study isn't that smart, even for a Sluagh puppet. Also, it looks like the lord is out of the manor, doing all sorts of nefarious things, most likely. Shall we have a look?"

Lorelei grinned at her then glanced back at Vandermere, biting her lip. He still hadn't woken. She didn't want to leave him here alone. Arachne might return.

As if reading her thoughts, Vaana said, "Go ahead. I'll stay here and make sure he's all right."

"Take care of him." Lorelei licked her dry lips.

"Just find what this bastard is up to," Vaana said.

Lorelei nodded and followed Amara down the hall with Wes behind her. She would indeed find what Lord Zaos was up to and put a stop to it. Even if that stop meant burying Murgleis in his chest.

❧

Amara paused at the end of the hall and touched a piece of chair rail. There was the sound of a click, and the panel of wall next to them flipped open.

"Secret passage?" Wes asked with a raised eyebrow.

Lorelei shot him a look. "Servants' passage. For when they don't want the servants seen."

Amara stepped into the narrow hall and glanced behind her. "Is this really a time for a noble lesson?"

Lorelei shrugged. "Let's go."

The hall was a tight fit. Dim yellow magelights lined the ceiling above their head.

Amara led them through a series of twists and turns, and then down a set of steep wooden steps, which were followed by more twists and turns. Finally, she stopped at a small door with a brass handle and turned it.

The door opened up to a dim room. The coals of a dying fire glowed in the hearth and the scent of burnt wood filled the air. Above the hearth hung a silver-lined mirror that reflected a large ebonwood desk full of a mess of papers to their left.

Amara stepped inside the room and pulled a candle and holder from her pocket. At Lorelei's raised an eyebrow, she shrugged. "He may have set his magelights to alert him if anyone is in here."

Lorelei nodded to the fireplace. "Looks like he was here a while ago."

"Now they are gone." Wes strode to the desk. "Let's find what he's up to before he comes back."

Amara joined Wes at the desk and began pulling open

drawers. Lorelei wandered over a set of tall bookshelves along the right wall. Her fingers trailed over the spines, the leather soft against her skin, as she read them. It was an odd assortment of religious texts and histories of the Empress.

Her hand paused as she touched the third row. Instead of the soft brush of leather, hard grain grated against the tips of her fingers. She tried to pull one out, but it wouldn't budge. It was as if the entire row of books were one piece.

"I think I found something," she said.

Amara dropped the small crystal ball she had been holding back in the drawer of the desk and joined Lorelei at the bookshelf. Her eyes narrowed as she studied the books.

"Wood. False shelf," she said. "Probably where he has his secret books hidden. There has to be a latch or something around here."

Lorelei scanned the bookshelf, searching for anything out of place. Lord Zaos wouldn't have been as lame as to have made the switch a false book, would he? She ran her fingers along the books on the top two rows, but unlike the third, they felt normal. She stepped to the side and scanned the wall for a hidden button. Nothing.

She turned her back to the bookshelf as her gaze passed over the room. A statue of a female with a snake body and long leathery wings sat on a side table next to a high back leather chair. The statue's gold surface reflected the dying embers of the fire.

That's a Sluagh, Murgleis said. *Or a depiction of one.*

Do I even want to know which one? Lorelei strode over to it and knelt for a better look.

The statue was well sculpted with minute details from the scowl on the creature's face to the ornate weapons in her six arms.

She is the Six Bladed Queen, Murgleis said. *Be lucky it is not she that this sorcerer has summoned.*

I'm guessing she is more powerful than you. Lorelei reached to pick the statue up, but it held to the surface of the table. "Huh."

She is equal to my creator.

The statue wiggled in its base, like it was removable. *You have a creator?*

She is the heart of the Demon City.

That's some pedigree for you, I suppose. Lorelei wiggled the statue again. Maybe it could turn.

Murgleis' mental sigh echoed in her head. *You are truly ignorant of my kind, little girl.*

We've already had this discussion about ignorance. That's why I'm asking questions. Lorelei placed her fingers around the shoulders and turned the statue to the right.

A series of clicks sounded from the statue followed by the sliding of wood upon wood from behind her. Lorelei turned. The false books on the shelf had flipped open to reveal the real shelf filled with thick books.

"Excellent work," Amara breathed as she leaned down to scan the titles.

Lorelei walked to the shelf and let out a gasp. These were books the lord would want to keep hidden. *The Secret Names of Gehenna. Sluagh and Their Progeny. The Gods of Celestial Bureaucracy.*

The last title stood out from the others. Gods like the ones Vaana had within her? What was the Celestial Bureaucracy, like a government for gods?

Lorelei pulled out the book and flipped it open to a page with notes written in the margins. An illustration depicted a long shark-like creature in an underwater setting. From the perspective, it had to be huge. She couldn't understand the language the book was written in, but she could read the margins. Something about the essence could lead to Apotheosis.

"Amara, what's Apotheosis?" Lorelei held the book out the show her.

Amara took the book and scanned the page, her face turning pale.

Her voice softened. "Lyr."

"That doesn't help my confusion," Lorelei said.

Wes looked up from the desk. "But I'm guessing you found something important."

Amara's throat moved and she swallowed hard. "She did. I know what Zaos is after and we have to stop him."

"What?" Lorelei asked.

"He's trying to become a god." Amara handed the book back to Lorelei. "And it looks like he's trying to do so by stealing the Aether from another god."

"I thought the gods were gone. Except the Empress, of course. Is this a remainder of a god, like..." Lorelei trailed off and cast a glance at Wes. She didn't need to reveal Vaana's secret.

"Not all," Amara said in a steely voice. "Several exist here on Threshold, despite the attempted purge of the Order."

The door of the study opened with a creak and they turned with wide eyes. Lorelei's hand hovered over Murgleis. A phooka male held open the door while two hobs slipped inside followed by a phooka female and an ankou male. All were dressed in the servants' livery of the manor.

Lorelei straightened her shoulders and lifted her chin, her voice taking on an annoyed tone. "We have been waiting for Lord Zaos for hours. How long does he expect us to stay here?"

"You can stop your games," the phooka male at the door said with a low animalistic growl.

One of the hobs, a female, stepped forward and pulled out a butcher knife from her skirts. "We won't let you hurt our mistress anymore."

22

The phooka male shut the door as his servant companions pulled out weapons. A male ankou held a pistol while phooka female had a brass fire poker.

Amara stepped back into a dark corner near the bookshelf and vanished.

Wes cursed. "I guess she's abandoning us?"

"I don't think so."

Amara wouldn't abandon them, would she?

Lorelei pushed away the sickening feeling in the pit of her stomach. She had to focus on the fight ahead. She pulled Murgleis out and raised him in a defensive stance. Her heart sank as she scanned the faces of the servants. Their eyes were narrowed as they glared at Wes and Lorelei and their faces were twisted in an expression of fierce hatred.

How had she earned such ire?

They're puppets of Arachne, Murgleis said. *Their minds, bodies, and souls belong to her. You are seeing an extension of her ire.*

Lorelei gripped her sword as they moved forward. Still, they were just faerie. They didn't deserve the fate given them.

The phooka male darted toward Wes, knife jutted forward. Wes yanked out his pistol and shot the phooka male in the shoulder. The echo rang out in the room. The phooka staggered back two steps, but he didn't even seem to register pain.

The phooka female raised the long brass fire poker and hopped over the couch to come at Lorelei. Tensing, Lorelei took a step back. The phooka lunged forward, stabbing the poker into Lorelei's side. Pain shot up and down her body. She stumbled back, blinking.

Had she just been attacked by a fire poker of all things?

This is why you shouldn't hesitate, Murgleis said. *Step aside and let me take over.*

How about no? I have this.

Lorelei swung Murgleis at the fire poker and twisted her wrist. The poker flung from the phooka's hand and sailed over the high-backed chair. She brought Murgleis across the phooka's middle, slashing into her stomach. Bright green blood flowed from the wound. The phooka dropped to the ground without a sound.

The male phooka pulled out a long knife, the kind used for skinning, and leapt at Wes. He plunged the knife into Wes' stomach. Wes gasped and shoved the phooka away from him with both hands. The phooka stumbled back, pulling the knife free.

Wes pressed a hand to his wound and stared at Lorelei with wide eyes.

"These servants are deadlier than I thought they would be," he said with a coughing chuckle.

"Stay with me Wes," Lorelei said.

"I still have some fight in me," he said.

Lorelei's eyes widened as the ankou rose in the air with his wings flapping and aimed a pistol in her direction. She ducked down as the gun fired. The force of the blast knocked the ankou back in the air and the bullet hit the wall a few feet from where she had been standing.

Amara materialized out of the ankou's shadow and snatched him from the air by his arm. He hit the ground and she was on top of him before he could react. A blade gleamed in her hand as it came down on the ankou. He stopped moving.

The phooka male charged at Wes again. Wes yanked his sword from its sheath on his belt and spun it in his hand. He jabbed the phooka male in the chest. The phooka gurgled blood from his lips and collapsed to the ground.

Pain flared in Lorelei's upper thigh. She screamed, grabbing at her leg, and then glanced behind her, gasping. The hob male was holding his butcher knife with the blade buried in her leg. How had she overlooked the hobs? She brought her sword down diagonally across him. He was flung back into the bookshelf and fell to the ground. He did not get up.

The second hob was sneaking up on Amara with her butcher knife raised.

"Look out for the other hob," Lorelei called.

Amara half turned, snatched the hob by her neck, and twisted. A snap echoed through the room and the hob dropped. Lorelei swallowed at the sour feeling in her stomach. Just how strong was Amara?

The room was silent except for their breathing. Lorelei leaned back against the wall, pressing her hand to the wound from the poker. The warm sticky blood ran through her fingers and down her side. Now that the fight was over, dizziness was setting in. Amara rushed towards her and ripped several pieces of cloth from her clothes to wrap around Lorelei's wounds.

"You should see to Wes," Lorelei said in a faint voice.

"I got it," Wes pulled a roll of bandages from a pocket

inside his jacket and began to wrap his wound. "That phooka was kind of a terrible fighter."

"I thought you said they were deadly." Lorelei leaned her head back and closed her eyes.

He chuckled. "Well, it seemed like an exciting thing to say at the time."

The far-off crash of metal resounded from outside. Lorelei sat forward. Wes hobbled to the window and stared out.

"We have a problem," he said in a grim voice. "It looks like half the town is converging here."

* * *

Lorelei hobbled back through the servants' passage and up the stairs to Vandermere's room. Amara and Wes had stayed in the study to search for a passage or any clues they'd missed.

Vaana spun around in her direction with her sword drawn as Lorelei stopped in the doorway. She gripped the sides, panting. Vandermere, awake and propped up against some pillows, glanced up at her with a wan smile. His expression changed to a furrowed brow.

"We have to go," Lorelei said between huffs of breath. "The Sluagh has sent her minions after us and it looks like it's half the damn town."

Vandermere swung his legs over the edge of the bed and started to stand. He wobbled, then lowered himself back on the bed with a groan.

"That's going to be a problem. The Sluagh poisoned him more than you." Vaana glanced at Lorelei and frowned at her wounds. "What happened to you?"

"Servants with household tools," Lorelei muttered. She turned to Vandermere. "Think you can walk if we lend you a couple of shoulders to lean on?"

He gave her a ghost of his smile. "You look like you need leaning yourself."

"Sit down," Vaana said to Lorelei. "You won't do us much good if you pass out."

Lorelei glanced back at the hall, biting the inside of her cheek. The mob could break in at any moment. She didn't want them to be separated from Amara and Wes when that happened.

"Fine." Vaana stood and strode to her. She held a hand over each of Lorelei's wounds, closed her eyes, and began chanting. Tingling warmth spread from the wounds and throughout her body. After a few seconds, the sharp throbbing that had been there disappeared.

"Great." Lorelei flashed her a smile, then rushed to the bed and held her hand out to Vandermere. "Do you have anything you can't live without in here?"

"Just my sword and my bag." Vandermere nodded to a table where both lay.

Lorelei helped him to his feet and looped his arm over her shoulder. "Vaana, could you get those?"

Vaana strode across the room, grabbed the bag and sword, and followed Lorelei as she assisted Vandermere through the door. Lorelei helped him down the hall, then stopped at the door to the servants' passage. She glanced at Vandermere then at the door.

"This is going to be a bit tricky," she said. "It's a tight fit for one person."

"If that's true, the walls should be able to hold me up," he said.

"Great," she said. "I'll go first, then you, and Vaana can take the back. That way one of us will be on either side if you fall."

"Where are we going anyway?" Vaana asked. "Do we have an escape plan?"

"Wes and Amara are searching for a hidden passage they think is in Lord Zaos's study."

"And if there isn't one?" Vaana asked.

Lorelei glanced down the hall that led to the main staircase and foyer. "We may have to fight our way out."

"Lovely," Vaana muttered. "I never thought I might die to a bunch of townsfolk with pitchforks."

"Well, you have gods within you," Lorelei said. "You'd probably survive."

"Let's not test that theory." Vaana waved to Lorelei to lead the way. "Shall we?"

Lorelei opened the door to the servant's passage and stepped inside. As she traveled down the hall, she kept glancing back at Vandermere. His face seemed to glow in the pale magelight. Several times, his hand rested on her shoulder with a slight pressure, and he leaned heavier when traveling down the steps.

Lorelei's chest tightened and heat rose in her cheeks when she thought of what Arachne had done to him. She would make that Sluagh pay.

As they reached the door to the study, a faraway crash from somewhere in the house caught her attention. She swallowed and pushed the door open with a silent prayer to anyone listening to let Wes and Amara have found something useful.

Inside, Wes and Amara stood near where the small table with the statue had been, leaning over an opening in the floor. The table in question was slid to the left along with the bit of floor it had been standing on.

"Looks like you could have turned the statue the other way," Wes said with a flourish of his hand. "And now we have his secret passage. Shall we see where it leads?"

A crash and the shattering of glass echoed from somewhere in the house.

"Let's do that." Lorelei strode forward to the opening. "I'll go first and check for anything to ambush us. Wes, can you give Vandermere a hand?"

Wes glanced at Vandermere who was leaning against the desk. During their short walk, some color had returned to his face. The water Vaana had used seemed to be working, just more slowly for him. Lorelei hoped he would be well once they reached the end of where this passage led. There was probably going to be a fight there, if not along the way.

She peered down into the hole. Bronze rungs were attached to a roughly hewn stone wall that descended into darkness. She bit the inside of her cheek. How was she going to see once she got down there? She didn't have a lantern she could attach to her belt and she didn't know a spell to create light.

"I have it," Amara said, as if she had read Lorelei's mind.

She flicked her wrist and spread her fingers. Tiny motes of white-blue light formed from each of her fingertips and floated to surround Lorelei.

"Thanks." Lorelei lowered herself on the ladder and began to climb down.

Vaana followed her, then Amara and Vandermere with Wes taking the end. The trap door closed after Wes, darkening their passage. However, Amara's floating lights were bright enough to guide their way.

Lorelei's feet touched the ground with a small scrape of dirt against her boots. She took a few steps forward and spun in a slow circle as the others climbed down. The ladder had ended in a small circular room. One lone tunnel made of stone exited from the chamber.

Lorelei stepped to the mouth of the entrance and stared at it with narrowed eyes. After about fifteen feet, the path curved to the right. A familiar warmth and scent moved close to her. Vandermere. When had his presence become so familiar? She glanced behind her, smiling at him.

She turned back to the tunnel. "Looks like this is the path."

Vandermere stared into the dark tunnel with faraway eyes. "It leads to danger and discovery. The sludge under the trapping of beauty."

Lorelei gave a soft chuckle. "Danger and discovery. Seems to be our life now."

He nodded.

Lorelei rested a hand on his arm. "Are you up for this?"

He glanced up at the ladder then to her with a wry smile. "Not that I have much of a choice, but I'll survive."

Lorelei pulled Murgleis out and stepped into the tunnel. "Let's hope we all do."

The tunnel wound around like a snake, but there were no turn offs.

Lorelei led the way, followed by Wes, Vandermere, Vaana, and Amara bringing up the rear. At one point, the muted swish of water flowed above the rock over their heads.

Lorelei lost track of time as they trudged onward. Finally, a light appeared around one of the bends. It glowed from an exit in the tunnel, but she couldn't make out what was beyond. However, the dull roar of falling water echoed from beyond. Her shoulders straightened and her breath caught in her throat. She tightened her grip on Murgleis.

She glanced behind her and spoke in a soft voice. "Be ready. This looks like the end."

She marched forward and stepped out of the tunnel into a huge cavern. In the center, water flowed from an opening in the ceiling into a large pool in the ground. The distorted form of a person floated in the center of the falling water. Small metal spikes surrounded the pool and waterfall. Tables filled with metal contraptions of beakers and shelves stood around the edges of the cavern. The floor of the cave ascended to a raised platform of rock that curved behind the waterfall.

"How is that even possible?" Wes muttered with his gaze on the waterfall.

"Magic," Lorelei said. "Certain spells can control the flow of water, though I think this is a binding circle of some kind."

"You would be correct." Lord Zaos's voice carried over the sound of the waterfall.

He stepped from around the waterfall on the raised platform and stared down at them with his lip curled and his eyes narrowed.

Lorelei stiffened as a chill prickled on the back of her neck.

This is what they had come for: the final confrontation to free the people of the town and unveil the ugliness that had been happening.

"It seems you wish to meddle. No matter," he said. "I have means to deal with busybodies."

He raised his hand. The scrape of rock sounded from above Lorelei and bits of dirt rained down on her. She lifted her gaze and gasped. White substance fell down in streams.

"Look out!" she yelled to the others as she tried to duck out of the way.

She crashed into the ground hard, scraping her knees on the hewn stone. A sticky, wet substance hit her legs, arms, and the back of her head. It held her fast to the ground, stretching with her movements. This had to be some sort of webbing from Arachne.

She had no leverage to move Murgleis and cut herself free. Her head barely turned, but it was enough to see Wes had not been able to move fast enough either. He stood, a sheet of white, like lace, wrapped around his body and covering his head. Despite his struggle, he couldn't take a step.

Vandermere moved past her peripheral and his hand brushed against her fingertips. "I'll have you out in a moment."

The tension on her right eased significantly, and she was able to inch her arm toward freedom. Just a little more and she could help cut herself out of this mess.

Vaana's boots moved into the view followed by the rest of her as she stopped in front of Lorelei and faced Lord Zaos.

"Spirit binding, Sluagh summoning," Vaana said in a low voice full of ire. "You trek in heresy so easily."

Lord Zaos threw his head back and laughed. "That matters little if I can achieve godhood."

"The Empress is the one true goddess," Vaana said in a hard voice.

She lowered her head and began chanting. Then, she pointed her finger to him.

Nothing happened.

He laughed and raised his hand up at Vaana as if to say "what now?" Amara appeared just behind him and raised her arm, which gleamed like metal in the pale light, and shoved it into his side. His eyes widened and he yanked away from Amara, turning to face her.

Amara gave him a thin-lipped smile. "Hello, Zaos. I'm delighted to see you again."

A shadow moved in Lorelei's upper vision.

"Vandermere, look out," Wes shouted.

The clang of a hard object on metal echoed behind her. Lorelei shifted her body, wiggling back and forth for a better view. A ripping sound was followed by a greater release of pressure. She could move her arm.

She rolled onto her side and raised Murgleis to the spot where her legs were still trapped.

Vandermere had his sword raised and was deflecting the attacks of three of Arachne's legs as she hung a few feet above the ground by a thick strand of webbing. His final blow sent her swinging backward.

Vaana shouted. Lorelei glanced back at her to find the white-haired female from the vault, the one who called herself the Morrigan, in Vaana's place.

Lord Zaos stared at her, unblinking. Amara struck him in his shoulder. He grunted, clutching his arm, and, with a glare, swished his other hand. A wave of force slammed into Amara, knocking her off the platform. She landed on the ground below.

He turned back to Vaana-Morrigan with a gleam in his eyes. "A goddess within a girl. You will do much to further my research."

He raised both his hands with his palms facing Vaana, then pushed them together with his thumbs and forefingers touching to form a triangle. From that triangle, black energy rushed towards Vaana-Morrigan. It hit the ground in front of her, creating a dark sludge.

Black tentacles erupted from the sludge. Vaana-Morrigan leapt back with a shout.

Lorelei's stomach tightened. If Vaana was taken by this madman, there was no telling what he would do to her.

Arachne's scream was followed by Vandermere's shout of pain. He backed away from her with one hand clutching his head.

Lorelei glanced down, then sliced through more of the webbing holding her. The last swipe cut the bindings on her legs, allowing her to roll over. With two quick slashes, she freed her other arm and stood. She sprinted to Wes, who was still cocooned in a web.

He looked up at her with a snarl on his face. His nose was that of a cat and tufts of fur covered his face. Lorelei's eyes widened. She's seen other phooka use their ability to shapeshift into animals, but she'd never seen them stuck halfway through the process.

"Every time I try to shift into something smaller, the binding shrinks," he said with a growl.

Her web is attuned to her, Murgleis said.

He couldn't even reach his sword in its sheath. She cut through the webbing on his arms and around his waist. He shook it off, spluttering. She pulled out his sword and handed it to him.

"Can you get yourself free?" she asked. "I need to help Vandermere and Vaana.

He glanced at Vaana-Morrigan. "Not sure what help she needs, but I got this."

"Good." Lorelei turned to survey the rest of the battle.

Vaana-Morrigan was slicing through the tentacles with her axe as they rose to attack. However, more rose in place of the ones she cut down.

Lord Zaos was engaged against Amara who had returned to the platform. Black bolts of magic shot from his hands, which she dodged or deflected, though she got no closer to cutting him down.

Arachne was closing in on Vandermere. She had given up hiding under numerous layers of cloth. Her breasts hung bare as did the large spider abdomen and eight legs. Vandermere stood holding his head. Lorelei knew from experience he was probably in a lot of pain.

She smirked. Arachne wasn't the only one who could use her vocal cords.

Lorelei sang a few verses, forming an intricate spell that ended on a high note. A wave of energy burst forth and slammed into Arachne. She flew back from the force of the energy and careened towards the pool in the center of the room. As she passed between two of the spikes lines of electricity formed between them and struck Arachne in her chest.

Lorelei sprinted forward and raised Murgleis in the air. He began to glow bright green. She swung, and the blade sliced into Arachne's neck with a flash of light that traveled down her chest. Arachne gave a low gurgle and went limp. She burst into motes of green light as she fell to the ground.

Lorelei took a step back, blinking. *Is she dead?*

Sluagh do not truly die. She will Change, Murgleis said. *Become something else.*

Before Lorelei could ask what Murgleis meant, Lord Zaos shouted something in a language she couldn't comprehend. Vaana-Morrigan slashed through the remaining tentacles and took a step forward. Lord Zaos's glare traveled over the lot of them, lingering on Vaana-Morrigan and Amara.

"This will have to be continued another time," he said.

"To Gehenna with that," Amara said with a snarl. "This ends now."

As she rushed towards him, Lord Zaos pushed his hand down with his palm towards the ground. Black smoke burst from the earth, concealing him. It spread quickly, filling the room and their lungs with heavy, choking air.

Lorelei leaned forward, heaving and hacking. By the time she had coughed enough to make her chest ache, the smoke had dissipated to a few remaining wisps.

Lord Zaos was nowhere to be seen.

23

Amara's scream of frustration reverberated against the walls of the cave, and Lorelei winced. She turned and slammed her fist into one of the nearby tables. It collapsed in a heap. With a growl, she turned her back to the group, shoulders stiff.

Vaana-Morrigan staggered and dropped to her knees. Her axe shifted back to Vaana's small sword as her white hair darkened to black. She shrank and within moments Vaana knelt on her hands and knees, panting with her face pale.

Lorelei strode to Vaana and leaned over her. "Are you all right?"

Vaana waved her aside. "I will be. Just give me a few moments."

Lorelei walked to Amara and placed a hand on her back. "We'll find him. He won't get away."

Amara gave a bitter laugh. "It was easy to find him here because he'd grown lazy. Now, he'll know I'm coming after him."

"He will slip up again." Lorelei glanced at Vandermere with a hopeful expression. "Right?"

Vandermere shook his head as he leaned against one of the walls. His face had lost even more of his color. The battle had taken its toll on him.

"Perhaps," he said. "I cannot see for certain."

Lorelei sighed. "Well, if this was his hidden lab, maybe there will be information on where he could have gone."

She moved to one of the tables and began sifting through the books and stacks of paper on it.

"What about him?" Vaana nodded to the figure in the circle of water. "That's a god, isn't it?"

"That is Lyr," Amara said. "The god of the sea."

Vaana snorted and shook her head. "He is a heretic god, then. He should be killed."

Amara strode down the stones steps to stand in front of the circle with her glare burning into Vaana. "You won't touch him."

"He is an affront to the Order," Vaana said.

"Not this again." Lorelei groaned and spun around. "How long do you plan to follow those laws, especially with what you carry?"

"I took vows to honor the Empress and her Order." Vaana pressed her hand to her chest. "And honestly, I feel everyday I'm following farther and farther. Perhaps I should just turn myself over to the Order."

"But you want to live," Vandermere murmured. "And you know you won't live if you do that."

"That doesn't mean I should keep ignoring my duties when I find more heresy." Vaana flung her hand to Amara and then Lyr.

Amara bowed her head to look at the floor. "In the time of the Miasma, the Empress set on a quest to tame the magic of Threshold. Her path took her to meet many of the gods of the world, including Lyr. It was the belief of the Order that every god had a part in the celestial order of the world."

Vaana snorted at her. "More lies."

"No." Amara raised her hard gaze to Vaana. "I believe your Order has become full of lies. Lies and conspiracy."

Vaana hissed between her teeth and gripped the hilt of her sword. Wes grabbed her arm before she could launch herself at Amara.

"Let's look at this reasonably," Wes said. "She's not completely wrong. You have doubts which appear to be well founded. We can look into the truth of things, starting here."

"How do you propose we do that?" Vaana jerked her hand free of his hold.

He spread his arms wide, waving around the room. "This so-called lord was working with your Order, was he not?"

"Yes," Amara said. "And we found a book in his study that showed he planned to take the Aether of a god to become one himself."

"So you say." A sneer spread across Vaana's lips. "The Order doesn't keep up with every faerie or what they do."

"But it is a possibility." Lorelei continued with her next words despite the glare Vaana shot her. "It is also a possibility he was looking for a way to end the god as a heretic on the Elemental Order's command. Perhaps they wanted to cultivate the remaining Aether. That is important to the Order, correct?"

"It is," Vaana said.

"Then maybe, in all this we can find evidence of his true purpose as well as where he went," Wes said.

"Fine." Vaana stomped past the pool to join Lorelei among the tables. "What are we looking for?"

"Letters, notes, anything, really," Lorelei said.

Vaana sifted through the stacks of papers on the table, scanning one at a time then slamming it down into a stack and moving to the next. After a few moments, the pile had grown.

The others had spread over the cave, searching through the boxes and other tables. With a sigh, Lorelei skimmed the books on the table. Most didn't have titles, and they proved to be journals. Some contained notes about various magical workings, mainly summoning and binding. Her gaze paused over the sketch of a being with the head and torso of a female and the lower body of a spider. That had to be Arachne.

Little is known of the origin of the Spider Queen. Legends say that she was created by Lilith, the Succubus Queen, in order to steal the hearts of faerie. Arachne is unable to shift her lower spider half but is able to spin a web of lies and deceit that only the strongest minds or most powerful magic can break through unless Arachne herself chooses so. She uses this web to draw faerie to them so she can steal their hearts. Those whose hearts she has taken become her puppets. Unfortunately, these souls are lost once their hearts are taken.

Lorelei flipped several pages to the depiction of a four-armed female with some sort of jewel in her forehead.

That is Abraxes, Murgleis whispered. *My creator. I have not seen her since before Kurnach.*

Creator? Like she forged you as a sword?

She is The Forger in Infinite Fire.

"Damn," Vaana muttered, jerking Lorelei out of her conversation with Murgleis.

"Find something?"

"Just a letter from one of the priests in Kirkwall asking the Lord of his progress with his summoning endeavor." Vaana held out the letter.

Lorelei took it and scanned it.

Lord Zaos,

I am writing you for an update as you have not reported in for several weeks. How goes your effort in claiming the Aether of the sea god? Remember, much glory awaits you in the Empress's name, perhaps even a governance over the lands recently claimed by the Empire here in the West. Contact us immediately with your progress.

Sincerely,

Father Vallio, Tradition of Water

"Hmm, this appears a bit damning," Lorelei said. "Though it doesn't say they were aware of his efforts of Apotheosis."

She handed the letter back. Vaana stared down at it and bit her lip. For an instant, she didn't seem like the confident lady she had been since they'd met. Lorelei put her hand on Vaana's shoulders.

"Hey, you still have us," Lorelei said.

Vaana shot her a glare and pulled away. She hopped off the dais and stomped across the cavern into the darkness.

"Good going, Lorelei," Lorelei muttered to herself.

She glanced back at the table and froze. Vaana had made a considerable dent in the papers. Where the papers had been strewn haphazardly was a small medallion made of onyx on a chain. It had a tall-legged bird with its head ducked beneath its wings which were spread in the shape of an umbrella.

The Black Herons.

Lorelei gasped and grabbed the stack Vaana had made. She tore through the papers for any missive about them. They had to communicate somehow. If Lord Zaos was one of them, there had to be more proof. After sifting back through the stack she set the papers down, fighting the urge to scream.

Nothing.

Among all the other damning evidence of the horrible things he did, Zaos kept nothing on the Black Herons. Still no proof. The insignia on the swords wielded by one of the Herons hadn't been enough. This medallion wouldn't be, either. She needed more. She needed names.

At least she had something now. If she could capture Zaos, she would have a member of the Black Herons.

"Find anything on the binding?" Amara asked, coming up behind her.

"No." Lorelei waved to the stack of books. "It's a lot to look through, though."

Amara pressed her lips together. "The longer we spend here, the more time Zaos has to get a bigger lead."

"You're chasing after him?" Lorelei turned and stepped closer to her. "Can I come with you?"

Amara smiled and rested a hand on her shoulder. "You have your own quest."

Lorelei held up the medallion. "This is my quest. He is one of the people I'm looking for."

"What about your allies?" Amara pointed to Vandermere and Wes still searching through the crates. Vaana leaned against the wall with her arms crossed. "Would you abandon them?"

Lorelei's grip tightened on the medallion as heaviness filled her chest. "But finding the Black Herons, proving they exist, is what I set out to do. I can't just abandon this."

"Who is to say your allies' troubles aren't connected?" Amara nodded to the table. "Haven't you found connections already?"

Lorelei glanced at the others and bit her lip. Amara had a point. They'd only stopped in Ebonshire in trade for passage from Wes's leader. If they hadn't, she wouldn't have found out about Zaos Nematona. He was connected to the Elemental Order and they were on the run from them due to Vaana's predicament.

Lorelei sighed. "All right. But, would you contact me if you find anything out?"

Amara touched Lorelei's cheek with a gentle smile. "Of course. I'm not leaving yet, however. We still need to free Lyr."

Lorelei turned to the waterfall and the figure within it. "Well, I could try what I did with you, though that had a major backlash. Like it flung me against the wall."

"I think I can aid with the backlash," Amara said. "I can dampen it"

"Why can't you do it yourself?" Vaana crept closer to them and the circle.

"Its crafting is made to bind creatures like me. It's also made to repel magic from us. However, he couldn't block faerie magic as he needs to access it."

"That means Vaana can't help either, because of the whole god thing," Lorelei said. "If she was so inclined."

"Which I'm not," Vaana said.

Amara nodded. "Her essence is bonding with the gods inside her. It would be detrimental."

"What about either of you?" Lorelei turned to Vandermere and Wes. "Any chance one of you has been hiding magic?"

Wes Looked up from the crate he was digging through and shrugged. "Sorry. I leave magic to others. Unless you need me to turn into a fish and swim around in there."

Lorelei sucked in a breath. Phooka could turn into all kinds of animals, but she always thought more on the cats, dogs, or birds. She never really thought about sea creatures.

"I wouldn't advise that." Vandermere straightened up. "As for me, I have enough with my visions. I don't wish to delve in the arcane arts."

Lorelei sighed and stared up at the swirling water. "That leaves me, then. I'm going to need something to house the Aether in. I don't think the heartstone I have will hold much more. It's still filled from when I freed Amara. I don't want to risk overfilling it."

She still remembered her professors drilling into her head the dangers of overfilling vessels with Aether. They tended to explode spectacularly.

Wes raised a finger and opened his mouth. He shut it, bounced to a bag near the crate he'd been searching, and pulled out a crystal. It was white blue and translucent with branching shards so it looked like a frozen flame.

"I was going to claim this heartstone." Wes sauntered to Lorelei and held it out. "But I guess, if you need it."

"Thank you," Lorelei said.

She took the heartstone and ran her fingers over the smooth planes. The tip stretched the length of her forearm. It didn't hum with Aether, but it was large enough to hold a vast amount.

"I think this will work," she said.

Amara touched the ground and chanted in an inaudible whisper. The ground shook and rumbled. The stone of the cave seemed to become liquid and rose up to create a wall waist high.

Lorelei gestured to her comrades, and they hurried over to join her and Amara.

"Sing your song," Amara said. "I'll raise the wall when the backlash hits."

Lorelei nodded and drew in a deep breath. Her voice started off soft and hesitant but gained power with each verse. She focused on the closest spike and willed the Aether it held to transfer into the heartstone. It flowed slowly, like sludge in a dam. Her voice rose and she gave a tug. With an inaudible pop, the energy entered the crystal. The metal of the spike corroded to a dark reddish brown. The other staves lit up with a high-pitched wail.

"Now!" Lorelei called to Amara.

The wall rose up around them, forming a semi-circle. The wail broke with the shattering of metal and the rushing of water. It crashed against the wall, causing it to shake, and flowed past them. After a few seconds, the sound of water calmed and only the splash of the waterfall remained. Amara whispered a soft chant and the wall crumbled.

Where the circle of spikes had created a standing surface

of water, it had now lessened to the waterfall flowing through the center of it. Stars twinkled in the night sky that could be seen from a large portion of the hole in the ceiling.

In front of the pool that the waterfall flowed into, a male stood with glowing sapphire eyes and wet, copper hair streaming down his shoulders and waist. Power radiated from him.

Lorelei sucked in a deep breath as her heart pounded. They were in the presence of a god. She didn't know whether to bow or not. She settled for giving him a respectful nod as his gaze swept over her. He stiffened as he looked at Amara.

"Amara," he said in a melodious soft voice. "I did not expect you to be the one who freed me."

"Technically, I only helped." Amara pointed to Lorelei. "She did most of the work."

He turned his attention back to Lorelei. "To whom do I owe my thanks?"

Lorelei cleared her throat. "Lorelei ap Moura, at your service...sir..."

He chuckled, a warm sound that tickled like sea foam against her skin. "You may call me Lyr."

"I wasn't the only one." Lorelei waved her hand at her companions. "Everyone fought Lord Zaos...He's the one who captured you."

"Oh, I remember him well." Lyr's voice grew cold and harsh.

"Pardon me, Lyr." Wes stepped forward. "How long have you been captured?"

"For me, but a short moment. To the faerie, years." He sighed. "Which means my faithful have been without me. I must return to them. However, should you need assistance, you may call upon my people, the Maren."

Lorelei gasped. The Maren pirates had been a thorn in her father's side for as long as she could remember. They roamed the seas, raiding and looting any merchant ships that had the ill fortune to come across them. Many of the sailors told tales of the Maren's ships just appearing out of nowhere. One even swore she saw the pirate ship emerge from beneath the water itself.

Still, having pirate aid could be useful.

"Thank you, Lyr," Lorelei said.

He bowed and dove into the pool of the waterfall, disappearing beneath the surface. Lorelei stepped forward, but nothing remained in the dark depths.

"He's gone. And I should be on my way as well." Amara rested a hand on Lorelei's shoulder. "Be well."

"And you," Lorelei said. "Let me know if you find anything about the Black Herons."

Amara nodded, stepped back, and spun away from them. She took a running leap towards the opening of the waterfall. In midair her body shifted. Feathers sprouted from her skin, and her arms became wings. In seconds, she'd taken the form of a small owl. With a hoot, she flew up through the hole.

Lorelei turned to Wes and held out the heartstone. "Here. You can keep it."

He raised a brow. "Really?"

"Your job was just to sail us along the river. You didn't have to come with us," Lorelei said.

"I wasn't going to do nothing while this town was suffering," he said.

"Still, it could help you," Lorelei said.

Wes took the crystal from her with a small smile. "Thanks. You're not too bad, for a sidhe."

Lorelei grinned at him. "You should be more thankful to me."

He shrugged. "Eh, I'll buy you a drink."

Vaana spoke for the first time since Lyr had been freed.

"Now that those gods are gone, we should see what damage has been done to the town."

"I suppose we're going to have to go back the way we came," Lorelei said with a sigh.

"Not necessarily," Vandermere said.

He walked around the waterfall to the back wall and ran his hand along the surface. He pressed against it with both his hands and a section slid into the wall and to the side with the scraping of stone.

Lorelei gasped and strode to Vandermere. The other side held a tunnel at an incline.

Wes came up behind them and gave a soft whistle. "Zaos really loves secret passages."

"It makes sense if you're doing heretical things," Vaana said as she joined them.

"Let's go," Lorelei said.

They traveled through the tunnel until they reached a small opening. After a bit of climbing up, they found themselves surrounded by ebonwood trees. Night had fallen, making it difficult to see. Without much to say, they started their trek back to Ebonshire.

When they reached the town, they came to a halt. Lorelei's heart twisted into knots.

Half the citizens of Ebonshire lay strewn about the streets, dead. All victims of Lord Zaos and his pet Sluagh.

24

They stayed in Ebonshire for two more days to help the remaining town members with their fallen, as well as to replenish the ship with supplies.

They also carved out some time to loot Lord Zaos' manor. Lorelei took several of the books she'd seen in both his study and hidden lab. It had useful information about Sluagh as well as gods. The way her journey had been going, she would need as much knowledge as she could get.

After the two days, their welcome in the town had waned. Most of the remaining people grew restless and blamed them for what had happened. Even though they hadn't been in the town when Arachne had turned half the town into her puppets, Lorelei and her companions had been the catalyst for the loss. They set sail before dawn with Wes at the wheel.

Lorelei leaned against the rail and stared down at the churning waters. Dawn had brightened the sky into a purple-blue hue and that color seemed to reflect in the river. They reached a confluence where the river met with a smaller stream. Wes leaned into the wheel as the ship hit a small rough patch of water.

Vandermere emerged from below deck and strolled towards her. She gave him a weak smile. It was the best she could muster. A heaviness had weighed on her chest since she had seen the death toll of Ebonshire.

"We are not to blame for the events that transpired in Ebonshire," Vandermere said. "You shouldn't hold yourself responsible."

"I know." She turned her back on the river and leaned against the railing. "But, wouldn't they have been better off if we hadn't meddled?"

"They would have continued to live the lie," Vandermere said. "Those people were already dead, thanks to the Sluagh." He shuddered and crossed his arms over his chest.

"As a sidhe, it is our duty to look after the other faerie," Lorelei said. "How did any of us help with that? Will that town even survive?"

"Wes has sent a message back to the Serpents. They will be sending reinforcements to assist Ebonshire," Vandermere said.

The corner of Lorelei's lip lifted in a half-hearted smile. The Serpents would have someone there to pick up the pieces soon.

Lorelei shook her head as she stared down at the deck. "Is this how the sidhe treat their people? This is our legacy?"

"Some use their power over the other faeries as an abuse," Vandermere said. "Others are different. They try to make circumstances better."

Lorelei raised her head to watch the passing clouds. "I always wanted to be good enough for my parents to accept me. To climb out of Freya's shadow, but maybe I should be striving for something else."

"What would that be?" Vandermere asked.

She wrapped her arms around herself. "I don't know. The

laws of the Quorum—hell, the Elemental Order—should have prevented Zaos from summoning that Sluagh."

"Just because the laws exist, doesn't mean that they will be followed."

Lorelei nodded. "And he even seemed to have the Order's blessing on his actions."

"Perhaps uncovering the truth of the Order is something you should be striving for," Vandermere said.

Lorelei's lips quirked in a smile. "Well, we were already searching for the truth about the gods, so why not?"

Vandermere patted her on the shoulder. "It's a beginning."

She stepped away from the rail and stretched her arms above her head. "I think I'm going to see what can be had for some breakfast."

"That sounds like a good plan," he said. "I think I'll join you."

❧

As the sun dipped below the horizon, Lorelei took the wheel from Wes. He nodded his thanks as he turned to head below.

"Wes, I'm sorry for what happened in Ebonshire," Lorelei said in a rush. "You weren't supposed to be caught up in it."

He stopped and shrugged. "I'm fine. At least I survived. I can't say the same for half that town. It seems to happen a lot when sidhe are involved."

"Zaos is a bad example of my people," Lorelei said. "He abused his power. And he will pay."

Wes spread his arms wide. "He seems to have gotten away with it. Things like what he did are why the Serpents exist. The ones in power are corrupt and no one looks out for us little guys."

"That's not true." Lorelei looked down at her hands gripping the wheel as heat rose to her face. "I mean, I helped you at Mourner's Hill in Winderward."

"You did and I'm thankful. But it also means you can help further, like by tracking down Zaos."

"Amara is hunting him down. And if she doesn't find him, I will." Lorelei reached out and rested her hand on his arm. "I promise."

"But not now," Wes said.

Lorelei sighed. "As Amara pointed out, I should continue with Vaana and Vandermere, though our predicament is tied to the Order and so is Zaos. This may lead back to him in some way."

"Maybe, but his trail is getting cold," he said.

"You doubt Amara can follow it?" Lorelei asked.

"She didn't stay long to search for anything."

"No, but she's something more than a faerie...a spirit, I think. She may have other ways." Lorelei tilted her head at him. "What about you? Did you find anything while we were in the lab?"

"A few things," he said. "I haven't got to sort through them yet."

"I need to look through the books I have. Depending on what we find and what is learned at the Tower of Fate, perhaps we can put a conscious effort into searching for him."

He gave her an unsure, but hopeful look. "You'd do that?"

Her grip tightened on the wheel as she stared at the river ahead with narrowed eyes. "Oh, I intend to. He is part of a conspiracy I want to shed light on."

"You know, I intended to just drop you off at the shore near the Tower, but maybe I'll stick around," Wes said. "You lot aren't so bad for Imperial sidhe. That Vaana is kind of a bitch, though."

"Yeah, she can be prickly." Lorelei gave a short laugh and

paused as something else filtered in her head. "What do you mean by Imperial sidhe?"

"You think all sidhe are a part of the Empire?" He snorted. "There are several families spread out through the West...bastards they are."

Lorelei blinked. She'd always thought that all sidhe belonged to one of the Houses. It had never occurred to her that other sidhe would be living in other parts of the world. It made sense though. With the coming of the Miasma, the old civilizations had been torn apart, but those civilizations had been spread across the face of Threshold and not just the Imperial Island. Though the Empress had set the Isle as the seat of her Empire, it didn't mean all sidhe would have moved there. Some would have rebuilt in their homelands of old.

"Hmm," Lorelei said. "The West has really turned everything I thought I knew upside down."

Wes patted her on the shoulder. "Glad to give you some insight. Now, I'm off to bed."

"Sleep well," she said.

With a wave, Wes walked to the stairs and disappeared below deck, leaving Lorelei with the river and encroaching night.

❧

The trip upriver stayed peaceful over the course of the weeks it took to reach their destination. There were no strange sea creatures rising from the depths of the water to attack them and no Sluagh seeking to control them. Even the river entities seemed to be at peace.

At the end of the first week, they passed the city of Kirkwall. Several stone buildings towered above the dock of the shore. Vaana stared up the gleaming spires of the Elemental Order's temple with her face pale and her lips pressed together. Lorelei stood beside her, leaning forward with her elbows resting on the rail as she watched the gleaming white.

"Ever since I was a child, I believed in the word of the Empress." Her voice came out soft. "I'd lost my parents when I was young and my aunt was busy with the task of running our House."

Lorelei blinked. "You're the niece of the head of your House?"

"My parents originally ran it..." Vaana shook her head and turned away from the city. "Anyway, I joined the Order when I was twelve. I'd always felt the calling. That I was meant for something great."

"You think it had anything to do with the gods you hold now?" Lorelei asked. "I mean, it's a little odd that you are capable of housing them."

She still wasn't sure how Vaana was capable of holding the gods. Over their trip, she'd seen no physical signs that they were harming Vaana. She'd thought that the Aether they were composed of would be too much for a faerie to house, even a sidhe.

"I don't know. I can feel their whispers...and when the Morrigan has taken control, she changes my form. But...it feels natural." Vaana stared up at the sky with a long sigh. "Does that make me a heretic? Have I truly lost my way?"

"Maybe the way you believed to be yours, isn't. However, it led you to this," Lorelei said. "After all, you were there on behest of the Order."

Vaana smirked. "You've been spending too much time talking to that Essus."

"And you," Lorelei said. "You said the Empress has a place for everyone in the Order."

Vaana's mouth pressed in a thin line. "None of this makes any sense. If I am a heretic, then how is this my place?"

Lorelei shrugged. "It seems that what the Order preaches is different from what some of them are practicing."

"If there is a conspiracy, it must be in Kirkwall," Vaana said. "I refuse to believe that Apostle Evangeline would be a part of it. Or the Voice of Wisdom."

"Why do you believe in them so much?"

"Because the Voice is the direct line to the Empress. She is the mouthpiece for her words," Vaana said.

"And the Apostle?"

"We were close as we both rose in the Order. She and Beth..." Vaana gulped. "And now, as a heretic, I'm their enemy."

Lorelei rested her hand on Vaana's arm. "Look. We'll find some answers when we reach the Tower of Fate. This lord should know something. He's the one who put the godstones in the Menhir."

"I doubt it," Vaana said. "This feels like a fool's errand."

Lorelei tilted her head. "Why do you say that?"

Vaana shook her head and turned back to Kirkwall. "It's good we didn't need to stop. I believe that the Apostle Evangeline has probably arrived. If she knew how close we were, she'd send an army of priests after us."

Lorelei stared out at the shrinking city. The Lord of Fate had to have the answers Vaana was seeking. If he didn't, where could they go afterwards?

25

Lorelei rested her palms on the railing and leaned forward as Wes navigated the ship to a slow-moving part of the river and set the anchor in calm waters. The shore was still a good distance from the ship, but they would be there soon. After weeks of sailing, it would be good to feel the ground beneath her feet. She loved the sway of the ship and sounds of water lapping against the hull, but she needed a break. She was ready to do some walking.

Vaana stood in the middle of the deck adjusting the straps of her stuffed backpack. She'd barely spoken since arising at dawn and didn't meet anyone's gaze. Her jaw was set in a hard line. She still seemed to be dwelling on her internal struggle between her faith and the gods now within her. What didn't make sense was that she wasn't thrilled to be visiting this Lord of Fate. Wouldn't she want to take any chance to get the gods removed from her?

Vandermere stood beside Lorelei with his arms crossed as he stared out at the shore. Two fingers tapped against his arm. His eyes held a shine to them and a small smile hovered on his lips.

Lorelei nodded to the shore. “So, how far do we have to go to get to the tower?”

“I’ve never been in person, but I think it is half a day’s travel to the southwest of here.” He stared up at the sky and as if checking the position of the sun with narrowed eyes.

Wes strode across the deck to the rowboat on the side of the ship and began untying its bindings. He whistled an upbeat tune as he worked at the knots.

Lorelei stepped away from the rail. “We should probably give him a hand.”

Vandermere smiled and held out a hand for her to go ahead of him. They strolled over to Wes.

“What can we do? Lorelei asked.

Wes shot her a quick smile, then nodded to some of the dangling ropes. “If Lord Vandermere is willing, he could take some of those to ensure the boat doesn’t fall too hard in the water.”

Vandermere took the ropes and held them taut. Lorelei stepped up and grabbed one of them before either of them could say anything.

“What? You want me to just stand and watch?” She glanced back at Vaana. “Care to join us?”

With a sigh that was loud enough to be heard over the river, Vaana trudged to them. “What do you want me to do?”

“How about untie those last few knots?” Wes asked.

Between the four of them, they were able to lower the boat into the water without incident and tie it off. Wes rolled a rope ladder down the side of the Winddancer. Vandermere climbed down first, followed by Lorelei, and then Vaana. Once they were all secured with the supplies, Wes descended into the boat. He took two paddles and began to row towards the shore.

Lorelei stared into the forest that sat just off the shore of the river. The brown trunked trees were thick, not permitting much sunlight through their tops. It seemed that much of her life had become traversing through forests. A smile curved at the corner of her lips. Still, it was much better than wasting away at Morningtide Priory.

Eventually, Wes brought them to the shallows. He hopped out of the boat. Vandermere followed suit and the two of them dragged the boat ashore. Lorelei climbed out, grabbed her backpack, and slipped her arms in the straps. She closed her eyes and breathed in the pine scented air as the others retrieved their equipment.

"The Lord of Fate's tower should be this way." Vandermere slung his bag across his back and trotted to the right. "We should head out so we can make it before it gets too dark."

"If it does, we'll have to make camp," Wes said. "I'm not traveling through the forest at night. Never know what could be waiting."

"Wild animals? Monsters?" Lorelei asked with an amused curiosity.

"Assassins," Vaana said darkly.

"All three maybe." Wes winked, then chuckled.

They trekked through the trees most of the day at a quick pace, leaving little room for conversation except for the occasional comment or muttered curse when someone tripped over a tree root. That someone tended to be Wes.

After the fourth one, Lorelei had to speak up. "Considering where I found you, I'd think you would have been more used to traveling through the woods than you are."

"I don't know why you would think that, considering where you found me," Wes said between pants. "I'm more of a city boy...and a river boy. Seeing the ports of call."

"If you say so," Lorelei said.

As the light in the sky turned pale orange, the top of the tower rose above the canopy.

"Not much longer," Vandermere called.

"Finally," Lorelei muttered. "How does this Lord of Fate get anything out here in the middle of nowhere? I don't imagine he hunts for his food."

"He may be the Lord of Fate, but he is skilled in other magics as well," Vandermere said. "Besides, my House aids its own. For the most part."

"Dimensional magics, then?"

"Among other things," Vandermere said.

They continued on. As the last rays of sun shot across the sky, they broke through the tree line and into a clearing that surrounded a brown stone tower that stood several stories tall. Dark green vines grew along the walls, invading the shuttered windows. A stone fence surrounded the towers and a small garden just inside, with plants that had overgrown their space.

"This place looks a bit neglected," Lorelei said. "Are you sure he is still here?"

"As far as I know, he is." Vandermere frowned at he gazed up at the tower.

"He's probably abandoned the place," Vaana muttered. "This is just a dead end, like I said it would be."

"We won't know until we knock. Besides, what are we going to do? Camp out in his front yard?" Lorelei strode forward and opened the wooden gate that led inside the tower's yard.

After a moment's hesitation, Vandermere took the lead and trod up the dirt path that lead to the ornate wooden door. A large brass knocker with the face of a dragon was set in the center of it. He lifted the ring in its mouth and knocked three strong raps that echoed through the air.

Lorelei wrapped her arms around her and shivered. The sun had set and the night had already cooled the forest. She hoped there was someone in the tower for she'd rather spend the night in a warm room if she had a choice.

"Looks like no one is here," Vaana said with a hint of smugness. "We should leave."

"Where to?" Lorelei asked. "Have you figured out anyone else to help you? I imagine if you had, you would have mentioned it. You haven't been keen on coming here at all."

Vaana's look turned to a scowl and she opened her mouth for a second before closing it.

"Well, I'm not sure about Vaana's problem, but we could always look for Zaos," Wes put in.

Lorelei glanced up at the dark sky. "Not tonight, we won't."

Vandermere took a step back and stared up at the tower with narrowed eyes. "Something is wrong."

Lorelei turned to him with her eyebrows raised. "What is it?"

He shook his head. "If he had left, we should have known. He should have told someone in the House."

Vaana crossed her arms. "What? No Essus has had a vision?"

"Not that I know of. But something feels off." He raised his hand to the door handle.

When he touched it, a purple glow surrounded him. He stiffened, his eyes growing wide. After a few seconds, the glow disappeared and the door swung inward.

"So, the door was spelled," Lorelei said. "I'm guessing only one of his House could enter without his permission."

"Indeed." Vandermere nodded and stepped inside.

Darkness greeted Lorelei as she followed Vandermere inside. She pulled a lantern from her pack, lit it, and glanced around. The stone floor was of the same brown color as the bricks outside. The foyer held three doorways and a spiral staircase that lead up to the second floor. A stale scent filled the air along with tiny particles of dust that had been disturbed by their entrance.

"He hasn't been here for a few weeks at least," Lorelei said.

Vandermere shook his head and walked to the doorway across the foyer. He leaned inside, glanced around, and turned back to the foyer with a frown creasing his lips and lines in his forehead.

"Kitchen," he said. "Looks mostly clean, though there are two glasses and a bottle of wine on the table."

"So, he had some sort of company before he disappeared," Lorelei said.

Vaana stepped inside and glanced around the room. With a sigh, she walked to the doorway on their right and peered inside, then turned around and did the same to the room on the left. Wes moved inside the tower and leaned against the wall near Lorelei, watching Vaana.

"Is it just me, or does she seem more agitated than usual?" Wes asked.

"There's nothing here," Vaana said. "Let's just set up and discuss what we're going to do next."

Lorelei nodded to the stairs. "We still have a few more floors to explore. Maybe we can find a clue on what happened to the Lord of Fate."

Vandermere led the way. Their steps echoed against the stones as they ascended to the second floor.

It was one large room, instead of divided into multiple rooms like the lower floor. Several long, curved marble tables lined the walls, their tops crowded with cauldrons, beakers, flasks, and pots. The center of the room was dotted with two shelves crammed with roots, dried flowers, and beakers filled with glowing liquid or dust of various colors. Diagrams of geometric shapes with arcane symbols and scripts covered the walls and floor.

"Wow," Lorelei said. "I haven't seen a lab like this since I snuck into one of the Halls at the Aimsir for a party."

Wes wandered over to the shelves and picked up a bottle. "I think this is blood of some kind."

"Careful. Some of this may be volatile." Vandermere passed by the tables and shelves with barely a glance at them and strode back to the spiral staircase.

Lorelei paused at one of the tables. Some beakers appeared to have dregs of burnt liquids inside of them. Several candles sat with their wicks extinguished. Vaana stood in the doorway with her hands in her pockets as she watched Vandermere ascend.

"Hmm, what would these experiments have to do with the working of Fate? I'd expect something more like crystal balls and such." Lorelei peered up at one of the diagrams. Instead of shapes, this one depicted a landmass. "Where do you think this could be?"

Vaana cast her gaze at Lorelei and the diagram and shrugged.

"What is with you? You haven't said one snarky comment since we dropped anchor."

Vaana shook her head. "We shouldn't be here."

"So you keep saying." Lorelei leaned one hip against the table, facing Vaana, and crossed her arms. "Would you care to elaborate?"

Vaana hesitated and then opened her mouth to speak. A loud scream from upstairs interrupted her. Without another glance at Vaana, Lorelei sprinted across the room and up the stairs. She paused at the third floor to blink at the disaster scattered about the large, open library. Shelves were toppled over with books strewn across the floor, their pages ripped from the spines and torn to thousands of tatters.

Vandermere was nowhere in sight.

Lorelei continued to climb to the next floor. A familiar,

metallic stench hit her nostrils when she reached the halfway point. She clenched her jaw, resisting the urge to grate her teeth as a chill crept up her spine and her stomach roiled. Iron. There had to be a lot of it if she could sense it from the stairs.

Vandermere.

Her chest tightened and she dashed up the remainder of the stairs. She came to a halt at the open room at the top. She covered her mouth with her arm, pushing down the bile rising in her. The iron smell was overpowering. Bits seemed to be embedded in the walls and the floor.

Vandermere knelt in the middle of the room, a bedroom from the looks of it. Tapestries and rugs filled the room, woven in strange abstract geometrical shapes that hurt her head if she did more than glance at them. An elaborate, oaken wardrobe stood next to one of the shuttered windows. In the back of the room was a large bed with ornately carved posts. In the center of the bed lay a skeleton, its skull tilted to stare at the staircase. A dagger was buried between its ribs. A dark, burned mark marred the purple sheets beneath the body and more iron shards lay strewn across the bed. It was as if a bomb of iron had gone off.

Vandermere screamed again and clutched his head.

Lorelei rushed to him and grabbed his shoulder. "Come on. We need to get out of here."

He stood, knocking her hand away, and turned her direction. His face was an emotionless mask. Shadows danced in his eyes as he stared down at her. That same aura of menace she'd felt when they'd first met emanated from him.

She was no longer dealing with Vandermere, but the Dark Lord.

26

Vandermere knew the skeleton when he saw it. Verdain ap Essus, the Lord of Fate was dead by iron. Forever lost.

A scream erupted from his lips before he could stop it and he fell to his knees. His chest heaved as his stomach twisted not only from the sight before him, but the iron surrounding him. His skin itched at the feeling of it in the air.

How could something like this happen? There were no signs that his attacker had forced their way in. They would have had to pass through the magical protections at the door. Knowing Verdain, there had been other protection as well.

His gaze trailed down to the side of the bed to where a pile of clothes lay. Next to it was a pair of lace panties. He'd had a female here, and it had been his doom. How could one of House Essus be tricked into inviting their assassin in?

He swallowed. He could force a vision and find out what happened. With this much iron, it was a risk. Even having a vision in such a place would be detrimental to him. It could give the shadow more leeway. Still, he *needed* to know and the vision would be easier in the place of Verdain's death.

He closed his eyes, drew in a deep breath, and let the vision come.

A purple light flashes.

A black snake slithers up an ivory road, leaving a trail of blood in its wake. It is surrounded in darkness.

Flash.

Golden eyes are filled with lies and secrets.

Flash.

The door to the tower opens. Verdain admits his death in.

Flash.

Vaana's face flashes as she stands over Verdain's body. A dagger is buried in his heart. She places a device on his chest and sprints out of the room.

Flash.

An explosion blooms. Fire and iron shards.

27

Lorelei backed from Vandermere until her back hit the railing of the staircase. He drew his sword and took another step towards her.

"Vandermere, it's Lorelei." She raised her hands up. "We're friends, remember?"

"Lies," Vandermere said in a deep voice. "No servant of the Shadow is a friend."

He lifted the sword up, so the tip was inches from her heaving chest. He wasn't outright attacking her, which was good, but any wrong move could set him off. With all the iron flung about in the room, a fight in here would be deadly to either of them.

She reached behind her, grabbing the rail. Slowly, she descended step by step with him following after her with his sword raised. Wes and Vaana stood in the library below near a fallen bookshelf. Vaana's eyes widened as she watched Lorelei descend. Wes shout a loud curse and rushed towards the stairs. Lorelei raised her hand to stop him, but it was too late.

Vandermere's head jerked in Wes's direction before returning to Lorelei. His face twisted into a dark scowl and he lunged forward to bury his sword in Lorelei's chest. She twisted her torso to the side and the blade slashed through her cloak.

She hopped back onto the rail and used her momentum to slide the remaining distance to the lower floor. At the end, she tried to stop but toppled forward and fell to the carpet. The blow reverberated through her bones and knocked the wind from her.

Wes leapt to stand in front of her as Vandermere sprinted down the remaining steps towards them. Wes pulled his gun from his belt.

"Don't," Lorelei cried in between gasps of air. "He's not in his right mind."

"Obviously," Wes said. "What happened?"

Vaana crept around the staircase to approach Vandermere from behind.

"Fiends," Vandermere hissed. "Servants of the Shadow. You'll not claim me."

"He must have had some vision from what he saw upstairs." Lorelei gulped and shuddered as the memory rose in her mind.

Wes kept his gun trained on Vandermere, who paused at the bottom of the staircase. Vandermere studied them with narrowed eyes, his forehead creased.

"I think he may recognize us somewhere deep in his consciousness." Lorelei raised her hands up and got to her feet. "We just need to reach him somehow."

Vandermere spun from them and slashed his sword at Vaana a few feet behind him. She ducked down and rolled into a ball to dodge him. In one smooth motion, she came out of the tumble and stood near Lorelei and Wes.

"Stop trying to attack him," Lorelei snapped. "It will only make things worse."

"Any ideas on how to calm him, then?" Wes asked.

A heaviness settled in her chest as her heart pounded. The last time this had happened, she'd sung and been able to pull him from his madness. Would it work this time? She had to try. Lorelei stepped forward, drew a deep breath, and sang.

"I've seen through your smile." Her words came out in a soft cadence. "Your pain speaks, through your silence."

She pulled the image of first meeting him, after he removed his helmet. The first smile he'd given her transforming his face.

"All I want is your joy. I want to heal your suffering and save you from the dark."

Vandermere stiffened, his grip on his sword shaking.

She focused her thoughts on the first night on the ship. How close he had gotten to her. She wasn't sure if she was ready to love someone again, but he had caught her attention.

"Give unto me your suffering. Let me share your burden and shine through your shadows."

She took another step forward to where the tip of the blade pressed into the fabric of her dress. Vandermere's hand dropped as he stared at her with a confused look on his face.

"Fear not the heat of my light. Let me be the sun in your world of shadows.

She laid her hand on his chest and met his gaze. "Fear not the heat of my light. Let me be the sun in your world of shadows..."

The gloom in his eyes faded and he stared down at her with recognition. With a loud groan, the sword fell from his hand and he collapsed to his knees.

Lorelei knelt beside him and wrapped her arms around his shoulders. He pressed his forehead against her breast as his entire body shook. She ran her hand through his hair as she let relief sink through her. It was as if a weight had been lifted from her chest.

"Shh. You're back with us," she said in a gentle voice.

After another moment, he pulled away and straightened. "I apologize. I lost myself." He smiled down at Lorelei. "You brought me back again."

"What was that all about?" Wes spoke up.

"The Lord of Fate is dead." Vandermere bowed his head. "I forced a vision to find out what happened."

"Did you see?" Lorelei asked.

Vandermere's head shot up and he glared at Vaana. "This isn't the first time you have been here. What did you do?"

Lorelei looked between Vandermere and Vaana as a queasy feeling settled in her stomach.

"What's he talking about?" Lorelei asked, landing her gaze on Vaana.

Vaana shrugged. "Who knows? Maybe the crazy hasn't settled."

Vandermere's fist clenched. "You're lying. I saw you. You murdered the Lord of Fate, didn't you? You set some sort of iron bomb to ensure his soul wouldn't reincarnate."

Vaana paled and her shoulders slumped. "Damn you, why did this vision have to be so accurate."

The room took on an eerie clarity for Lorelei as a chill ran down her spine. "You really did this? That's why you haven't wanted to come here. Because you knew you'd left nothing behind."

"I was following orders. Verdain ap Essus was a heretic. Worse. He didn't just collect information on old magic, he actually collected the essences of old gods."

"So, the Order told you to kill him...with *iron*?" Lorelei asked.

"Doesn't sound in line with the Order's principle of Reincarnation," Wes spoke up.

"I had my doubts about it, but it was given to me by the Apostle of Fire and by the Voice of Wisdom herself. How could the one who speaks for the Empress be wrong?" Vaana met each of their stares with an expression of determination.

"And do you believe these things now?" Lorelei asked.

Vaana crossed her arms and stared down at the floor. "I don't know. Things have been...unclear...since the Menhir."

"What happened?" Lorelei asked. "He didn't have the essences here, so you got where he stored them, somehow?"

"She seduced him," Vandermere said in a cold voice. "Verdain had a predilection for courting females."

Vaana nodded. "I knew this from the information I'd gathered on him. He was surprisingly forthcoming. I had expected more resistance."

Vandermere's jaw tightened and he was on his feet in an instant. His fist clenched and he stepped towards Vaana. Lorelei put a hand on his arm.

"Wait," she said. "Violence isn't the answer to this." She jerked her head in Vaana's direction with the curl of her lip. "We do need to decide what to do about you, though."

"What, you plan to kill me?" Vaana said with a snort. "I'm not easily felled. Especially now."

Lorelei's stomach twisted at the thought. "No, but we need to think about this. I knew you were using us to get the tablet...but you kept what you did from us."

"This is why I didn't want to come here." Vaana threw her hands in the air. "I knew it would be for nothing...and it would break what we have built."

"What have we built?" Vandermere said in a growling voice.

"Yeah, I used you in the beginning, but that's changed. I've grown to like you." Vaana stared down at her clenched fist. "And I've been pretty useful. I've healed you and saved your lives."

"So, what? You want to go on with them like you've been?"

Wes looked at Vandermere's face. "I don't think they're gonna be happy about that."

Lorelei held up her hand. "Look, I think we need to step back from this for now. Let's take the night to let some emotions settle and discuss what to do in the morning."

"She may leave," Vandermere said. "To escape whatever punishment is owed to her. She abandoned the Order, after all. I doubt she has any problems with abandoning us."

"She doesn't have many places to go," Lorelei said.

"Actually," Wes said, "she has almost the entire West to get lost in and people willing to aid her for the right price. I'm sure she knows where to look for them."

"Fine," Lorelei said. "How about we lock her up for now?"

Vaana let out a short laugh. "You're not about to lock me up in some broom closet."

"As much as you think you can win, it's three against one," Lorelei said. "We know your tricks."

A strange light glittered from Vaana's eyes. "You haven't even begun to see my tricks."

Vandermere reached down and grabbed his sword. "By all means, show us then."

"Wait!" Lorelei held up her hand. "Let's not destroy what is left of the library. Vaana, I know you think that fighting your way out is your only option..."

Vaana sent a glare in Vandermere's direction. "Isn't it? He plans to mete out some sort of punishment for my transgression against his House."

"And it's probably well deserved," Lorelei touched Vandermere's arm again. "But...what will it get us in the end? We came here to learn more about the gods within Vaana. If we kill her, what will happen to them?"

"I don't know." Vandermere's brow furrowed. "I could find out."

"None of that. Also, we are considered heretics and wanted by the Order. That isn't going to go away. If we turned her into the Quorum, we'd be arrested as well." Lorelei looked to Vaana. "We are in the middle of nowhere, and as far as I know, you don't know how to sail a ship. You can at least wait for the night."

"Fine," Vaana muttered in a low growl. "Which room do you want to stick me in?"

Lorelei turned the key, locking Vaana in the storeroom. They had found a ring of keys on the wall of the kitchen that worked for most of the locks in the tower. They'd considered locking her in the small sitting room, but it had windows. In the end, Vaana had predicted her prison, though she'd been left with a bedroll and pillows as well as food.

Lorelei turned and leaned her back against the door with a long sigh. "What now?"

"Well," Wes said, "there is a lab and a library to explore. Maybe she didn't destroy everything."

Lorelei nodded. "She left the sketches on the wall intact. Maybe she left more."

Without a word, Vandermere turned and marched up the stairs.

"Maybe we should give him some time," Lorelei said softly. "This has all come as a shock to him."

"Huh," Wes said. "Is he supposed to be a seer or something?"

"Something like that," Lorelei said. "But it doesn't make him omniscient."

"Still, you'd think he would have looked into this place before coming here. Had a vision or something."

Lorelei stared up at the ceiling and bit her lip. "I don't

think Vandermere likes to have visions for fear of what could happen."

"You mean like earlier? What was that all about?"

She shook her head. "All of his House is cursed with a madness. It appears that his becomes uncontrollable when he has visions."

Wes shook his head. "You all are a weird lot."

Lorelei chuckled. "I guess you're right. But, you're still here."

He shrugged and bumped her shoulder with his. "Maybe I like weird."

"Doesn't that make you weird too?"

Vaana's voice came muffled from behind the door. "If you're going to flirt, pick another room."

Wes gave a fake bow and stretched his arm to the stairs. "Shall we?"

They climbed the stairs to the second floor. Vandermere was nowhere to be seen. Lorelei sighed and paced the length of the room. She wanted to go to him, to let him know she was there for him, but he probably didn't want the company at the moment. Her gaze drifted to one of the sketches on the walls.

"Some of these look like maps," Lorelei said, "But to places I've never even heard of."

"There are tales of gateways that lead to other worlds," Wes said. "There's supposed to be one somewhere to the West."

"We are in the West," Lorelei said. "I mean, we've been traveling West for the past two weeks...on a river. How much more West is left?"

"A lot," Wes said with a chuckle. "And no one knows where this gateway would be. At least, no one I've talked to."

"Were you interested in going there? You don't seem like the type to follow fancies."

"You just don't know me," Wes said. "I'm here, aren't I? And you found me under Murgleis's thrall."

"True." Lorelei frowned down at the sword. *You've been silent a lot recently.*

I'm not here to provide a running commentary on your exploits. We made a pact and I am waiting for it to be fulfilled.

You knew we would come here first.

I did. I am patient. I have time, after all.

What do you think of Vaana's betrayal?

It is to be expected. The Order is filled with evils you can't comprehend... Well, perhaps you can.

What do you mean by that?

Silence met her question.

Lorelei let out a sigh and turned to Wes. "So, maybe we should check out the library before messing around with anything in here. We don't want to blow this floor of the tower up."

Wes glanced up the stairs. "What did you see in the bedroom?"

Lorelei shook her head as the image flashed in her mind. "You shouldn't go up there. It's deadly...The whole room is covered in iron shards and dust."

"I'm surprised you're not sick from it. Or Vandermere."

"I covered my nose and mouth when I realized what it was...but Vandermere..." He didn't. Lorelei's brow furrowed. "Strange."

"What?" Wes asked.

"Vandermere was on his knees, kneeling in it, and yet he didn't seem affected at all."

Wes's eyebrows raised. "I thought your people are supposed to be affected by it more."

"We are...unless in Vandermere's madness and anger he didn't notice." Lorelei gasped and sprinted towards the stairs. "What if he's upstairs sick?"

She raced up the steps as her body broke into a cold sweat. Visions of Arryn raced through her mind. Arryn had been stabbed with iron and it had crippled him. What would happen to Vandermere if he breathed it in?

The library was empty. Lorelei paused, catching her breath as her gaze rose to the ceiling. What madness had compelled him to return to the room filled with iron?

She barely spared Wes a glance as he joined her. Instead, she took the steps two at a time to the top floor.

Vandermere stood near the headboard of the bed, holding a medallion with an emerald the size of her fist in it.

28

Lorelei took a step back as Vandermere turned her direction. His brow wrinkled as he looked at her. For a second, her heart pounded as she stared at his face.

Not again.

"What are you doing here?" He strode towards her. "This room is poisonous to you."

Relief flooded through Lorelei and she pressed her mouth and nose in the crook of her arm as an afterthought. Vandermere touched her shoulder and turned her in the direction of the stairs. He was all right. He'd not slipped back into that madness as before. She descended the stairs with light steps and he followed behind her.

Once they reached the library, she turned back to them. "Why were you up there? It's just as poisonous to you, isn't it?"

A smile ghosted his lips. "No, actually. House Essus doesn't fear iron. It doesn't burn our flesh or sear our lungs like other sidhe."

Lorelei's eyes widened and she had to keep her mouth from falling open. Wes gave out a low whistle.

"That's some trick, from what I hear," Wes said. "Other sidhe would probably pay a pretty penny to learn how to accomplish that."

"None of my House has ever truly found out why, but it's widely believed among us that it has something to do with the madness." Vandermere stared down at the medallion.

Wes shot Lorelei a look and she could practically read what he was thinking. Maybe their belief that iron didn't need to be feared was just part of the madness. Lorelei bit her lip and nodded to the medallion.

"That's emerald, isn't it?" she asked in a soft voice.

Wes's attention turned to the emerald and he took a step forward with an almost reverent look on his face. "Seriously? That's huge. Something like that could set all of us for life."

Vandermere's fist tightened around the medallion.

"Where did you find it?" Lorelei asked.

"I had an urge to return upstairs. I needed to...see the body, to inspect him." Vandermere's hand fell to his side, the emerald still in it. "I found this around his neck."

Lorelei reached out and squeezed his arm gently.

"Emeralds are supposed to grant wishes, right?" Wes said. "We could use it to get everything we want."

Vandermere shook his head. "I think even emerald has limitations."

"Like what?" Wes crossed his arms. "The stories I've heard said emerald can give a heart's desire. Right, Lorelei?"

Lorelei licked her lips as she stared at the emerald. "I've heard the same."

Her heart's desire. She'd set off on this journey to learn the truth of the Black Herons. Could the emerald show her that truth, provide her proof?

Or it could give you Arryn's heart.

Her stomach rose at the thought. Even after a year, did she still want him?

"No wishes yet." Vandermere stared down at the medallion. "I was led to it for some reason."

"Probably so we could finish up with this god business," Wes said. "With one wish, Vaana and all of it could be over."

Vandermere's fingers brushed across the emerald and a flash of green light filled the room. Lorelei cringed at the brightness. When she opened her eyes, the image of a tall sidhe stood before them. His form was semi-translucent and had a greenish tint to it. A smile lit up his face as he gazed at them.

Lorelei's eyes widened. She had come across some outrageous things during their journey, but she never expected to come across a ghost, if that's what this thing was. Could they fight a ghost if it got violent? What magic could she call forth with her song that could harm one?

"Thank the Empress," the ghostly image said. "You found the emerald. I couldn't predict how long I would be trapped in that room."

"Verdain?" Vandermere's voice took an incredulous, breathy quality.

Lorelei's blood raced through her veins as his back stiffened. The world seemed to fade as the ghostly image came sharply into focus. Lorelei had seen a ghost before in the Citadel of Night, but that ghost had died to the citadels plunge into the ravine. No soul survived iron.

The image nodded. "It's the spirit, as my flesh is useless now."

"But how? Your room is covered in iron." Lorelei raised her hand to the ceiling. "An explosion went off in there...or something."

Verdain crossed his hands behind his back. "I'd had visions of my impending death for days. I knew it was soon, so I took precautions. I performed certain magics that allowed my soul to escape to the emerald upon my death. It was protected there from the iron bomb my assassin laid."

Lorelei's breath caught in her throat. Her heart seemed to stop for an instant before speeding up to a thrum. She'd heard tales of how emerald could grant wishes, but to know it had saved Verdain from iron...

She ran a hand through her hair. Iron was beyond deadly. It was the end of someone's soul. There wasn't even hope of reincarnation. And yet, here was Verdain, existing despite an iron bomb that had exploded in his room, all thanks to the emerald medallion.

"And the emerald is maintaining you now?" Vandermere asked.

"Yes," Verdain said with a sigh. "Though it seems to be taking up most of the emerald's power to do so."

Wes's shoulders slumped. He'd been staring at Verdain with a look of shock and wonder. Now, lines of disappointment creased along his forehead and brows.

"I guess that means wishes are out," he said.

"I'm sorry," Verdain said.

"No." Wes waved his hand. "It was yours in the first place."

Lorelei shot Wes a small smile. She knew how he felt. That medallion could solve half the problems they were dealing with. However, that might cost Verdain what was left of his existence. Lorelei wasn't sure if she was prepared to do that. She knew Vandermere wouldn't sacrifice Verdain.

"Lord Verdain." Lorelei turned back to the spirit. "We believe we have your assassin locked in a storeroom below. We...uh...unknowingly brought her back here."

The image's eyebrow rose. "I can't see how she would unknowingly return."

"I believe she returned in hopes of finding more information on the predicament she was in," Vandermere said. "She has bonded to the essences of fallen gods."

"Hmm, interesting." Verdain tapped his cheek. "My assassin did indeed come asking about certain godstones. Of course, I did not have them here. I had them stored in a safe place."

"She found them, with my help." Lorelei bowed her head and crossed her arms.

Vandermere touched her shoulder. "It was meant to happen. I saw it. It was the event that brought us together."

Verdain tilted his head at Vandermere. "You are of my House?"

"Vandermere ap Essus." Vandermere gave a slight bow. "And this is Lorelei ap Moura."

"Ah, I see. An Essus and a Moura." Verdain smirked. "That would do it. And you saw what was to happen with my assassin?"

"Not your death...not until I arrived here." Vandermere swallowed. "I saw her taking the godstones...and that it would start a journey for us. If I had known what she'd done..."

"You couldn't have stopped it or what came after," Verdain said. "It was meant to happen."

"But it all ended here," Lorelei said. "For nothing, really."

"Perhaps not," Verdain said. "It is interesting that she could house such power. No faerie should be able to hold the power of a god."

"Gods," Lorelei said. "There were six stones. The lighting from all of them struck her. From what she says, she has them all. They speak to her."

"Very interesting," Verdain said. "What do you know of this sidhe girl?"

"She's of House Aoife," Vandermere said.

"She joined the Elemental Order when she was still a child," Lorelei said. "From what she told me, she was trained under the Voice of Wisdom...I think. She is close to the Apostle of Fire, or was until the stones. Now she's wanted for heresy. We all are."

Verdain chuckled with the shake of his head. "Ah, yes, heresy. A favorite crime of the Order. Some of the best people I know are wanted for heresy...some of the worst as well."

"This speculation is great," Wes said. "And it's let me know what craziness I've gotten myself into, but what are we going to do about her? I mean, we can't leave her locked in the storeroom forever."

"We need to learn more about how she can house the essence," Lorelei said.

"And how to remove it," Vandermere said.

"Perhaps you should start by asking her about her past," Verdain said.

Vandermere shook his head. "Would she tell us anything? Or just make up lies?"

"I don't think she lied about everything," Lorelei said. "And she wants to know just as much as we do. She came back here, after all."

Vandermere stared at the floor for a few minutes before shaking his head again. "Fine. We will speak with her."

"If you knew about the godstones, do you know about the gods they once were?" Lorelei asked.

"Not a lot," Verdain said. "I know they were once a pantheon from a world other than Threshold. Though they affected Threshold as well. There were many gods that did. I believe they were called the Danann."

Lorelei rested her hand over her mouth as she stared at him, trying to comprehend what he just said.

"Other worlds?" She asked in a strangled voice.

"Well, yes. Before the Miasma came, there were many worlds that were connected by gates of some sort. However, contact was lost during the time of the Miasma, and most of the knowledge has been lost."

Wes cleared his throat. "Not sure how that helps us now. We should probably focus on Vaana and her special capability."

"You're right. Despite what gods they are, Vaana is the key in this." Lorelei looked to Verdain's image. "Will you be able to move on now?"

"Not yet." Verdain's gaze shifted to Vandermere who was staring off with his lips pressed in a thin slash. "I think some of you may need my guidance. I'll reside here in the emerald for now."

Wes sighed. "Definitely no wishes, then."

"Ah, but you have knowledge." Verdain's voice echoed around them as his image disappeared. "And with it, power."

❦

When they opened the door to the storeroom, Vaana was sitting with her back against the wall. She stared up at them with a resigned expression.

"Is this my execution then?" She raised her tied hands up. "I mean, you have me at your mercy and all that."

"I doubt you're that subdued," Lorelei said. "And no. We've come to ask some questions."

Vandermere glared at Vaana. His voice came out artic. "Tell us of your family. What led you to join the Order?"

Vaana gaze shifted to the floor. "I felt it was the right thing to do."

"But you were young, right?" Lorelei asked. "Did your family push you into it? Are you second born or something?"

"What does that have to do with anything?" Wes asked.

"Second born don't inherit," Lorelei said. "They usually have to take up a career in the military, or the Order."

"But, what does this have to do with anything that's happened?" Vaana said.

"We're trying to determine how you can contain the essence of these gods," Vandermere said.

Vaana let out a sigh. "Do you think, if I knew, I would be here, of all places?"

"So, this isn't something you knowingly underwent," Lorelei said. "So, it is something with your birth...or did the Order do something to you?"

"I don't know." Vaana raised both her hands and ran her bound hands through her hair. She let out a long sigh. "I'm an only child. My parents died when I was little and my aunt raised me. I don't remember much of my parents...and my aunt was always busy."

"Poor noble," Wes muttered under his breath.

Lorelei elbowed him and turned her attention back to Vaana. "So, you decided to join the Order."

Vaana hesitated. "My aunt felt it would benefit me...I'd been having, I don't know, visions?"

Lorelei shivered and glanced at Vandermere. Visions. She had something similar with her nightmares. Her parents had always considered them an embarrassment...and they'd even urged her to join the Order only a few months ago. And Vandermere suffered from the visions of his House's curse, or gift. Perhaps it wasn't just the Menhir that drew the three of them together.

Vandermere cleared his throat. "Do you remember anything odd with your initiation or your training?"

"The Voice of Wisdom took a special interest in me. I was actually trained alongside Apostle Evangeline...and Beth." A look of sadness crossed Vaana's face as she stared at her hands. "As for the training, I don't believe so. I was trained for special tasks of eliminating heretics and retrieving relics."

"An assassin and thief," Vandermere muttered.

Vaana's tone became sharp. "It was for the safety and peace of the Empire. Faeries are easily led astray."

Lorelei put a hand on Vandermere's arm before he opened his mouth to argue. "That argument aside, there was nothing else?"

"Well, after a few years, I was sent to Kirkwall for more practical application of my training, as was Beth and the Apostle. The West is under the domain of Evangeline."

"Strange," Wes muttered. "You would think it would be under the Apostle of Earth. After all, most of the spirits here use Earth magic."

Vaana's brows drew together. "There were times I was taken to a dark room with a single light to meditate and strengthen my relationship with the Empress. However, I don't remember what happened after the meditations began. The Voice of Wisdom always told me I would remember when I was ready."

Lorelei bit her lips and glanced at Vandermere as an uneasy feeling settled in the pit of her stomach. Did this conspiracy really go as deep as the Voice of Wisdom herself?

"Is there anything else you can think of?" Lorelei asked.

Vaana shook her head. "There should be no reason that I'm stuck with these things inside of me. I'm guessing you couldn't find anything here?"

"You destroyed most of the books and killed the Lord of Fate." Vandermere's voice turned cold again. "I'd say you did a decent job of making sure nothing would be found."

Vaana sighed. "I'd hoped I missed something..."

Vandermere muttered and turned away. He stalked out of the storeroom. Lorelei spared Vaana a glance as she filed out with Wes. Wes locked the door behind them and headed to the parlor. Lorelei bit her lip as she stared at the door. With a shake of her head, she turned and joined the others.

"Well, that wasn't much to go on," Wes said.

"I think we need to go to Kirkwall." Vandermere flopped into an armchair and rested his hand on his forehead. "We may discover more information there."

"How?" Lorelei said. "The church there is pretty big and there are probably a lot of priests guarding it. They're not exactly going to let us in to snoop, not when they want to kill us."

"Yeah," Wes said. "Up until a year ago, it was the biggest in the West."

"All right. How are we supposed to break in?" Lorelei asked. "I'm sure it is well guarded...especially against shapeshifting phooka."

"You shouldn't go. Someone needs to stay and keep watch over Vaana. Besides"—Vandermere nodded to Murgleis hanging at Lorelei's side—"The Order will most likely detect it...and you aren't the best for stealth with your magic."

Lorelei felt her face heat up. "And you are good at stealth?"

"I have my powers to foresee and avoid possible trouble," Vandermere said.

Lorelei crossed her arms over her chest. What he said made sense, but the idea of getting relegated to prison guard rankled at her nerves. She gritted her teeth, searching for any point to argue.

"You can't go alone," she said. "Even with your powers, you were still caught by that Arachne."

"He won't be alone," Wes said. "I have some contacts there I can talk to. And he needs someone to sail him there."

Vandermere grinned at Wes and turned to Lorelei. "I think things are settled then."

Lorelei glared at him. "Fine, but if you're not back in three weeks, I'm coming after you."

Lorelei watched Vandermere and Wes disappear into the tree line. She sighed. They were going off to a dangerous place without her. She wasn't sure if it was worry for them, or the loss of doing something adventurous that annoyed her. Perhaps it was both. Muttering under her breath, she returned inside and ambled into the parlor in search of something to do.

She glanced at the mirror on the wall and gasp. The blonde hair, pulled into an intricate style of curls around a face full of annoyance, didn't belong to her. No, that was Freya glaring at her instead of her own reflection. Her sister had used her magic to create a two-way communication between mirrors.

"It took you long enough to stop moping," Freya said.

"This is a surprise," Lorelei said. "Though it's not pleasant. How did you find me?"

"It took a while and Mother and Father had to pull some strings, but we were able to scry your location. It seems you finally stopped moving again."

"You should have told them not to go through the effort," Lorelei said.

"You have some nerve. Why couldn't you just stay on that island?" Freya asked in a high hiss.

"What? Upset I didn't willingly hide away while you stole my fiancé?" Lorelei crossed her arms and tilted her head.

"You lost him yourself," Freya snapped. "And you've done much worse than just run away. You spit in the face of one of the Apostle of Fire and cavort with heretics. Clearly, you have lost your mind."

A chill ran up Lorelei spine at her words. "What have you been told?"

"Enough. It has the whole city talking." A sneer lit Freya's lip as she looked down her nose at Lorelei. "The embarrassment we have to face."

"It's not true." Lorelei's fists clenched. "There is something very wrong with the Order and we are trying to find out the truth."

"Even if any of that was true, where do you get off thinking it's your place?" Freya gave a soft sniff. "This is what got you in trouble before."

"Isn't it the place for any of us to right what is wrong?" Lorelei said. "We are supposed to look after the lesser faerie, and the Order we believe in is not only using them, but we sidhe as well."

A vein throbbed in Freya's temple as a look of rage subsumed her. She closed her eyes and took a deep breath. "You're to return home and submit yourself to the Order authorities for questioning. They have agreed to give leniency if you turn over information on your companions, especially the sidhe female."

Lorelei's stomach tightened and her fingers dug into her palms. Did her family really believe they were being magnanimous with this offer? At best, she would be forced to stay with her parents or shipped off to another priory. A heavy weight settled over her at the thought. Even if Vaana assassinated Verdain, Lorelei wasn't going to turn her in to the Order, not before Vandermere returned with information on Vaana's history. She certainly wasn't going to betray him or Wes.

"No," Lorelei said. "I'm not coming back. I've gotten this far on my own."

Freya's face twisted into a scowl. "Fine. You deserve everything you are going to get."

The mirror clouded over with a bluish mist. It faded, leaving only her reflection.

She had to wonder when her sister had become so ugly.

29

The noise of music, laughter, and clinking glasses flowed around Vandermere as he sat at a small table in the corner of the tavern, nursing a sour ale. Wes had brought it to him and then sauntered off in search of the contact they were supposed to be meeting.

Over the last two days, Wes had dragged him through several dingy, wooden ramshackles masquerading as ale houses in search of a lead. Wes seemed to have a lot of contacts, because he spent most nights talking to his contacts which ranged from tavern owners to merchants to craftsmen. All congregated for drinks at the end of the night. Despite these numerous contacts, they found nothing. Tonight, might be different though. Wes had said this could be their big chance to uncover any information on the Order, especially the church in Kirkwall.

Vandermere hoped he was right. He'd given Lorelei a promise of a week, three with ship travel. If he didn't return, she was coming after him and bringing that traitorous bitch with her.

Vandermere gritted his teeth and his hand slid under his

shirt to grip the medallion hanging underneath. Why had Fate tied him to Vaana after what she'd done? It'd always had a sense of irony, he supposed. Though, without Vaana, he would never have met Lorelei. A smile touched his lips; she'd been a salve to his madness.

Wes's head bobbed among the crowd as he made his way back to their table. A sidhe female with lemon yellow hair pulled back into a bun followed behind him.

Vandermere raised an eyebrow. When Wes had mentioned a contact, he hadn't expected a sidhe.

"Vandermere, this is Lady Tanila ap Aoife." Wes gestured towards her. "A good friend of mine recommended we speak."

"A pleasure." Tanila sat in the chair across from Vandermere in one graceful sweep.

A member from Vaana's House. Vandermere gritted his teeth. Was this a plant? Surely, Wes was more cunning than that. His gaze met Wes's, who widened his eyes, and tilted his head to Tanila.

Vandermere cleared his throat. "Pardon me. It is a pleasure and a surprise. You were not what I was expecting. Tell me, how is it that we can help each other?"

Wes sank into the last chair with his side turned to the back of the chair. He glanced around the crowd with narrowed eyes. Tanila swept her gaze across the room, then leaned forward, ducking her head closer to Vandermere as she threaded her fingers together.

"I'm a reporter investigating a story concerning my House and the Order," she said.

"Oh?" Vandermere asked. "I didn't know there was a connection between the two. To be honest, House Aoife is more concerned with gaining riches and secrets."

"We are interested in the lost histories of our people, for the most part. However, it is true of the Order as well.

Usually, they are considered to be rivals in the search for artifacts, which makes this all the more interesting."

"What do you mean?" Vandermere asked.

"A number of our girls have been joining the Order over the past decade, most notably, Lady Vaana ap Aoife."

Vandermere's back straightened. "Why is Vaana important in this?"

"Lady Vaana is the daughter of the previous head of our House, Lady Tiere. She was expected to succeed her mother when she became of age. However, she joined the Order."

"Who sits in the Quorum now for the House?" Vandermere asked.

"Lady Corin, Vaana's aunt."

Vandermere sat back and rubbed his cheek. "And Lady Kara was Vaana's guardian after her parents' death."

Tanila's eyebrow raised. "You know more of this than you are letting on."

"I know a little," Vandermere said with a smirk. "I'm from House Essus. We're supposed to know things."

"All this is interesting, but what does it have to do with Kirkwall?" Wes asked. "Why are you here?"

"Lady Vaana was sent here to Kirkwall at the beginning of her training. She was only transferred back to the Elphyne Empire a few years ago." Tanila leaned back and stared off for several moments. "Vaana returned from here changed. She used to be more of a friendly, lively girl."

"She's still lively," Wes muttered. "Not so much on the friendly."

"You know her?"

"We've met," Wes said.

"You believe that something happened to Vaana here?" Vandermere broke in. "But how do you know it wasn't just the training that changed her?"

"I can't explain it," Tanila said. "I just have hunches for these things. So, I did a little digging..."

"And?" Vandermere asked.

Tanila leaned farther forward and motioned for Wes and Vandermere to inch closer. When they did, she spoke in a low voice, barely above a whisper. "I found a secret lab in the church here."

"You have?" Vandermere said. "What's inside?"

Tanila sighed and leaned back again. "I didn't get a chance to look around. A group of monks came and I had to leave before I got caught."

Vandermere's shoulders slumped.

Tanila pulled a small key from her pocket. "I still have a way in, if you're interested in coming with me."

Vandermere smiled. "We'd love to accompany you. We have questions of our own."

Tanila closed her hand around the key. "And what are those questions? I'm curious to know what interest you have in the Order...and Vaana. You've met her, it seems."

Vandermere stared at her. The last time he'd trusted an Aoife, she'd been an assassin. Still, that had been due to the Order. Tanila seemed just as interested in digging up secrets as they were. Besides, he didn't have to tell her everything.

"Vaana has been traveling with us for the past several months," Vandermere said.

Tanila let out a soft coughing laugh. "You're the heretics that led her astray? I expected more like him." She nodded to Wes. "No offense."

Wes shrugged. "I guess I might fit a look."

"That's what they are saying?" Vandermere scowled. "I suppose I shouldn't have expected less."

"That's not what happened?" Tanila asked.

"No," Vandermere said. "She was affected by several artifacts she found...The Order seems to believe that turned her into a heretic."

"Is she here in the city?" Tanila glanced around the tavern as if she expected Vaana to be sneaking up on her.

"No," Vandermere said. "That would be dangerous She is somewhere safe, with a friend."

And hopefully still locked away.

"All right, so you're here because...?" Tanila asked.

"Because we believe that what the Order did to her is the reason she was affected by the artifacts. We're here for close to the same reason as you."

"How was she affected?"

"That's our business," Wes said. "We gave you why we are here. So, are we going to do this?"

Tanila looked between them with narrowed eyes. "I'm not sure what I'm getting out of this."

"Two males having your back." Wes crossed his arms. "Extra eyes and ears."

"Two males who could get me caught," Tanila countered. "I mean, do either of you know anything about stealth?"

Wes snorted. "Please, I'm a phooka. I can shapeshift into something small and stealthy. And he can see the future."

Tanila shook her head. "Still not enough. How about this? I take you with me, and you bring me to Vaana after we're done."

Vandermere shared a glance with Wes. Could they trust this woman? "I thought you already knew Vaana."

"We met when we were younger, but it's not like we were close or anything." Tanila waved her hand. "I'm just looking for an interview on her perspective on this."

"If you do find a story where do you expect to publish this?" Wes asked. "This is the Order we're talking about. They have so much control that getting your truth out will be difficult."

Tanila smirked. “Darling, I’ll make a place.”

“All right.” Vandermere raised his hand. “If you get us into this secret lab and we find information, we will take you to her.”

“It’s a deal then.” A satisfied smile curled on Tanila’s lips.

The door to the tavern swung open and two redcaps in bronze chainmail with tabards with the symbol of the Kirkwall guard stepped inside. Tanila stiffened and hunched her shoulders.

She turned back to Vandermere and Wes. “Meet me at midnight tomorrow on Deveron Street across from the church.”

She stood and pulled the hood of her cloak over her head. She moved between standing patrons along the edge of the tavern, skirting around the movement of the redcaps as they scanned the room.

“We should probably wait here for a few more minutes so not to catch their attention. Ale?” Wes signaled to the barmaid for two drinks.

Vandermere chuckled. “You just want to drink.”

“After that, I could use one,” Wes said. “She was intense.”

“No more than Lorelei...” Vandermere said. “Or Vaana...”

“No, Vaana would take the award on that,” Wes said.

The barmaid returned with two mugs filled with foaming ale. Wes took his and drained half of it. He set the mug down with a satisfied sigh and leaned back.

Vandermere took his mug and sipped as he scanned over the crowd, keeping his eye on the two redcap guards. They’d taken a place at the bar and were laughing over their own drinks. Tanila had been particularly paranoid at them. What had she done to get that key?

“Lorelei must be going crazy by now,” Wes said with a chuckle.

Vandermere smiled at the thought of her pacing the

tower. "Most likely. She'll get her chance to see more action though. This is just one step."

"Do you think we can trust Tanila?" Wes asked.

Vandermere closed his eyes, searching his feelings, his gift for any insight. Nothing came to him. He sighed.

"I can't say for certain, but she seems to be our only option if we want to learn more," Vandermere said. "I only hope she doesn't lead us into a trap."

❧

The following night, Vandermere leaned against the wall of a shop in the alley off Deveron Street. He peeked around the corner to peer up at the clock tower that rose above the gabled rooftops of the city. One minute until midnight. A chill ran up his spine. Tanila had avoided those guards in the tavern the night before, but what if she'd been caught by others? She clearly had been up to no good.

He let out a long breath and glanced at Wes, who was cleaning underneath his nails with the point of his dagger.

"How can you do that and not cut yourself?" Vandermere asked.

"Care and precision," Wes said. "Besides, we phooka are agile."

"Doesn't that depend on what animal shape you take? I don't see a bear being all that agile."

"You haven't seen a bear fishing, then," Wes said. "I prefer smaller animals, anyway."

"Like rats?" Tanila's voice rose from farther down the alley.

Vandermere stood up straight as she stepped out of the dark shadows in the back.

Wes pointed from the front where they stood to the back. "How did you...?"

"I've been scouting this city for weeks. I've learned a few secrets." Tanila sauntered towards them. "On time, early even. I like that. So, are we ready?"

"When you are," Vandermere said.

"Let's see what secrets this church holds then." Tanila stepped out of the alley and strolled along the sidewalk with her hands in her pockets.

Vandermere followed behind her. Wes strolled after them, whistling a low tune. Vandermere glanced over his shoulder every few steps but the street remained empty. At this time of night, most of the city had fallen asleep or had taken refuge in the many taverns.

Tanila led them through the backstreets to the right side of the church. It loomed above them, three stories of white stone that appeared grayish-yellow because of the nearby streetlamps.

Tanila stopped as a smaller stone building added onto the greater structure. Its windows were shuttered and dark.

"This is the Agora," she whispered. "The main building has no exit I could find aside from the front. However, there is a secret entrance through here. We need to hurry. The guard's route passes this way in a few minutes."

Wes put his back to the wall and scanned behind them. Vandermere turned the opposite direction and watched for any coming lights as Tanila pulled out a key. She stepped up to the small wooden door on the side and unlocked it. The door swung open with a creak.

She had to duck her head to slip inside. The door had been made with smaller folk in mind, most likely the hobs. Vandermere paused, then shrugged and stooped to follow after her. Wes grunted as he contorted himself to squeeze through.

The lingering scent of roasted meat and grease greeted them in the darkened kitchen. Pots of various sizes hung from the low ceiling. Vandermere had to stay in his bent position as not to hit them. Wes closed the door, and Tanila lit a lantern.

"Don't worry," she said with a smirk. "The next room is more our size. Just be quiet. The cook sleeps above, as does the guests who stay here."

They made their way around the small counters of the kitchen in an awkward crouching shuffle. The doorway into the next room was more fitting for their height. Vandermere stepped into the next room and stood straight with a sigh of relief. A dull ache lingered in the small of his back and probably would for some hours. If that was the worst pain he would have to endure here, it would be worth it to learn more about Vaana's ability.

Tanila moved past the long wooden table and six chairs in the room to a door on the other side. She unlocked it and swung the door open.

Wes raised an eyebrow.

"Skeleton key," Tanila said. "I pulled some favors to have it specially made."

The next room held two rows of shelves filled with books and scrolls. A large desk sat in the middle of the room with a thick tome on top. Tanila stalked past to the shelf in the back and fiddled with something on the wall beside it. There was a click and the shelf and the wall swung towards them with a soft scrape of wood.

Tanila waved her hand at the dark hole. "May I present the entrance into the Church of Passionate Embers."

Vandermere crept forward into a small stone stairwell with brass reinforced steps leading up and around. The scent of incense clung to walls. Wes entered, hands in his pockets. Tanila pulled the wall closed behind them.

"Where is this secret lab?" Vandermere whispered.

"It's in the catacombs, but we're going to need to travel up to the second floor to get to the stairwell with the entrance to it." Tanila nodded to Wes. "Here's where we could use that ability you were boasting about. Want to check that the hall upstairs is clear?"

Wes gave her a mock salute and turned his back on both of them. His form seemed to collapse in on itself as fur sprang out all over his body. He grew smaller and smaller, his clothes engulfing him and fluttering to the floor. A small lump shifted from his shirt and a small orange cat shimmied out of the neck hole. It stared up at them, its green eyes reflecting in Tanila's lantern light, and gave a soft mrow.

"Well, go on." Tanila waved her hand up the stairs.

The cat raced up the stairs with a grumbling trill and disappeared in the dark. Tanila leaned against the corner of the stairwell with her hand resting near the secret opening. She was ready in case they had to hide from any late-night corridor walkers.

Vandermere reached for the medallion around his neck and his fingers brushed against the emerald.

All this for a female that had murdered one of his own House. Verdain had been a legend. Vandermere's uncle had told him about Verdain when he had been a boy. Verdain had been one of the most powerful mages to graduate from the Aimsir. He'd excelled in three different schools of magic. He had been a pride of House Essus, who had to deal with the ridicule of other Houses for their curse.

And he'd been slain by a girl.

A girl who has most likely been tricked and used by everyone she's looked up to.

Vandermere started at Verdain's voice in his head. He hadn't known he could do that.

You're touching the emerald. Therefore, I can communicate with you. Verdain's voice held a hint of amusement. *As for the girl, give her some leniency. It seems she's had a hard life.*

So? I lost my own parents when I was a child. I didn't become an assassin, Vandermere thought back.

Ah, but I assume you had someone who cared for you?

My uncle.

From what has been said, I doubt this girl has had that.

Vandermere's fingers twitched. *We'll see. Hopefully, we'll find out tonight.*

And if it is true, do you think you can forgive her?

I wouldn't say that.

You need to let this go. I have, and I was the one who was killed.

Vandermere didn't have a response for that.

After several minutes, Wes trotted back down the stairs, sat in front of his clothes, and began licking one of his paws.

"Well?" Tanila asked with a hiss.

Wes stared at her for a few moments before turning his back to her with a sigh. His fur shortened as he began to grow larger and soon a naked Wes stood in the shadows. Tanila rolled her eyes and looked away while Vandermere picked up Wes's clothes and held them out to him. Wes took them and pulled on his pants.

"I think we picked a good time," he said softly as he slipped on his shoes. "The upstairs hall is empty and the guards seem to be on the opposite side of the church."

"We should hurry, lest they make their way to this hall," Vandermere said.

Wes pulled his shirt over his head and turned to Tanila with a grin. "Lead the way."

Tanila led them up the stairs and through a narrow stone hall to another stairwell, which they took back down into a small room. She crept to the left wall and ran her hand along the corner. A crease appeared in the wall and it swung inward leading into a storeroom. In the center, a set of stone steps led down into nothingness.

"It goes to the catacombs," Tanila said. "Stick close to me.

It's a bit of a maze down there."

They descended into a roughly hewn, stone room with a narrow hall leading off into darkness. Vandermere had expected the air to be damp, but a musty dryness filled the air, leaving an itch in his lungs. He covered his mouth with the back of his hand and coughed.

Tanila pulled a folded piece of paper from a pocket in her pants and opened up a map. She held her lantern up to it and scanned it for several minutes before nodding to herself.

"This way." She set off down the only hall available.

"Obviously," Wes muttered but followed behind.

The sounds of dirt scraping against stone from their footfalls filled the halls as Tanila led them through a small maze of twists and turns. They passed several rooms with deep recesses in the walls. Finally, she stopped at a brass door that glittered in her lantern light. It seemed too new and shiny compared to the rest of the catacombs.

Using her skeleton key, she unlocked the door with a metal click.

"Even this one?" Wes asked.

"Of course. I paid a lot of money for the enchantments on it." She swung the door open and sauntered inside.

Vandermere stepped in and scanned the room. Six stone tables with a strange series of metal tubes filled up most of the space. Two females lay upon them with their eyes closed.

Vandermere's brow furrowed and he inched closer to them. Something seemed off about these females. They were as tall as a sidhe, but their features seemed more rounded. He gasped as his hand brushed against one of the empty tables and a vision overtook him.

A young sidhe girl with black hair lies on the table with her eyes closed. Her chest rises and falls in a steady rhythm.

Vaana.

A shadowy robed figure leans over the girl and slips a needle attached to a small tube into her arm. Chanting in a strange language fills the air as the figure moves away from the table. A gold liquid races through the tube and into Vaana's arm. Symbols light up along the edges of the table.

Vandermere jerked his hand away from the table with a gasp. Tanila turned from a shelf full of scrolls that she'd been scanning and raised an eyebrow.

Wes took a couple of steps from the doorway. "You all right?"

"Vaana was here. They did something to her...some sort of ritual...experiment...combination of the two."

Tanila's face lit up, then she turned back to the shelf and started digging through the scrolls with more fervor. "They had to have recorded it. There has to be some sort of proof."

"Wait." Wes raised his and turned back to the door.

He crept closer and leaned his head out, staring down the hall. Vandermere sucked in his breath and listened. Was that the sound of voices off in the distance? Wes met his gaze and nodded. Vandermere strode across the room and grabbed Tanila's arm.

"We have to go." He pulled her from the shelf.

"Not until I get my proof." Tanila yanked her arm from him.

He grabbed her again. "It will be of no use to you if we are caught. We'll have to find something else."

Tanila's lips pressed into a thin line and she gazed at the shelf one last time before following them out of the room.

"What about the females?" Tanila's breath came out in a huff.

"No time." Wes turned his head to let his voice carry as he ran. "We'd be caught for sure trying to carry them around."

They scampered down the hall in the opposite direction they had come with the sounds of voices and footfalls growing closer.

30

Vandermere leaned against the rough wall of the catacomb and panted as Tanila scanned the map with narrowed eyes. Sweat beaded his brow and his ribs ached with each breath.

"Are you sure you can read that thing?" Wes asked.

Her glare was visible even in the dim lantern light. "You didn't have a problem following me up until now."

"I'm just hoping you can lead us out as well as you led us in," Wes muttered.

"Well, I intended to leave the way we came, but there are complications." Her gaze slid from him to the hall behind them.

The voices had faded a while ago. However, they'd rushed through a maze of so many twists and turns that Vandermere wasn't sure Tanila knew where they were at the moment. He rubbed his eyes. He could try to force a vision, but for what purpose? Did he really want to risk losing himself to the Shadow for the chance he could see a way out?

Tanila bit her lip as she continued to study the map. Vandermere turned and stared down the hall ahead of them.

Were those a set of double doors at the end? He walked to the end of the hall and stared up at the entrance. A four-pointed star surrounded by flames was embossed on the brass doors with the crease running through the center. Why was the symbol of the Elemental Order of Fire emblazoned here? As far as he knew, Kirkwall wasn't dedicated to a particular element.

"I don't remember going through those," Wes said from behind him.

Vandermere half turned. "We didn't. Tanila, do you see anything like this on your map?"

She joined them with the sound of rustling paper. "There's many doors on here, but I don't see any emblems on the map."

He moved around to peer at the map over her shoulder. Most of the tunnels were straight passages with little curving or winding, much like they'd been traveling through. He narrowed his eyes as he found a straight part of the wall that looked similar to where they were standing. There were two doors marked on the map.

He placed his hand on the doors. "Think this could be it?"

"Maybe, it looks like it leads to old tunneling." Her finger trailed along a hall past the doors to where it intersected with a group of tunnels. "Though that part of the map seems unfinished."

"Old tunnels could lead to the city," Wes said. "It's a way out that would ensure we don't get caught."

"It's in the early hours of the morning," Tanila said. "How many could possibly be awake?"

"Depends on how long we've been down here, and how long it will take us to get out," Vandermere said. "We could arrive back in the upper floors as most are rising."

Wes looked to the doors. "This may be a better option."

"And if there isn't a way out?" Tanila asked.

"We can wait until nightfall and have Wes scout the temple," Vandermere said. "However, I'd rather not risk the temple tonight. We've already almost been caught."

"Fine," Tanila said. "Lead the way."

Vandermere pushed the door open. A wave of hot dry air hit his face from the hall beyond, stealing his breath for a moment. He took a step back, wiping the perspiration that beaded his face with his sleeve.

He glanced at Wes and Tanila. "Do either of you know if this church was connected to the Path of Fire?"

"It shouldn't be," Tanila said. "All my research indicates that all the Paths are practiced here equally."

"I wonder what else they are hiding down here," Vandermere said.

"We may find out." Tanila pushed past him and stepped into the tunnel.

She raised her lantern, revealing a hall similar to the one they had just come through. Vandermere glanced behind, took a deep breath, and joined her. Wes brought up the rear and shut the doors behind him.

He gave Vandermere a quick smile. "Wouldn't want anyone coming to investigate why the doors were open."

Vandermere nodded. "Alright, Tanila, let's at least go until the map ends."

She glanced at the paper and traveled ahead. Vandermere followed, side by side with Wes. They stopped where the bricks of the hall gave way to a hewn tunnel.

Tanila looked at the map and then looked back at them. With the nod, she turned right. In the dark of the tunnels, Vandermere lost sense of time. The tunnel went on endlessly. At last, it opened into a cavernous room. The air stood in a thick, white haze, obscuring the farthest wall. Vandermere's boots sank into the loose dirt as he stepped inside.

"This isn't on the map," Tanila said. "We reached the end a few turns ago."

"And you didn't say anything?" Wes asked with a huff.

"I was keeping track of what turn's we'd made," Tanila said.

"It might be a good idea to write them down." Vandermere said. "In case we need to go back."

Tanila nodded and pulled out a small pen from a pouch on her belt. As she scribbled on the map, Vandermere moved along the right side of the room while Wes inspected the left. Vandermere paused about three fourths of the way in. Two tunnels stood ahead, close to each other. The second had a wider mouth than the first and a faint orange glow seemed to brighten and dim from it. An uneasy feeling filled the pit of his stomach.

"Help…I…trapped…"

Vandermere started at the voice that drifted from the tunnel without the light. It sounded almost feminine and like fire at the same time.

"Release…"

He took a step forward. What had the Order trapped down here? Perhaps it had been the Path of Fire that had done so, thus their symbol. It could be another god, or a spirit. He frowned. It could also be a Sluagh.

"What are you doing?" Tanila called.

Vandermere turned her direction. "There's something here."

"A way out?" Wes appeared through the haze in the center of the room. "There's another tunnel over here."

"No," Vandermere said. "I think they bound something here."

Wes's gaze moved past him and his eyes grew wide as an intense heat suffused Vandermere's back.

"Look out!" Wes shouted.

Vandermere turned to look. An icy sensation crawled up his spine, despite the heat that filled the room.

A reptile creature emerged from the tunnel, so large that its sides scraped against the edges of the opening. Two eyes glowed like orange fire, dimming and brightening with each breath it took. The light reflected off dark, red scales along its muscular four-legged body.

Vandermere stared up at it as it towered over them. Now he knew what had been giving off the light.

"Great Empress." Tanila's face paled. "They have a fire drake down here."

The drake snorted and two tiny flames erupted from its snout. With a rumbling growl, it opened its maw and emitted a ball of flames that flew in the air towards Vandermere. Vandermere leapt to the side, but the flames caught his clothes. He hit the dirt and rolled, snuffing the flames.

The drake charged towards him. Tanila pulled out a pistol and fired at the creature. The booming echo filled the hall and the shot went wide, hitting the wall behind the drake.

The drake veered towards Tanila and snapped its large jaws at her, catching her in the side. Her screams burst through the cave.

Vandermere rolled to a crouching position, hopped to his feet, and drew his sword. A loud growl sounded to Vandermere's right. Before he could react, a large gray wolf leapt onto the back of the drake, clamping its jaw around the back of the creature's neck. Vandermere glanced towards the middle of the cavern in search of Wes and found a pile of clothes. The wolf had to be him.

The drake released Tanila and reared its head up with a roar, shaking side to side to dislodge the wolf. Wes's claws scraped against its scales as he lost his footing and went flying off. He landed a few feet away with a soft yelp.

Vandermere lunged forward and buried the point of his

sword into the rear flank of the drake. The creature gave him a baleful look and snapped its teeth.

"Wes, get Tanila and escape. I'll hold it off!" Vandermere shouted.

He straightened his shoulders and raised his sword. A multitude of regrets rose to his mind. He would never be able to find a cure for his House's madness. He would never reclaim his parents' house from his uncle. He would never see Lorelei again. Strange that was the one that stuck out the most. Still, if he was going to die here, at least it would be defending others.

Wes sprung to his feet and bounded over to Tanila, shifting from wolf to phooka form in the air. He landed with a grunt, scooped her up, and sprinted towards his clothing.

The drake glanced at Wes and Tanila. Vandermere jabbed the sword in its flank and the creature let out a low growl. It slammed its tail into Vandermere, catching him in his midriff. The air rushed from his lungs and he was knocked off his feet toward the center of the room. Pain flared as the burns on his arms and shoulders scraped against the stone.

Wes moved up beside Vandermere with a pistol in his hand. He raised it at the drake, now turned in their direction, and fired. Wes's bullet didn't miss. It stuck the creature in its right eye.

The drake let out a high-pitched screech and reared his head from side to side. It lowered its head on the ground and pawed at the wounded side of its face.

"Come on," Wes said, panting. "We should run."

Vandermere rose to his feet and nodded, following Wes to where he'd lain Tanila next to his clothes. Blood dripped from her into the cavern floor. Vandermere lifted Tanila up while Wes grabbed his clothes.

"Is there a way out not past that creature?" Vandermere asked.

Wes pointed to a tunnel ahead of them. "Hopefully it leads out."

Vandermere hurried behind Wes's naked form towards the tunnel. He spared one glance behind him as he reached the entrance. The drake's nostrils flared as it inhaled. Its head snapped their direction and it let out a growl.

"Run," Vandermere said in a low voice.

They took off down the tunnel. The hairs rose up on the back of Vandermere's neck as he focused his attention for the sounds of the creature pursuing them. Its roars and the scraping of stone grew fainter the further they ran. They came to a turn where the tunnel narrowed enough for one person to travel comfortably. The drake would have no chance of fitting through.

Vandermere staggered a few more feet and set Tanila down as Wes pulled on his clothing. She'd passed out sometime in their run. Her tan skin had taken on a pallor and her clothes around the wound were soaked dark blue with blood. There wasn't as much as he expected given the size of the drake's maw. He knelt beside her and gripped his knees as his hands began to tremble. He needed to stay calm. Tanila needed someone with a clear head if she was going to survive.

Gritting his teeth, he slid her blouse to the side. A row of puncture marks as wide as his fingers lined her shoulder, breast, and side in a semicircle. The edges of the wounds were charred, as if the drake's teeth had cauterized upon biting her.

"Is she going to be all right?" Wes leaned over him to inspect her.

Vandermere shook his head. "I don't know. Ironically enough, I wish Vaana were here."

Wes shrugged. "She does have her uses."

"We need to get her to a healer."

Wes snorted. "Another irony. The best healers in the city

are the ones above us...and they would wonder how she got injured."

"Where else can we take her?" Vandermere asked.

Wes scratched the back of his neck. "We could take her to the Twisted Root Tavern...There's a girl I know there that could patch her up. No magic, but she'll look after her."

Vandermere pulled his shirt off and ripped it in two. He wrapped the strips around Tanila's chest and abdomen. Once he was finished, he gently lifted her as he stood.

"Find us a way out then," Vandermere said.

With Wes leading the way, they traversed more of the tunnel. Vandermere had lost track of the time they had spent below the church. Weariness pricked behind his eyes like burning needles, but he pushed on.

Please let this be a way out, he prayed to whatever gods were listening.

Wes stopped at a large hole in the right wall and peeked his head through. His shoulders straightened and he looked back at Vandermere with a grin.

"Looks like sewers," he said. "These should connect with the rest of the city."

Vandermere raised his gaze to the ceiling with a soft groan. The god that answered appeared to have a cruel sense of humor.

He tilted his head at Tanila. "This isn't going to be good for her with the wet and the filth. Find us a way out as soon as possible."

"Wait here," Wes said. "I'll scout it out."

Wes's form shrank and his face elongated with fur and whiskers sprouting. In a few seconds, a small rat emerged from Wes's clothing and scurried through the hole.

Vandermere adjusted Tanila and rolled his neck side to side, wincing at the ache from his burn. He closed his eyes, trying to push the pain from his mind. Something else filled it instead.

Verdain's tower stands before him, smoking and smoldering. A large portion of the top is missing, though chunks of rock lay about in the clearing around the tower.

Order priests buzz around the towers in robes of red, white, blue, and green.

"Vandermere? Please don't tell me you're having one of your episodes," Wes's voice called.

Vandermere gasped and blinked as Wes's fingers snapped him out of the vision.

Wes raised his hands in a symbol of surrender. "Please say something."

"It's still me," Vandermere said. "We need to leave now... Lorelei is in danger."

"What about Tanila?"

Vandermere stared down at the woman in his arms. He had to get her help, but Lorelei needed him. He had a sense the vision was still in the future, but he had no idea how soon it would come to pass.

"Take her to your friend and I'll make for the ship and prepare it. I've learned a few things while traveling with you," Vandermere said. "Hurry."

Wes led their way through the sewers to a ladder that ascended to a small alley in the city. Vandermere passed Tanila, still unconscious, to Wes. Without further conversation, he rushed towards the harbor.

He hadn't seen Lorelei or Vaana in the vision. The ominous feeling in his stomach grew.

31

Lorelei looked out the window of the sitting room and sighed. Over two weeks had passed since Vandermere and Wes had left and there had been no word. She stared down at the book propped up on her knees and tried to concentrate on the words. After reading the same sentence several times but not comprehending anything, she closed the book with a groan.

Playing guard was starting to drive her crazy. She hated waiting. It didn't help that her eyes ached from the restless sleep she's gotten over the past week. Her nightmares had reared up with a vengeance. She stood and stretched, her gaze falling to the window again. Maybe a stroll around the tower would help.

She grabbed Murgleis off one of the stairs and strapped him to her belt as she strode to the foyer. She glanced at the storage door and bit her lip. Vaana should be all right for a short time. Before they had left, Wes and Vandermere had helped Lorelei make the storeroom a little more habitable, though Lorelei still let Vaana come out for short walks around the tower. Despite all she did, keeping her locked in the tiny room seemed cruel. She of course made sure Vaana's hands were bound and kept a close watch on her.

Should she let Vaana go outside with her now? She shook her head to herself. She didn't want to deal with a conversation with Vaana at this point.

She opened the front door and stepped outside. A sweet scent of lavender from the garden flitted on the air and she drew in a deep breath with a smile. Some of the tension that hung in her shoulders and neck lessened.

She ambled towards the garden with her hands behind her back and came to the stone wall. She turned and stared at the wall on the opposite side of the yard. It wasn't more than thirty paces from her. Even the cloister garden at the priory had been larger than that. Lorelei crossed her arms and gritted her teeth.

Damn Vandermere and Wes for leaving her here while they went into danger. Didn't they know how crazy it would drive her?

Murgleis's voice whispered through her mind. *You could always leave here on your own. We have a bargain, after all, to travel to Kurnach.*

"I'm not going to abandon my friends," Lorelei hissed. "And I haven't forgotten our bargain. We're not even near Kurnach."

Your friends seemed to have abandoned you.

"They haven't. They have a few more days. Besides, I can't leave Vaana locked up here alone."

Why not? Or set her free even?

Lorelei bit the inside of the cheek as an uneasy feeling grew in the pit of her stomach. Leave it to the Sluagh to try and convince her to take the selfish route. It suited him, after all.

No, she wouldn't be that selfish, or childish, to leave her friends because they had her stay behind. Besides, she wanted to learn the truth about Vaana and the Order as much as they did.

"No," Lorelei said. "They have less than a week. Then I go after them."

As Lorelei turned back to go inside, something large and hot flew over her head. It crashed into the tower with a deafening boom. The ground shook beneath her. She ducked as bits of rock rained down from above. Between her arms, her gaze lifted to the gaping hole in the top of the tower.

Whatever had hit it had come from behind her. The woods.

She twisted around. Three priests in colored robes with the symbols of the Elemental Order marched from the tree line towards the tower. One was dressed in the deep red of Fire, one in green for Earth, and one in white for Air.

Lorelei's heart raced as she rushed, crouching, towards the door of the tower. The danger of the moment mixed with the tiny spark of excitement that burst within her chest. Thoughts rushed through her mind, one after another.

They're here for Vaana. I have to get to her first. Finally, some action!

She was mere feet from the door when a flaming rock the size of her head came flying at her. She stopped short and ducked. The projectile hit the ground to her side. She stood back up, her heart skipping a beat.

The Earth priest, a phooka, stood at the gate with a circle of large stones floating around her. To her right, the white robed sidhe held his hand out, chanting as did the redcap Fire priest. Flame spewed from the redcap's hand and surrounded one of the stones. The Air priest pushed his hand out and the rock shot towards Lorelei.

She hopped back and the stone crashed into the ground at her feet with a burst of flame. Lorelei straightened her shoulders and drew in a deep breath. If they wanted to play at the elements, Lorelei could do that.

Her voice sang out through the air in a hard and fast tempo. With it, she reached out to the wind currents and summoned them to form a wall around her and the tower. The shrieking of the wind added to her song, creating counter melody that blended well with it.

The next rock they sent was caught in the wall, its flames dashed. It shot out and flew back at the priest. The Air priest's eyes widened and he tried to stop the momentum, but it was too fast. It hit him in chest and knocked him to the ground. He didn't move.

From behind the three, nine more priests came out of the wood line. Lorelei's eyes widened. She wouldn't be able to take all of them. She had to get Vaana.

Vaana would help.

Lorelei pushed the wind out towards the two standing priests. It ripped through the stone wall and the gate and crashed into them, knocking them back with the body of the Air priest. Lorelei rushed to the door, flung it open, and dashed to the storeroom.

Her fingers fumbled with the key and it took three tries until she was able to get it into the lock. She turned the key and yanked the door open.

Vaana stood in the center of the room with her brow furrowed. "What's happening?"

"Order priests," Lorelei said between gasps. "They've come for you."

"Looks like we're going to have to fight our way out," Vaana said. "Where are my weapons?"

Lorelei searched her memories. Where had they put Vaana's things?

She untied Vaana's bindings and raised her finger. "Kitchen!"

As she said the words, an explosion sounded from outside and above. The entire tower shook. It looked like they were back to throwing rocks. Vaana pushed past her and rushed into the sitting room.

"Try to keep the place from falling around us!" Vaana called from over her shoulder.

Lorelei sprinted to the wall near the door and pressed her hands against it. She sang a deep, slow melody as she connected with the stones of the tower. She imagined them as strong as a mountain. One whole instead of a building consisted of tiny pieces with cracks. A mountain could withstand this assault. The tower shook again, the stone trembling beneath Lorelei's hands. Tiny pebbles and debris fell from the ceiling.

Someone outside was countering her.

Lorelei dug her fingers in the rock as her song began to falter. She couldn't keep this up for much longer. The wind outside had cost her a large amount of Aether and this was a constant drain as well. She needed to reserve some for her escape.

Vaana burst from the sitting room with her backpack slung on her back and her daggers in hand.

Lorelei dropped the song and stepped back from the wall. "There are twenty of them out there. You really think you can fight all of them with daggers?"

Vaana smirked at her. "That's why you need to provide a distraction."

A second of doubt filled Lorelei. "You aren't going to leave me to them if you get a chance?"

Vaana gave her an unreadable look. "What choice do you have?"

The tower shook again, and Lorelei lifted her eyes to the ceiling. Vaana had a point. If she stayed here, she would probably be buried under a mountain of rubble.

"Fine." Lorelei pulled Murgleis from his sheath. "I'll try to open up a way out and we make a run for it."

Lorelei took the lead outside the door with Vaana behind her. This was a losing battle—they were sorely outnumbered—but she would go down fighting.

The priests stood in a semi-circle around the now broken wall of the tower. As she drew a deep breath, one of the white robed Air priests began chanting. They probably expected her to go with another wall of wind. A smirk lit her lip. She would surprise them all.

Instead of any particular element, her song dipped deep and called a frigid cold down on the group of priests. Puffs of steam exited their mouths as all began to gasp. Three of the priests—a Fire, Earth, and Air—dropped to the ground.

The Air priest's chanting shifted and it was joined by his fellow Air priests. Lorelei's control over the surrounding temperature began to slip. They were attempting to warm the area.

Instead of fighting them, Lorelei helped them. The air became hot and dry. The sudden shift hit the priests hard and the three remaining Air priests dropped to the ground along with two Water priests. Another, a green robed Earth priest, dropped to one knee, clutching his chest.

Five priests remained. Beads of sweat rolled down the phooka Water priest's face but his glare was fixed on Lorelei. A second Earth priest stood near his fellows with his shoulders straight. Two Fire priests stepped forward, the redcap wearing a grin. They didn't make another move. Were they waiting for their friends to get up?

Lorelei stopped her song and shouted to them, the command ringing in her voice. "I've taken more than half of you down in seconds. Leave now and you'll live through this day."

The Earth priest, an ankou, lifted his Earth companion up and began to back away. The redcap Fire priest and the phooka Water priest followed suit.

"Stop!" the remaining Fire priest, a sidhe, shouted.

Lorelei gritted her teeth. The priest had to have been of the same level of nobility as her. It had been worth a shot. She honestly didn't want to kill these people.

The red robed sidhe turned in her direction. "Heretic. Surrender yourself and turn over Vaana ap Aoife. If you do so, perhaps you will be granted leniency."

The authority washed over her, forcing her to her knees. He was of a higher standing than her. Her fists clenched. She'd always hated the feeling when her parents had used it on her as a child. She had a need inside her to obey, even though a tiny part in the back of her mind screamed defiance.

"Don't surrender." Vaana's voice called from inside the tower, ringing with command. "Stand up and fight for our freedom."

Lorelei stood and raised her sword, her heart pounding. Vaana had said her mother had been the head of House Aoife. By birth, Vaana outranked most sidhe. Lorelei narrowed her eyes at the Fire priest. Vaana stepped through the door.

"You were supposed to make an opening," Vaana muttered.

"Well, I created a distraction," Lorelei said. "I guess I got a little carried away."

"They didn't bring enough to take us in." Vaana looked over the priests, who seemed to be uncertain whether they should attack. "You heard my friend Lorelei. Turn around and go back to your temples. Stop hunting me."

"Oh, Vaana, that's not going to happen," a familiar voice called from around the side of the tower.

Beth swaggered into view, flanked by two phooka dressed similar to her in dark leather armor. Lorelei's chest tightened. Order assassins, like Vaana had been. It seemed the Order had gone all out in bringing them in.

Lorelei spared a glance to the side. Still caught in Vaana's command, the priests were retreating into the woods, leaving their fallen behind.

Lorelei turned back to Beth with a smirk. "You lost to us last time and now you've lost your support. You really think you can take us?"

Beth waved her hand dismissively at the priests. "They were just the distraction. Fodder, really. Which, I must say, you handled excellently. I now see why the Apostle chose you. She even planned to convince you to join the Order under her. Pity you threw it all away."

Lorelei's lips pressed into a thin line. "I never intended to join the Order."

"Wait," Vaana said in a cool tone. "Distraction for what?"

"Oh, Vaana," Beth said in an oddly sad voice. "Why did you betray us? Why did you turn you back on the Empress? On Apostle Evangeline?"

"I didn't turn my back on the Empress..." Vaana said testily. "And you are stalling."

A chill ran down Lorelei's spine. Vaana was right. The last time they encountered Beth, she didn't waste much time talking. Lorelei scanned the area in search of a trap. The priests had all but disappeared, their forms now shadowy flickers between the trees. Were they planning something?

Beth's gaze rose to the tower behind them and she grinned. The sound of whistling filled the air, like something falling fast. Lorelei lifted her gaze and her eyes widened. Her heart skipped a beat. Two figures descended upon them, propelling down the side of the tower.

The figures landed, the ground shaking under them, and

rose to stand tall. They towered over Lorelei and Vaana. The metallic stench of iron wafted from them, sending Lorelei's stomach roiling. These were of no race she could identify. Their skin was as pale as an ankou but they had no wings, and their ears were rounded. No faerie had rounded ears.

Iron pieces replaced the right eyebrow, cheek, and jaw of the creature on the left. How could that even be possible? The skin around the metal should have deadened and turned black, yet it was just as pale as the rest of her.

Golems. The word echoed in Lorelei's thoughts. Ilia, her friend from school, had told her about them when they had traveled to the depths of the Citadel of Night. The golem there had been working for the Shadow Court. And these, the Order.

Look out! Murgleis's voice rang through her mind.

The golem with the iron face rushed forward. A blade folded out from her forearm, made of grim dark iron. She thrust her arm forward and buried the blade into Lorelei's abdomen. The breath vanished from Lorelei as she doubled over. Her skin felt cold even as a burning sensation raced through her veins.

Clutching her stomach, Lorelei took two steps back from the golem, drew in a gasping breath, and began to sing. Her voice came out unsteady, broken. She concentrated on calling the air for one strong wind gust that would knock this creature, Beth, and the two phooka down.

The smooth faced golem on Lorelei's right waved her hand and the wind shifted to her direction. The gust hit the golem full on, sending her flying. The golem's back slammed into the side of the tower. Lorelei gulped. The creature had just reverted the attack upon herself.

Beth sneered at Lorelei as she drew her blades. In a blur of movement, she rushed past Lorelei to Vaana. Lorelei turned her head in time to see a flash of metal followed by a clang. One of Beth's blades flew from her hand and hit the ground a few feet away.

"You seem to be worse than when we were training together." Vaana's voice held a hint of snide satisfaction. "Or I've gotten better."

"It's because of that heretical power inside you." Beth hissed, and the last words seemed to go on forever in Lorelei's mind. "Don't worry, we have something for that."

The world seemed to slow down around Lorelei, blurring and taking on a gray color around the edges. The two phookas she'd brought with her had pulled out crossbows at some point. They fired simultaneously. Green electricity raced across the bolts as they flew past Lorelei to Vaana.

Vaana leapt backwards, and they hit the ground.

She raised her head and said something, but Lorelei could not make out the words. Sound had become muted and slowed, even her own song. She was so hot. Sweat rolled down her forehead and neck in waves.

"Murgleis." Was she speaking or thinking? "I'm dying, aren't I?"

That wound would be deadly even if given by a normal blade.

Murgleis didn't say it but she knew what he was inferring. With the iron, her death was assured. A cold feeling formed in the pit of her stomach. She fell to her knees. All around her the sounds of battle continues.

A shadow passed over her.

Help me. Please. I don't want to die. Tears pricked at the edges of her eyes as she clutched her stomach.

She wasn't ready. She had so much she hadn't done.

There is only one way I can save you.

At this point she didn't even care what it was. "Do it."

She felt Murgleis push her consciousness aside and take control of her body. *Rest now.*

As the world faded to darkness, Vaana's scream rang out.

32

Vandermere raced through the trees, the branches whipping at his face. Wes was just a few feet behind him. They'd used every sailing trick Wes knew to speed up their journey back to the tower. Traveling downriver helped as well. Vandermere sent a silent prayer to any god listening that they would make it in time.

The sounds of a battle drifted from ahead of them. Vandermere's heart sped up. Silhouettes moved through the trees ahead. Vandermere slowed his pace and motioned for Wes to stop. He slipped behind a tree and peeked out around the side.

Four Order priests in their colored robes trudged towards them. The green-robed Earth priest carried another of his path in his arms. Their faces held expressions of loss. Had the battle already been fought?

No, there were still sounds of clanging metal and shouts in the directions of the tower. Why were these priests leaving?

One of the red-robed priests, a sidhe, jerked his head in their direction. His eyes narrowed as he searched.

Vandermere pulled his head back behind the tree and rested his hand on the pommel of one of the swords he'd gotten from the ship to replace the one he'd lost in the tunnels under the church.

"Halt," the sidhe priest called in an imperious voice. "Someone is here. Spread out."

Vandermere glanced in Wes's direction and nodded as the sounds of footsteps on fallen branches drew closer. Just a few more moments and the priests would be upon them. Vandermere sucked in a quiet breath and waited, counting silently.

The priests were mere feet away. They would see him any minute now.

He drew his sword and twisted around the tree, slashing at the priests. His blade hit the arm of the green robed priest, slicing into the fabric of his sleeve, but rebounded with a spark and the sound of metal on stone. Vandermere muttered a curse under his breath. The damn earth priest had turned his skin to rock.

The priest's right arm shot out in a backhand that caught Vandermere in the chest. He stumbled backwards as his breath whooshed out of him. His hand gripped his sword to keep from losing it and he steadied himself. His whole chest throbbed. The brute Earth priest had barely made an effort with that. Vandermere needed to be careful; one solid hit would break bones.

The boom of a pistol echoed through the trees followed by a male cry. Wes stood several feet away with his smoking pistol tilted in the air. One of the Fire priests knelt, holding his chest. He turned with wide eyes.

"Drop your weapon and surrender," he barked at Wes.

Wes lowered his gun.

"No!" Vandermere shouted, putting the force of command in it. "Don't surrender. We need to get to Lorelei!"

Wes shook his head as if coming out of a stupor. His eyes

narrowed and he snarled at the Fire priest, then reloaded his pistol.

The priest glanced at Vandermere with a mixture of incredulousness and annoyance. "By the Goddess, why are there so many of you high-ranking nobles here! What has made you turn to heresy?"

"Perhaps you should ask your Order why it's considered heresy," Vandermere shot back.

The Earth priest swung a fist at him, ending the conversation. Vandermere ducked to the side and put a tree between him and the priest.

Three priests were accounted for. What about the others?

He scanned the trees.

There. Where the trees split apart, the blue robed priest knelt by the unconscious Earth priest. That made sense. With barely any water except for perhaps what the priest carried on him, there was little use for the Water priest except for healing. That did mean, though, the priest could get his fallen companions up.

It might be best to take this one out first, then worry about the others. The idea of striking down an unarmed opponent left a sour taste in his mouth. He wouldn't kill this person.

Vandermere dashed through the trees at the Water priest. He turned, eyes going wide. Vandermere raised his sword and smashed the pommel into his face. The priest crumpled to the ground.

"How dishonorable! What kind of sidhe are you?" the Fire priest exclaimed.

"He's still alive," Vandermere shot back. "That can remain the case for all of you if you retreat to your ships with your wounded. Let us pass to the tower unimpeded."

The Fire priest's gaze shifted from Vandermere to the

fallen priest beside him, then to the direction of the tower where the sounds of combat drifted.

"We can take them," the Earth priest rumbled. "At least we will have two."

"No, you can't," Wes growled.

His skin shifted and rippled as he began to grow three times his size. The seams of his clothing split when it could no longer fit on his body and fell to the ground in tatters. Within seconds, a giant black bear stood on his hind legs and let out a roar.

Both the Earth priest and the Fire priest took steps back.

"We have no qualms with you personally," Vandermere said. "Just with your superiors."

The Fire priest pressed his lips together as he stared up at the bear. A vein throbbed in his temple in a bluish hue.

"Stand down," he called to the Earth priest. "Let them pass. Beth and her retinue can deal with these two. I doubt they will be much trouble for her."

With that, he knelt by the Fire priest who was still holding his chest, trying to staunch the bleeding. The Earth priest cast an icy look at Vandermere and pointed to the unconscious priests beside him. Vandermere stepped back away from them and nodded to Wes. As the Earth priest rose and stomped to his companions, Vandermere and Wes took off in sprints towards the tower.

Vandermere hoped they weren't too late.

The sight of the clearing made him stop short. Priests of all four orders lay strewn across the grounds in front of the gate. Beyond the gate, Lorelei fought a pale skinned female with metal on her face.

An ill feeling filled Vandermere's chest. Something was off about the female. She didn't quite look faerie and the dark metal on her face—was that iron? A chill raced up his spine as the female brought her blade, also iron, down upon Lorelei.

In a flash of green, Lorelei swung Murgleis in an upward motion and parried the blade. He'd never seen Lorelei move so fluidly. It was as if she and the blade were one. And why wasn't she singing?

The female spun and brought her sword to Lorelei in backward slash. Lorelei darted to the side and met the blade with Murgleis again. This time, the iron sword of the female was ripped from her hand and flew into the air. In a blur of motion and light, Lorelei brought Murgleis down and across the female's neck, decapitating her. The female's body dropped to the ground.

Vandermere found his voice. "Lorelei!"

She turned his direction, her eyes glowing with an eerie green light. A smirk lighted on her lips as she tilted her head at him.

That wasn't Lorelei.

"Quickly," the thing in Lorelei said in her voice. "You should find a way to save her. She doesn't have much time and my way wouldn't benefit either of us."

With those words, she closed her eyes and collapsed to the ground.

❧

Vandermere rushed through the gate and to Lorelei. All the time, fear built up within him. She lay on her side with one arm flung out in front of her. Murgleis was still clutched in her fist. Vandermere knelt and rolled her onto her back. Coldness crept through him as the sight of her blood-soaked abdomen.

Please let this be from a different sword and not the iron sword that female thing had been wielding, he prayed.

He pulled aside the cloth of her shirt and sucked in a gasp. Her skin had already started to gray around the wound.

Dark lines extended from the wound in a spider web pattern across her stomach.

He turned his head back to Wes. "Check the tower and see if there is anything to fight iron poisoning." As an afterthought, he added, "Find me Vaana, damnit."

He returned his attention to Lorelei as Wes began to shift back to his phooka form. Vandermere ripped her blouse apart to get better access to her wound. The least he could do is try to staunch the flow of blood. By the amount soaked in her clothes and the pallor of her skin, she'd been bleeding out for some time. Why had she let it get this bad?

She hadn't been in control of herself.

A chill filled him as his gaze fell upon Murgleis, still in her unconscious grip. Had the Sluagh taken her over and led to the wound?

He swore under his breath. "I'm sorry. I should have pushed you more to abandon that damn sword."

"On the contrary," a feminine voice said behind him. "If you had, the girl would already be dead."

Vandermere turned, still kneeling by Lorelei. A copper-skinned female stood at the gates. She wasn't a faerie. None of the races had four arms. The bottom two she held behind her back as the top two crossed over her chest. She would have towered over him even if he'd been standing. Her hair seemed to be made of a pale metal though it flowed with an unnatural movement, like a wind that wasn't there. In the center of her forehead, a viridian gem glowed.

She tilted her head as she looked at Lorelei. "As much time as my dear Murgleis has given her, her life force is all but gone."

Vandermere narrowed his eyes at her. "Who are you?"

"The answer to your prayer." She gave him a smile that glinted in the sun. "You called and I heard. And since my

Murgleis was here, I decided to come and see what is so special about this girl. She's not very impressive looking."

"She's dying," Vandermere said through gritted teeth. "And I didn't pray to you."

"You didn't pray to anyone in particular. You should be careful of that." Her voice softened. "All can hear such prayers. You never know who will answer."

"Like you?"

"Indeed."

"What is your name?"

She smiled. "You may call me Abraxes."

A chill ran through Vandermere's spine. Lorelei had read through some of the books she found on the Sluagh. He thought he remembered her mentioning a connection between Murgleis and a Sluagh named Abraxes.

He straightened his shoulders. "And what can you do to help her?"

"The iron will kill her and her soul will be lost." Abraxes took two steps closer. "However, I have claim due to the bargains she made with my Murgleis. All I have to do is kill her and take her soul. I can craft her into something new. One of my children."

"No!" Vandermere rose to his feet and drew his sword. He would be damned is he let a Sluagh turn Lorelei into one of them.

Abraxes crossed all four of her arms in front of her chest. "Then she dies and you lose her forever."

"Not yet," Amara's voice drifted on the wind.

From the gloom of the doorway, Amara materialized and stepped outside. She leaned against the wall of the tower next to the doorway. Wes stood a few feet away with his mouth agape.

Abraxes shot Amara a glare and took another step forward.

"Back off, Abraxes," Amara said. "She is mine."

Abraxes stopped and her face stretched into an odd smile. "This is a surprise. You've been gone for so long, we thought you lost."

Vandermere blinked. Did this mean Amara was indeed a Sluagh? Even if she was, he trusted her more at this point than the others. With a shake of his head, Wes stepped back into the tower. He at least was smart enough not to get in between two Sluagh.

"I was found. So, you can spread new rumors of my return." Amara marched over to Lorelei and knelt beside her. "As for the girl, I claim her."

"I already have a claim," Abraxes said. "My Murgleis has ensured that. We can fight for her soul."

"No." Vandermere stood, allowing more room for Amara, and faced Abraxes. "Lorelei will still be dying as you two battle it out. What would it take to release your claim?"

Behind him, Amara whispered over Lorelei. He wanted to turn to make sure she was being healed, but he wouldn't turn his back on Abraxes.

"Amara, don't you dare. We have not come to an agreement." Abraxes tilted her head as she studied Vandermere. "You are an Essus, yes? One of the prophets?"

"I am."

"Then give me a vision. And nothing small...Tell me something major...something secret."

Vandermere gritted his teeth as she grinned at him. Such a vision would surely bring the Shadow upon him. Did she know that? It seemed as if she was egging him on just for that purpose.

He stared down at Lorelei. She was deathly pale against the green grass. Amara's hands hovered over the wound with a slight glow.

"I can hold off more bleeding, but not for long," she said softly. "You need to make a decision on this."

Vandermere nodded to her as much as to himself. Lorelei was worth it. For her, he could endure the madness that came.

He turned back to Abraxes. "Very well. I agree. But you will allow Amara to heal Lorelei now."

"Done." She nodded and spread her arms out. "Do you need anything? A dark room, soft cushions, incense, perhaps?"

"No." Vandermere strode forward and sat in the front of her with his legs crossed under him. "This place will work and the sooner this is finished, the better."

He rested his hands on his knees and closed his eyes, reaching for that part inside himself that was so tantalizing. The ability to know.

Everything faded away except for that part.

Vandermere floats bodiless in darkness as the world shifts around him. His heart pounds as he feels the Shadow encroaching on his mind. He needs to hold it off for a short time. Everything spins and there is a flash of light.

The silhouette of a woman stands before a portal of brilliant pulsing light, arms raised towards it as she is consumed from the inside by boiling pitch.

Flash.

A brightly burning amethyst star shoots downward from the night sky, briefly illuminating a fleet of warships on the ocean before crashing into the water.

Flash.

A man awakens from a nightmare and screams silently as he is consumed by flickering shadows. In a burst of light, the shadows are driven away, but the man is now only a translucent image floating above his gnawed remains.

Flash.

From the roiling sea, a burst of steam shoots forth a massive iron tower that twists itself into the night sky, rending it like a spear would pierce flesh.

Flash.

A woman uncovers a dusty box in a long-forgotten tomb. As she slides open the stone lid of the box, the look of wonder is replaced with agony as thin iron tendrils pierce her cheeks and forehead and begin wriggling through her veins. She rips the iron from her face and then slides the box lid shut.

Flash.

Howls of agony fill the air as a monstrously large, thorn vine winds its way up and around the iron tower, drinking the blood that pours from the wounded sky.

Flash.

A librarian almost finishes cataloging his books before turning to a gold leafed tome with the crescent moon on it. As he lays his hands upon the book, seven eyes open within the crescent and, enraptured, the man does not notice as his library burns down around him. In the last moment, he blinks and the eyes on the book are replaced with his own.

Flash.

The thorny vines reach their apex and bloom into a blood-colored rose from the petals of which emerge a monstrous snake that begins to devour the rose and wind its way back down the iron tower.

Flash.

A single ship on the ocean burns with green Sluagh-fire as a battle rages onboard. The ship sails into the horizon before it explodes in a flash of greenish light.

Flash.

The cries of agony are replaced with shouts of triumph as the serpent makes its descent.

Flash.

A golem made of quciksilver is beaten in an iron forge. Its cries sound almost faerie-like. In a final attempt to free itself, one hand reaches outward and strangles its forger. It then claws its broken form out of the forge and into the night.

Flash.

The lights in the top of the iron tower come to life, burning a fierce unwholesome red.

Flash.

A lone figure writes furiously in a book, then closes it and tosses it into the standing portal of brilliant pulsing light.

33

Light. It blared just behind Lorelei's closed eyelids, dragging her from the depths of unconsciousness. Her eyes fluttered open. A blurry shape formed in the light. After several blinks, her vision cleared and she found Amara leaning over her. The sky was bright that Lorelei had to squint to look at her.

Amara's face had a wan look to it with shadows under her eyes. Relief filled her smile as she gazed down at Lorelei.

Memories of what had happened flooded Lorelei's mind. She tried to sit up and winced at the sharp pain in her stomach. She lay back with a groan.

"No sudden movements," Amara said. "It took much Aether to heal the wound, and it will still take you time to recover."

"Vaana?" Lorelei croaked.

Amara shook her head. "You have more pressing things. Vandermere has made a deal for your life."

"You forced him to make a deal?"

"Not me." Amara nodded to Murgleis on the ground

several feet away. "There are consequences to wielding him, as you know."

She gazed towards the gate and Lorelei followed that direction. A four-armed female stood over Vandermere as he sat with his head bowed.

"Who is that? And what has he done?"

Murgleis answered the first question. *My creator. Abraxes.*

Lorelei sucked in a short breath. She'd read a bit about Abraxes from the books she'd confiscated from Zaos's manse. Abraxes was the great Forger who took souls and created new Sluagh that filled the Demon City. Long ago, when Threshold was young, she forged Murgleis to claim more souls for her.

Why is she here? She sent the thought to Murgleis with demanding feeling. He needed to answer her.

She has a claim on you through me. My...assistance comes at a price. Every time you called upon me, there has been a price. Saving you from iron allowed me to claim your soul...for her.

Lorelei gritted her teeth. *And you neglected to tell me until now?*

I have allowed the price to be taken by the lives you claimed. And yes, I kept it from you. Telling you would have impeded on my goals. I am Sluagh after all.

Lorelei drew in a breath and tried to quash rage growing in the pit of her stomach. She'd been warned that Sluagh were treacherous. This is what Amara had meant. Vandermere had made some sort of trade.

Lorelei drew a deep breath and sat up with a soft groan. Amara leaned back with a frown.

"What deal did he make?" Lorelei whispered to Amara fiercely.

"A vision for her to release her claim on you."

"But that could drive him mad."

Lorelei glanced back to Abraxes and Vandermere, wincing

at the twinge in her stomach. Would she be crippled as Arryn had been? That was a bit of justice.

"It most likely will...but you can help with that, can't you?"

Lorelei closed her eyes and began to sing a soft song. Abraxes's eyes flashed to her and narrowed. Amara stood up, glowing white.

"You specified a vision, nothing else," Amara said. "Let the girl sing."

"Very well," Abraxes muttered.

Lorelei reached out with her song, willing it to surround Vandermere, to stave off any madness that would come to him. The tension in his shoulders relaxed and he inhaled. Minutes passed. Then, he shook his head and climbed to his feet. Without a word, he turned from Abraxes. His gaze fell on Lorelei, and the creases in his forehead smoothed. He rushed to her and, stooping, pulled her into a tight embrace.

"I thought I lost you," he murmured in her ear.

She gave a weak chuckle. "I'm harder to kill than that."

"No joking," Vandermere released her, but held onto her hand. "You almost died."

Lorelei pressed her lips together and nodded. Her gaze landed on the fallen body of the golem with the iron face. If it hadn't had been for Murgleis, she would have succumbed to the iron poisoning long before defeating it. One of the two phookas who came with Beth lay a few feet away as did the second golem. There was no sign of the other assassin...or Beth...or Vaana.

Abraxes cleared her throat. "I believe we have a bargain you need to fulfill."

Vandermere nodded and turned her direction. "We do."

"Well?"

Vandermere's chest rose and he closed his eyes. "There

was a woman who opened a door of some sort. I believe she brought the Miasma long ago."

Abraxes crossed all four of her arms. "That's old news, not a secret."

"It is to me," Lorelei said.

"Of course. You are an ignorant girl," Abraxes said.

Lorelei gritted her teeth and took a stand. Amara grabbed her arm, shaking her head. Abraxes crossed her arms, watching Lorelei for a moment, and then threw her head back and laughed.

"My, aren't you a bold one? I see why Murgleis likes you." Abraxes turned her attention back to Vandermere. "Is that all you have? Say it is so, because I would like to claim this girl."

"No." Vandermere's voice took on a throaty edge. "There is more...A librarian and a book with a crescent moon. It has seven eyes that open. His eyes replace those on the book."

Abraxes's eyebrow twitched. "That's more interesting. Any idea where this book is?"

"No, there was no location. Though I think it may have been thrown into some portal. White light."

"Pity," Abraxes said.

"There is one more thing." Vandermere raised his gaze to her. "This felt like it has not happened yet. There is a ship burning with the green fire of the Sluagh as a battle rages on its decks. It sails into the horizon and explodes."

"Any idea of who the Sluagh was?" Abraxes asked.

"No." Vandermere pointed to the viridian jewel in her forehead. "But the explosion reminded me of your gem."

"Interesting." Abraxes nodded, smile settling on her lips. "Consider this bargain complete. I release my claim upon Lorelei." She held out her hand. "Come, Murgleis."

The sword shuddered on the ground where Lorelei had left it. Lorelei pressed her lips together. She should let Murgleis go with Abraxes. He'd saved her though, even with the cost. Also, she didn't like the idea of Murgleis being used for whatever plans Abraxes had. With Murgleis with Lorelei, she could watch him.

"Wait," Lorelei said. She pulled away from Vandermere and scooped up Murgleis. "I made him a bargain. And it isn't complete."

Abraxes raised an eyebrow. "My, you are a glutton for punishment."

"You can't be serious," Vandermere burst out. "After everything that just happened?"

"You nearly lost your soul to Abraxes," Amara added. "You can't possibly be considering carry that thing any longer."

Lorelei stared down at the pommel of the sword. *Do you wish to go with her or do you still want to return to Kurnach?*

There was a moment of silence before Murgleis's voice filled the air. "I will remain with Lorelei ap Moura until she has brought me to Kurnach."

Vandermere jumped, jerking around to look at the sword. Amara shook her head and, throwing her hands out, turned to stride into the tower. A scowl fell over Abraxes' face.

"You can't be serious," she muttered. "Still mourning that boy from so long ago. I liked you better as my Harvester of the Fallen."

"I have changed, as we all do," Murgleis said. "And a bargain had been struck. Until our terms have been satisfied, I will remain with Lorelei."

Abraxes let out a breath in a short huff and stood up straight. Her gaze narrowed on Lorelei and the smile returned.

"Very well, you may keep my Murgleis," she said. "Who knows, you may be mine yet."

With that she vanished in a burst of viridian light, leaving behind the smell of hot metal.

Lorelei turned to Vandermere. "I will be more careful

next time."

Vandermere shook his head. "I don't understand this. Why keep that thing when your soul is in danger? All I just did will be for nothing."

Lorelei bowed her head. "It's hard to explain...his loss is something I can relate to..."

Vandermere gripped her shoulders and pulled her to face him. "I don't understand it and I don't agree with it. You are worth a thousand of him, and I don't want to lose you."

Lorelei's heart pounded at being so close to him. "Please trust me on this. He can be a valuable ally, and compared to the Order, we are very lacking in those."

For several moments, Vandermere stood there, staring at her with an intensity she had never seen before—on anyone. She could hear the blood rushing through her ears. Was he going to kiss her? Was she even ready for such a thing? He closed his eyes and let out a deep breath, releasing his grip on her. He took a step back and rubbed his face with his hand.

"All right," he said. "I do trust you. Just don't make any more bargains with him."

"I'll try not to," Lorelei said.

Wes rushed outside from the tower and threw his arms around Lorelei. "I'm so glad you're safe."

She laughed and hugged him back. Amara stepped out of the tower and leaned against it with her arms crossed. Her eyes narrowed on Murgleis and her jaw stiffened.

She punched her arm. "Don't do something crazy like that again."

"I'll try to remember not to get caught by a large attack on the place I'm living," Lorelei said.

"What happened, anyway?" Vandermere asked. "And where is Vaana?"

Lorelei took a deep breath. "Let's go inside. It's a long story."

Lorelei finished retelling them the events of the battle and leaned back in the chair of the sitting room.

Even though Amara had healed her, she still ached. She ran her fingers along her abdomen. A long thin scar stretched across her stomach that she would keep until the end of her days, though Amara assured her that it shouldn't impede on her ability to move once she'd recovered.

Vandermere sat across from her with his fingers steepled and his elbows resting on the arms of the chair. Wes slouched in another chair next to her and Amara hovered near the window, staring out through the trees.

"How did they even know to come out here?" Vandermere mused out loud.

Lorelei bit the inside of her cheek and stared down at her hands. "I've been thinking on that. A few days before it happened, I was contacted by my sister. I think she used the contact to learn my location."

"And she gave it to the Order?" Wes snorted. "What a bitch."

"Freya has always had a problem with me. I never thought she would go this far." Lorelei closed her eyes with a sigh. "She probably convinced herself she was doing the right thing."

Lorelei gulped down the rising ache in her chest that threatened to steal her breath. Why did her sister's actions always hurt her so much?

"So, are you sure this Beth took Vaana?" Wes was quick to change the subject.

"I didn't see it happen," Lorelei said. "But they are not here, so Beth has most likely taken her back to the Order. We need to get her."

"Why?" Wes turned to Vandermere. "I mean...you don't

owe her anything, except vengeance for your Lord of Fate."

Vandermere rubbed the medallion hanging from his neck, lost in thought. He sighed heavily. "From what we learned on our trip to the church, well, underneath it, I don't think it's a good idea for Vaana to remain in her hands."

"Despite what she's done, Vaana was with us for a long time," Lorelei said. "She aided us and fought by our side in Ebonshire. She saved your life, Vandermere, and she didn't have to."

Vandermere bowed his head. "So...how do we save her?"

"If the Order took here, wouldn't they return to Kirkwall?" Lorelei said.

"Kirkwall is dangerous for you," Amara said. "If they returned there, they may be expecting a retaliation."

"They probably think I'm dead," Lorelei shrugged.

Amara pointed outside. "Not if their projects don't return."

"Golems," Lorelei closed her eyes as a shudder ran through her. "I believe they're called golems."

Amara smirked at her. "I'm aware."

"You know about them?" Wes asked. "Well, you could have saved us a trip under that damn church."

"I came across one when I was in school... Well, when I was out on an unauthorized outing." Lorelei tapped her fingers against the arm of the chair. "She had been part of a group known as the Black Herons. I didn't know they were connected to the Order, though. And Vaana's not one of them. What did you learn?"

"Someone at the church in Kirkwall is creating them," Wes kicked one leg over the arm of his chair.

"Or experimenting with them," Vandermere leaned forward and rested his hands on his steepled fingers. "Same with Vaana."

"But Vaana isn't a golem," Lorelei said. "She's sidhe."

"I don't know," Vandermere said. "It looks like they took her as a child and performed some sort of methods that made her capable of housing the essence of gods."

"Why, though?" Lorelei asked.

"That's something we weren't able to find out," Vandermere said.

"We need to," Lorelei adjusted in her seat and winced at the tightness in her stomach. "And we need to get Vaana back."

"How are we going to do that?" Wes asked. "And what do you plan to do with her once you do get her back?"

"We'll figure the second out when we get to it," Lorelei said. "As for the first, how did you find out about the experiments?"

Wes cleared his throat and sat up. "Someone led us into a secret area under the church.

"Can you find your way back? Or can this person help again?"

Vandermere shuddered, and Wes paled slightly.

Vandermere cleared his throat. "The lady unfortunately was injured. I don't think she'll be able to help. And the way is guarded by a creature...a drake."

"Drakes aren't that much of an issue," Amara said. "There are probably some things here that can put it to sleep. What type?"

"A fire drake." Vandermere stared down at the medallion in his hand for several moments and then added, "Verdain says there should be supplies to create a sleep dust for it."

"Good. Can he guide you through concocting it?" Amara asked.

Vandermere raised an eyebrow at the medallion and then nodded.

Amara straightened in her seat. "Next, we're going to need a distraction for the guards of the city."

"We?" Lorelei asked with a scowl.

"You said the golem you met was part of the Black Herons? Zaos was too, correct?"

Lorelei nodded.

"Then, I'm coming with you. This is my best chance to get into the church to find him, and besides, I'm not letting you run into danger so soon after nearly dying."

"You seem very worried about me," Lorelei said. "This goes beyond freeing me. I mean, you saved my life. We should be even."

Amara gave her a long sad smile. "One day, I will tell you why. For now, let's worry about getting into Kirkwall and rescuing your friend."

"Not our friend," Vandermere's hand sliced through the air horizontally in a swift motion. "A tool we don't wish to see in the hands of the Order."

Lorelei pursed her lips at him. "My friend."

Vandermere shook his head and stood up. "You shouldn't waste such words on her. I'll see to working on the sleeping dust."

With that, he strode out of the room. Lorelei stared after him, biting the inside of her cheek. She needed to find a way to reconcile Vaana and Vandermere. Even in the beginning, he had said they would be together on this journey for a while. He was letting his anger blind him from the truth he should have been able to see the most. They needed each other.

Amara touched her arm. "Worry about it later. We need to plan."

With a nod, Lorelei pushed those concerns away. She needed to worry about getting in and out of Kirkwall with Vaana.

They had a city full of elemental-wielding priests to contend with.

34

They moored the Winddancer in an inlet near Kirkwall and snuck through the gates when the moon was high in the sky. Wes led the way to an entrance to the sewers.

Lorelei wrinkled her nose at the stench that rose from beneath the ground. She sucked in a deep breath and held it as she climbed down behind Vandermere. They followed Wes through a series of tunnels until he stopped at a large hole in the sewer wall.

The roughhewn walls and ground held a slight dampness, but nothing compared to the refuse of the sewers. She climbed through, strode several feet away from the sewers, and drew in a deep breath. The air still held a faint stench, but it didn't permeate everything.

Vandermere came up behind her. "You shouldn't wander too far. This place is like a maze."

She turned to him. "But you know the way?"

"I remember." Wes approached with Amara in tow.

"I hope you remember the way to this room with the tables and golems as well," Amara said. "I wish to see it."

"We're going to have to pass it to get to the stairs. It shouldn't be a problem." Wes pulled out a torn and bloodied map. "Besides, I borrowed this from Tanila."

"Tanila?" Lorelei asked. "Is that the person who helped you?"

"Yes." Vandermere peered into the gloom of the tunnels ahead of them. "I hope she's recovered."

"My people are doing what they can." Wes opened the map and inspected it. "We're going to have to pass through the room with the drake to get to the other tunnels. From there we make our way to the double doors."

"This place really is like a maze." Lorelei turned to Vandermere. "I know it may be a bit much, but will you be able to see where they are holding Vaana?"

Vandermere let out a sigh. "When I tried before, I got a sense of darkness and movement. I believe they were still on the move."

Lorelei bit the inside of her cheek. "That was days ago, right? You can try again now that we're here?"

"I might be able to make a stronger connection at the table. I had a vision of her there."

Lorelei unsheathed Murgleis and nodded. "Great. Let's deal with this drake first."

Vandermere pulled out a small glass bottle with a pink dust inside and held it out to Wes. "I think your aim is the best. Stand back and toss it at the drake when it unleashes its fiery breath. The ingredients should react with the fire and cause an effect to put the drake to sleep."

Wes cut his eyes at Amara. "Can't you just put the thing to sleep?"

Amara let out a sigh. "If I use too much of my power, I fear it will draw the priests' attention. Then we'd have the whole church after us."

"Why are you here then?" Wes asked.

In a blur of movement, Amara dashed to Wes and snatched the bottle from his hand. He teetered back, caught off balance.

She held out the bottle in front of him. "I'm still quick and I'm still capable of fighting, if needed. Besides, I can shift into anything, including a bright-eyed priest."

Wes's shoulders slumped as he took the bottle from her. "Now, I'm wondering why I'm needed."

She patted him on the shoulder. "You're the bottle thrower and more importantly, the map bearer. So, lead the way."

With a sigh, he pointed to the hall behind them and then started toward it. Vandermere followed after him, with Lorelei in the middle and Amara bringing up the rear. Lorelei slowed until she was walking side by side with Amara.

"You probably shouldn't tease him," Lorelei whispered to Amara. "I think he feels like he's out of his depth."

"But it's fun," Amara murmured. "And besides, he *is* out of his depth with the lot of you. It's actually admirable that he chooses to stay, considering the trouble you get yourselves into."

"He wants vengeance on Zaos," Lorelei said. "For Ebonshire."

"Hmm," Amara said. "Venerable, but it will probably get him killed. You should have him return to his people."

Lorelei flashed her a frown. "Are you suggesting I command him to do so?"

"It's what your people do," Amara said. "And if it saves his life..."

Lorelei gritted her teeth and sped up. She liked Wes, even considered him a friend. It seemed wrong to force him to leave when he didn't want to. During their talk, she'd let Wes and Vandermere move farther ahead. They'd paused at a large opening and were staring back at her and Amara.

"The cavern is just ahead," Wes said in a low voice as Lorelei and Amara joined them. "The drake will most likely be in a tunnel to our right."

"It is hard to see inside," Vandermere said. "You need to stay alert."

"So," Wes said, gripping the glass bottle, "who is going to play distraction?"

"You were already burned." Lorelei glanced at Vandermere. "And I'm good as a distraction. I'll do it."

"You're recovering from your wounds," Amara said. "I'm fast enough to avoid its fire. I'll do it."

Wes nodded with a smirk. "Let the shapeshifters handle it."

Amara shook her head with a silent chuckle and took the lead. She and Wes crept into the room along the side of the wall. Lorelei let them get far enough for the mist in the room to obscure them before stepping inside. She slunk down, keeping their shadowy figure in view.

They paused, as if conferring, before Amara's figure stepped away from the wall and crept towards the middle of the room. The scrape of her boots against the stone echoed through the cave.

A roar reverberated off the walls, coming from Lorelei's left. A bright orange light flared up, illuminating a tunnel in the mist, and the drake rushed out. Lorelei's eyes widened and her mouth hung open. Vandermere had said it was large, but she hadn't fully understood the size of it.

It stopped at the entrance of its tunnel, nostrils flaring as it scanned the room with its one good eye. Its sight landed on Amara and it roared again. Its maw opened and a flame erupted from its mouth.

Amara leapt to the side, clearing the flame's reach. "Now, Wes!"

The bottle flew into view and disappeared into the flames. The sound of breaking glass and a sizzling hiss rose over the crackling. A bright pink cloud swelled from the flames and surrounded the drake. Its fire breath died with a quick snort from the creature. It shook its head, batting at its snout as it teetered from side to side. With a huff, the creature collapsed on the ground.

Lorelei gripped Murgleis and took several cautious steps forward. Vandermere grabbed her arm and pulled her back, but even from this distance she could see the drake's sides heaved in deep, slow breaths. It was sleeping.

Wes moved up beside them and whispered, "Woohoo."

"Great," Amara said softly. "Now, let's get out of here. Which way?"

Vandermere's hold tightened on Lorelei's arm as he stared at a tunnel near the one from which the drake had emerged. "Do you hear that?"

"Hear what?" Lorelei tilted her head.

Was that a female voice calling? She couldn't quite make out what it was saying.

"I heard it before..." Vandermere stared with his forehead creased. "Before the drake attacked."

"It's probably a trap," Wes said. "Like the drake."

"Or something the drake was guarding. I need to see." Vandermere's eyes glazed over.

"You can't be serious," Wes said. "Vaana's not going to be down that way and we are wasting time."

Vandermere's gaze locked on Lorelei. "We *need* to see her."

"See who?" Lorelei asked.

"The Fire," Vandermere said. "We need to see her...for the truth."

She reached out to touch his arm and he gripped her hand

in his. He was speaking to her and she sensed no menace from him. He wasn't in one of his episodes of madness, but he was speaking so strange.

"What do you mean?" she asked.

Amara stared down the hall with a narrow-eyed gaze. "I can't get a feel for what he's speaking of. It could be a trap...or something bound."

"Which could also be a trap," Wes said. "I'm not going down there. It's just crazy."

"Fine, I'll go alone." Vandermere marched toward the tunnel.

Lorelei pressed her lips together and looked between Wes and Vandermere. "Wes, go on ahead with Amara. Leave us some sort of marks so we can catch up."

Wes's eyebrows rose. "You are seriously going to let him do this? He's crazy."

With a glare at Wes, Vandermere disappeared down the tunnel.

"Sometimes," Lorelei said. "But he's also a prophet. Besides, he's had my back. I'm not leaving him alone."

Amara frowned. "I don't like this. We shouldn't be splitting up."

"Then wait here with Wes," Lorelei said. "If we run into something bad, I'll sing."

"And if you can't?"

"Then wait for twenty minutes. If we don't come back, come after us."

Wes shook his head. "This is stupid."

"Maybe," Lorelei said. "But it's not much different from things we've done already."

With that, she took off into the tunnel after Vandermere. She wasn't about to let him wander off alone into a possible trap.

I *dislike this,* Murgleis' voice rang through Lorelei's mind. *I sense something powerful and it is not your Vaana.*

We know it's not Vaana, Lorelei shot back as she rushed through the tunnel.

What other god do they have trapped down here?

That gave Lorelei a pause. *You think it is a god?*

Murgleis was silent for a moment. *I do not know. It is not Sluagh.*

Vandermere's back disappeared around a corner. From the edges, bright firelight flickered, beckoning. Lorelei quickened her steps and sent a silent prayer to the Empress.

Please don't let it be a bigger drake...or something worse.

She rounded the corner and let out a gasp. She and Vandermere stood at the entrance of a small stone room. Bricks carved with intricate sigils had been laid with care to create the walls. A stone bed was pushed to one side of the room, along with a table.

A female paced the center of the room as much as her chains would allow her as they were attached to the ground between the center of the room and the bed. Her face was hidden in a deep hood but her robes clung to her figure. Two fiery wings sprung from her back and her hands were wreathed in flame. She turned and looked at them, tilting her head.

Lorelei's breath caught in her throat.

"You came." Even the female's voice held a smoky, burning quality. "I was beginning to lose hope that anyone would answer my call."

I dislike this... Murgleis repeated. *She is...holy...more holy than anything else in this church.*

The female's gaze fell on the sword and bowed her head.

"Murgleis, Light of Lament. I mean no ill will toward you, nor am I capable of harming you in these chains."

"Who are you?" Lorelei asked.

"I am Hesiah, the Apostle of Fire," the female said.

Lorelei's eyebrows lifted as a bubble of disbelieving laughter rose from her chest. "What? But Evangeline is the Apostle..."

"A puppet put in place by the Pretender. She bound me here when I ascended to Hesiah." She held up her hands. "These chains funnel my Aether to the false Apostle so miracles can be performed under the Pretender's bidding."

"I barely understood any of that." Lorelei glanced at Vandermere who just stared at Hesiah with wide eyes. "What do you mean ascending? And who is this Pretender?"

"Hesiah is the name of the great Elemental Dragon of Fire. As an Apostle, I have reached the pinnacle of my faith and have taken her name."

"And the Pretender?"

Vandermere let out a low groan. "The Vampire Queen...the lost goddess. She has been pulling the strings."

Hesiah nodded. "Your prophet sees correctly. The Mother of Vampires has wormed her way in the Order under the guise of the Voice of Wisdom."

A cold sweat broke over Lorelei's body despite the heat Hesiah generated. The room seemed to grow smaller as her chest tightened. It couldn't be true.

"This has to be some sort of joke," Lorelei choked out. "How could the Empress allow such a thing? The Voice is her conduit to the faerie...She would know!"

Hesiah shook her head. "I fear the Empress has been lost to us since she disappeared from Threshold."

"She didn't disappear." Lorelei jerked her head in Vandermere's direction. "She ascended...back to her celestial realm."

Vandermere shook his head and let out a bitter laugh. "It seems things are more dire than even my visions let on."

Lorelei swallowed. It felt as if tiny needles were pricking the corners of her eyes. This was too much. She had to focus on their task, their reason for coming here.

"We have to find Vaana." Lorelei clutched at Vandermere's sleeve. "She's somewhere in this church, right?"

"The girl the false Apostle has been seeking?" Hesiah asked. "She is with her now, but they are not in this church."

Lorelei glanced at Hesiah. "How do you know that?"

"I catch glimpses through the eyes of the false Apostle." Hesiah raised her head to stare up at the ceiling. "She is taking the girl, your Vaana, to the Pretender."

Fear shot through Lorelei. Daan had attacked them with the intention of taking Vaana. It all made sense now, why the Order had been bent on chasing them. They'd experimented on Vaana to give her the ability to house gods or more powerful spirits to bring to Daan.

"Daan plans on draining the Aether of the gods, doesn't she?" Lorelei asked.

"Most likely," Vandermere said in a grim voice. "They were her siblings, after all."

"Wait, what?" Lorelei turned to Vandermere.

He let out a sigh. "In the Menhir, I had a vision."

"I remember," Lorelei's voice took an annoyed edge. He was choosing now to tell her?

"I saw Daan's creation...her battle with her siblings, and her defeat by the hands of her sister, the Empress."

Now even Hesiah focused on him. "What do you mean by this?"

"The Empress is supposed to be an incarnation of the One True Goddess," Lorelei said.

"But you know there are many goddesses...or were. Daan was one and the Empress was her sister. Though she was more..." Vandermere rubbed his forehead. "I don't understand all I saw...and now isn't the time to explain it."

"Fair enough." Lorelei turned back to Hesiah. "We can try to free you?"

Hesiah shook her head. "I'm afraid you won't succeed. As long as the false Apostle lives, I am bound here."

Lorelei took a step back and bit her lip. "But..."

Vandermere rested his hand on her shoulder. "We have to deal with the false Apostle first."

"Do you know where she is?" Lorelei asked Hesiah.

Hesiah bowed her head and closed her eyes. "She is traveling the Damerel at this moment."

Vandermere frowned. "That's upriver, on one of the branches. If she plans on returning to the Empire, that is a roundabout way to do so."

"She wishes to avoid the Legate...I'm sorry, I cannot ascertain why," Hesiah said.

Lorelei let out a sigh. "It's fine. At least we know which direction to head to. We may be able to catch up if Wes is fast—"

Her words were cut off by a high-pitched whistle from Wes. Lorelei sent a wide-eyed look at Vandermere.

"I think that's our cue that we need to leave." Lorelei glanced to Hesiah. "We'll come back for you. We will free you."

The burning in Hesiah's voice died down, taking a sad quality. "Thank you for your thoughts, but I've long ago given up hope on such things. I'm glad to see a face aside from my captors."

Vandermere took Lorelei's arm, leading her away. She glanced over her shoulder before picking up her pace. They rushed down the tunnel towards the cavern.

At the entrance, they stopped short. Wes and Amara stood with their backs to the tunnel and weapons drawn, facing figures across the cave: Zaos Nematona stood in the center with three priests and a golem.

His gaze landed on Lorelei and Vandermere. "Ah, you again. Well, I hope you enjoyed your little chat with our experiment. I fear you won't be leaving with her secrets."

35

Lorelei scanned the room with her brows furrowing. "How did you even know we were here?"

Zaos let out a harsh laugh. "Do you think we wouldn't have an alarm system set on such a valuable asset?"

A chill ran through Lorelei followed by a flush of anger. "You did it. You bound the true Apostle of Fire here."

"I was called upon to bind a rebellious spirit and was rewarded quite well." Zaos shrugged.

"By the Mother of Vampires," Vandermere said with a low growl.

"So, what? Is she working with the Black Herons to take the Empire down?" Lorelei stepped forward with her fists clenched. "Did you help Daan steal the place of the Voice of Wisdom?"

A redcap Fire priest's incredulous look passed between Zaos and Lorelei as his eyes bulged. "What is she talking about?"

"She speaks blasphemy, as a heretic would." Zaos kept his glare on Lorelei. "Wake our guardian so we can arrest these four."

"Like Gehenna you will," Amara hissed.

She clapped her hands and ripples of force spread from her towards Zaos and the priests. The golem leapt in front of Zaos and spread her arms wide. The wave slammed into her and knocked her back a few steps. The energy of the attack dissipated around her before it could hit the rest of the group.

Amara's head jerked back and her hands fell to her sides as her mouth dropped open.

Zaos smiled. "She's a beauty, isn't she? We developed her to deal with upstart spirits like you."

"She can't handle all of us," Lorelei said and drew Murgleis.

Wes pulled his pistol and let off a shot as Vandermere drew his sword. The explosion of the pistol rebounded off the walls. One of the two priests in the back, both of the Earth path, raised his hand. A wall of dirt rose from the ground. The bullet hit the wall and the entire thing collapsed back into the earth.

The Fire priest sprinted towards the sleeping drake. Vandermere dashed to the side to intercept him. The other Earth priest shifted his hands in a rising motion as he chanted. Several small rocks lifted into the air.

Lorelei drew in a deep breath and let out a few notes of her song. She concentrated on the air, attempting to snatch it from the lungs of Zaos and the Earth priests. Zaos raised two fingers up towards the ceiling and rotated them in a circle.

Lorelei's song died with a gurgling choke as the air rebelled and snatched the breath from her lungs, instead. She clutched her throat as a sharp ache formed in her chest. So, this was how it felt.

Zaos smirked at her. "Your lot caught me by surprise before, but not now."

Amara's hand rested on Lorelei's shoulder and she whispered a chant in her ear. The weight in Lorelei's chest lightened and she gasped, sucking a lungful of precious air.

"Thanks," Lorelei said between pants.

Amara nodded. "You're going to have to take out that golem. Let me deal with Zaos."

"I'm on the golem," Lorelei said. "I think the one I saw at the tower fell quickly to Murgleis's blows."

Does this mean I'll be taking control again? Murgleis asked.

Lorelei sent a scowl to the blade. *No. But I could use some guidance.*

Very well.

"Wes, we could use some cover fire." Lorelei called back before rushing forward.

Another shot echoed through the cavern in response. She ducked as rocks flew at her and leapt forward, landing near the golem. Amara rushed Zaos and the priests. Lorelei yanked Murgleis out. It whooshed through the air as she spun and aimed a blow at the side of the golem. It sliced through the pale flesh and a dark liquid spurted out.

The golem thrust her hands out and her palms hit Lorelei in the chest. She went flying back a few feet and landed on her knees with a shaking jar that traveled through her bones. Her lungs squeezed and, for a moment, she couldn't find air. She glanced up in time to see an assault of rocks raining down on her. She covered her head with her arms, brought her knees up, and rolled so the stones bombarded her back. Each hit sent a sharp jolt through her. She gulped in a breath and squeezed her eyes shut. How long did she need to endure this?

Let me take control, Murgleis murmured. *They would be no issue against me.*

Not after what happened a few days ago. The cost is too great. Vandermere and Amara would never forgive me. Besides, I think Zaos may have a few tricks to stop you.

He's busy with Amara.

I have my friends to help me. We will get through this.

Wes's shot rang through the air as if to reinforce her words. One of the Earth priests circled out and the stony assault ended.

Lorelei pulled her head from her arms and scanned the fight. Amara was locked in a battle of magics against Zaos and the golem. Her hands were raised as she fended off a blast on black energy from Zaos. One of the Earth priests lay on the ground, unmoving. Another flung a series of stones at Wes. Vandermere darted forward to stab the Fire priest with his sword. The priest ducked to the side and blocked Vandermere's blow with a flaming blade.

Lorelei sucked in a soft breath and stood. Amara needed her help the most. She charged forward and slashed at the golem just as she was going to step in the way of an attack from Amara. The sword sliced through the golem's upraised arm, severing the wrist.

A beam of light erupted from Amara's hand and slammed into the Zaos's chest. He stumbled back several steps with a grunt. Amara sent a triumphant grin in Lorelei's direction.

It died with the roar of the drake.

A cold weight filled Lorelei's chest. Despite Vandermere's efforts, the Fire priest had managed to awaken it. Amara's gaze darted from Lorelei to Zaos. With a nod, she darted to Lorelei, grabbed her, and tossed her towards Wes.

Lorelei hit the ground with a groan and glared up at Amara.

"What the hell was that for?" she shouted.

"I'm sorry, but you can't linger here..." Sadness filled Amara's eyes.

With those word she lifted her hands, one in the direction of Zaos and the golem and one in the direction of Lorelei, Wes, and Vandermere. Her fingers moved in a series of movements on the hand facing them while a blast of light emitted from the other hand. Lorelei caught a glance of the golem leaping forward before her vision was consumed with a flash of light.

She blinked several times, trying to recover her sight. Something was wrong. The ground she was sitting on was no longer dirt, but wood instead. The smell of fish and water filled her nose.

She gasped as the world came into focus. She sat on the Winddancer. In the distance, the lights of the city gleamed. Wes was lying in front of her, staring with a dazed look in his eyes. To her left, Vandermere pulled himself to a standing position with the help of the rail. Amara was nowhere to be seen.

"Amara is still in the church. We have to get her." Lorelei leapt to her feet and rushed towards the gangplank.

Vandermere moved in front of her and caught her by the arms. "Lorelei. We can't."

Wes scanned the horizon toward Kirkwall. "Priests are probably scouring the city..."

Lorelei pushed at Vandermere's chest. "We can't leave her! He's going to bind her again."

"She stayed behind to give us a chance to escape and teleported us here," Vandermere said. "We need to find the false Apostle and Vaana."

Lorelei met his gaze as her chest tightened and tears pricked her eyes. Every fiber in her wanted to rush back to Amara, but Vandermere was right. Things would be worse if Daan got ahold of Vaana. But, Amara...

Vandermere raised his hand to touch Lorelei's shoulder, but she shrugged it away. She didn't want his comfort.

With a sigh, he turned away. "Wes, let's get out of here before any patrols find us. What do you need me to do?"

She let their voices fade to the background as she sank to the deck and stared at the city.

I'm losing my sister again...

She didn't know where that thought came from, but it felt so right.

Lorelei stared out at the passing trees along the river without really seeing them. Aside from the occasional fishing village, trees were all that could be seen along the godforsaken river.

Wes had been sailing the ship upstream non-stop for the past two days with Vandermere and Lorelei relieving him when he needed to rest.

Lorelei's gaze drifted behind them, staring downstream. The way they had come.

Kirkwall lay in that direction and it held Amara.

The boards creaked as Vandermere joined her at the railing.

"She's clever," Lorelei said in a small voice. "She could have gotten away."

"Maybe." Vandermere's voice didn't hold any optimism.

Lorelei's shoulders slumped and she bowed her head. "I don't understand it, but abandoning her feels like abandoning family."

"Perhaps because she treated you better than family?"

Lorelei let out a soft breathy laugh. "Yeah. Funny, that. My own sister probably turned me over to the Elemental Order."

"And here you have someone who has come to your aid when you have been in need. She saved your life."

"Both of you did," Lorelei said. "And I couldn't save her. Now Zaos has her again."

Vandermere rested his hand on hers. "We will go back for her. Once we get Vaana away from the Order, we will save Amara."

Lorelei nodded. "I know...it's just, what if it's too late? Or what if Zaos lays a trap?"

"We'll figure out a way. I mean, we've gotten this far."

Lorelei groaned and threw her hands in the air. "But how far have we gotten, really? Most of the time we have been on the run. On this damn river."

"We've discovered much, about the Order and other gods, and about your Black Herons." Vandermere leaned against the rail and bumped his shoulder to hers. "Gaining knowledge is always important before a plan can be made."

"You don't seem as upset about Amara."

He sighed. "I am sad that it turned out this way and I admire her sacrifice, but I don't feel the same kinship with her that you do."

"I don't know, maybe it's connected to this past life I keep dreaming about. To my Reincarnation Sickness." Lorelei stared up at the stars. "Maybe I'm just crazy."

"Trust me, you're not." Vandermere took her hand and gave it a gentle squeeze. "It's not crazy to care for someone."

She nodded. "But you're right. We need to rescue Vaana first. Any plans for that? Do you know what Damerel is like?"

"I've never been there myself," he said. "But from what I know, the town is built around a grotto near the river. They supposedly have many statues built before the Miasma came. No one really knows who they're of."

"Why would Evangeline take Vaana there?" Lorelei tilted her head.

"Evangeline probably wishes to avoid Nearon. The last time she was there, there was a huge fanfare. Other ways are going to take her longer though. Most of the tributaries join the Silverbourne River, and Nearon sits at the mouth. So, they are going to have to travel by land to get to the sea." He sighed. "But it is farther than Kirkwall, so...perhaps there is something they wish to retrieve there."

Before Lorelei could respond, a bright, bluish light lit up the night sky above the ship. She looked up, blinking. Was that a person in the center of the light?

"Amara?" Lorelei said in a breathy voice as she took a step closer.

Something was wrong with Amara though. Dark sigils covered her skin and her eyes were pure white. She stared down at the ship with no expression and pointed to the mast. Wes shouted and leaped towards Amara from behind the wheel of the ship.

Behind Lorelei, Vandermere gasped and grabbed her around the waist. "Look out!"

As Vandermere yanked her back, a burst of white fire erupted from Amara's hand and hit the mast of the ship. A deafening boom filled the air as fire and shards of wood burst out. The force slammed into Vandermere and Lorelei. They flew over the side of the ship and dropped into the river as flames roared to life.

The frigid water covered Lorelei's head, and shock rolled through her. She stared up at the burning ship, distorted in the surface of the water.

Zaos Nematona had somehow turned Amara against them. There was no saving the ship. And Lorelei was going to die in this river.

36

No.

The word resounded in Lorelei's head as she sank lower in the ice-cold water.

She'd survived the Mother of Vampires, and she'd survived iron. She would survive the river, too. She kicked her feet, propelling herself towards the surface.

Where was Vandermere?

She'd lost touch with him once they'd hit the water. She needed to find him. Wes too. He'd been at the wheel when the explosion had hit.

Concentrate on getting us out first. Murgleis's voice rang through her mind.

Lorelei pushed herself up towards the surface, kicking her legs. Within seconds, she broke the surface. Sweet air surged into her lungs and she took a deep gasp.

She floated in the middle of the river with the shore several yards from her. A short distance away, what remained of the ship was sinking into the river, the flames from the mast being engulfed in water. Amara had disappeared. Lorelei needed to move, or she would lose what little energy she had if she wanted to get to the shore. Her chest already ached from her time under water.

Drawing in a deep breath, she swam towards the shore at a direction that was diagonal with the slow current. It pushed her farther back, but if the others hadn't made it to shore, they would be in this part of the river. Her chest tightened.

Let them be all right.

They made it. They had to have.

Halfway through, her arms began to ache. She gritted her teeth and pushed on. Her limbs were screaming at her by the time she dragged herself on the muddy shore. She coughed and sputtered, spitting up water and muck from the river.

Panting, she stood and scanned the river with narrowed eyes. The light of the ship was a bare ember in the distance. There, down the river about ten feet, a dark figure bobbed as it floated downriver. It had to be Vandermere.

Lorelei shook her limbs, then jogged along the shore until she was aligned with Vandermere.

"Don't fail me now, body," she muttered before taking a deep breath and diving in.

Even though she'd been in it a few moments before, the water was like a cold shock to her body. She struggled to breathe. Her arms cut through the waves and her legs kicked with all her might. She had to duck to the side to avoid a grouping of rocks.

His head dipped under the surface.

"Vandermere!" Her cry echoed along the river.

She gripped the rocks as a spasm hit her leg.

Shit, she wasn't going to make it.

Help me, she cried to Murgleis. *Give me strength.*

You know there will be a price for it, Murgleis said.

My soul again? Like last time?

Perhaps not...but you will owe me.

Fine!

With her last word, the pain in her limbs faded and a surge of energy shot through her. She dove beneath the water and swam in the direction to where she'd last seen Vandermere.

To your right, Murgleis called. *I can sense his life force. Hurry, it is fading.*

Lorelei adjusted her direction and reached out. Her fingers brushed against cloth. She pushed forward and gripped an arm.

Got him!

She rose to the surface, dragging Vandermere with her. She broke through with a loud gasp and pulled him up. His head flopped to the side in a limp motion. She wrapped an arm under his arms and around his chest and began an awkward back paddle towards the shore.

When she reached land, she groaned and dragged him out of the river. She lay him on his back and pressed her ear to his chest. He wasn't breathing. Trembling suffused her. The sailors who worked for her father had taught her how to remove the water from a man's lungs. She'd never had to use that knowledge until now.

She pressed her hands to his chest and pushed down in firm, quick movements. She drew a deep breath, pressed her lips to his, and breathed into his mouth. His chest rose slightly under her hand. If she'd imagined a kiss between her and Vandermere, these weren't even near the circumstances of her fantasies.

She repeated the chest pressing and air transfer for several moments. A shudder passed through Vandermere and he lifted his head, coughing and spewing water. Lorelei sat back, resting her weight on the balls of her feet as he rolled over to continue coughing. Relief shot through her and she closed her eyes.

She couldn't relax yet, though. Opening her eyes, she rose

to her feet and marched to the shore. Her gaze searched the black river for signs of Wes.

Nothing.

She picked up a branch nearby and with a quick verse, set the tip on fire. The flames reflected off the darkness of the river's surface.

You felt Vandermere. Can you sense Wes? she asked Murgleis.

Every second he was silent filled her with dread.

Finally, he replied. *I can sense nothing but the river life.*

No, it couldn't be. Her chest tightened, making it more difficult to breathe than in the river.

She spun to Vandermere who was leaning between his knees with his shoulders heaving. Within a few steps, she reached him.

She knelt by his side and placed her hand on his leg. "Hey, I know you're recovering, but Wes is still out there. Could you see where he is?"

He nodded, his mouth hanging open slightly. His hand rested over hers, clasping it, and he closed his eyes. After a few moments, he shook his head.

He had to find him. Even if Wes was farther down the river, they would save him. Lorelei's grip tightened on Vandermere as she turned her gaze back to the river.

Wes was raised on the river. He knew ships. He had to have gotten away. Maybe he turned into a fish.

His soul would have been the same, Murgleis said. *I would have sensed that.*

She shook her head. Murgleis had to be wrong.

Vandermere let out a gasp and teetered forward.

Lorelei rose up on her knees, pressing her hand on his back. "What did you see? Did you find him?"

"I'm sorry." Vandermere turned a sad gaze to her. "I only saw darkness."

"No." Lorelei jerked away from him, leapt to her feet, and ran to the river.

It couldn't be real. Wes had to be alive. She wouldn't lose another person in a matter of days, not after Vaana and Amara. Murgleis and Vandermere just hadn't searched hard enough. She drew in a deep breath, ready to pull Wes from the river somehow with the power of her song. She would risk the last of her Aether in saving him.

Vandermere's hands gripped her shoulders. "Lorelei...he's gone."

His words rang through her head, bringing the truth with them. All at once the tidal wave of grief washed through her. Her shoulders trembled as tears sprang from the corners of her eyes. Her knees gave out and she sank to the ground, sobs racking her body. Vandermere followed her, wrapping his arms around her. She buried her face in his chest and let the grief take her.

Lorelei cried herself out, but stayed curled up in Vandermere's arms. She didn't think of anything. After a while, her thoughts returned. She pulled away and stood up, rubbing the dried tears from her eyes.

"Thank you," she murmured in a hoarse voice. "We need to move on though. Vaana still needs us."

Vandermere snorted and crossed his arms. "And how are we going to do this with just two of us?"

"How were we going to do it with three? We first need to scout out Damerel and see how many forces Evangeline has with her. Wes..." Lorelei paused and drew a shaky breath. "Wes would have been the best, but now we need to figure it out for ourselves."

Vandermere sighed. “We don’t even know if we’re on the right side of the river.”

“But knowing is your thing.” Lorelei gripped his hand. “Vandermere, please. I need to do this. We can’t have lost Amara and Wes for nothing.”

Vandermere sighed and closed his eyes. He was silent, his hand giving the slightest twitch in hers. Then, he opened his eyes, raising his head, and pointed to their right.

“That way,” he said. “It will be a bit of a hike. We should set a fire to dry ourselves and rest before we go. We can leave at dawn.”

Lorelei nodded and set about gathering branches and wood. Vandermere joined her. They worked on setting up a meager camp without speaking. With a short song, Lorelei had a fire blazing. She stripped down to her thin chemise and sat down beside the fire, shivering. Most of her clothing was still damp. Vandermere removed his clothes, as well, and the two of them sat side by side.

Lorelei swallowed and stared into the flames as a different kind of heat suffused her. Ever since the Menhir, she hadn’t had a chance to seek out a lover. They’d been on the run so much and she hadn’t wanted to cause any tension between herself and the others. But now, she was here alone with Vandermere.

She cleared her throat. “How far to the town?”

“It will probably take several hours to get there.” Vandermere kept his gaze on the river. “Longer if we left now in the dark.”

“Too bad,” she said. “We could have used the cover to enter.”

“We’ll have to make do.” He sighed and stretched out on the ground near the fire. “We should get some rest.”

Lorelei nodded and curled into a ball. A shiver went through her.

"You know," Vandermere said, "it would help if we slept next to one another. For warmth."

Lorelei couldn't help the grin on her face. "Is this your way of flirting?"

He laughed. "No...just being practical."

"Oh, well, for the sake of practicality." She shifted until she was laying with her back to him.

He rested his arm across her waist. She scooted back and drew in a breath at the heat that radiated from him. She wanted to roll over and wrap herself in that warmth...to press her lips into his and run her hands along his body. Maybe she could lose herself in him and forget the ache in her chest for Amara and Wes.

No, this was Vandermere. She wouldn't use him like that.

She stared into the fire for a long time before she drifted off into an uneasy sleep. Even then her dreams wouldn't grant her peace.

Hands clasp hers as she falls. But the fall is endless, and she can't hold on. She drifts away from her sisters and plummets into darkness.

Lorelei awoke with a start. The sun was above the horizon and the gentle roar of the river filled her ears. The fire had died to ash and wisps of smoke.

Vandermere stood across from the fire, fully dressed, with his back to her. She sat up and stared at the river. A few wooden planks of the Winddancer had floated onto the shore, but other than that it was impossible to tell the ship had sank.

Lorelei swallowed back tears and shoved to her feet. She pushed aside thoughts of Wes as she dressed. The sinking of the ship meant they'd lost most of their equipment, including her heartstone. Vandermere didn't appear to have his sword either. Going against Evangeline and whoever she had with her would be difficult.

"We should head out," she said. "Not much point in staying here."

He turned her direction and nodded. Together, they hiked through the woods without speaking but the forest spoke for them in the sounds of singing birds, rustling trees, and cracking branches.

Lorelei's stomach growled. When was the last time she'd eaten? She couldn't remember. She felt exhausted and sore with a piercing ache forming just behind her eyes. Her Aether was low. She shook her head with a sigh. No food or alcohol in sight. Things were looking grimmer by each passing moment.

They walked for hours before the trees began to thin out and rooftops appeared near the horizon. Their steps slowed, becoming softer as they crept close enough to see the wooden buildings of Damerel.

Vandermere tugged at her sleeve and pointed to a group of tents that were a few hundred yards to their right, just outside of the town.

"That's most likely them. It's probably easy to keep watch for anyone coming in. Like us," she whispered. "How are we going to scout anything out? Evangeline knows me."

Vandermere paused and turned her direction. "I can go in alone, if you like. I might be able to get an idea of what we are facing."

"Beth is probably with Evangeline and she knows you."

"Then we will need a distraction," Vandermere said. "Something to keep them busy. Could you create a storm?"

Lorelei shook her head with a sigh. "I don't have the Aether to do more than create a breeze, much less a storm."

Vandermere rubbed his chin as he stared off at the village. "Then we're going to have to rely on me to at least see what we are facing."

"Even if we do, how can we succeed? You have no sword,

and I have no Aether." She pressed her back against a tree and slid to the ground. "This is hopeless."

Vandermere knelt beside her and rested his hand on hers. "Hey, we'll figure this out. You are powerful...you just need a boost."

Lorelei raised her hands and looked around, tears running down her face. "Do you see anything around here I can use to regain Aether? Not a wine bottle in sight. We've lost Amara and Wes and now we're going to lose Vaana because I'm weak."

"There are other ways for you to gain Aether. Better ways."

Lorelei sniffed in a silent laugh. "You see a Wellspring around here?"

"No, you have me."

With those words, Vandermere leaned forward and kissed her. She blinked, her mouth partially open under his, as a ripple of shock went through her. It was followed by a small surge of Aether. With a soft sigh, she responded to his kiss, opening her mouth to allow his tongue to brush against hers. Her blood began to sing as the Aether spread through her. Better than wine. She hadn't been this full, this high on Aether since before she'd been stuck on Kiste Isle with nuns. Her hands gripped onto the lapels of his coat as she pulled him closer. She needed more; she wanted all of him.

"Well, well, well," a female's voice broke through Lorelei's euphoria. "I find the most interesting things on patrol."

Lorelei jerked away from Vandermere and turned a wide-eyed gaze to Beth and the two leather clad males with her.

"Well, this can go two ways—peacefully or not." Beth drew a thin rapier from her belt. "I'm hoping for not."

37

Lorelei drew in a deep breath. If she could sing a quick song, she could knock Beth back.

With a nod from Beth, one of the males, a phooka, raised his crossbow.

Beth wagged her finger at Lorelei. "One pretty note and Marlin, here, will plant a bolt in your throat. Now, both of you are going to come along quietly."

Vandermere rose to his knees, leaning close to Lorelei as he made to stand. "Duck."

With that, Vandermere turned, lifted one hand clutching a rock, and hurled it at the phooka holding the crossbow. The phooka shouted as the rock hit the crossbow, knocking it out of his hands. Lorelei rolled away from the tree. The bolt hit another tree with a soft *thunk*.

"Oh, good," Beth said. "You chose to resist."

She darted forward and jabbed her sword at Lorelei's chest. Of its own volition, or Murgleis's, Lorelei's arm rose with the blade in hand and deflected the blow.

"Hey!" she shouted.

Let me handle the swordplay, Murgleis said. *Just sing. Your friend is going to need your help.*

The second male, a redcap, gave a soft growl and yanked a broadsword from his belt. He tromped towards Vandermere with a bloodthirsty grin on his face. The phooka scooped up the crossbow and fumbled with reloading it. A chill went through Lorelei. Vandermere had no weapon. He was going to get perforated by that brute headed his way.

Lorelei drew in a deep breath and began to sing. She got two notes out before Beth planted a kick to her abdomen. Lorelei let out a choking grunt and stumbled back a few steps.

"None of that." Beth closed in on her.

Fine, Lorelei thought to Murgleis. *Give me an opening.*

Lorelei's shoulders and back lost the tension that had been building since she'd woken that morning. Murgleis swayed her body, moving from one foot to another with the sword held loosely.

Beth tilted her head. "You're grinning. Almost like you're looking forward to this."

"Am I grinning?"

Just concentrate on the singing, Murgleis said.

How is this working anyway? I need to control my breathing and position to sing.

You have control of it. I'm just supplementing a few moves for your arms and legs. Besides, you know how to fight and sing.

Lorelei stopped asking questions and waited for Beth to make a move. Waited for the right opening.

Beth spun toward them, following through with a slashing blow. Lorelei's hand rose and knocked the attack back. Metal clanged against metal as they clashed in a series of attacks. On the last, Lorelei's wrist rotated in a swift motion and Beth's sword flew from her hands. It landed on the ground a few feet away.

Before Beth could recover, Lorelei burst out a quick verse, concentrating her will on the pressure in the air. It increased and shot out at Beth and the bowman behind her, slamming into them. Beth and the phooka with the crossbow were knocked off their feet.

"Vandermere, grab the sword!" Lorelei called.

Vandermere leapt away from the redcap as he swung and darted towards the sword. Lorelei stepped in between Beth and her sword with Murgleis raised in her hand.

Lorelei glared down at Beth. "Not as fun as you thought I would be."

"On the contrary, the fun is just beginning."

Beth spun on the ground with one leg thrust out to sweep Lorelei off her feet. Lorelei hopped back with a soft curse. Beth lunged up and forward, drawing a dagger from her boot in a fluid motion. The dagger buried itself in Lorelei's left shoulder. Lorelei let out a small cry and wrenched herself away from Beth.

Damn it all to Gehenna, Beth was fast.

Panting, Lorelei raised her sword. She was doing well with Murgleis before. They needed to keep up the strategy. Vandermere faced off with the redcap, the clang of their swords echoing through the trees. The phooka behind Beth raised his crossbow and aimed it in Lorelei's direction. Lorelei drew in a deep breath and let out a quick song.

Beth flicked her wrist and sent a dagger flying at the first note that left Lorelei's throat. Murgleis flashed green in the sunlight and deflected the dagger, and it careened into a tree trunk to the side. Lorelei concentrated on the air around the phooka and snatched it away. The phooka clutched his throat, his face turning gray-blue and chest heaving. It was a shock, but he was still standing. She'd have to keep up the song for a little longer in order to take him out.

Vandermere rushed the redcap and buried Beth's sword

into him. The redcap cried out, dropping to his knees. With a nod to Lorelei, Vandermere darted toward the phooka.

Beth's glare darted from Lorelei to Vandermere. A smirk lighted on her face. She flicked her wrist, a small throwing knife appearing in her hand from some hidden area beneath her sleeve, and flung it at Vandermere. Lorelei took a step towards him, her song breaking off in a warning cry. The blade embedded itself into his right thigh. He stumbled forward for several feet before he hit the ground. The sword clattered from his hold.

Lorelei's gaze snapped back to Beth and her grip tightened on Murgleis's hilt. She charged towards Beth with a loud battle scream. She was tired of this female taking and hurting her friends. Beth's eyes widened and she darted out of the way of Lorelei's first swing. The second caught Beth in her right hip.

Beth let out a cry and stumbled back a few steps. Lorelei darted forward, her arm guided by Murgleis. The sword flashed in the sun at it slashed and cut. Beth twisted to the side as she attempted to avoid the attacks. Lorelei spun and brought Murgleis across Beth's abdomen. Beth let out a gasp and clutched her stomach. She collapsed to the ground in a ball.

Vandermere had managed to pick himself up and recover Beth's sword. He stood facing off with the phooka's raised crossbow. With Lorelei's song gone, the air had returned around him and he'd been able to regain his breath.

Lorelei sang a quick verse in his direction. A wave of force shot off in his direction. It hit him, knocking him off balance, and the crossbow fell from his hand. Vandermere lunged at the phooka and plunged the rapier into his chest.

Beth glared up at Lorelei, one hand clutching her middle while the other seemed to search the ground for a way to save herself.

"You may have bested me, but I wounded your friend over there." Beth let out a pain filled laugh. "You expect to save the heretic by yourself?"

"I think you should be more worried about yourself." Lorelei took a step forward and raised the sword.

This soul is mine, Murgleis said. *As payment for my assistance.*

Wait. That's not part of our agreement. An ill feeling filled Lorelei's stomach.

Hers or a part of yours...that's the way things are.

Lorelei swallowed the bile rising in her throat. Sluagh were notorious for taking souls. Had she really thought Murgleis would be so different?

Fine, she said. *But I won't do it.*

No need.

With that, Lorelei's hand raised and Murgleis plunged into Beth's chest. Beth gave a scream that was cut short as blood spewed from her mouth. She shuddered and fell still, slumping forward. Shaking, Lorelei dropped the sword, closing her eyes and drawing a deep breath.

She turned her attention to Vandermere. He sat and propped himself up against a nearby tree with his wounded leg raised. Lorelei rushed and knelt beside him.

"Are you all right?" Her chest tightened.

He gave a gravely chuckle. "I don't think she hit anything vital, but it's bleeding a lot."

"Hold on. There has to be something we can use to stop the bleeding," she said.

She scanned the ground and her gaze fell on the fallen faerie. They may have been scouts, but they had to have something to tend to their wounds in case they ran into anything. Maybe they had some of that healing water Vaana had been carrying.

Lorelei returned to Beth's body first. If any of them possessed the water, it would be her.

She crept over to her. Beth stared up at the sky with glassy dead eyes. A queasy feeling filled Lorelei's stomach and she swallowed hard. With a deep breath, she leaned down and closed Beth's eyes, then began searching her body. She found a roll of cloth bandages and a small bottle of some sort of alcohol in a large pouch attached to Beth's belt but no healing water. The search of the other two proved just as fruitless. More bandages.

Lorelei returned to Vandermere with her armful of bandages and alcohol. "This was all I was able to find."

"It will have to be enough then." Vandermere gave her a pain-filled smile. "Think you can dress me up?"

"I can try." Lorelei knelt beside him, using her lap to hold the bandages. "I'm not great at it. If I knew how to heal with my song..."

Vandermere raised an eyebrow. "That's possible?"

"Ilia, one of my friends, could do it, but she was a higher initiate than I was. I just learned the basics of controlling the elements before I was kicked out." Lorelei leaned down, trying to get a better view of the knife and wound. "I think you're going to need to roll over."

With a groan, Vandermere shifted away from the tree and rolled onto his stomach. The knife was still embedded into his thigh and blood had soaked through the leg of his pants. She ripped his pants for a better view. That was usually how Vaana started. Lorelei bit her lip as she stared down at the wound.

"Should I remove the knife?" She reached for the handle.

"Don't." Vandermere reached back and caught her hand. "Neither of us know how to do this, but it may be worse if you do. Just bandage around it."

She nodded, ripped a part of the bandage from the rest of the roll, and poured some of the alcohol on it. He hissed as she dabbed it on the wound and rubbed the blade down. She took the rest of the roll and wrapped it around his leg and the knife with his help.

"You can't fight like this," she said. "I can try to heal you."

Vandermere shook his head. "You need the Aether for Evangeline. Remember why we are here."

"But not at the cost of you." Lorelei's eyes stung. She couldn't lose another person.

"I'll be all right," he said. "We'll find a healer soon. Or I can sneak into the town or something. You worry about getting Vaana back."

Lorelei's fingers tightened around the bandage. "It's just me and Evangeline is an Apostle who most likely has a lot of guards and priests with her. What if I'm captured?"

"Lorelei, you are more than enough. Trust me, your control of the elements goes well beyond the basics. You are more than a match for her and whatever she brings with her."

She raised her gaze up to the sky as a tear slipped from her eye. "I could call a storm, like you said. Thanks to you, I have enough Aether."

"Do it and stop worrying about me," Vandermere said. "I'll be fine. Trust me. I'm a seer, after all."

Lorelei let out a soft laugh and wiped the tears from her cheeks. Leave it to Vandermere to see what she didn't. She had done many great things on her journey. She'd freed gods with her songs. She could take Evangeline.

"I'll save Vaana and bring her back here to heal you. It's the least she could do," Lorelei brushed a kiss across his forehead and stood.

She closed her eyes and drew in a deep breath, holding it in her diaphragm. Her song started out low, with a heavy beat as she called the clouds to form. Within minutes, the sky became the color of slate with the clouds shifting and churning.

She increased the intensity of the melody and stomped

her foot with the rhythm. Lighting flashed in the clouds above and thunder rumbled from a short distance away. At the crescendo, the rain poured from the sky in a violent frenzy.

Vandermere ducked his head, wrapping his coat around his head.

Lorelei continued to sing, pulling at the strings of the storm to ensure it would stay after she ended her song. She let the last note die.

The storm pelted harder.

She retrieved Murgleis from where she'd dropped him and stood straight, facing the town.

She and her demon sword had a false apostle to defeat.

38

The storm raged through the town of Damerel and through the temporary encampment. Rain pounded on the tops of the tents with their emblazoned symbols of the Apostle of Fire like battering rams at the gates of a keep. Within minutes, the ground turned to a muddy swamp.

In the camp, several of the priests withdrew into the tents, leaving only those unlucky enough to be on duty.

A smirk lit Lorelei's lips. Those unlucky few would be the first to feel her wrath.

Their gazes snapped in her direction as she approached the tents. One raised a sword in her direction. The other held a crossbow, loaded and ready.

"Halt!" a guard with the sword called. "This area is off limits. If you are seeking the Apostle, she will return to Damerel in the morning."

"Oh, I'm looking for her, but it can't wait until morning," Lorelei said. "I have words for her. But I suppose I should get her attention."

With that, she sang a short verse and the rain around the

guards froze and sharpened into tiny shards of ice. Both men let out screams as hundreds of tiny daggers slashed at their skin, turning the ground beneath them a multicolor of blood. As the guards attempted to duck away from the falling shards, Lorelei darted to the guard with the crossbow and swung Murgleis in a downward arc. The blade cut him open from shoulder to hip. His scream as he collapsed echoed over the storm.

Four other guards darted out of the tents along with a red robed priest. Their eyes widened as they took in the scene of Lorelei standing over one fallen guard and another clutching his chest with blood flowing down his body.

"Halt!" several shouted in a chorus as they rushed towards Lorelei.

Lorelei grinned and shifted her weight in preparation. Her voice rose above the falling rain in a short verse, once again turning the rain into tiny blades of ice. The shouts turned into screams as they rushed into the downpour of pain. The guard nearest her came at her with his sword aimed at her neck. Lorelei dodged to the side and brought Murgleis up to parry his blow. They danced the dance of combat for several blows, the clang of their swords ringing out as the rest of the guards struggled through the shards to reach them. With a swift spin, Lorelei got past his defense and cut him across his midsection. The guard clutched his stomach and collapsed.

She turned back to the remaining guards. The fire priest had managed to back out of the mess and stood a few feet away, chanting with his eyes closed and his brow knitted. The rain must have been impeding his ability to call flames. He raised his hands up and clenched his fists with his body rocking in a rhythm. An orange flame burst over the heads of the guards and the shards of ice evaporated in puffs of smoke. It wasn't much, but it gave the guards enough time to rush forward out of the icy onslaught.

Lorelei sighed and shook her shoulders. Four guards and one priest weren't bad. She'd taken down more at Verdain's tower. However, she needed to conserve most of her Aether for dealing with Evangeline. She would have to play this carefully.

The guards stopped several feet from the entrance of camp where Lorelei stood and took up a formation.

"Surrender, heretic!" the one in front, a redcap, called.

"Heretic?" Lorelei asked. "The heresy is the state your Order is in now. But I plan to change that, starting today."

The redcap snarled and raised his sword. The two guards behind him raised their crossbows. Lorelei drew in a deep breath, prepared to knock their weapons from their hands.

"Wait!" Evangeline's authoritative voice called out.

She stood at the largest tent in the camp with one hand holding the flap open and a bronze spear with a flame-shaped point in the other. She was dressed in chainmail over thick red robes and the flaming star, symbol of the Apostle of Fire, around her neck. Her stern gaze remained on Lorelei as she marched to the center of the encampment.

"This is a surprise," Evangeline said in a calm voice. "I didn't expect you to be so foolishly loyal to come here alone. What do you expect to accomplish here?"

Lorelei looked around at the encampment. "I came here for Vaana. I'm not leaving without her."

"You should have run," Evangeline said. "You would have survived for at least a little longer."

Lorelei tilted her head. "Nope. Couldn't do that. I wasn't going to leave Vaana to be dissected, or whatever you people plan to do."

"We people?" Evangeline's eyebrow twitched. "She is fallen. I am taking her to be cleansed by the Voice of Wisdom herself."

Lorelei let out a laugh. "Your Voice is a fake, as are you, Evangeline."

Evangeline's face twisted into a scowl. "That's Apostle of Fire, heretic!"

"No, you're not the true Apostle of Fire," Lorelei said in a soft voice. "I'm sorry if you believe the lies your fake Voice has been telling you, but they are just lies."

Evangeline stared at her with narrowed eyes. Then, she threw her head back and laughed. "You truly believe what you are saying. Your family was right. You are mad."

Lorelei gritted her teeth. "Really? I'm mad? Come on. Surely you have seen some signs of this. Maybe your power isn't up to what it should be? Some prayers not getting through?"

There had to be something to shake Evangeline. How was she connected to the real Apostle? She was drawing power from her.

Murgleis, can you detect how it is happening? she asked.

I will try.

Evangeline jerked as if slapped and for a second her face contorted, her brows drawing together and a frown forming on her lips. Then it smoothed out as she drew a deep breath and straightened her shoulders. She nodded to the guards. They hurried to surround her in a shield formation. She waved the priest towards her tent. With a nod, he turned and sprinted inside.

"I won't allow a heretic like you to sway my faith," Evangeline said. "Today, Vaana shall witness what happens to those who defy the Elemental Order."

With her words, the priest stepped out, dragging Vaana behind him. Her hair was still in its braid though the rain glued the flyaway hairs to her face. Deep shadows marred her face under her sunken eyes. Lorelei sucked in a deep breath and shot a glare at Evangeline.

"I'll be the one to kill you," Lorelei said. "And I hope your mistress is watching because I'm coming for her too."

With that, she burst out a quick song. In a flash of brightness, a bolt of lightning struck Evangeline. The force of the strike blew outward, sending the guards flying. They hit the ground in all different directions, convulsing and shuddering as electricity raced across their bodies.

As the bolt hit, Lorelei changed her verse, willing the air around her and Vaana to cool and buffered the force of the blowback. The priest holding her was not so lucky. The wave lifted him off his feet and slammed him into Evangeline's tent.

A cloud of steam filled the area, obscuring Evangeline. Lorelei turned, waiting for it to clear. When it did, Evangeline stood where she had been with her spear in hand, untouched. Lorelei scowled. This was ridiculous.

She has to be using the Apostles Aether to protect herself. Were you able to detect how she's channeling it? she sent to Murgleis.

It's the symbol around her neck, Murgleis said.

That made sense. She was using the symbol of the Apostle as a conduit between the two.

"You are powerful. More than we'd expected. However, it's not enough," Evangeline said. "It is my turn."

She slammed the butt of the spear onto the ground. Heat filled the air as fire burst into existence in a circle around Lorelei. With a gasp, she sang a quick song, willing the wind and rain to form a shield. Even with it, the fire broke through, licking her arms and torso. She forced the shield to torrent out and douse the flames. With a hissing sound, steam rose up around her.

Lorelei glared at Evangeline, sweat beading along her forehead. Her Aether was growing low. She had enough for maybe one more large effect, perhaps a few smaller, quick effects.

She needed to get that symbol from Evangeline. It was time to rely on Murgleis.

Evangeline spun her spear in a swooping motion with one hand. As she did, fire flared from the tip down the shaft until the entire thing was burning with a bright flame. The rain hissed as it hit the spear.

Evangeline gripped the weapon with both hands, pointing it at Lorelei, and charged her. Lorelei spun to one side and knocked the spear to the other with her sword. Murgleis screamed in her head as he made contact with the spear.

What is it? What's wrong? she asked in a silent panic.

His mental voice was filled with pain. *That spear is holy. It burns me.*

Before Lorelei could respond, Evangeline brought the spear back and jabbed Lorelei in her shoulder. Lorelei bit back a cry as searing agony flared in her shoulder. She jerked back several faltering steps and brought Murgleis up in a defensive stance.

We need to disarm her and get to that symbol, Lorelei said. *Can you take another clash with the spear?*

Too much contact with that spear would force me to Change, Murgleis said. *If I'm going to risk such harm, I expect a payment. Her soul would do.*

Lorelei pressed her lips together as she and Evangeline circled one another. She'd let him take Beth's soul. Was this any different? How far down this soul taking path was she willing to go?

There had to be another way.

No, she told him. *I'll do this on my own.*

She dropped him to the ground and brought her hands up with her fists clenched.

Evangeline threw her head back and laughed. "Have you given up already?"

Lorelei smirked and gestured for Evangeline to make a

move. Evangeline charged her with the spear aimed at her chest. Lorelei stepped back and let her pass. As she did, Lorelei grabbed the shaft of the spear, gritting her teeth against the burning. She twisted the spear and yanked it free from Evangeline's grip, hooking the chain with the symbol and ripping it from her neck.

Evangeline let out a cry and she stumbled, falling to the ground on her knees. The flames around the spear died in Lorelei's hands. Lorelei twirled the spear around with the point at Evangeline.

Evangeline stared up at her with her mouth agape. "My power, what have you done to me?"

"The power was never yours. I simply took the bauble that allowed you to channel it," Lorelei said.

Evangeline stared down at her hands with her brows knitted together. She glared back up at Lorelei. "You are lying. This is some sort of trick."

"Even now you deny the truth." Lorelei sighed.

"I know the truth," Evangeline hissed.

Madness crept into the false Apostles eyes. Her face twisted in a snarl, and she leapt at Lorelei with her fingers spread as if she intended to claw Lorelei's face. Lorelei raised the spear and thrust it forward so Evangeline impaled herself upon it. She gave a gurgling sound as blood seeped from her lips and then went limp, pulling the spear down with her weight.

Lorelei pushed the dead woman off the spear with her foot. She drew in a deep breath, closed her eyes, and raised her face to the sky, letting the rain wash away the blood.

She'd done it. No demon sword, no help from others. She'd defeated the false Apostle on her own and she would probably carry the burn scars to prove it for the rest of her life.

Someone cleared their throat from the side.

Lorelei looked. Vaana stood over the body of the Fire priest, free of her chains. She held a small dagger. A smirk played across her lips.

"I was going to help," Vaana said. "But it seems you had the whole thing handled."

Lorelei grinned at her. "You came to me because I am capable of great things, right?"

"Not exactly, but we can go with that," Vaana said. "We need to see to those wounds. Where is everyone else?"

An ached filled Lorelei's chest and her eyes widened. "Vandermere! He's in the woods. You have to see to him first. Do you know if they have any of that healing water?"

Vaana shook her head. "I'm not sure. Let's not waste time now searching for it. I should have enough Aether to heal at least one of you. Are you able to take me to him?"

Lorelei looked down at herself. Her skin throbbed from the burns across her torso and hands as did the cauterized spear wound.

She gave Vaana a faint smile. "My legs still work. Let's go."

Lorelei led Vaana the short distance to where she'd left Vandermere. He stood, leaning against the same tree, soaked and shivering with his jacket still over his head. His chest heaved and his face had taken a grayish tinge. Vaana pushed past Lorelei and moved to his side. He shot her a halfhearted glare but didn't move away as she touched him.

"Where are you hurt?" Vaana asked.

"Leg." He turned to give her better access.

Vaana muttered under her breath as she removed the bandages. She pulled the blade from the wound, eliciting a groan from Vandermere, and placed her hand on the wound. Her chants were a soft cadence.

He looked in Lorelei's direction. "I take it you won."

Lorelei nodded. "Evangeline has been dealt with."

"Good." He gave her a gentle smile. "Could you end the storm then?"

"Oh, right." Lorelei sang a calming song and willed the clouds to depart.

The rain stopped and the clouds began to drift away. By the time Vaana had finished her chanting, the sun was shining down on them.

"That was fairly easy." Vaana turned to Lorelei with a glare. "You made it seem like he was worse than you."

"He was bleeding," Lorelei said.

Vaana shook her head with a light chuckle. "Well, come here and let's see what I can do for those burns."

As Lorelei took a step forward, the boom of an explosion echoed from the direction of the encampment. Lorelei started and spun in that direction.

A flaming figure stood in the center.

39

As Lorelei rushed towards the figure, her mind raced. Had Evangeline somehow risen from the dead? Had Daan done that? She barely registered the footfalls of Vandermere and Vaana behind her. She stopped short at the entrance and breathed a sigh of relief.

Hesiah stood over the fallen body of Evangeline with the spear in her hand. She pulled back the hood of her flaming cloak to reveal a dark-skinned sidhe with brown hair. Her eyes were tiny flames, bright and orange.

Vaana stopped beside Lorelei with her dagger raised. Lorelei held her hand out in front of Vaana as Vandermere joined them.

"It's all right," Lorelei said. "Vaana, this is Hesiah. The true Apostle of Fire."

"What do you mean, true Apostle?" Vaana asked in a high pitch.

"It's a long story," Lorelei said. "I'll tell you later."

"If there is a later," Vandermere muttered.

"I owe you my thanks." Hesiah smiled at Lorelei. "You freed me as you said you would."

Lorelei nodded and bit her lip. "Hesiah, would you know anything of the people in the church you were bound beneath? Especially about any mages they were working with?"

"I'm sorry," Hesiah said. "I know very little. I was visited occasionally by priests of Fire, however, I was bound by Daan herself."

Vaana's eyebrow shot up and she took a step forward. "All right, you need to tell me who or what this...thing is...and what she means by being bound under a church by the Mother of Vampires."

"We told you, she's the real Apostle of Fire." Lorelei rubbed her face and scanned the encampment. "Look, it's complicated and we shouldn't waste time here when someone from the town will probably be showing up soon. I really don't want to have to fight off anyone wanting to arrest us for killing members of the Order, especially the alleged Apostle of Fire."

Vaana opened her mouth and shut it. A grimace formed on her face. Lorelei couldn't help the smile that came to hers. This time, she was the one rushing Vaana along without answering questions.

Vandermere snorted. "We're really letting her come along? After what she did to Verdain?"

"That was before we met. And she just healed you. She could have freed herself and left when I was fighting Evangeline," Lorelei said. "We need her and not just for her healing. I think we're going to need her other skills as well."

Vandermere closed his eyes and inhaled slowly. His eyelids fluttered. After several moments, he exhaled and nodded.

"It appears she'll be in our company for the foreseeable future," he said through clenched teeth.

Lorelei smiled at him and turned to Hesiah. "What do you plan to do now? Will you be joining us?"

"No." Hesiah stared off into the distance. "I intend to find the other Apostles. The Mother of Vampires has them bound like I was. But I'm sure we'll see one another again."

A chill ran down Lorelei's spine. "They didn't just capture you?"

"For Daan to pose as the leader of the Order she would have to subdue all of us."

Lorelei's mouth went dry as the enormity of Daan's machinations hit her. And somehow the Shadow Court, especially the Black Herons were involved.

"We'll look as well, wherever our path takes us," Vandermere said.

"Thank you again. Now I must be off. As should you." Hesiah nodded in the direction of the town. "You are right. They're going to grow curious soon."

"We should gather what we need and head out." Vaana strode toward Evangeline's half-standing tent. "We can tend to your wounds along the way."

Hesiah stooped and picked up the false Apostles holy symbol. Flames flared from her hand, consuming it. A wave of heat wafted from her as the metal liquified and dripped to the ground. Lorelei's eyes widened and all she could do was stand there and gape. The power of the Apostle of Fire was immense.

With one last nod to Lorelei and Vandermere, Hesiah raised her hood. The flames around her swelled up to cover her. When they died down, she was gone.

Vandermere shot Lorelei a wide-eyed glance, seemingly as speechless as she was. He took her hand and squeezed it, then moved to one of the tents that wasn't Evangeline's.

Lorelei's gaze drifted to the ground to where Murgleis lay. She marched to him and picked him up.

You dropped me. His voice sounded petulant.

I'm sorry, but it was something I had to do on my own. And selling her soul wasn't a price she was willing to pay again so soon.

Does this mean you wish to lay me down for good?

Not yet. We still need to get you to Kurnach. We have a deal, after all.

Good, Murgleis said in a satisfied voice.

Lorelei smiled as she stared up at the sparse clouds that remained. She knew she had only a few moments. There was still so much to do. Zaos had Amara. Daan would continue to pursue Vaana. The Apostles were being held captive. She and her comrades had a long journey ahead, but they now had a path to discover the truth.

Even with the threat still looming over them, Lorelei took a second to bask in the glory of her victory.

Lorelei's adventure continues in Hymn of Ascension on Amazon. Get it today!

Interested in adventures from Lorelei's past? Want to learn what led to her parents believing she's crazy? Sign up for my newsletter and receive Nocturne, a prequel Novella on www.natalyacapello.com.

NATALYA'S NOTES

Thank you so much for reading *Song of Shadow*! I'm very happy you decided to pick up my book and here you are now, reading this.

So, a little about myself... I have always had a love for fantasy since I was child. It started with fairy tales and progressed to epic quests to save worlds. It's little wonder that I started roleplaying in my teens. Lorelei, the main character of *Song of Shadow*, is actually one of the characters I played. She became so dear to me that I wanted to tell her story.

Lorelei started out as a bard, though with more magical powers. This is why she became a lyrist in the books. She's had a love for singing, music, and tales from heroes of bygone ages since her inception. That's probably why she gets into so much trouble in this book and in Nocturne. By the way, if you haven't read Nocturne, it is available for free by signing up for my newsletter on my website www.NatalyaCapello.com.

This book couldn't have been possible without the love and support of my husband Jayson.

I also want to give special thanks to J Scott Sharp for his

great notes. The story is much better because of his efforts. Thanks to Rainy Kaye for her brilliant editing as always. My lovely cover was illustrated by Jackson Tjota and the typography was done by Christian Bentulan. Special thanks Lucy Smoke, Kel Carpenter, Felicia Beasley, Ines Johnson, and Jasmine Walt for your support in the finishing touches.

So, what's in store for Lorelei now?

Well, the Daan and the Elemental Order aren't going to let her, Vandermere and Vaana alone. Especially not since Lorelei killed Evangeline. There's also Zaos to deal with and Amara to find. You can find out what happens in book 2 Hymn of Ascension which will be out early November.

If you enjoyed this book, I would really appreciate it if you would be kind enough to leave a review. Reviews help other readers see what a book is like. Also, I have a readers group! It's a great place for my readers and me to get together and talk about books, life, and just have fun in general. I'd love it if you joined Natalya Capello's Acapellas on Facebook.

Once again thank you for your support.

Forever Yours,
Natalya Capello

P.S. Head to the next page for a tiny taste of Hymn of Ascension.

HYMN OF ASCENSION CHAPTER 1

The black rooftops of Valda rose up out of the tree line as Lorelei leaned forward gripping the reins of her stolen horse. She gave a gentle kick to its sides to make it speed up its pace. Behind her, Vaana and Vandermere urged their horses on as well. Lorelei's shoulders ached and her head throbbed from exhaustion. They'd been riding for two days with little time to rest in between. Still, it was better than getting caught by whoever would have been chasing after them. The Elemental Order was never going to stop chasing her after she'd killed a high-ranking church official.

Lorelei pressed her legs into the sides of her brown mare and urged her forward. Only a short distance left to go and she could rest in a bed and have a bath. Even the thought of it sent a shiver of anticipation through her.

She let out a short breath as they broke through the trees. Ahead the town sat, sleepy in the fading afternoon light. Crossroads divided the community into four parts with wooden buildings lining the roads. A phooka woman with bright green feathers in place of her hair swept dirt off the porch of a small store. A pixie child hovered in the air above two other faerie children with her wing buzzing as she tossed a ball at them. Their laughter and shouts echoed into the air.

Vandermere pointed to a three-story building that sat on the edge of town. It had a wooden sign hanging over the door with a sheep holding a large mug of ale.

"That has to be the inn," he said in his low, calm voice.

He looked as tired as Lorelei felt. Streaks of dirt marred the paleness of his face with one prominent one just under his sharp cheekbones. His pointed ears jutted from the tangled mass of long, black hair he'd tied back from his face.

Vaana, who sat on her horse to Lorelei's right, didn't look much better, though her black hair hung in a braid down her back. She looked paler than usual and dark circles had gathered under her eyes.

Lorelei could only imagine she looked just as bad.

She ran a hand over her face. "Good. I could use about a week's sleep."

"Too bad we really only have time for a night." Vaana pressed her knees into the horse and set it in a trot towards the inn. "Come on."

At a one-story wooden stable next to the inn, they stopped and dismounted. A tall male with a square chin and a shock of golden hair came out of the double doors of the stable. His eyes were large, even for his broad face. He had to be a phooka, one of the shape-shifting Faerie.

The phooka looked at them with his eyes widening. Lorelei stifled a laugh. He'd probably hadn't seen many sidhe, if any, much less three bedraggled ones.

Though they were the ruling race of the faerie, Lorelei hadn't seen many sidhe in the West beyond the trade city of Nearon. Most tended to stay in the Elphyne Empire that lay in the lands of the Central continent. Lorelei herself was from the Empire, though she could not go home for several reasons. One of them was that she'd killed an Apostle of the Elemental Order a mere two days ago.

Lorelei gritted her teeth, pushing the thought to the back of her mind and smiled at the stable hand. "Hello, is there room available for our horses?"

The stable hand's gaze roved up and down her and he gave a clumsy bow. "Of course, milady."

Vaana stepped forward and held out her reins to him while addressing Lorelei. "Handle this, and I'll get us rooms."

As the stable hand took the reins, Vaana turned and marched towards the inn without a chance for Lorelei or Vandermere to respond. With a soft chuckle, Vandermere shook his head and leaned his shoulder against the side of his horse. Lorelei reached in her belt pouch and pulled out three small silver coins.

"This should be enough for one night?" she asked.

The stable hand's eyes widened, and his head bobbed up and down. "That's more than enough, milady."

"Good." She pressed the coins into his open hand.

They passed their horses off to him and walked to the inn in silence. Lorelei was too tired for idle conversation and anything important shouldn't be discussed out in the open.

When they stepped inside, Vaana was waiting for them, holding a key for each of them. "Here. The innkeeper is having baths drawn in our rooms. You can have food sent up as well."

"When are we going to speak?" Vandermere asked, taking his key.

Vaana held up her hand. "I need that bath and some rest before I can coherently think."

Lorelei knew how she felt. After the two days of riding from the encampment of the Apostle, a haze had seemed to settle over her mind. Trying to focus on anything only increased the dull throb in her head.

"Morning then?" Lorelei asked, plucking her key from Vanna's fingers.

Vaana nodded. "We'll meet in my room."

Lorelei moved away from the door and scanned the inn as Vaana marched to the stairs to the right side of the room. The scent of roasted chicken and vegetables filled the air. A small bar took up the left side of the room with four round tables near it. Small lanterns hung on the supporting beams of the upper floor, giving off a soft yellow light.

Vandermere placed his hand on Lorelei's shoulder. "I'm heading up, unless you want me to stay with you?"

She gave him a smile and shook her head. "No, I think I'm going up as well. I could use some time alone to decompress."

"We'll walk up together then." He held his hand out for her to go before him.

Lorelei swallowed her suddenly dry throat and shuffled to the stairs. The back of her skin prickled with the awareness of Vandermere's presence behind her on the way up. They'd shared a kiss before she'd gone after the Apostle. At the time, it had been to refresh her Aether, the energy that powered her magic. She hadn't been thinking of the implications of afterward.

With other males, it wouldn't have meant anything. They would have been a passing fancy. This was Vandermere, though. In their few weeks together, she'd come to trust him above almost anyone else, even her parents.

She chuckled to herself. It was strange that she would trust an Essus. The whole noble House was cursed with some sort of madness. Lorelei had seen it in Vandermere multiple times over the course of their adventure together. She could understand the fear and awe that others viewed House Essus with. Still, she could also sympathize with Vandermere as her own family had had her committed because they thought her crazy. Her sister Freya had pushed her parents for it in order to clear the way to get to Arryn. Lorelei blinked several times as tears pricked at her eyes.

Despite how much she'd come to rely on Vandermere, she wasn't ready to give her heart to anyone. Not after Arryn.

Lorelei gritted her teeth and focused on the hallway at the top of the stairs. She was too exhausted, physically and emotionally, to make any rational decisions about anything. She glanced down at the key in her hand. The wooden edges of the rough oval scratched her skin. A "4" had been carved into the center of it.

Numbers had been carved into the fronts of the doors with "7" being the closest to the stairs. Lorelei let out a sigh. She guessed she was in the middle. It seemed to be her relationship between Vandermere and Vaana. She trudged down the hall to her door and turned to face Vandermere.

"This looks like me," she said.

He'd stopped across the hall at the "6" door. "I'll be here if you need anything."

She gave him a wavering smile. "Thanks. At the moment, I'm looking for that bath and then to collapse in the bed and sleep until Vaana bangs on my door."

He chuckled. "That sounds like an excellent plan. I shall see you in the morning."

She turned, unlocked her room, and opened the door. A young phooka woman in a brown, woolen skirt was pouring a bucket of steaming water into a copper tub in the middle of the room. She glanced in Lorelei's direction and gave a small curtsey. The smell of a strong, flowery perfume filled the air. The girl had obviously scented the water with something.

"I'm almost all done here, milady," she said in a high-pitched voice.

Lorelei nodded to her and scanned the rest of the room. It wasn't very large. Perhaps the size of her dressing room at her home. A single bed had been pushed against one wall and a small table and two chairs stood on the opposite side of the room. She crossed to the outer window in five steps and stared down at the town below.

People hurried along the streets in all directions as the sun set. A group of three males walked towards the inn with their laughter carrying on the night air. One, a phooka male with sandy colored hair had glanced up at her and winked one of his golden cat eyes with a grin.

"Your bath is ready, milady," the maid called. "Will you need anything else?"

Lorelei turned from the window and smiled. "Dinner and a bottle of wine would be lovely."

"Shall I send someone up to remove the tub along with the dinner?"

Lorelei nodded. "An hour should be sufficient time."

The maid gave another curtsey and slipped out of the room. With a sigh, Lorelei walked to her bed and dropped her backpack on the floor next to it. She unbuckled her belt to which her sword, Murgleis, was attached and set it on the bed, followed by her clothes.

She stepped into the tub and then let out a small hiss as the hot water surrounded her aching muscles as she slid into a sitting position. She leaned back and rested her head on the lip of the tub, letting the steam caress her skin. Her gaze traveled to the ceiling with its rough wooden slats. The wood had discolored slightly, giving the brown a grayish tint. Lorelei's nose wrinkled.

Her mother would have given a tongue lashing to her staff if they had missed the tiniest spot of dirt, even on the ceilings. No, this place was nothing like her home, but she couldn't go back.

Why am I thinking about home so much? She mused. It's not like they would let me stay even if I wasn't a fugitive.

That last time Lorelei had spoken to her parents, they'd all but banished her to the Morningtide Priory on the tiny island of Kiste, which stood on the edge of the Empire.

The continent of the West lay beyond Kiste Island. Many of the sidhe of the Empire didn't venture outside of the Empire. They preferred to stay safe and comfortable in their bustling cities and sprawling estates. The West was too uncivilized for them. Only the adventurous sorts, like Lorelei, or the ambitious left the Empire to see what lay beyond.

Well, that wasn't exactly true. Others had come and settled in some of the cities and towns that lay in the West recently, like Vandermere. He'd come to watch over the Menhir du Moura in the name of his House. That was until Vaana and Lorelei had come searching for secrets. And secrets she had found, along with a few lost treasures.

She tilted her head, her gaze drifting to the sword on the bed.

You consider me a treasure? Murgleis's voice filled her mind, dripping with amusement. I would have thought your naivety would have disappeared at this point.

"Not exactly, though you have been very useful," Lorelei said. "I've learned how double edged your gifts are, though."

Murgleis was more than just a magical sword. In fact, the sword was just a form he took. He was actually a Sluagh, a demonic being from another world summoned to this one at some point by an ambitious sorcerer.

When Lorelei had first come across Murgleis, he'd been atop of a hill with a group of enthralled Faerie around him. Lorelei had taken him from his spot and begun a battle of wills between the two of them, which she had won. The other Faerie had been freed and Murgleis had been her weapon and companion since.

Speaking of our time together, what of our bargain? Murgleis asked. When will we travel South to Kurnach?

Lorelei sighed. In the beginning, Murgleis had tried to take control of her body on several occasions. They'd made a bargain that he'd aid her without trying to control her if she would take him South.

I don't know. Lorelei slipped into a mental conversation him as she picked up a washcloth and soap from a tray the maid had left and began to scrub. Honestly, this probably isn't the best time. There are several other things we need to do first.

We? I don't need to do anything except return to Kurnach.

And you need me to take you there, which I will, Lorelei thought to him. But I have more pressing things to worry about at this moment.

He was silent for several moments before speaking. Very well. I can wait. I have eternity, after all. However, you do not. I can only do so much to keep you alive.

Lorelei's lips lifted in a slight smirk. I think what you have is more than enough. Just no more calling your creator.

She shuddered as the vision of the four-armed female rose in her mind. His creator had come to claim Lorelei's soul when she'd been on the brink of death. Thanks to Vandermere, she had been saved.

Neither of us wish that, Murgleis said.

Lorelei finished washing herself and lay her head back against the lip of the tub with a sigh. The water was cooling, but it was still warm enough for her to feel wrapped in a cocoon.

A knock shook her from the light sleep she had drifted into. She sat up with a start and glanced around the room. Where was she again?

"Milady," the door muffled the maid's voice. "I've brought food, and we can take the tub if you are finished."

"One moment," Lorelei called as she stood and climbed out of the tub.

The tray the maid had left also held a towel. Lorelei grabbed it. The cloth was rough against her skin as she rubbed herself dry. She sprinted the few steps to the bed and hopped on it, pulling the blanket up to cover her breasts.

"Come in," she called out.

The maid came in first with a large wooden tray filled with a plate of food, a wine bottle, and a copper goblet. She was followed by two males each holding two buckets.

The maid set the tray on the bedside table. "Shall I serve?"

"Just the wine please," Lorelei said. "I'll get the food in a little while."

The maid poured the wine into the goblet and held it to Lorelei. "Here you go, milady."

Lorelei smiled at the maid as she took the cup. The sweetness danced on her tongue at the first sip, leaving an aftertaste of cinnamon. The maid joined the males and they drained the bathtub while Lorelei looked on, drinking her wine.

They finished quickly and hauled the tub out of the room, leaving Lorelei alone with her food and wine.

She was asleep after one cup and never touched the meal.

She drifts in a place of warmth and light. Her sisters' laughter floats through the air and surrounds her. She steps into a glowing room and her two sisters turn in her direction. Their faces are blurred but their hair shimmers. One copper and one silver.

She goes to speak and the world around her trembles.

Crimson and black vein-like cracks form in the white walls. The coldness of the Empty seeps in from the outside.

Her copper-haired sister raises her face to the ceiling. "It is coming."

"Other worlds have been destroyed by the battle," the silver-haired one says. "If they reach Threshold, all the others will fall."

"We have to do something," she says.

"What can we do from here?" the copper-haired sister says.

"Not enough." The silver-haired one bows her head.

"Then we fall," she says. "We fall to a place we can do something. Our followers are dying. If we do nothing, what good are we?"

"If we fall, we won't be the same," her copper-haired sister says. "We will lose so much."

"That doesn't mean we can't regain it, or more," She says.

Her silver-haired sister looks at the cracks. "And if we stay here, we may be doomed."

"Have you seen as much?" her copper-haired sister crosses her arms. "Because I haven't. Nothing has breached these walls, ever."

"Until now," her silver-haired sister says. "You know I haven't seen anything. We can never see past the Shadow."

"It blocks us at every turn," She says. "We have to fall. Are you with me?"

FAERIE RACES

Sidhe: The sidhe are the ruling race of the Faerie. They are known as the Lordly Ones or the Good People. The Sidhe stand between 5 1/2 to 7 feet tall with pointed ears and have an ethereal beauty about them. They also have an authoritative presence and the ability to command the lesser Faerie.

The Lesser Faerie:

Phooka: The phooka are the shapeshifters. They are considered liars, tricksters, and thieves, which in many cases is true and most phooka tend to have a mischievous nature. They are able to take the shape of different animals, however, some of that animalistic nature always stays with them in their Faerie form, whether it is feathers for hair or the ears of a wolf.

Pixies: Pixies are generally friendly, mischievous, short of stature and attractively childlike; they are fond of dancing and gather outdoors in huge numbers to dance or sometimes wrestle, through the night. They tend to work well with the phooka, though they are much more interested in revelry than playing tricks. Pixies also love travel and to tell stories of the adventures they go on. pixies are known to excel at the magical arts and work as magicians for other faerie. Pixies are the smallest of the races standing about 2 to 4 feet tall and have wings of various shapes and sizes. Their skin and hair color also varies.

Ankou: The ankou are keepers of the dead. Ankou act as reapers and perform the rites so the faerie can move on to its next incarnation. It is believed that the first ankou was originally a Pixie that made a compact with the Empress to carry the souls of the faerie to reincarnation. Ankou have a natural knack for necromancy. They need no formal training, nor do they require Aether to speak with the dead. They stand 4 to 6 feet tall, wings, pale skin, dark hair. Have death sense.

Hobs: Hobs are faerie who are obsessed with domestic affairs and usually take up household positions. Can be fiercely loyal to those they serve until they become insulted. Then they wreak havoc. Hobs are short, around 3 to 4 feet tall, large, pointed ears, their skin tone ranges from yellow to green, large multi-colored eyes. Hobs possess powerful hearth magic, so they are able to warm a meal without a fire or command a broom to sweep a room without touching it.

Redcaps: Redcaps are known for their feral and brutish nature. For them, the thrill of the hunt and the fight flows through them. This doesn't mean they can't be civilized, but even then their brutish nature lurks just under the surface. Redcaps are considered to be some of the most capable fighters in Threshold. All redcaps are born with red hair. In fact, it is the reason for the name of their race, as the redcaps themselves never bothered to take another name. Their sharp pointed teeth are another defining feature. It is said a redcap can bite through anything. Along with this, redcaps have enhanced strength and endurance.

GREAT HOUSES OF THE SIDHE

House Moura: House Moura, known for their bravery in battle. Lady Moura was said to be a great warrior as well a very beautiful. The most famous story of her was the tragic love between her and Essus. Moura thoroughly immerse themselves in Earthly pleasures. Moura sidhe are overly fond of food, drink, drugs, and sex, and are often called away from higher pursuits by appeals to their baser needs. Anything that gives them a rush is fine with them.

House Aoife: House Aoife has a craving for adventure and discovering the secrets of forgotten places as well as finding treasure. The Clan is a matriarchy with the line being passed along the mother's side. Most men are seen as second class.

House Essus: House Essus are the seers and historians of the sidhe. All are plagued with a madness that curses their House. Essus wasn't the true founder of his House, but he was one that is looked upon as the true leader. The actual found has been lost to history. Very few of House Essus even know the origin.

House Nematona: Several ago, a several high standing

member of House Nematona attempted to overthrown the Quorum and take down the Elphyne Empire. The attempt obviously failed, and the would-be assassins were tortured to death, but the rest of the House was placed under a dark shadow of suspicion for its ignorance of the conspiracy and for not moving to stop it. Those individuals sought the sanctuary of the Elemental Order and were granted it. From then on, many of the house joined the Order, or ended up working for it.

House Nemain: Members of Clan Nemain tend to be masters of politics, intrigue, and manipulation. They make the most of their talents and have an innate arrogance and supreme confidence in their ability to handle any situation and come out ahead. They love creature comforts, fine clothing and other evidence of their noble standing, taking these as their due, but they love power even more than the trappings that come with it.

ABOUT THE AUTHOR

Natalya Capello lives in a world of oddballs, weather wizards, and big dreams. Really, it's just Texas.

She loves chocolate and spaghetti (but not together!) and writes about fantastical worlds with strong heroines and lots of magic. When she's not writing she enjoys spending time with her cat and playing video games and tabletop RPGs.

Website: www.natalyacapello.com

Made in the USA
Columbia, SC
16 December 2023

28699087R00228